Rock & Roll is wasted on the young!

The year was 1970 and Zack Black & the Blues Attack was poised to be the hottest band in America. Radio loved them, demand for their record exceeded supply, and everywhere they played seats were sold-out. But when stardom seemed within their grasp, they let it slip away. Will Black thought that chapter of his life was closed forever. He had not been in touch with his former bandmates since he moved to New York some forty years ago. But now a mysterious woman has approached him with an unusual request: will he help her carry out her husband's dying wish?

Incredibly, Will finds himself tasked with putting the Blues Attack back together to prove to the world, and themselves, that they still have what it takes. But to do so means that the one-time friends will have to confront the secrets and lies that had contributed to their demise. Given a second chance, will they make the same mistakes?

KUDOS for *Hello, I Must Be Going*

In *Hello, I Must Be Going* by David Meyers, Will Black was a member of the band, Zack Black & the Blues Attack. Forty years ago, they were one of the hottest things going. Then egos and petty jealousies broke them up. Now, the widow of the band leader wants to get them back together to finish the tour their breakup interrupted forty years ago, and she wants Will to help. But will their adoring fans from so long ago remember them? And if they do, will they even care? A warm, sensitive, and entertaining story of camaraderie, friendship, betrayal, and tragic misunderstandings, this is one you will enjoy all the way through. ~ *Taylor Jones, The Review Team of Taylor Jones & Regan Murphy*

Hello, I Must Be Going by David Meyers is the story of a widow's quest and the effect it has on the lives of all those involved. Audrey Taylor's late husband Zack was one of the leaders of a band called Zack Black & the Blues Attack. Forty years ago, they were on the verge of success with a hit record and a sold out tour. But the band broke up mysteriously in the middle of the tour and left fans and backers hanging. Now Zack is dead and Audrey wants to revive the band in his memory and finish the long over-due tour. She gets Will Black the other leader of the band to help her, offering to finance the whole thing. Will is unsure at first, then he meets Audrey and discovers that Zack truly regretted the breakup of the band. Giving us glimpses into the far-from-glamorous life on the road for new bands, one who haven't yet found stardom, *Hello, I Must Be Going* seamlessly combines the past and present for a tale that will keep you enthralled from beginning to end. ~ *Regan Murphy, The Review Team of Taylor Jones & Regan Murphy*

ACKNOWLEDGMENTS

This is a work of historical fiction or semi-fiction, if you will.

While Zack Black & the Blues Attack never existed, the times, the music, nearly all of the places, and most of the people mentioned did or do. However, I may have changed them somewhat to fit the narrative much the way a tailor alters a suit.

Take Teddy Robinson, for example. To the best of my knowledge, the biographical facts are true. But he never befriended a musician named Will Blecker (a totally fictitious character) or, if he did, it was a different Will Blecker. So their interactions are, obviously, invented. The same is true of many of the other musicians, bands, venues, etc., that play a part in the story.

Over the years, I have interviewed well over 500 musicians. A number of them were in the same bands at the same time. Yet, they frequently could not agree on the facts pertaining to a particular event or incident. Memory is like that. And everyone has an angle. In in a few instances, I have appropriated a story that was told to me about one band and given it to my imaginary one. But very few.

As far as the song lyrics are concerned, they're my own invention, as the White Knight said, except for "Amazing Grace," the well-known hymn, and "Clickety-Clack," which is hardly known at all. I wanted to preserve the words to this apparent folk song for posterity (i.e. my grandson). Several of them have been set to music, either by my frequent collaborator, Scott Michal, or, in one and one-half instances, Arnett Howard, and in another, the late Frank Pierce. While I have tunes in mind for all of them, I can only sing them and not very well at that.

I would like to extend my heartfelt appreciation to the following individuals for their feedback and encouragement: Randy McNutt, Tara Narcross, Evelyn Keener Walker, and Karen Wilcox. Asking a friend to give up several hours to read something you've written, not knowing whether it will be a pleasant experience, is a hard thing to do, at least it is for me. I am always relieved when they agree to do it more than once.

Also, thanks to Andy Downing, whom I don't know, for his article on Don Bovee, whom I didn't really know, either, except as a character on campus. And, for the record, I've never met Eric Clapton. On the other hand, I feel I know Spoolie Johnson better than he knows himself.

Finally, I owe a special debt of gratitude to Joel Brown and Chuck Wilson for permission to use the photographs of The Toads. I saw the band perform live only once, but I never forgot it. Maybe, it had something to do with the fact that they were all green.

HELLO, I MUST BE GOING

DAVID MEYERS

A Black Opal Books Publication

GENRE: HISTORICAL FICTION/MUSIC/SUSPENSE

HELLO, I MUST BE GOING
Copyright © 2019 by David Meyers
Cover Design by David Meyers
Cover photos used with permission
All cover art copyright © 2019
All Rights Reserved
Print ISBN: 978164471695

First Publication: OCTOBER 2019

Published by Black Opal Books **http://www.blackopalbooks.com**

DEDICATION

To the many musicians I have known and called friend.
My life would have been poorer
—and my bank account richer—without music.

CHAPTER 1

She's the Kind of Girl

It was a typical crowd for a Tuesday—typical, that is, until she showed up.

I was a couple of songs into my second set, working the piano bar at Joe's Pier 52. For the past two weeks, I had been holding down the bench for Teddy Robinson while he took a well-deserved vacation. But how do you fill in for a legend? You don't. You can't. The most I could hope for was that no one spilled a drink on me. Or threw one. Not very likely in place like Joe's, but in a career spanning four decades you learn to expect anything.

Teddy was one of the first people I looked up when I got to New York. I had been given his name by a mutual acquaintance. All I knew about Teddy was that he was from Columbus, got discovered by Jackie Wilson when he was sixteen, and could sing and play with the best of them. And he was blind. Comparisons with Ray Charles were inevitable. And deserved. Played a mean harmonica, too, kind of like that other kid—Little Stevie-something.

Once Teddy was satisfied, I wouldn't embarrass him, he began tossing jobs my way, ones he couldn't do. And I became his walker, though he really didn't need me. Through our excursions up and down the streets of the Big Apple, I quickly learned the ins-and-outs of his adopted city and, in time, mine. That first year, I would have starved if it hadn't been for Teddy. You don't forget things like that. At least I don't. We made it a point to keep track of one another,

Teddy and I. But I had always gotten far more out of our friendship than he had. There's nothing I wouldn't do for the guy. Give him a kidney, even.

Always working, that was Teddy, but it had started to catch up with him. So when he decided to take a vacation, he asked me to cover. Which is how I chanced to be at Pier 52 when she walked in: tall, willowy, and wearing a black dress—the kind a woman keeps in her closet as a reminder of how slim she used to be. She immediately called to mind a Hollies' song. But, then, I tend to associate song lyrics with nearly everything. That's what happens when your mind is a jukebox.

It was a slow night. The regulars knew Teddy was off, and I didn't have any regulars. I spotted her as soon as she entered the room. That is, I saw the reactions of the other red-blooded males—straight, gay, or whatever—and my eyes followed their gaze. She was alone and sat at a table in the back. A Hitchcock blonde, the kind that could class up Tiffany's. I took her to be in her thirties or well-preserved forties and wondered if she wasn't a model or a movie star. Not that I'd recognize most of the current crop. But Joe's gets a lot of theater traffic.

I thought I'd drop by her table on my next break, just to exchange a few pleasantries. Buy her a drink, maybe. I didn't flatter myself to think anything would come of it. Though I was wearing my best suit, the powder blue number, the one I always wore when I was performing. It marked me as a professional. And would have made me feel like I was part of the Rat Pack if I had owned more than just the one.

But before I had the chance to act, Marcie, one of the wait staff, handed me a cocktail napkin with a brand-new Benjamin folded inside. "Looks like you've made an impression," she said, nodding in the direction of the mystery woman.

I sat up straight and looked across the room at her. Holding a martini glass at eye level, she seemed to tilt her head and smile slightly in acknowledgment. When I glanced at the napkin, I saw that it had the words "Broken Wings" written out in neat, block letters.

"Broken Wings" was a song by John Mayall, the godfather of British blues. I hadn't thought about it since I was in my old band, the Blues Attack, when I was still in my teens. It had been the flip-side of our first record. I had heard it on the *Blues Alone* album and studiously applied myself to learning it as a showcase for my developing organ chops. It was heart-breakingly sad—and obscure. Certainly not the type of material I'd normally choose for the patrons of Pier 52. On the other hand, it was my last night. No matter what I did, Teddy would be occupying the piano bench tomorrow. I stretched my fingers and prepared to pour on the charm.

"This is a special request," I said in my best Barry White voice, "and I always try to honor requests—as long as you don't ask me to stop playing."

The reaction to my little attempt at humor reminded me why I was better off leaving the jokes to others.

I couldn't remember ever attempting "Broken Wings" on the piano before. I didn't have the lush organ fills and I struggled to retrieve the stark lyrics from the deepest recesses of my memory. Still, I was a little better keyboard player than Mayall—although not half the musician. I eased into it with this improvised introduction, starting on the high end and stair-stepping it down until I reached the opening chords.

"Some-buh-uh-uh-uh-dy," I sang in a bluesy murmur with just a touch of grit. The lyrics were a little awkward—the ones I could remember—but Mayall made them work. I tried to emulate his phrasing, syllable by syllable, as best I could. Even as I was singing, I couldn't help but wonder why the mystery woman—I dubbed her Goldilocks—had wanted that particular song. There was no reason for her to expect me to know it unless she knew something of my history. But she was too young to have ever seen my band.

And the record had barely been released. She certainly didn't impress me as someone who collected garage band 45s. I didn't even own a copy of it anymore. The last one got away from me during the nomadic phase of my life, which as pretty much the last forty years.

Eyes half-closed, I whisper-sang my heart out, hoping to make a psychic connection with the one person in the room I knew would care. I didn't realize how much I had missed the song until I found myself awash in associated memories. Mostly of playing in the band. But also of young love. A trace of a smile may have even bowed my lips. Someone once said that the interruption of a song was like the stopping of time itself. That's the way I felt. For a few moments, our souls had touched.

Or maybe not.

Because when I looked up again, Goldilocks was gone. She hadn't even stayed for the last verse. There was something I wasn't seeing in this picture.

Even without the Hammond B-3 and with some muffed lyrics, I had acquitted myself fairly well. I had tried my best to give Goldilocks her money's worth, although I doubted I had won over any new fans.

When Marcie passed by me in her orbit again, I hailed her. "Did the customer who made the request say anything before she left?"

She shook her head and mimed, "Sorry," the way women do.

She wasn't the only one who was sorry. Like the Hollies sang, she had it all.

As I turned it over in my mind, the whole thing didn't make much sense. I might have thought I had imagined it all if it weren't for the $100 bill stuffed in my breast pocket. Taking it out, I noticed a phone number written on the inside of the napkin. The area code was Westchester County—at least it was before the cellphone era. Westchester usually meant money. Paul Newman and Joan Woodward had lived there and lots of other celebrities still did. And a mobster or two. Or so I read in the *Post.*

As I thought about Goldilocks, I flashed back on a song I had written when I was still in high school, one of my first. I had "written" it—in my head, not on paper—for a doo-wop group I had joined, the Clintones, although I would quit when they went barber shop. Even then, I knew most girls were allergic to boys in striped vests, sleeve garters, and straw boaters.

It was a bouncy affair.

> *She's the kind of girl that you wanna*
> *take home to meet Mama.*
> *She's the kind of girl who will only have eyes for you.*
> *She's the kind of girl makes you pinch yourself*
> *to see if you're dreaming.*
> *She's the kind of girl who is almost*
> *too good to be true.*

I remember trying to teach it to the other three Clintones, singing the different parts as best I could. Actually, I only had the melody and the bass part. I wasn't much of an arranger, yet, so it was kind of every man for himself.

> *She's the kind of girl always looks like a million dollars.*
> *She's the kind of girl who could never be a sometime thing.*
> *She's the kind of girl that you only find once in a lifetime.*
> *She's the kind of girl who can make a guy feel like a king!*

From the beginning, I was a stickler for true rhymes: moon, June, spoon. It killed me if I had to resort to a slant rhyme: town, bound, fount. That's because I grew up with show tunes, the whole Great American Songbook. Lyrically, guys like Cole Porter and Lorenz Hart were my idols. Stubbornly—make that stupidly—I kept myself aloof from blues and rock and roll for a long time.

> *So is it any wonder my head's in such a whirl?*
> *All the world's an oyster and I have found the pearl*

Ev'rytime I see her my heart begins to twirl.
She's got that kind of magic, she's that kind of girl!

Why I threw in a bizarre bridge, I can't say, except I was something of a geek—science fairs and all of that. Even built a cloud chamber. I remember I had been intrigued by the mnemonic Mr. Wood, the science teacher, taught us so we could remember the planets back when Pluto still qualified: Mercury (Mary's), Venus (Violet), Earth (Eyes), Mars (Make), Jupiter (Johnny), Saturn (Stay), Uranus (Up), Neptune (Night), Pluto (Panting). So I dropped it into the song.

Mary's violet eyes make Johnny stay up nights panting.
Johnny has never seen eyes that looked so enchanting.
Sometimes you can hear Johnny when he's ranting.
And chanting and descanting and....
She's got that kind of magic, she's that kind of girl!

I especially liked the abrupt change after "descanting." It was like the record skipped.

She's the kind of girl always looks like a million dollars.
She's the kind of girl who could never be a sometime thing.
She's the kind of girl that you only find once in a lifetime.
She's the kind of girl who can make a guy feel like a king.
Can make a guy feel like a king!
Can make a guy feel like a king!
Can make a guy feel,
Make a guy feel,
Make a guy feel like a king!

I may have had a specific girl in mind, but at that stage of my life it was more likely any girl who reciprocated my interest. I was extremely shy, which was another reason I dropped out of the Clintones. Surprisingly, a lot of musicians are—except for the ones who aren't. Most bands had at least one member who will do anything to hog the limelight, several who are happy to let him, and at least one who hates him for it. I always believed that my musicianship would bring me more than enough attention. But in rock and roll, a keyboard can't compete with a guitar unless you set it on fire or knock it over a la Keith Emerson.

A few years later, I revived the song when I joined my first serious band. Because I knew most people weren't interested in hearing our originals, I combined it with "Expressway to Your Heart," the Soul Survivors hit. The bass parts are almost identical so it was easy to start out playing "She's the Kind of Girl," switch to "Expressway," and then back again. I thought I could fool them into liking my song by camouflaging it.

After "Broken Wings," I sleep-walked through my last set of the night, reminded everyone that Teddy would be back on Wednesday, then headed downtown to my apartment. I decided to hoof it just to clear my head—and think about Goldilocks.

The whole thing was a puzzle. Who was this person? Rich, beautiful, a lover of English blues. Of all the gin joints in all the towns, right? Clearly, she was either the perfect woman or a whack job. I wanted to call her right then, but decided tomorrow would be soon enough. Musician's time. Late morning.

CHAPTER 2

Top of the Mark

She picked up on the third ring, catching me by surprise like an errant fishhook in the ear. I was expecting a maid or a husband or, more likely, a recording. But I knew it was her—Goldilocks—even though I'd never heard her speak before. Her voice was perfect.

"Hi, this is, uh, Bill Black," I stammered. I should explain. Billy Black was the name I used professionally. For a time, I went by Billy Martin until I learned Billy Joel called himself that back when he was playing piano bars in LA. But my real name is William Blecker—Blecker being German for someone who shows off his teeth. I picked up the nickname Blackie in my childhood.

"Oh, hi, Bill," she said. "Thanks for calling. I wasn't sure you would. I don't usually give my number to total strangers, but I don't feel we are."

"I'm sorry, but have we met?" I couldn't imagine how, but there was always that chance. She could be a cousin, for all I knew. I'm not really good at keeping track of such things.

"No, but I feel like I know you. My name is Audrey Taylor—Mrs. Zachary Taylor." Her words hung in the air like the chiming of an antique clock.

"You're Zack's wife?"

Zachary Taylor had been my best friend growing up, although I hadn't seen him in years. He was responsible for my becoming a musician. We formed the Blues Attack when we were in high school. He was the smartest and most-talented person I had ever known. I immediately began kicking myself for not keeping in touch.

"I was," she said, followed by a long pause. "He passed away."

"Passed away?" I struggled to remain upright in a world that had suddenly turned upside down.

"Seven weeks ago."

I was stunned. Words wouldn't come out. Sure, we may not have sent each other Christmas cards, but I still took comfort in knowing Zack was out there somewhere. We had once shared the same dream and, as long as we were both alive, I could maintain the illusion that we still might achieve it. Now, the dream was dead, too. I just hadn't known it until this minute.

"Are you still there?"

"Yeah." I didn't know if I was feeling sad, lonely, or just sorry for myself. I knew I would be spending a lot of time sorting it out.

"Maybe I shouldn't have been so blunt. I've had some time to deal with it. I forget that there might be others who cared about him, too."

"No, that all right. It just caught me off guard. How…"

"Cancer. Prostate"

"I'm sorry." And I was. Men don't like to hear that kind of thing, especially about someone their own age.

"Thank you." The words sounded tired and worn out from overuse.

"How…"

"Two years. After he was diagnosed and began treatment, he survived for two more years. It was very aggressive. What's the word? Metastasize? It metastasized."

Now, I really felt guilty. I had been in New York all that time and could have dropped by to see him had I known. But I should have done it anyway. Looked him up. Years ago.

"Is there anything I can do?" I asked lamely. "I mean, I

don't really know what, but if I can do—something." I felt like an idiot. I hadn't even known Zack was married, and now I was asking his widow if I could be of any help to her. Of what possible assistance could I be? Change a light bulb? Take out the garbage? Paint the kitchen?

"Actually, that's why I looked you up."

"Well, I'll do whatever I can. Zack and I were once very close. Almost like brothers."

"I know. I know. He felt that way, too."

I didn't know whether to believe her. I certainly wanted to, but Zack and I hadn't exactly parted on the best of terms. When bands break up, it's like a marriage that has gone disastrously wrong. Over the years, the level of acrimony had subsided only a little. Still, I felt her loss; it was my loss, too. I began to regret every angry word I had ever said to him. I couldn't have felt worse if I had cut off my hand— my left one. And I have a strong left hand, great for pounding out octaves.

"That's why I feel I can ask you this favor."

"A favor. Of course." I was hoping against hope she didn't need money. Most musicians I knew weren't rolling in dough. I started thinking of how I could scrape some cash together, maybe a thousand or fifteen hundred bucks. Pawn something, maybe.

"It's a little bit hard to explain," she said. "But if you could come up to our house this weekend, I could show you."

"Your house?"

"It's just outside Tarrytown. You can take the train. You'll come, I hope. I mean, if you're free."

She had caught me between gigs, as we say. I used to work three or four nights a week at this jazz club in the Village, but it had gone punk when management realized they wouldn't have to spend as much money on maintenance. Overnight, the restrooms became vomitoriums. Since then, I had subbed where I could, played for auditions and rehearsals, and took an occasional wedding job.

"Sure," I replied. "When do you want me?"

"How about Friday? If you can arrange it."

"You sure I won't be an inconvenience?"

"No, I have plenty of room. Let me know when you're coming and I'll pick you up at the station."

She hung up when she was finished. I would have preferred to prolong the conversation, just to hear her voice, but she had apparently said what she wanted to say. There were questions I wanted to ask her, but those could wait until we were face-to-face. I would miss Sunday's meeting of the Roxy Morons—an old timers group—which I didn't mind, except I would have to let them know or else they would assume I had died. We got together every week to eat, play, drink, and lament the sad state of the music business.

After I got off the phone, I peeked out the window. It was raining. *Good*, I thought, *this city needed a bath, And maybe a good cry*. But then it stopped.

For the rest of the morning, I turned my apartment upside down, looking for any mementos that might have survived from the Blues Attack years. Most of them had been stored in my parents' basement back in Ohio along with other mementos of my childhood and were disposed of in the auction following my dad's death. At the time, grief trumped any sentimentality I might have felt. Now, I wish I had held onto a few more things. What I was left with was a yearbook and a dozen or so newspaper clippings that were pressed between the pages. Also some fragments of songs.

There was one I had written while I was on a trip to San Francisco with my parents. A tour bus had dropped us off at the top of Nob Hill, right in front of the Mark Hopkins Hotel, and I remember trying to imagine what it would be like to stay in a grand place like that. For some reason, I saw myself looking down from the very top. It must have been fifteen or twenty stories tall. As I read the lyrics, the melody began to play in my mind.

They come and they go,
In the streets far below,
Passing into and out of the dark.
Just who they might be,
Is a puzzle to me,
From here at the Top of the Mark.

Where do they come from?
And where do they go?
And what are their secrets?
Well, I'll never know.

Still I can't look away,
From this strange shadow play,
Peering down from the Top of the Mark.

Not bad for a ten-year-old kid. A few years later, I had
flown out to San Francisco. It was my first time on an airplane. On the return flight, we had a half hour delay when it
came time to land at Chicago's O'Hare Airport. Later, I
made up this song, working out the chords on my banjo—
long neck, folk-style—when I got home.

I'm stacked up in Chicago,
Can't get back on the ground.
Yeah, I'm stacked up in Chicago,
Can't get back on the ground.
My baby's down there waitin',
But this plane keeps circlin' around.
I'm stacked up in Chicago,
Can't get back on the ground.

At the time, I had no idea that I would become a musician—or have a girlfriend—but the desire to express myself
musically was already evident to anyone who bothered to
listen. It just needed a catalyst. It needed Zachary Taylor.

Zack Taylor had been our class president. He was also

the valedictorian, homecoming king, and all that other stuff that once seemed so important. In fact, in almost every way possible he made me feel inadequate without ever intending to. Fortunately, when it came to forming a band, he couldn't do everything—not at the same time, anyway. True, he could play bass, drums, keyboards, and even a little sax, but he preferred the guitar and dedicated himself to becoming a virtuoso. He might have been the best I ever heard. Someone once said that Paul McCartney could play Bach on a tugboat whistle. Zack was better.

Until I took up the piano, I had thought I would be a writer. Then Zack asked me to jam with him one day when he heard me pecking out some tunes on the band room piano. I learned that was a big no-no when Principal Swain came up behind me and dug his talons into my shoulders. According to Kurt Vonnegut, every author he knew would have preferred to be a musician.

I didn't really know how to play, but Zack could tell I had a good sense of pitch and rhythm. Soon, I was spending all my free time at his house while he was patiently teaching me the fundamentals. Later I added some lessons at Coyle's Music, but Zack had laid the foundation. I still felt like he was looking over my shoulder when I played.

Because Zack was one of the coolest—no, he was the coolest kid in school—I liked that we hung out together. I would never be cool on my own, but I could pass for it when I was around him. And when he suggested we form a band, I was all in. I began practicing twice as hard so I wouldn't lose my spot. Along with learning the piano, I began to discover I had a knack for arranging. I had an ear for chords and knew which notes to fill in.

As our friendship developed, we became inseparable. He started calling me "Blackie" while I nicknamed him "Liz." This was because one of Zack's few flaws was his terrible handwriting—as bad as a doctor's—which once resulted in a substitute teacher mistaking Zachary Ellsworth Taylor for Zachary Elizabeth Taylor. As a result, I wound up writing down the arrangements. No one would be able to read them otherwise.

From time to time, other musicians invited themselves to jam with us. A few of them sounded pretty good to me, but Zack wasn't as easily satisfied. He auditioned various drummers and bass players in different combinations until he found two—Evan Bishop, who we called "Stuka"—and Wes Kennedy. They seemed to be opposite sides of the same coin. The four of us became the nucleus of the original Zack Black & the Blues Attack. I thought we were the heaviest band on earth—or at least in Ohio.

Like everybody else—even The Beatles—we had started out covering other people's songs. The very first song we attempted was "Hi-Heel Sneakers," with me on a Farfisa organ Zack had wrangled from somewhere. It had been a hit for Tommy Tucker a year or two before, so we all knew it, in theory anyway. But getting us to play it together was another thing. At first we sounded like so many radios tuned to different stations.

Very early on, it became apparent that this would be Zack's band because he was the only one of us who had any idea of how to fix what was broken. And there was a lot. But I took it as a good sign that it wasn't long until we sounded competent enough to be invited to play a sock hop after school. I say "invited" because we didn't get paid.

Then a funny thing happened on the way to the gym— the gym being where the sock hops were held and the preservation of the gym floor being the reason the dancers had to do their hopping in their socks. We became rock stars. Even before we had played a single note, there was a gaggle of teenage girls ready to swoon over us or, more accurately, Zack, and the rest of us were indirect beneficiaries of all the swoonage. If we hadn't already decided we were going to be a band, their reaction sealed it.

Other than being warned twice to turn down the volume—with a threat to pull the plug if they had to tell us again—our first gig went well. Afterward, we accepted the praise of our mostly female fans, while their boyfriends glared at us and seemed poised to yank them away if we said or did anything untoward. There was also a nerdy guy who reminded me a lot of myself about ninety minutes earlier. He volunteered to be our roadie. We let him. He went on to start his own construction company and retired a wealthy man. I, on the other hand, elected to pursue fame and fortune in the music business. Fifty years later, both continued to elude me.

CHAPTER 3

Clickety-Clack

When it came to making a trip up the Hudson Valley, I welcomed almost any excuse. I seldom got the opportunity to commune with nature, even if it was from a speeding metro train. Living in the city, you tend to forget that most things don't naturally grow from concrete, that the sky doesn't come with a frame, that Noah had more than pigeons and rats on the ark. Central Park was just a tease.

However, this time I had an even greater incentive: I had been invited to spend the weekend with a woman I didn't know for reasons she didn't explain and yet I was committed—emotionally, anyway—to doing whatever she asked of me—short of breaking the law. At least not a big one. The combination of beauty and mystery was irresistible. Besides, it's not like I had any plans.

As I boarded the train, I thought of something Hans Christian Anderson once said: "Life is like a beautiful melody, only the lyrics are messed up." I don't know why he said it—and I suspect it sounded better in Danish—but it has always resonated with me. The lyrics of my own life had certainly been messed up—ironically, because I was the one person in the band who was most concerned with the lyrics. Even when we were playing cover songs, I had to fight the temptation to tweak a word here or there to "improve" them.

Before I could write a note, I was pushing for my band

to do originals. Few rock and rollers before Buddy Holly, The Beach Boys, and The Beatles had ventured to write their own material. But almost overnight, the musical world was divided into two camps—those who did and those who didn't. And for those who didn't it was like being left holding a slice of pizza after the toppings had slumped off. So I would write lyrics, Zack and I would come up with the melodies, and we would both work on the arrangements.

I still caught myself writing lyrics or snatches of them, but it had been a long time since I bothered to turn them into a finished song. There was no point. I no longer tried to foist my "children" on an indifferent public. The sad truth is that most people want to hear only the songs they know. So most working musicians have to swallow their pride and play "covers." Either that or take a day job.

As we got underway, I started thinking of all the train songs I knew. I had never written one myself, maybe because there were so many good ones already: "City of New Orleans," "Atchison, Topeka & the Santa Fe," "People Get Ready," "Clickety Clack (A-Clunk A-Clunk)"—the last learned on my mother's lap. Cisco Houston had recorded it, but it wasn't quite the same. For the definitive version, you had to hear my mother's.

Sitting there the passenger car, I sang it in my head while quietly tapping out the percussion on the arm rest with my fingertips.

> *Clickety-clack, a-clunk, a-clunk.*
> *A train's a-comin', a-chunk, a-chunk.*
> *Clickety-clack, a mile away,*
> *It hasn't a second of time to stay.*
> *It sings a noisy, rackety song,*
> *A rickety, rackety, rockety song.*
> *Get off the track, it isn't where you belong!*

I always thought of this song as something precious, something to preserve, protect, and, eventually, pass along to a younger generation like an old photo or an antique book. At the same time, it was a living, breathing thing. I didn't have to consciously learn the words, no more than I did many of the other songs my mother sang to me: "The Walloping Window Blind," "Go Tell Aunt Rhody," "The Big Tin Pan Parade." They were engraved in my soul.

Over the hill, across the lake,
A mile a minute it has to make.
A wiggling snake with flaming eyes.
It wiggles and wriggles along the ties.

Even as a child, I was aware that there were different talents at work in crafting a folksong such as "Aunt Rhody" and the more polished "Tin Pan Parade." I delighted in the line that rhymed Napoleon with linoleum"—although, as it turned out, my mother wasn't above changing a few words, either. And, I suspect, buried somewhere in there was the spark that ignited my desire to be a musician.

The cinders fall in fiery rain,
A tunnel is waiting to swallow the train.
Goodbye, goodbye, tomorrow we'll come again.

Later on, I was surprised to discover that other people my age didn't know the song at all. I suspect it had to do with the fact that my parents were older, at least ten or twenty years older than my friends' parents. They were from a different generation. And they both died prematurely. So I suddenly became an orphan in my early twenties. Overnight, I felt like an old man.

Unwittingly, I found myself composing a song in my head. *I took the train to Tarrytown,* I began. *Didn't know what I would find.* Then my mind leap-frogged ahead to possible rhymes for "find"—mind, blind, grind, unwind, remind, behind. I would go with behind; leaving the city behind. For what? I could see trees, now, and not just in parks. *Out among the trees / I felt at ease / As I left New York behind.* Maybe I should add an extra beat—*find there.* Then I could go in another direction—*I took the train to Tarrytown / Didn't know what I would find there / Maybe gain some peace of mind there / Or maybe find my way.* "Way" would make for an easy rhyme. *As I left New York behind / It felt like all my cares were lifted / While through space and time I drifted / Back to yesterday.*

That was the first verse. It needed work, but it would do for now. The melody had pretty much written itself as I assembled the words like boxcars on a train. So I switched to the chorus. What did I want to say about Tarrytown? Nothing—yet. But that didn't matter. I would stumble onto something. Brown, clown, down, drown, gown. I wanted an exact rhyme if I could find it. That was the challenge, like working a crossword puzzle. Writing songs was my own sort of game. I cringed when I heard some of the "rhymes" they got away with in pop music. "Still is" and "Bruce Willis." "Juiced in it" and "used to it." "Through the door" and "nuclear war."

But then I realized I was taking the easy way out. No, this song wasn't about Tarrytown. I knew I would have to go back to the verse and tweak it some more, but the chorus would need some clever turn of phrase like in a country song. Maybe that I left New York, but New York didn't leave me. What did that mean? It didn't matter. Pop songs thrived on ambiguity. *It was peaceful / It was pleasant / It was nice as nice could be. / But even though I'd left New York / New York didn't leave me.* I debated whether "still" or "but" was better and ultimately couldn't decide. So, too, with "didn't leave me" or "hadn't left me." I was leaning toward the former.

With the Hudson River unspooling over my left shoulder, the stations ticked by on the Metro-North route: Ludlow, Yonkers, Glenwood, Dobbs Ferry, until at last I reached Tarrytown. I had been this far before, but not much farther, and I had promised myself one day I would ride it all the way to Albany. But I knew I probably wouldn't.

The train ride ended too soon. Like a thirsty man draining the last drop of water from a canteen, I wasn't ready to let go of it yet. I knew the trip back to the city wouldn't be as satisfying. As I stepped down from the car, I had two rough verses and the chorus in my head. It still needed some work, but I doubted I would ever bother with it again. It had merely filled the time, taken me from Manhattan to Tarrytown.

ぐろぐろ

I had been waiting about a quarter of an hour at the station when a white Mercedes coupe pulled up. Although I hadn't really gotten a very good look at her at Pier 52, I had no doubt this was Mrs. Zachary Taylor. She opened the door and swung her legs out as though it was a red-carpet entrance, the type usually accompanied by the flash of cameras. After adjusting her skirt, she took several quick steps toward me. "Hope you had a pleasant trip," she said, extending her hand. "I feel like we're meeting again for the first time."

"That's a good way of putting it."

"Is Billy what people call you? When you're not performing, I mean."

"That's the name most people know me by."

"But is that what you'd like me to call you?"

She had already tapped into something most people never even bothered to find out. The fact was I didn't really care for the name "Billy." Most people just assumed that because my given name was William, I answered to Bill or Billy and so I did. I had been saddled with it since I was a kid. "I'd prefer William or Will."

"Will it is, then."

She popped open the trunk, I threw in my overnight bag, and in a moment we were cruising through Tarrytown. Sit-

ting off to the side of the highway was a sculptured reminder of the fact that this was the setting for the Headless
Horseman of Sleepy Hollow. We passed an appropriately
creepy cemetery, tombstones sprouting like broken teeth,
and I wondered if Zack was buried there.

"I'd give you the chamber of commerce tour, but there
will be time for that later," she said as we left the town
proper behind us. She must have sensed that I was confused
about what she meant, so she added, "I'm assuming we're
going to be good friends, Will. And there will be other vis-
its to Tarrytown."

We were passing large estates, judging by the wrought
iron gates and fences that would keep out stray dogs or
rogue elephants, although most were set so far back from
the road that I couldn't see them. Occasionally, I caught
glimpses of chimneys and slate roofs.

"I hope you don't think this was all a come-on," Audrey
suddenly said out of nowhere. "I started thinking about it
after we talked on the phone."

"I—"

"Don't," she said. "No lies."

I didn't know what to say, so for once I said nothing. I
felt as though I had been dowsed with the bucket of water.

"I didn't mean to put you on the spot. You had every
reason to believe it was a come-on. I'm sure women throw
themselves at musicians all the time."

"That might be overstating it a bit."

"And if I had met you before—before Zack—who
knows?"

"Actually, that's not the first time I've heard that." I was
thinking back to high school.

"The thing is, what Zack and I had was perfect. A fairy
tale. I keep thinking that any moment he'll walk through
that door. And when he does, I'll be waiting for him. I don't
want to settle for less."

All I could think is Zack was dead and I still felt inadequate compared to him. At least I knew what the ground

rules were. I didn't realize I had dropped out of the conversation until she said, "Is there a Mrs. Blecker? I'm sorry, I should have asked sooner."

"Was."

"And?"

"It was a romantic triangle that ended when she either fell out of love with the piano or me." Audrey probably wondered why I smiled, but it was because I remembered how a friend dubbed my wife "Mrs. Black du Jour." There had been other relationships before her, but none that made it to the altar—or, in this case, the captain's bridge. We were married on a cruise ship. We saved some money because I had been booked to play the lounge. Free room and board. I was happier about it than she was, though.

Audrey swung the car up a long, serpentine drive that led through a woods, over a rise, and into Shangri La. As her home hove into view, I asked, "Have you always lived in a castle?"

It was a modest place, bigger than a breadbox, but smaller than the White House. There were several towers and a glass structure on one end that was undoubtedly a conservatory, the non-musical kind. I had played a few gigs at places like this, mostly out in the Hamptons for the Great Gatsby set. You could always tell they didn't trust musicians, but I suspect they didn't trust anyone.

"It was Zack's idea," she said, opening the trunk so I could get my bag. "His ideas tended to be big. Me, I could be just as happy in a two-room apartment. When you start with nothing, you appreciate everything." And then she was sad for a moment like a cloud had passed over her face.

I don't know if she intended for her remark to pique my curiosity, but it certainly had. I made a mental note to delve a little deeper later.

Standing at the curb, bag in hand, I asked, "Does this hotel have room service?"

"It's off season. I only keep a skeleton crew," she said, shutting the trunk. "Me."

Feeling like I had stepped into a movie, I followed her inside her "humble abode," as Jane Austen might say.

CHAPTER 4

Won by One

People once thought that a goldfish could grow no larger than its bowl. Then some scientist or, more likely, science fair student discovered that if the bowl is too small, the fish dies. I couldn't help thinking about that—and how many fish may gave their lives in the name of science—as I compared the size of Audrey's place to my own. She should have been a Brobdingnagian giantess and I should have been dead. Which just goes to show people aren't fish.

I had been in a few mansions before, but I had never felt that the people living there were real. Audrey was real. The place was elegant, but warm, if that makes any sense. The scale was immense—the foyer was at least two stories high. Clear out the furniture and you could have played a game of half-court basketball. But still it was homey in a Citizen Kane sort of way. Every choice, from décor to furnishings had been exactly the right one. I was immediately drawn to the bay window in the great room which provided an unobstructed view of the Hudson River.

"You could charge people for tours," I said as I stood there absorbing it all. I had forgotten how many shades of green occurred in nature—colors for which there are no paint samples.

"Yes," she said softly. "It doesn't seem right that anyone should own it, does it?" Again, a certain sadness had descended on her, but then was gone after a few moments.

"Are you hungry? I've got some cold cuts and could fix you a sandwich."

"Musicians are always hungry."

"And thirsty?"

"Especially thirsty."

As I retraced my steps, I noticed a black lacquered box resting on the fireplace mantle. It could have been a music box or jewelry box, but I suspected it contained something more precious—that it held all that remained of Zachary Taylor. I had to resist the temptation to take a peek inside.

Having left my bag parked by the front door, I followed Audrey into the kitchen. I sat on a tall stool at the island, while she laid out a spread of sliced deli meats, cheeses, several kinds of bread, and various other sandwich fixings—enough to feed a half-dozen football tailgaters.

"You expecting company?" I asked.

"I guess I did overdo it a bit. It's been a while since I've entertained."

"Your house—your home—is incredible. Absolutely beautiful. Zack must have done well for himself." Mentally, I included her in the tally.

"He was very successful at his job."

"And what was that?" I was hoping she wouldn't say musician.

"I guess you could say he was an inventor. He made medical devices. He held a number of patents—hundreds, I would guess."

"That doesn't surprise me. I always expected him to succeed at whatever he put his mind to."

Back in our band days, Zack was always tinkering with the electronics—his guitar, my keyboard, our amps—trying to improve the sound. He was sort of a self-taught engineer even then. If ventriloquist Paul Winchell could make an artificial heart, then I'm sure Zack Taylor could make other medical gizmos if he set his mind to it.

"It's ironic," Audrey said. "He saved thousands of lives, but couldn't save his own."

Although I am more sensitive than you might expect, I am not outwardly warm and fuzzy. As Audrey once more slid into her reverie, I knew that I should probably do or say something to comfort her. But I didn't know what. After a few awkward moments while I debated whether to take her hand and utter a few bromides cribbed from sympathy cards, she snapped out of it.

"There I go feeling sorry for myself again." She lapsed into silence for a few more moments as she busied herself sprucing up the kitchen and I decided not to disturb her. When she spoke again, she said, "I feel like I already know you."

"Really? What did Zack tell you?"

"It's not what he told me. It's your music. I've been listening to it a lot."

"Listening?"

"To your album."

I did not have an album, but we—the Blues Attack—did. Once. "I'm sorry," I replied, trying to make a joke.

"No, I like it."

"I do, too. Mostly. So what did you learn?"

"Well, you're from Columbus. I know that." And then she laughed. She laughed because "I'm From Columbus" was the lead-off song on the album. "Is there a story behind it?"

"Yeah. We played this club once and the owner had been promoting us as a Cleveland band. So I wrote it to let people who were seeing us for the first time exactly who we were—and who we weren't."

"Sounds like you had a chip on your shoulder?"

"I guess I did. But he wasn't the only club owner to do stuff like that. A lot of bands found themselves being billed as 'from England' if they had a name that sounded at all British." I remembered how the one Columbus band, The Epics, got hired by Super K Productions to masquerade as the British Road Runners to push a single, "Do Something To Me." And another local band, The Dantes, got passed off as Them, Van Morrison's band, because the bass player owned the name or something.

"Do you still know it?" she asked.

"Probably. It's been half a lifetime or more since I played it, though."

"Well, I won't put you on the spot—not yet, anyway. I want you to get comfortable first. But I do have some questions."

"Ask away."

"You wrote the lyrics and Zack wrote the music, right?"

"It was more complicated than that. Zack was the teacher, I was the pupil. He was already an incredible musician when I met him. He would give me a musical phrase or a title and I would work on it and then throw it back to him. We were collaborators, but I became responsible for the final form the lyrics took and we worked on the music together. Then I would finalize the arrangement. We both contributed equally, I would say."

"So the songs say what you wanted them to?"

"I've always been pretty particular about lyrics. I hate the way many pop songs are just a jumble of phrases that don't scan, don't rhyme, and don't really say anything. They're neither profound nor poetic. People read all kinds of things into them because they are mostly incoherent. ."

"So who is a good lyricist?"

I didn't have to think about it. "Joni Mitchell. There are others who have written songs that compare to her best—Kristofferson, Prine, Frishberg, Lehrer, a few others—but she's probably the most consistent."

"Frishberg?"

"Dave Frishberg. Wrote 'My Attorney Bernie.' You should check him out."

"Not Dylan?"

"No. I've always thought his songs have a kind of a studied illiteracy. You know he's a smart guy writing down to people."

"You're joking, right?"

"If anything, the universe is playing a joke on me." I was overstating it a bit. I could think of some Dylan songs I liked, but I didn't put him on a pedestal.

"So who are the bad ones?"

"Whoever writes the songs for Journey."

"That's harsh."

"Hey, I don't blame them. The formula works. And I'm not even certain they try to make them rhyme. 'Believin' and 'feelin', 'boy' and 'Detroit,' 'city' and 'city.' People loved them and they made money hand over fist. It's easy for me to say I wouldn't sell out, but I've never had the chance."

"You seem to know a lot of their songs."

"Guilty pleasure, I guess." I noticed Audrey hadn't touched any of the food. "You aren't eating?"

"Haven't had much of an appetite," she said and I realized I had wandered into another mine field. "Tell me, Will, why did you come here?"

I almost choked on my sandwich. "You-you invited me," I said, covering my mouth while I tried to swallow. I wondered how many more sucker punches might be coming. First the one in the car and, now, this.

"I know that. But why? You don't know me."

"You're the wife of my best friend."

"Your best friend—a guy you hadn't seen in what? Thirty or forty years?"

"I didn't say I was his best friend."

"But you were. That's what I don't understand. How could two friends stay so far apart?"

That was an imponderable. The question hadn't been far from my mind ever since I learned of Zack's death. All of us our aware that the sand is running through the hourglass. That fact was driven home to me from watching the opening of my mom's soap opera, "Days of Our Lives," throughout much of my childhood. And yet we act like we have all of the time in the world.

"I hope you don't expect me to say something profound," I said, "because I don't have anything. I just know our lives went in different directions. He went off to college, I stayed with music. I would stop by to see his parents when I went home, just to hear how he was doing. But after my parents died, I didn't have any reason to go back to Columbus. And I just assumed he left New York after college."

"I'm not blaming you, Will. Zack was equally at fault. I just want to understand how men can be like that."

"We're not talking about Zack and me anymore, are we?"

She got that deer-in-the-headlights look. "I'm sorry," she said. "I'm feeling a lot of anger and I don't know why."

"That's normal," I said. I suspected she was asking me questions that she never got around to asking Zack or else she was hoping for different answers.

"Is it?"

I didn't really feel I had anything to offer, so I kept silent.

"I tried to get him to look you up. He kept saying he would and I think he would have if he hadn't... " And her voice trailed off.

It wasn't a conversation I wanted to continue because it only made me feel guiltier.

"He wasn't a happy person, you know. I tried to make him happy, but there was a part of him I couldn't reach."

From what I could see, Zack seemed to have it all. Successful career, beautiful wife, amazing home, more money than a third world country.

"Are you a religious person, Will?"

"I would like to think so. Some days more than others. It helps to get out of the city."

"So you believe in God?"

"That's the easy part. Like Vonnegut said: 'Music is the proof of the existence of God.'"

"But what kind of a God?"

I didn't want to get dragged into a discussion of why

God allows evil, suffering, and all kinds of stuff to exist because I knew my answers wouldn't comfort a grieving widow. "If you are asking me why God allowed Zack to die, I can't tell you. That's a religious question. And the answer ultimately comes down to whatever works for you. But I do know this: everything has a cause and, if you remove one link in the chain, starting from before you or I even met Zack, we wouldn't be here right now, the two of us. So I guess it depends on how you feel about this moment."

She took a few moments to ponder what I had just said. Normally, I preferred to speak through my music. I wasn't even sure I had made any sense.

Finally, she asked, "Do you belong to a church?"

"There's one I go to sometimes."

"Why?"

"Well, because there's music and I sometimes think God might be hanging out there, too."

"Do they ever have you perform?"

"Occasionally."

"What do you play? Hymns?"

"No. More contemporary things."

"Like what?"

I gestured toward the piano near the bay window. "Would you like me to play one?"

"Yes, please."

After wiping my hands with a paper napkin, I took a seat at the piano. It was a vintage Steinway, probably a Model B, with a flame mahogany finish. Much more than a piece of furniture. I began to sing:

> "Won by one!
> Who was sent to save us.
> Won by one!
> None is greater than He.
> Won by one!
> Who our sins forgave us,

When He died upon the cross
At Calvary"

I had written it for a Vacation Bible School program, but
it had morphed into a praise song for the contemporary service.

"Won by one!
With His words He taught us.
Won by one!
He has opened the door.
Won by one!
With His blood he bought us,
So we can be justified
Forever more."

When I first started attending the church, I was annoyed
by a lot of the praise music I heard where they simply took
lines from the Bible and repeated them ad nauseam with
little regard for rhyme scheme and a few "Yay, Jesus" cho-
ruses thrown in. But then I got dragged to a Twila Paris
concert and realized that I had tarred their ilk with too broad
a brush. She gave me something to aspire to.

"Just as the sun has divided
The day from the night.
The line has been drawn between
What's wrong and what's right.
Into a world that had fallen,
The Lord sent His son.
Though the battle still rages,
The war has been won."

Looking up, I saw that Audrey was looking beyond me,
through the window and over the lawn that rolled down toward the river.

"Won by one!
Won by one!
Won by one!
Won by one!

"Won by one!
Sin need not enslave us.
Won by one!
He has shown us the way.
Won by one!
For new life He gave us,
When He rose up from the tomb
On Easter Day."

After I had finished, I sat quietly until Audrey returned from wherever her mind had gone. "That's nice," she said.

"I'm glad you like it."

"So, do you believe there's a Heaven and that good people go there?"

"I want to. I would hate to think that this is all there is."

"I want to believe that, too. So what do you think it's like—heaven?"

"That's anybody's guess. What people believe is mostly Hollywood. The Bible doesn't go into much detail." One of my interests was comparative religions and I had read a number of books on the subject.

"Well, if there is one, I'm sure Zack's there."

"So maybe you'll see him again." Personally, I wasn't at all sure that heaven worked like that, but I was trying to be as positive as I could.

"I don't know."

"Why not?'

"Because heaven is just for good people."

There were at least a dozen follow-up questions that sprang to mind, but I was not inclined to ask any of them.

"Well, I hope not too good," I said. "I'd kind of like to make the cut."

CHAPTER 5

What's Love?

Halfway through my second sandwich, I finally asked the sixty-four dollar question, the one that we had been dancing around ever since we spoke on the phone. "So what is it do you want my help with?" Taking another bite, I awaited her answer.

"Ah, yes. The reason I dragged you all the way out here." Slipping off the stool across from me, Audrey wiped her hands on a towel, then tossed it on the counter. "Let me show you."

I quickly drained the rest of my beer and reluctantly abandoned the sandwich, a rather nice pastrami and Swiss on rye. My mother always said my eyes were bigger than my stomach, but she would not think so if she could see me now.

A circular stairway led down to what I had grown up calling a basement, but this was more like a medieval wine cellar, though without the dust and cobwebs. A cellar with maid service. The walls were cut stone, the ceiling arched brick, and the floor a checkerboard of quarry tile. It was all video game perfect. Stepping through the doorway, I was transported back in time. Audrey turned to look at me, waiting to see my reaction.

I found myself in the Cracked Cup, a coffee house where the Blues Attack used to play. Located in a downtown church basement, its walls were lined with old wooden doors, the cross-and-Bible-type, salvaged from buildings

that had been razed when the freeway was being construct-
ed. We performed on a small platform about a foot off the
floor, hardly large enough to hold our equipment. In fact,
my Leslie speaker had to sit on the floor. And here it all was
again.

Somehow, Zack had recreated the Cracked Cup in his
rec room—although architects probably have a grander
word for it. The walls were hung with framed memorabilia,
from ticket stubs to newspaper articles to fliers and small
posters. There was a Rock-Ola Bubbler jukebox in one corner and an old Curtis Mathes TV in another. Stealing a look
at one of the posters, I saw it advertised an appearance by
the Blues Attack. Beside it was a *Columbus Citizen-Journal*
clipping from when we placed second in a battle of the
bands at the Ohio State Fairgrounds Beef and Cattle Barn.

"This is truly amazing," I said, although amazing didn't
go far enough. "How…"

"Zack had a bunch of pickers keeping an eye out for
things. Same folks Terry Stewart used for the Rock and
Roll Hall of Fame." Apparently, they were friends with
Stewart, the museum's former CEO.

"I wouldn't have believed most of this stuff existed anymore."

"Well," Audrey said, "you did have a fan club. Turns out
the president kept a couple of scrapbooks. That's where
Zack got most of the posters and things. Her picture's over
there."

Above the jukebox, there was a framed photo of a couple
of teenage girls I immediately recognized, but whose names
I no longer recalled. They were posing with Zack. It appeared to have been taken during one of our appearances,
probably at a school dance. Or maybe an armory—all the
small towns had one. It didn't surprise me that I wasn't in
the picture. I was generally the third or fourth favorite Beatle.

"These are letters from some of your fans," Audrey said,
pointing to a cluster of framed items on another wall. I saw

I was mentioned in one of them, while Zack was mentioned in all—no surprise there.

"And look at this."

I glanced over to where Audrey was fiddling with the knobs on the TV. As the image bloomed on the screen, I found myself watching a video of Zack Black & the Blues Attack performing on Jerry Rasor's "Dance Party." It was the Valentine's Day show and there were paper hearts taped up all over the place. Although I was watching a younger version of me playing and singing, I felt a disconnect. It was hard to imagine myself back in the body of the rail-thin teenage boy standing behind the massive Hammond organ.

I listened for a moment. During my career, I had learned thousands of songs and I discovered along the way that I never truly forgot any of them. All I had to do was think of myself playing the notes and the words would come back to me. And for a moment, I felt like I was back there.

"'Hush,'" I said, answering the question I had asked myself. "Deep Purple." After years of playing requests, I automatically cited the original artist whenever I played a song like the old radio deejays would do. It had become part of the title. I remembered buying the first Deep Purple album at Lazarus Northland. A friend's sister worked in the record department.

I stood mesmerized by the video. I had copied Jon Lord note-for-note. As I was critiquing my own playing, my gaze gradually shifted to the elephant in the room. I had seen it when I first came in, sitting in the middle of the floor. It would have been impossible not to. And I had been giving it furtive glances ever since. I had wanted to rush right up to it. After all, it's not every day you see a statue of yourself. But, instead, I decided to act nonchalant.

The centerpiece of Zack's little museum was an elevated platform on which four life-size figures were posed playing the guitar, bass, drums, and organ. There was no mistaking that Zack intended them to be us. The figures were stylized and not creepy like waxworks, but each one had something that gave it a specific identity. Zack's was wearing his old fringe vest with the pockets for his harps. Mine had on a pair of Buddy Holly glasses identical to the ones I wore back then. Evan Bishop, our drummer, sat up high behind his kit, ramrod straight, and twirled his sticks like they were airplane propellers. His playing style owed a lot to the great Dino Danelli of the Rascals. And Wes Kennedy, our bass player, had a Daniel Boone hat, like a bargain basement Felix Pappalardi. The logo I had designed was painted on the drum head.

"I can't believe it. Everything looks authentic."

"It better be. Zack paid a small fortune for it."

I had worked my way around to the B-3. I don't even own one now, but for years I nearly ruined my back hauling it to our gigs. It was even worse when I learned how to use the pedals and had to take them everywhere, too. Well, not exactly had to, but wanted to. I felt like the captain of the Enterprise when I sat behind the console.

"Does it work?"

"Sure. Want to try it?"

"What do I do with...me?" I gestured toward the life-size mannequin that was hunkered over the keyboard.

"Just push him aside," she said. "Here, I'll help." She slid "Billy" over to the end of the band, then held onto his shoulder to make sure he didn't topple off.

Taking a seat, I flipped on the power and listened. There is nothing like the hum of an old vacuum tube amplifier coming to life. I then punched the Leslie—a rotating speaker—and it emitted its distinctive warble. After doing a little dance on the pedals, I was ready to take requests.

I decided to kick it off with "Chest Fever." Channeling Jimmy Greenspoon—I never liked the mix on Garth Hudson's version—I began slowly pounding out the chords like a man giving CPR. It came as no surprise that the acoustics in the room were great. After the first chorus, I paused just to listen to the halo of sound around my head.

"Don't stop," Audrey said. "I didn't realize how much I

missed live music. I was used to hearing Zack play all the time."

"Do you play an instrument?"

"I played second clarinet in the school band, but that was in a different life."

"So what would you like to hear?" I was doodling around on the keyboards, waiting for her to reply, when I spotted something that stopped me cold.

"What is it?" Audrey asked.

I ran my fingers across a series of deep scratches on top of the console. They were initials...exactly whose, I had forgotten. They had been carved there forty years before by some guy in a road band who thought he was Keith Emerson. He had asked to sit in with us one night and then rewarded us by leaving his initials—KB—like a horrible scar. "I used to own this. Where did he find it?"

"Like I said, he had pickers scouring Ohio and elsewhere for anything related to the Blues Attack. It became an obsession, especially after he became ill."

I almost expected to see James Brown's Afro Sheen still smeared on the cabinet. We had opened for him a couple of times and I had never wiped it off.

"There's a lot of history here," I said. "I got these bass pedals from Chickadee. I needed some and he never used his because he played bass on the lower register. Sold them to me for twenty-five dollars."

"Chick-A-Dee?"

"Johnny Albert. Used to work a lot of black jazz clubs all over Ohio and up into Detroit. Sometimes worked with a drummer they called Chickadoo. I just can't believe Zack tracked it down."

"Money was no object. I think he always hoped to get the band back together again."

"I don't think that could ever happen," I said and immediately regretted it. Audrey looked at me with an expression I couldn't decipher. She then sidled over to the jukebox and made a selection. The machinery jumped to life. A record was picked off the carousel and deposited on the turntable. The tone arm arced across to the spinning disc and settled lightly on the outer edge.

There was a brief crackling like the crumpling of cellophane followed by the opening riff of an electric piano. And then Zack's voice dropped in like a bouncing ball:

"My friends keep telling me to see a doctor."

Wes and I answered, "*Doc-tor!*"

"They just can't imagine what's wrong with me. (Doc-tor!)
If I'm not sick I must be going crazy. (Doc-tor!)
But maybe there's another possibility."

I joined on the bridge:

"'Cause these symptoms appear
Whenever you are near.
Can't keep my knees from shaking
And I know there's no mistaking
When I get that awful aching in my heart–
That a spell's about to start."

For the chorus, Wes and I, maybe even Evan, answered Zack in a call-and-response:

"What's love (What's love?)
But a kind of fever.
What's love (What's love?)
But some social disease.
What's love (What's love?)
But an endless heartache.
Won't someone tell me, please,
What's love?"

In 1968, "What's Love?" reached the top of the charts

across much of Ohio, except Toledo for some reason. Rusty Bryant once told me that "nothing good ever came out of Toledo," which made me think he had some bad experiences, too. It was one of a dozen or so original songs Zack and I had written during a week at Rocky Fork Lake when we realized we wouldn't get much further as a cover band. Our biggest rival, The Dantes, had learned this the hard way when they went on tour, wound up in Los Angeles, and found themselves pitted in showcases against the likes of Rhinoceros, Illinois Speed Press, and Chicago Transit Authority.

"This could turn into an epidemic. (Doc-tor!)
Got the worst case that they've ever seen (Doc-tor!)
And if I don't respond soon to their treatment, (Doc-tor!)
They might have to put me under quarantine."

"That's the song that got us the record deal."
"I know," Audrey said.
Of course she did. She was our biggest fan—Zack's anyway. She had started dancing to the music, one of those people who just couldn't keep from moving whenever she heard a song playing. Personally, I was never much of a dancer, even when we were performing. The keyboard kept me anchored to one spot. Shy by nature, I was also glad to have a piece of furniture to hide behind.

"Still what's hardest to explain
Despite the misery and pain
That even though my head is reeling
There's something so appealing
That I wouldn't trade this feeling or this strife
'Cause I've never felt any better in my life!"

There was a lot of bubblegum music on the radio in 1968…still is, come to think of it. The 1910 Fruitgum Company and Ohio Express were charting in the top twenty. But The Beatles' "Hey Jude" would go on to be the number one record of the year. Still, when the A & R man for Capitol Records called around the major markets to see how it was doing, he kept hearing it was sitting at number two in Ohio.

"What's number one?" he would ask.

"'What's Love?' by Zack Black and the Blues Attack."

"Who's that?"

"A Columbus band."

Finally, after hearing it often enough, he decided to fly out to Ohio to investigate. He had us do a showcase at one of the better campus hangouts, Ruby Tuesday. Of course, we packed it with as many friends and fans as we could, but we were already a good draw. We played five of our best originals for him before he waved us off. "That'll do," he said. "Thanks." And then he walked out.

Zack looked at me and I looked at him. Apparently, we had failed the audition or whatever it was, but we didn't know why. Without saying another word, we began to pack up our gear. "So that was it? What happens now?" Evan asked.

"We get better," Zack said.

> "What's love (What's love?)
> But a kind of fever.
> What's love (What's love?)
> But some social disease.
> What's love (What's love?)
> But an endless heartache.
> Won't someone tell me, please,
> What's love? (What's love?)
> What's love? (What's love?)
> What's love? (What's love?)
> What's love? (What's love?)
> What's love? (What's love?)
> What's love? (What's love?)"

Two days later, Stan Billups, the A & R guy, called our agent and the day after that we drove to Detroit to sign contracts. We had a deal for two singles and one album with an option for four more. I remember everyone but Zack congratulating each other. When I asked him what was wrong, he said, "This is the end." I didn't know what he meant and wouldn't until much later. But it was the end—the end of innocence.

CHAPTER 6

A Hole in the Heart

The grand tour of the Zack Taylor American Museum and Cabinet of Curiosities was starting to get me down. All these reminders of our glory days were making me second-guess my part in the whole fiasco. "Fiasco" being the term my old friend Chuz Alfred used to describe the various reversals in his own musical career. So I decided to get right to the point. "What's this favor you want, Audrey?"

"Not me," she said. "Zack. It's a favor for Zack."

She walked toward a wooden, arch top door and took hold of the handle. For a moment I expected Zack to jump out shouting, "April fool!" But, of course, he didn't. Instead, she swung it open and tilted her head, directing me to enter.

The lights came on as I stepped into the room. They reminded me of a planetarium, mimicking a sunrise. I found myself standing in a recording studio, as up-to-date as any I had seen. There was a good assortment of instruments, including a Yamaha grand piano, as well as various electronic keyboards, a drum kit, and a half-dozen microphones. But it was the guitars that really caught my attention. There were dozens of them carefully stored in cabinets behind glass. Most guitar players I've known were collectors, but Zack was light years ahead of them. He could have opened up his own music store like Mark Chatfield did with Cowtown Guitars.

Audrey had removed one guitar from its case and held it out to me. I took it, but not being a guitar player—easy to play, hard to play well—I couldn't do much more than admire the workmanship. It was a beauty. But all I knew for sure was that it was immaculate—restored, I assumed—made by Fender, and probably dated back to the 'fifties.

"It's a 'fifty-four Fender Stratocaster," Audrey said. "It was his favorite."

Now, I remembered Zack playing three or four guitars, but I didn't think this was one of them. Maybe it was a later acquisition. "It doesn't look familiar." Of course, I wasn't one of those people who could identify car models, either. But ask me about electronic organs...

"It's the one he learned to play on. It belonged to Spoolie Johnson."

Elmore "Spoolie" Johnson. That was a name from the past. Zack had family in Mississippi, and his parents used to take him there on vacation every summer. One year, he heard an elderly black man playing guitar on a park bench and he was hooked. He begged his father to buy him one and pay for lessons. For several summers, Johnson became his teacher and mentor. He had been a blues musician, working juke joints throughout the south or something. Zack got his love of the blues from Johnson. And, so the story went, this guitar.

"He made me promise to give it back," she said.

"Back? Back to whom? Spoolie must be dead by now."

"His family, then? I don't know. There must be someone. I've got to try, anyway. Will you help me?"

This wasn't what I expected at all when she invited me to her place. I thought maybe she wanted me to assist her in getting Zack's affairs in order, maybe sort through his music or organize some photos. But I never anticipated she'd want me to go on a cross country jaunt.

"I don't know..."

"Please, Will. I don't know who else to ask."

I started talking before I even knew what I was going to say. "I have my work—"

"I'll pay you for your time. You can get someone to fill in for you, can't you?"

The fact is my dance card was mostly open at the moment. I didn't have any regular gigs and had been hustling jobs wherever I could. Piano players are a dime a dozen in the city. I was reduced to working children's birthday parties. Almost.

"I suppose," I said. I was stalling for time, hoping something brilliant would come to me, but failing miserably.

"I wouldn't have asked, but Zack always said he could count on you."

That did it. "All right. I'll have to make a few calls. And you don't have to pay me anything."

"But I insist. I have more money than I can ever possibly use. Let me spend a little of it to make this trip worth your time. Besides, it'll be fun."

As a musician, it wasn't like me to turn down a job, knowing each one could be my last. And Audrey wouldn't want me to be less than authentic. "I'll just have to clear my calendar." I was fibbing a little bit there. My calendar was so bare I could almost use it over again. "When did you want to go?"

"Monday."

"Monday?"

"If that's okay. The sooner, the better, right?"

"But all the clothes I have are what I brought with me."

"We can run over to White Plains and pick some up."

What choice did I have? None. The people I needed to reach—most of them, anyway—would be working at that hour, so I texted them all the same message, listing the available dates and asking them to contact me with the ones they could cover. Normally, I would have my agent handle it, but he hadn't landed me any gigs in months. I suspect he had dropped me but didn't say so, just in case I stumbled into something big. There was the time one of the songs I had written was used for a car commercial. That was a nice, fat paycheck and he, of course, got his cut for doing nothing.

While I was taking care of business, Audrey was searching for something in a four-drawer, oak filing cabinet. When I looked up, she was holding a file folder carefully labeled "Elmore Johnson." She handed it to me and I began leafing through it. There were a handful of black and white snapshots from 1958-1960, all of which had Oxford, Mississippi, written on the back of them. In one photo, a kid—obviously Zack—was sitting on a bench in front of a barber shop, posing with the same Stratocaster Audrey had shown me. There was also a brief, typewritten bio, which included a discography or, rather, photocopies of record labels. There were ten altogether, almost enough songs for an album. I hadn't known until that minute that "Spoolie" Johnson had done any recording.

"I would have loved to have heard some of these." Old records were almost like religious artifacts to me.

"So let's do it."

"But these have to be really rare."

"I don't know about that, but I'm sure we have them."

"You own them?"

"As I said, Zack had—"

"—these pickers. I get it."

Audrey stepped out of the studio and crossed to the other jukebox, a Wurlitzer, the kind that played CDs. She scanned the selections, punched a button, and in a few moments the recording began to play. I could hear surface noise, so it was obviously a recording of the original record, probably shellac. I suspect Zack hadn't want to risk damaging it through repeated plays.

I stood in the doorway so I could listen better. It was a blues song that I didn't remember hearing before. The lyrics were earnest and dark, but otherwise unexceptional, sung by somebody...Spoolie?...who sounded a bit like B. B. King. However, what really pinned my ears back was the instrumental break. It wasn't exactly note-for-note, but it was highly reminiscent of Zack's inspired playing on "Hole in My Heart." I say "inspired" because we had really thought it was Zack who came up with it. What we didn't know was that it was lifted from an old Spoolie Johnson 78.

"Zack stole that riff," I said, smiling for some inexplicable reason, and immediately thought better of it when I realized I had spoken aloud. After all, I was in the presence of his grieving widow. "I'm sorry. I didn't mean for it to come out that way."

"That's okay," she replied. "Zack felt the same. When he got this record about ten years ago, he was stunned. He hadn't realized he had done it. He said he must have heard Spoolie play it when he was a kid, but he didn't consciously remember it. And that wasn't the only one. There are a couple of others on the Blues Attack recordings."

Of course, musicians had been "borrowing" from each other for years. And since Zack learned to play blues guitar at Spoolie's knee, it's not surprising that you could hear the influence. But this was more like plagiarism—or would be if it were done consciously. Spoolie should have gotten a cut of the royalties at least, but in the topsy-turvy world of music, none of us saw any.

He could have gotten all the royalties and wouldn't have been any better off. The same was true for other bands I had crossed paths with in my younger days: The Music Explosion, The Lemon Pipers, The Ohio Express. Even The Byrds got robbed. I guess the mob has always been behind the music business. The Beatles and Stones were about the only ones who always got paid.

Audrey had made another selection and as soon as Spoolie's record came to an end, the juke box pulled another one from the rack, dropped it on the turntable, and it began to play. Like a contestant on "Name That Tune," I knew it within three notes. It was Zack's voice singing.

"I stay up all hours,

I can't get to sleep.
Tried counting my blessings,
Even tried counting sheep,
But that won't do,
No, it just won't do.
'Cause I've got this great big hole in my heart
And it's shaped like you."

It was our record. I had wanted to build a song around the line "there's a you-shaped hole in my heart" or "there's a hole in my heart shaped like you," but I wasn't getting anywhere. Then one day we were jamming after practice and I just began tossing out lyrics off the top of my head. The fact that Zack had to double time the line when he was singing it made it even better.

"Tried drowning my sorrows,
Tried drowning my pain.
But each time I put the bottle down
It all comes back again
And that won't do.
No, it just won't do.
'Cause I've got this great big hole in my heart
And it's shaped like you."

The band then launched into an extended instrumental break that almost compensated for my underdone lyrics. I had wanted to polish them some, but Zack wouldn't hear of it. He liked the roughness, something I, with my love of show tunes, bristled at.

When it came to the bridge, it was just Zack singing over drums for the first four lines before the while band joined in.

"Went down to the crossroads
And called the Devil's name.
Hung around an hour or two

But the Devil never came.
Guess he must have known the
Hell you put me through,
'Cause I've got this great big hole in my heart
And it's shaped like you."

The thing about this lumbering blues tune was the crowd loved it, even if it was written by a white boy, and we loved playing it. Some nights we just kept it going for ten or twelve minutes.

"Won't you show me some mercy?
Won't you throw me a bone?
Don't wanna face another day,
Another day alone!
No, that won't do.
No, that just won't do.
'Cause I've got this great big hole in my heart
And it's shaped like you."

Here we created some room for the horns to do their thing.

"Got this great big hole
And it's shaped like you.
And it's shaped like you.
Got this great big hole
And it's shaped like you.
Got this great big hole
And it's shaped like you.
Got this great big hole
And it's shaped like…"

Then it just trailed out, something I suspect songs didn't do until people began recording.

"You wrote that?" Audrey asked when it was over.

"It was a group effort."

"It's catchy."

"Well, there're shots you can get for that."

"No, really."

"We were pretty good, weren't we," I said, focusing on the performance. Personally, I thought we could have held our own with a lot of the second tier bands, the ones that are fondly remembered, but didn't quite get the gold ring. "At least we didn't embarrass ourselves." I was thinking of some of the Columbus bands that went into the studio without giving any—or, perhaps, sufficient—thought to what they would record. That's how you ended up with things like The Sidewinders covering the old Girl Scout song, "Three Chartreuse Buzzards Siting on a Fence."

"I think so. I wish I could have seen you back then." And then her voice grew softer. "I wish I could see you now." She turned her attention back to the guitar. "I think returning the guitar to Spoolie's family is his way of trying to make amends."

So that's what this was about: Zack trying to put things right for a wrong he felt he had committed—the conscious or unconscious appropriation of some guitar licks. Damn. Now, I had no choice but to help her out. Not that I was complaining about being stuck for a week or so with a woman who would ordinarily be out of my league.

Someone said, "Where words fail, music speaks." It might have been Hans Christian Andersen, again. If so, he probably listened to a lot of blues or country, or whatever was the nineteenth century Danish equivalent, because his love life was a disaster. We had that in common.

Audrey turned the record over. The flipside was our cover of "Broken Wings." I sang the lead on this one, possibly the most mournful song in our repertoire. It was kind of embarrassing hearing my younger self trying to sound like I was a world-weary old black man twice my age. My voice was never rough enough for this kind of material, which was why I was eager for us to create our own.

"Why did you request 'Broken Wings' at Joe's that night?"

"After Zack died and I started listening to all the old Blues Attack recordings, I found myself returning to them again and again. That little bird with the broken wings—that was me. Some days it still is."

"I often think how we all have a soundtrack running through our lives," I said. "Everyone born since World War II has, if not before. We are surrounded by music everywhere we go. I can hear a song and remember where I was when I first heard it. Take 'Cherish' by the Association. I remember my friend, Joe, and I were on our way to pick up our tuxes for the senior prom when it came on the car radio."

"I know what you mean. I was going through a bad time when 'Don't You Forget About Me' was a big hit. So whenever I hear it, it's like I've jumped into a time machine and gone back to 1985."

There it was again—the gulf between our ages. Music should bring people closer together, but that song pushed us further apart. She could have been my daughter. "I'm not sure if it's the same for young people today. Maybe I'm just getting to be an old fogey—actually there's no 'maybe' about it—but I don't hear many songs that I think would invoke the same sort of nostalgia."

"Everyone thinks they grew up in the best possible time for them, don't they?"

"True. But I actually did." I loved having been a child of the 'sixties. The music felt more important then. It was important.

"I wish I could have known you back then. All of you. Then I might have had more time with Zack."

"Well, I'm not sure you would have wanted to know all of us—back then, anyway. And it could be you met Zack at just the right time. If you had met him any earlier, it might not have turned out the same."

"You're right. He probably wouldn't have liked me."

"Why's that?"

"I wasn't very likable."

"I find that hard to believe."

"It's true. I was an entirely different person. I don't even recognize myself."

"Well, we all have our secrets."

She did not respond. I was beginning to think Audrey had as many layers as an onion. And then it occurred to me that would be a good idea for a song. I would try to remember it for later.

CHAPTER 7

Make the Most of Ev'ryday

I awoke to the sound of rain on the window—just rain. In the city, there would have been a cacophony of sounds—sounds rising from the street, sounds broadcast through the building, sounds generated by my own apartment. Gershwin would turn it into music. But here in the countryside, it was like the gentle drumming of fingertips on the glass, and almost too quiet to sleep.

Audrey was already awake and moving about when I padded into the kitchen and took a seat at the island. The lights were low and it was still dark outside. There were flashes of lightning in the distance like the flicker of a fluorescent fixture going bad, but without the annoying hum.

"You're up early," I said. "Or late. Unless I missed a day."

"I didn't sleep well."

"Didn't or don't?"

"Both. I guess you're starting to understand me."

"There're two kinds of people: those who have trouble sleeping and those who do little else."

"Like some coffee?"

"No, thanks."

"You don't think I can make good coffee?"

"I'm sure you make fantastic coffee. I'm just not a coffee drinker."

"Well, we'll see about that," she said. "Help yourself to whatever's in the fridge." So I did, pouring myself a glass of freshly squeezed juice—pomegranate?—from a carafe.

"How long have you lived here?"

"About a year."

"A year?" I was taken somewhat aback because that meant Zack had barely unpacked his suitcase before he died. "Zack hardly got to enjoy this place, did he?"

"For Zack, the enjoyment was in the planning. He made it for me—a place to house memories. He knew he wouldn't be here for the long haul."

"So he wasn't well when he built it?"

"I don't think so. Of course, he didn't bother to tell me he was sick."

I detected a note of bitterness or regret, I wasn't sure which. I had enough trouble sorting through my own emotions, let alone those of a woman twenty or twenty-five years my junior. She was staring out the window. "Looks like it's going to be a dreary day." She might not have been talking about the weather.

The house was clearly designed for entertaining. There were two groupings of couches in the great room on either side of a fireplace you could park a Volkswagen in. The Steinway sat off to the left of the French doors which opened onto a patio overlooking the Hudson River. I wandered over to it and took a seat on the bench.

There were several sheets of manuscript paper curling on the music rack. I recognized Zack's handwriting by its illegibility, which was another reason why I had done the arranging for the band. I tried to absorb what I could of it. More Bach than Beatles or Beach Boys,

"Play me something," Audrey said, plopping down in a nearby chair where she could watch me.

"What would you like to hear?"

"You choose. You're the professional entertainer."

She might not have meant it as a test, but that was how I took it. I knew next to nothing about her except she was the wealthy widow of my one-time best friend. She had a flair for the dramatic. And she was still grieving. While I ran my

fingers along the keys, checking—through force of habit—
to see if the piano was in tune, a song flashed into my mind
that I hadn't played in years. Maybe it would cheer her up, I
thought.

"I once wrote several songs for this off-off-off-
Broadway show—*Pollyanna of the Seven Gables*. It was
supposed to be a spoof on 1930s-style musicals, so I was
trying to imagine Fred Astaire and Ginger Rogers doing
them. This was probably the best of the bunch." I began to
sing in a sprightly manner, my hands leaping like gazelles
high above the keyboard.

> "So what if the sun's not shining?
> Who cares if the skies are gray?
> Just look for the silver lining
> And make the most of ev'ryday."

Pausing after the first verse, I glanced at Audrey. She
had turned her face so I couldn't see it. "It's a dumb song.
You want me to play something else?"

"No," she said, still hiding her face from me. "Go on."
So I did.

> "It seems like it's always raining
> When you're going out to play
> But don't waste your time complaining
> Just make the most of ev'ryday."

My voice was kind of froggy. That's me: the velvet frog.
It would be a couple more hours before I could sing decent-
ly. Fortunately, the song didn't require much range so I continued to croak through it.

> "Well, some days are good and some days are bad,
> But I never keep track.
> For good days or bad days, once they are gone,
> You can never, ever, ever, ever get them back!"

"This," I said, "is where you imagine Bernadette Peters tap dancing up a storm."

"Bernadette Peters? Really?"

"I was told that that Bernadette Peters—or maybe her sister or cousin—would be doing it. But I'm pretty sure she never even saw it—at least I never saw her. And the show closed in rehearsals."

"Too bad."

> "So what if the wind is blowing?
> As long as you don't blow away.
> The secret of life is knowing
> To make the best of ev'ry day.

> "So get up, get out, and get going,
> And make the best of ev'ry.
> Make the best of ev'ry.
> Make the best of ev'ry,
> Ev'ry,
> Ev'ry,
> Day!"

I ended with a Liberace-like flourish at the end. "I know," I said, "it's pretty silly."

"No, it's not. Play it again." She turned her face just enough that I could see a single tear glistening on her cheek, and then added, lowering her voice, "Sam." So I played it again. And I would have kept playing it as many times as she wanted me to, but twice seemed to have satisfied her.

"Did you ever meet her?"

"Who?"

"Bernadette Peters."

"No. No. Not really. But once she did come into a place where I was playing. At least it looked like her. But you get a lot of people trying to look like other people in New York."

"Bernadette doesn't know what she missed."

"It's probably for the best. This way she wasn't forced to choose between Sondheim and me."

"So tell me about yourself," Audrey said. She sat on the arm of the couch nearest the piano.

"There's not much to tell. I'm a musician. End of story."

"But you were married, right? At least once?"

"Just once."

"What was she like?"

"She was great. Really great."

"So what was the problem—you?"

"No, I was great, too. We were both great. We just weren't great together."

"Why was that?"

I wasn't ready to dissect my marriage in front of a woman I had just met, so I made like an octopus and began filling the water with ink to cover my escape. "A great man once said, 'Marriage is like a three-legged race. In the best of them, the partners are equally matched. In the worst, they don't even face the same direction.'"

"Who was it?"

"Who?"

"This great man."

"I think it might have been me. And I might have exaggerated the 'great' part."

"So are you still friends?"

"Sure. We're just not in touch."

"Doesn't sound like you're friends, then."

"I don't keep in touch with anyone. It doesn't mean I don't like them."

"I think I understand why you weren't great together."

"No, I don't think you do."

"You're probably right." Now, she was the one who was backtracking.

"What about you? Was Zack your first?"

"First what?"

"Marriage."

"He was my first everything. I didn't exist before I met him."

"Are you talking Pygmalion or Frankenstein?"

"Do I look like a monster?"

"No, but those are the scariest ones."

"Are you scared?"

"Just a little. But it's a good kind of scared—like riding a roller coaster."

"I never liked roller coasters."

"Too scary?"

"Too tame."

As we talked, I continued to play, going from one song to another in my piano bar way, not even consciously thinking about it, really. I had just finished playing some show tune—I couldn't tell you which one—when Audrey asked, "What makes you write songs?"

I was taken aback by her question. It had been a long time since anyone had shown more than superficial interest in me. "I never really thought about it. It's just what I do. Didn't you ever write poems when you were a teenager?"

"Not really. Sometimes I'd try to write down my feelings, but I wouldn't call them poems."

"I've always written. When it wasn't songs, it was stories or even plays. I just had this need to express myself. But I liked putting words with music the best. It's therapy."

"So you're your own therapist?"

"Can't afford a real one."

"It must be a wonderful feeling to perform your songs." She stood up and started moving aimlessly about the room.

"It is. Not that I do it much anymore."

"So how do you do it—write a song? Do you write the words or the music first?"

"So you want to see how the sausage is made."

"I doubt it's as bad as that."

"No, sometimes it's worse."

"So which is it: words or music?" She had circled back until she was looking over my shoulder.

"Words have their own music. Usually, I get an idea for a lyric and it will have its own rhythm which suggests a musical phrase. I try to come up with a chorus or verse, go back and forth from words to music until it starts to take on a form or shape."

"A shape?"

"I imagine that I am building something. Sometimes, it might be something simple like a road or a bridge, but other times, if I do it right, it's a cathedral—a cathedral of sound."

"Can you show me?"

"You want me to write a song, now?"

"Can you?"

"I'm not a songwriting machine. I need something to inspire me. Usually, I'm taking a shower or riding on the subway or reading and it just comes to me."

"Oh." She seemed disappointed.

I vamped a little more, stalling for time while glancing around the room. What could I write a song about?

"You should write a song about birds," she broke in.

"Birds?"

"Sure. People like bird songs. 'Freebird.' 'Blackbird.' 'White Bird.' 'Surfin' Bird.'"

"Rubber Ducky?"

"I love 'Rubber Ducky." She began to sing it, but then stopped when she realized I was listening. "I'm sorry," she said, covering her face with her hand to hide her embarrassment. "I'm not very good."

"Who told you that?"

"No, one. But I'm not really a singer."

"I disagree. You have a pretty voice. It has a very listenable quality. You should do more of it."

"I'm kind of shy."

"All singers are. Some just hide it better than others."

"Is that true?"

"I don't know. But here's the deal: I'll help you write a song, but you have to sing it. Try this." I laid down a few

chords while singing, 'If only the birds that sang the best.'
Now, you try it."

She sang, tentatively, "If only the birds that sang the
best."

"Good. Now, 'If only the birds that sang the best were
allowed to sing."

"If only the birds that sang the best were allowed to
sing."

I continued. "Then when you walked through the forest."

"Then when you walked through the forest."

"The silence would be—deafening."

Audrey sang, following my inflection exactly.

"Good. Now, the whole thing."

"If only the birds that sang the best were allowed to sing
/ Then when you walked through the forest the silence
would be deafening."

I stopped. "Very nice."

"So are you going to teach me the rest of it?"

"I don't know the rest of it."

"Well, who's it by?"

"Me, just now. You wanted to see me write a song, well
there it is—at least all that I've got so far. That'll be the
chorus."

"So what do we do next?"

"Well, usually, I would come up with some dummy lyrics for the verse."

"Dummy lyrics."

"Just some nonsense stuff that establishes the rhythm
and rhyme scheme. Do you know the song 'I've Got
Rhythm?' Well, Ira Gershwin wasn't sure how George
wanted to rhyme the verses so they came up with some
dummy lyrics: 'Roly poly / Eating solely / Ravioli / Better
watch your diet or bust!'"

"Good thing they changed them."

"Sometimes, I think they don't. Take 'Thunderball.'
Tom Jones didn't want to record the line about striking like
Thunderball because he didn't know what it meant. The

songwriters admitted that they didn't either."

"I guess the important thing is he sounded like he did when he was singing it."

"All songwriters do it. At least, I think they do. In the end, Ira didn't use the rhyme scheme at all. I want the verse to be something urgent that builds momentum." Taking up a piece of blank manuscript paper, I turned it over and started jotting down ideas as fast as they came to me in rhymed couplets. "Something like—

"We all have our talents / No matter how small.
We all have our voices / To answer the call.
We all have our issues / We must rise above.
And we all have our passions / The things that we love.

"That's crap," I said, "but you get the idea. It's just something to work with."

"Okay, so what's next?"

I handed her the piece of paper. "You put them some-where. Later, you come back to them when you're fresh."

"So that's it?"

"For today. You can't rush these things. Or maybe you can. Most of what they play on the radio sounds rushed. You hear a lyric and you wonder why they couldn't have spent fifteen more minutes on it."

"I agree."

"I mean they have the opportunity to create something truly great and they toss it away."

"Maybe they don't know any better."

"No, I suspect what they know is that most people don't care. Music has been called the literature of the heart. They treat it more like a post-it note. Here's an interesting fact: it wasn't until the 'fifties and 'sixties that songwriters began to realize that pop songs might have a life beyond their ini-tial release. The whole concept of 'oldies' caught them by surprise. That's why so many of them got burned when it came to publishing rights."

"My favorite songs are all oldies."

"You can chalk that up to the sorry state of the recording industry."

Back in the kitchen, I poured myself another glass of juice and imagined it was a cocktail.

"Well, the next time you write a song, don't do it without me," she said.

CHAPTER 8

Waking Dreams

From the moment I arrived in Tarrytown, I had had this gnawing apprehension like I was waiting for test results to come back from the doctor. I couldn't put my finger on it exactly, but I felt it had something to do with the artificiality of the situation: Miss Scarlett and Professor Plum in the kitchen with the coffee maker. And, now, I had agreed to accompany her on a road trip. It was so unlike me—at least the image of me that I carried around in my head. But maybe that wasn't a bad thing.

I had packed for the weekend, although I really thought I would be there only one night. It would have added several hours to our trip to swing back to my place to pick up some more duds and, to be honest, I didn't really have anything suitable. My wardrobe consisted of several dinner jackets and a tux I wore for my wedding gigs and a two or three other outfits I knocked around in. So that afternoon, we went to White Plains, about twenty minutes away.

There were several clothing stores to choose from and Audrey seemed to take particular delight in having me model "outfits" for her. I felt like a toddler being dressed up by his older sister. It had been a long time since I had dressed to please a woman.

When it came time to pay, she had her credit card out before I could even find my wallet. "You don't need to do that," I said and I meant it, although I didn't know how I would come up with the money. If my credit card wasn't already maxed out, it would be.

"No, my treat."

"I'll pay you back," I said, more a wish than a promise.

She loaded me up like a Sherpa with more shopping bags than I had hands and I trailed her sheepishly to the car.

Back at the castle, I hung up my new wardrobe in an empty closet. I felt like I was moving in—and I didn't want to feel that way. I didn't want to get too comfortable. This was still Zack's home and Audrey was still Zack's wife. I was just a friend, a friend who would be here for a couple of weeks and then return to my previous existence.

After dinner, we sat in the living room. Several times I had thought we were going to run out of things to talk about. I'm not a talker by nature, but I didn't have to be. When I was working, I could fill in any awkward silences with music. However, it's different when you are one-on-one with someone, especially someone you want to like you. But I needn't have worried. Audrey kept introducing new subjects.

"What were you like as a kid?" she asked.

"I was a nerd, a nobody, just this kid obsessed with music."

"What kind of music?"

"All kinds. Jazz, folk, Broadway, even some classical."

"Not rock and roll?"

"Not at first. To tell the truth, I was kind of dismissive of it."

"What changed your mind?"

"The Animals."

"Not The Beatles?"

"No. It was Alan Price's organ playing. That and their choice of material. It spoke to me in a way The Beatles didn't, although I did admire their songwriting skills. It was around that time I met Zack and he made me believe that we could be The Animals. Other than 'House of the Rising Sun,' nobody seemed to be covering them. I'm pretty sure we never played any Beatles or Stones, not even in practice. Of course, we weren't immune to them, but their sound—or sounds—wasn't ours. Zack was partial to the great blues guitarists.

"I cut my eye teeth on the likes of 'Please Don't Let Me Be Misunderstood,' 'I'm Going to Send You Back to Walker,' and 'We Gotta Get Out of This Place'—all American tunes, as it turned out. Like me, Price was basically self-taught. Unlike me, he felt underappreciated. In our band, the B-Three was up front and Zack's guitar wove these intricate patterns over and around it. From the moment Zack and I formed the Blues Attack, I was just happy to be part of something bigger than myself."

"Do you remember when you first discovered music?"

I stopped to think. Some of my earliest memories were of sitting alone in the basement, playing 78s on an old portable record player. My brother had a handful of recordings by the Sons of the Pioneers and my favorite was "Ghost Riders in the Sky." But I also had some of my sister's 45s and remember listening over and over to Gogi Grant singing "The Wayward Wind." Mine would have been a lonely childhood if it hadn't been for that record player.

"When I was a kid, I heard this record by Rusty Bryant. He was a local sax player and he had a hit called 'All Nite Long.' It was a double-time version of 'Night Train' and I thought it was the most exciting thing I had ever heard. It was recorded live at the Carolyn Club in Columbus, and you could hear the excitement in the crowd. He did this call-and-response where he would play doobie-wah doobie-wah and the crowd would answer, chanting 'All nite long.' Doobie-wah doobie-wah, 'All nite long.' You could practically smell the beer and the smoke and the sweat. I don't think I've ever heard a live recording that was any better. That record has been the touchstone for everything I've ever done. Is it as good as 'All Nite Long'?"

"And?"

"And it still is."

"Did you ever meet Rusty?"

"Yeah. I even sat in with him a couple of times. He and Hank Marr, a keyboard player, were local heroes. They worked as a sax-organ combo for years off-and-on. Hank recorded with Rusty and Rusty recorded with Hank, depending upon who had the record deal. Hank was this incredible B-Three player. But that was later."

I remembered when Rusty invited me over to his house. There was the metal silhouette of a train on his mailbox—a reminder of "Nite Train."

"But the first person I ever met who had a hit record was Joey Powers," I said.

"Who?" Audrey asked, and I wasn't surprised. His name doesn't come up much anymore, in part because he wasn't on a major label.

"Joey Powers," I repeated. "His real name was Joseph Ruggiero and he was a student teacher at my high school. One afternoon, I was sitting in audio-visual room and Joey came in with about a half dozen girls trailing behind. He had this forty-five record in his hand and asked if I would play it. So I set up a record player in an empty classroom and we listened to 'Meet Me at Midnight Mary.'"

"I don't think I know that song."

"Most people don't. But it reached the top ten. Even earned a gold record, but it was his only hit. Anyway, I was surprised to discover that a regular guy—a student teacher—could have a hit record."

"So what happened to him?"

"He was still in college at the time, working on his master's degree, I think, but he also had a record to promote. I don't know if he dropped out or what, but he hired this local band, The Vanguards, to back him and began playing gigs in Ohio and Pennsylvania."

"How did a student teacher in Columbus, Ohio, manage to get a hit record?"

"Well, to begin with, he was from Canonsburg, Pennsylvania, Perry Como's hometown. And his parents knew Perry, who helped him get a job at NBC in New York. He had already recorded a number of singles before he returned to Ohio State to work on his master's degree. But I didn't know any of that—the part about his connections—back then. Joey was a lot older than we were. Funny thing is, a couple of years later it seemed like everybody had a record on the radio."

"What do you mean?"

"It was 1966. The Rebounds—who went to Brookhaven, my high school—recorded 'I'm Not Your Steppin' Stone,' and it was a big hit locally. And another Brookhaven band, The Epics, had 'White Collar House,' which supposedly got banned from the radio."

"Why was that?"

"The rumor was that they had written it about a brothel, although one of the Pence brothers told me it was about this teen club in Newark where they used to play. He said they wore these dark blue shirts with white collars and cuffs and the black lights made them glow. Then then were was The Dantes with 'Can't Get Enough of Your Love' and The Fifth Order with 'Goin' Too Far.' It just seemed like every band in Columbus had a record so we wanted one, too."

"Which of your songs is your favorite?"

"That's hard to say. It's like asking which of your children is your favorite. Which is yours?"

"Well, my favorite is 'Waking Dreams,' but you wouldn't know it. Zack wrote it just for me." She started singing softly:

> "My dog goes chasing rabbits
> Sometimes when he's asleep.
> I don't know if he's ever caught a thing.
> But I can see him running
> Through the gardens of his mind,
> In a canine heaven where he's king."

As she sang, two thoughts crossed my mine. The first

was that Audrey had a beautiful voice. Really good. And the second was that Zack didn't write the song; I did. Even the dog was mine; he never owned one. It was incomplete when I brought it to a recording session and we never worked on it any further because it didn't fit the concept of the album. I had forgotten about it until this moment.

"Aren't the lyrics wonderful?" she said, pausing between verses.

"Yeah," I replied. When it came to songwriting credits, Zack and I had done the Lennon-McCartney thing; we shared credit on every song, whether it was a collaboration or not. In this case, it was all my song. I had never concerned myself with who got credit back then and, like McCartney, didn't mind that my songwriting partner's name came first: Taylor and Blecker. Now, like McCartney, I was starting to regret it. I wondered whether Zack had told her he wrote the song or had she merely assumed it.

> "We're not so very diff'rent,
> That lop-eared dog and I,
> Dreaming of a life we've never had.
> But each day when he wakes up,
> He takes things as they are,
> And never worries if they're good or bad."

I noticed her eyes were getting moist. "He gave it to me for our first anniversary," she said, her voice suddenly soft. Maybe someday I would tell her the truth about the song, but not today. I didn't have the heart to snatch his gift away from her.

"You can sing," I said.

"Not really. Just for fun."

"No, you're good. Did you ever perform?"

"Just in the shower."

"That would sell a lot of tickets."

"Would you buy one?"

"No."

"No? You wouldn't buy a ticket?"

"I'd buy them all."

"It's hard for me to sing in front of people."

"I'm people."

"You're my friend. That's different."

"When you're good, the whole audience wants to be your friend. And you're good. Didn't Zack ever tell you?"

"Yes, but he was my husband."

Hearing Audrey sing was like seeing Gomer Pyle break out in song for the first time and wondering where that voice came from. She reminded me of this mousey little girl I used to know in high school. Nobody would have looked at her twice. And nobody suspected she could sing. But then she married this musician and the next thing I knew she was all feathered hair and spandex, fronting one of the most popular bands in town. If I had the opportunity, meaning if I was around long enough, I was going to help Audrey develop it if she let me.

"We've got a long drive ahead of us," I said. "I think I'll turn in early."

"All right."

"What about you?"

"I think I'll stay up a little while more."

Watching someone in mourning was one of my least favorite things to do. Even though Audrey had invited me to her home, I felt like an intruder. I tried to walk the line between respecting her privacy and making myself available of she needed me for any reason. Although I fully intended to get some sleep, I lay awake for an hour or more mulling over the circumstances in which I now found myself. People are strange, as a not particularly good poet once said.

As I nodded off that night, a song was running through my head—my song:

> *My dog goes chasing rabbits*
> *Sometimes when he's asleep.*
> *I don't know if he's ever caught a thing.*

It had taken over fifty years, but I knew now that there was at least one area in which Zack may have envied me.

CHAPTER 9

Nothin' to Lose

T he Huckleberry Finn in me had long lay dormant, left behind on the banks of the muddy Olentangy, I suppose.

I had grown up in Columbus—a city that is ten times the size of Manhattan, but with half the population. Most people don't walk, ride the bus, or take taxis. We didn't have a subway system and passenger trains had pretty much stopped coming there by the ''seventies. So we drove cars. Boy, did we drive cars.

As a boy in Ohio—to reference a Phil Ochs song—I took any opportunity that presented itself to get behind the wheel and go. Once I was out barhopping with some friends and they wound up driving all night just to see the sunrise at Niagara Falls. Fortunately, I had bowed out for once. Still, I was on this perpetual quest. For what, I didn't know. But I knew there was something more waiting for me out there.

Once I got to New York, however, I gave up looking for it. I guess I figured if it wasn't there, I wouldn't find it anywhere. And I never mentioned the Blues Attack. That would have been like wearing your high school letter jacket to college.

☙☙☙

Anxious to hit the road, I was up before dawn or even the thought of dawn. When Audrey came down, she caught

HELLO, I MUST BE GOING   71

me sitting at the Steinway, playing nothing in particular. "You're addicted to that thing, aren't you?"

I learned long ago that I never felt lonely or homesick or depressed when I was sitting behind the keyboard. It could have been that the musicians on the Titanic didn't even notice the ship was going down. I might not have. "If I'm not playing, I'm wishing I were," I replied.

"That must make relationships tough."

Relationships are tough, I thought. But what I said was, "It's a symptom, not the disease."

"So you have room for both?"

"In theory."

"Not in practice?"

"A musician lives in an upside down world. Sleeping and waking are reversed."

"Maybe it's everyone else who lives in an upside down world."

"Try convincing them of that."

"People can convince themselves of anything if they have a reason."

"What reason?"

"Any reason. Love usually—or hate."

"Are you going to elaborate?"

"Not now. Maybe some time." As I continued to play, she changed subjects. "Why do you think people like certain songs?"

"You tell me," I said.

"I think that songs puts feelings into words in a way that many people can't."

"Are there any songs that do that for you?"

"Lots."

"Like what."

"I don't know. Things I hear on the radio. Oldies. What about you?"

"Hymns, mostly—" I began playing "What Wondrous Love is This?" and then segued into "Amazing Grace." "—I can't sing them without getting choked up."

"Are there any you wrote?"

"That choke me up? No."

"No? Why do you think that is?"

"I don't know. You can't tickle yourself, I guess." Trying to raise her spirits, I asked, "What would you like to hear?"

"Could you play me another song from *Pollyanna*?"

"Another song? Wasn't one enough?"

"I kind of liked it. It made me happy."

For some reason, I always had the most trouble remembering my own songs. It's not like I got many requests. None, in fact, for *Pollyanna*—which the cast came to call "Polyandry" for reasons best forgotten—but I set my mind to dredging one up. "If you know the story, Pollyanna would play 'The Glad Game.' No matter how bad things were, she'd focus on something positive. So, of course, all kinds of disasters befall her. In this case, it was a zombie plague." I played a brief intro and began to sing, slowing the tempo as I struggled to remember the words:

> "There's no need to wear a frown,
> Just dance away those blues.
> 'Cause if you've got nothin',
> And I've got nothin',
> Then we've got nothin' to lose.

> "Be a mope or be a clown,
> It's up to you to choose.
> Cause if you've got nothin',
> And I've got nothin',
> Then we've got nothin'to lose.

> "Now, nothin' may not be a lot,
> But when it's ev'rything you've got,
> It seems to me
> The only sensible course is
> Poolin' our resources.

"There's no reason to complain,
We all must pay our dues.
'Cause if you've got nothin',
And I've got nothin',
And nothin' plus nothin's
Still lots of nothin',
Cause if you've got nothin',
And I've got nothin',
Then we've got nothin' to lose.
Doobie-doos."

"I wish I could play the piano," Audrey said. "My dream is to learn how to play one song. Then if I'm at a party where there is a piano and someone asks me if I play, I could say, 'A little.' And then I would play my song and everyone would be impressed."

"I could teach you."

"I don't mean 'Twinkle, Twinkle, Little Star.'"

"I don't either. I was thinking Bach, 'Minuet in G.'"

She stood up. "Maybe we should be going. What do you think?"

⌒⊃⌒⊃

The distance from Tarrytown, New York, to Oxford, Mississippi, is over 1,000 miles. Audrey wouldn't fly—not sure why—and I preferred not to. Not being a native New Yorker, I didn't have the same contempt for "flyover country" that many of them did. To me, it was just another term for "heartland" and I had no predisposition to avoid it.

The drive would take two eight hour days. Since moving to NYC, I had not driven more than a handful of times each year. I used to enjoy it, but I was concerned that my reflexes would be a little rusty and, at my age, I had difficulty sitting for prolonged periods of time. We would have to make a number of rest stops along the way.

As we pulled out of her drive, Audrey said, "When we moved here, I felt like a princess. Now, I feel like a prisoner. It'll be good to get away for a while."

Some prison, I thought.

"So are you ready to get on the road?"

"Normally, not," I said, "but this time it's different. It's more like a vacation and it's been a long time since I've had one of those."

"I'm glad."

We would be following interstates almost the entire way. I caught I-287 west over the Hudson River and set it on cruise control. Although I hadn't gotten much sleep—I never do when I stay at a strange place—I knew I could drive eight or nine hours without any problem. But neither of us was in any particular hurry.

"Have you traveled much?" Audrey asked.

"Some. There aren't many states I haven't been to at one time or another."

"I'd never been anywhere until I met Zack."

"Most people haven't. I read that the average American has only been to a dozen states."

"I've been to Canada and Mexico, but that's about it. I'd like to see more of the world."

"Well, it looks like you can afford it," I said and immediately wished I hadn't.

She shut down for a few minutes, apparently mulling something over. When she was ready to talk again, she said, "What's the point if you don't have someone to share it with?"

"I know what you mean. I guess that's why I haven't done more."

After a while, Audrey pulled out her phone and began checking something—email, I supposed. I was not as involved with the devices as most people are. In fact, my phone was about as primitive as you could get. I used it primarily for business. Most of contacts were other musicians. Although we pretended to care about one another, most of our communications were about jobs. Years ago, I called Billy Maxted, composer of "Manhattan Spiritual," down in Florida because I heard he was practically on his death bed. I called him out of the blue because I was a fan. The first thing he said to me was, "Is there any work where you are?" Now, I was becoming that guy.

We had driven for about an hour or so when Audrey said, "He loved you," apropos of nothing. I was learning she was prone to throwing these verbal boomerangs that caught me off guard.

"What?"

"Zack loved you—the band, the music. You were his first love. He loved me, too, of course, but I always knew I was further down on the list somewhere. I've wondered for years who I was competing with."

Of course, I knew that when she said Zack loved me, she didn't mean it in the same sense that she did when she said he loved her. That was romantic love. We—Zack and I— were more like brothers. But some brothers are closer than others, and we were the kind who were seldom in contact.

I had the feeling she was analyzing my face, trying to read my physiognomy maybe.

"Before he died, he told me that the only thing he ever regretted was breaking up the band. And I think he hoped someday you would get back together again just one more time."

"Well, that won't happen."

"Why?"

"Why? Because it was Zack Black and the Blues Attack. It was his band. Without Zack Taylor, it's nothing. He's irreplaceable. If anyone would know that, you should."

That last remarked seemed a little—actually, a lot— preachy. I hoped she didn't notice.

"So tell me the story of the band. I want to know every-thing."

"Zack must have told you."

"Yeah, but I want to hear it from a different perspective.

Like where did the name come from?"

"Well, we thought about calling it the Zack Taylor Band, but Zack didn't want people to think it was all about him, even though it was his band. Since we were playing a lot of blues, we started thinking that we should have a name with 'Blues' in it like the Blues Project, Moody Blues, Hughes Blues, Blues Magoos. We considered Red, White, and Blues. Then someone came up with the Blues Attack, probably a riff on the Bluesbreakers, and we all thought it was good. It quickly evolved into Zack and the Blues Attack. I think Zack changed it to that because it had a real aggressive, in-your-face quality. Of course, we weren't really a blues band, no more than those other bands were."

"Why not?"

"Because we quickly realized we weren't fifty-year-old black men. As soon as we started writing our own stuff, we became something else. It's like when Al Kooper called the Blues Project the Jewish Beatles. Sure they played some blues or blues rock, but also jazz rock, folk rock, garage rock."

"So when you started, did you play for birthday parties and things like that?"

"In the beginning. Dances at recreation centers, after school sock hops, you name it. We also played on 'Dance Party' in Columbus and 'UpBeat' in Cleveland. By that time, it was on a hundred stations, I think."

"So what was it like being on 'Dance Party'?"

"It was a big deal. Jerry Rasor was like our own Dick Clark. He was in his thirties, handsome, well-dressed, and had a very engaging personality. His show was a big deal and every band wanted to be on it. And we played live. All the teenagers watched it."

"That must have made your very popular."

"It did. But it wasn't just us. They had other teenagers who were featured dancers on the show. We all acquired a certain degree of celebrity on the weekends and then would carry it with us through the week when we were at school.

It's a wonder we all didn't get big heads, especially the bands that had hit songs."

"What do you mean?"

"There was a time when the local Top Forty would include recordings made by two or three Columbus bands. They would be outselling the big name groups. They were usually bands that had some sort of connection to the local radio or TV stations. Many of the behind-the-scenes guys managed bands on the side."

"So did you have long hair like The Beatles?"

"I didn't. I kept it right at the length required by the school dress code. But other guys, like Tommy Williams, challenged it."

"Tommy Williams?"

"He was the lead guitar player for The Rebounds. He wore this Little Lord Fauntleroy suit and a Dutch boy haircut. The school principal went crazy. I think Tommy may have gotten suspended for it."

"Fast Times at Brookhaven High."

"You're making fun of me," I said, noting the smile that had crossed her face.

"No, I'm not. Truthfully, I'm jealous. It sounds like you had a lot of fun when you were growing up."

Thinking back on it, I had to agree. It was a wonderful time to be a kid. "The teenager had just been invented. And for the first time ever, they could pick out their own clothes, choose their own music, eat whatever they wanted. For a brief period of time, teenagers ruled the world—until big business figured out how to control all of that buying power. Suddenly, the genie was back in the bottle."

"You still haven't told me how you got together, what you did, everything. I always felt there were some things Zack was holding back."

I'm sure there were, I thought. But I wouldn't tell her about those things, either.

"We were just a bunch of guys who lived in the same neighborhood," I began. "Zack and I went to Brookhaven.

Wes was Catholic, so he went to DeSales, which was right across Karl Road. And Evan was from Linden-McKinley because he lived south of Oakland Park. I knew him from junior high, but not well. It's kind of funny. I was sitting in study hall one day—this was at Medina Junior High—and the band teacher asked me if I wanted to play bass in the orchestra. I had played a little trumpet when I was younger, but hadn't really been involved in music for a year or two. But I was tall, which was the main criterion, so I found myself in the music room instead of study hall several days a week. Evan Bishop was one of the percussionists, but we didn't hang out together or anything.

"So you can play bass, too?"

"No. The bass they gave me had only three strings. They never got around to replacing the fourth one—the G."

"That's too bad."

"The piano player told me not to worry. Said it was two more than I needed."

Audrey started to laugh, then caught herself. "Are you serious?"

"Serious as a visit from the IRS. But I did enjoy fooling around with the thing. *Bump, bump, bump, bum-buh, bum-buh-bump.* When the music teacher caught me giving it a doghouse spin like some rockabilly musician, I was invited to go back to study hall."

Audrey laughed.

"I was kind of a dorky kid. I liked folk music and show tunes, mostly. I was aware of rock and roll, but didn't really follow any of the groups. Then when I got to Brookhaven, I met Zack. We were in some of the same classes and were on speaking terms, but he was off doing his own thing and I didn't really know what that was. Then he heard me picking out a tune on the music room piano one day—I had gone there to see this girl I had a crush on—and decided I should be in this band he was forming. I don't know what it was he saw in me, but he made it his mission to teach me how to play keyboards. My parents weren't in any position to buy me one, so Zack loaned me his. Next thing I knew, we were jamming in his basement every spare minute."

"At first, I was just playing chords behind him while he explored the different sounds he could get out of his guitar. He was already quite accomplished technically, but was looking for a way to make the instrument truly his. He also played bass, of course, and knew his way around a drum kit. Then one day he hauled out a tenor sax and taught himself how to play that, too. He was just a natural. A musical genius, really. I knew someday people would be paying to hear him. It just never occurred to me that I would be part of it all—the phenomenon that was Zack Taylor."

"You must have been getting good, too. Doing all that practicing."

"Yeah, it turned out I had a small talent as well. And since Zack couldn't be a band by himself, I was figuring out ways to make myself useful. Ever since I started listening to music, I would make up my own arrangements in my head. As I became more proficient on the piano, I would show Zack some of my ideas. We developed this sort of musical short-hand. People started to call us Lennon and McCartney, but we were actual collaborators. Most of the time Lennon and McCartney were really Lennon *or* McCartney. This was especially true when we began writing songs, but I'm getting ahead of myself. And I'm probably boring you."

"No, you aren't," she said. "I want to hear it all."

I wasn't so sure I wanted to tell it all, particularly the unflattering parts. In Zack Black & the Blues Attack, we took turns being jerks—all of us. I still regretted some of the stupid things I did. And now I knew I would ruminate about them unless I could distract myself somehow.

"I think it's time for a stretch," I announced, and pulled off at a plaza. When I was younger, I could drive for twelve hours with hardly a break. Now, I had to stop and stretch every two or three hours just because. Truck drivers and piano players have to mind their backs.

CHAPTER 10

The Sheik

My legs weren't stiff, yet, nor my neck, for that matter, but nowadays I tried to make a point of getting up and walking around every hour or so just to keep the circulation going. And assure myself that everything was still working. I knew I had to pay more attention to my body than I did when I was younger, that is if I wanted to stay on the right side of the grass. It was hard not to contemplate my own mortality with Zack gone. Our birthdays were only a month apart. He was always older. Now I was and would be forever.

While I topped off the gas tank, Audrey ducked inside the convenience store. When she returned to the car, she had two cups of coffee. I could count on two hands the number of times I had drunk a cup of coffee. I just never developed the taste for it. Apparently, she forgot. But rather than seem ungrateful, I drank it after putting a couple of creamers and a packet of sugar in it. That was the thing about coffee: the more people become coffee snobs, the more they disguise the actual flavor by adding all kinds of things to dilute it or turn it into a milkshake. I could do that.

We had entered Pennsylvania a while ago and, as the song says, there's plenty of it. When I used to make the trip back home to Columbus, I drove it length-ways on many occasions. It was novel the first few times, especially the tunnels through the mountains, but anymore it was one long snooze. Fortunately, halfway across the state we dropped down into Maryland and then West Virginia. I wasn't as familiar with this landscape so I didn't find it as boring. And the highways were better, uncorrupted by harsh winters.

I knew it was just a matter of time before Audrey asked me to continue telling her the history of the band. When she did, I jumped ahead a little. "We started picking up jobs here and there, playing for little or nothing. We were all under age, so we didn't even think of trying to break into the bar scene, not that we were good enough. But things started to really get rolling when we were heard by Webb Webster, a deejay on WCOL. That was the big AM station in Columbus. He became our manager, so we would accompany him to record hops. He would spin records and greet his fans, then we would play a set when he took a smoke break. Since the teens weren't there to see us, it took the pressure off and we could concentrate on honing our skills."

"Evan, our drummer, was the youngest member of the band. I'm not sure why, but there were a lot of good, young drummers in Columbus at the time. The Rebounds had David Day. Glen Cataline was in The Edicates. Dean Francis fronted The Soul Rockers. And we had Evan. I don't know where Zack found him, but I suspect it was while he was taking guitar lessons from Chuck Dailey at Coyle Music. Chuck taught the lion's share of the guitarists who came out of The Beatles generation."

"The only member of The Blues Attack who had been in a band before was Wes. It was a Catholic youth folk group—The Candlelight Singers. He sang and played upright bass with two other guys and three girls. He looked like Dick Smothers. Very clean cut. I remember being impressed that they had an album—until I actually heard it. But he could read music and quickly acquired an electric bass, so he was in—the last member of the original group. Wes was particularly good at working out three-part harmonies."

I noticed that Audrey had closed her eyes and was resting her head against the door frame.

"I'm not keeping you awake, am I?"

"No," she said. "I'm listening. You were telling me about Wes."

"Well, Wes was different. For one thing, he had wanted to be a priest."

"A priest?"

"Or a cop. It was that kind of family. Those were the only two choices, except maybe open a pizza place."

"So did he become a priest?"

"No, and I kind of feel bad about that."

"Cop?"

"No. We turned him into a rock and roller, and it was all downhill from there."

"Why?"

"Every band has at least one druggie. I'm afraid Wes was ours. But we broke up before Zack got around to kicking him out."

"What happened to him?"

"I've often wondered. I used to hear things, but I lost track after I moved to New York. Just like I lost track of everyone, including Zack. But I do know it kept him out of the draft."

"What did?"

"Drugs. Actually a drug conviction. The armed forces are particular about who they let kill people."

"What about you? Did you get drafted?"

"I had dropped out of college. We all had. It was a calculated risk, given the way the war was heating up under Johnson and McNamara. I knew it was just a matter of time before I would be drafted, since I had a low lottery number, but I tried not to think about it. Wes came up with what he thought was a foolproof plan to evade the draft: he would commit a felony. His reasoning was that the Army wouldn't induct him if he had a felony conviction on his record and that was generally true. I don't know what exactly gave him the idea of getting arrested or buying drugs, but I suspect it was one of the widely publicized drug busts that had taken place—maybe Roky Erickson's. He had been the leader of the Thirteenth Floor Elevators and wound up battling mental illness for the next forty years of his life.

"So, unbeknownst to me or Zack—although I suspect Evan knew—Wes began venturing off to make drug purchases in the hope that he would be caught. The fact that we were in cities he knew nothing about did not deter him, but did add an element of difficulty to the task. We noticed that he would wander off with some of the fans after our concerts and not return until the early hours of the morning. We could smell marijuana on his clothes.

"Since we had a no drug rule, Zack called Wes out on it, but there was no evidence that he was bringing any weed back with him. In fact, I wasn't even sure he was smoking the stuff. He claimed that he couldn't help what other people were doing around him. So Zack backed off, not wanting to create something out of nothing. But it wasn't nothing. And as soon as he got his draft notice, Wes got himself arrested for possession of marijuana. At least that's what I heard."

"So did he go to prison?"

"For a couple years, I think."

"What about you?"

"High blood pressure." There was a little more to it than that, but she didn't need to know.

"And that got you out?"

"It did."

"Do you still have it?"

"No."

"No?"

"It was a transitory condition. I immediately got better when Uncle Sam stopped knocking."

Because she had closed her eyes, I thought Audrey was taking a nap. But then she asked me to sing another song. Although I never considered myself a great singer, I had become accustomed to doing it when I was behind a keyboard. But it wasn't quite the same when I was sitting behind the wheel.

"What are you in the mood for?" I asked.

"What've you got?"

"That's what Marlon Brandon says in *The Wild One*." I turned just enough to see Audrey's reaction if she had one, but she didn't. Apparently the movie title meant nothing to her, so I thought I would explain. "Brando plays the head of this motorcycle gang and someone asks him what he's rebelling against. He answers, 'What've you got?'"

"I don't think I ever saw it."

Of course she didn't. I hadn't, either, until they ran it on "Saturday Night at the Movies."

"So tell me more about the band."

"I don't remember where I left off."

"It doesn't matter. I can probably fill in the missing parts."

While I'm sure she thought that was true, I knew that it was unlikely Zack would have told her everything. He probably revised it as he went along, just as I was doing, to eliminate the really stupid stuff—and there was a lot of that.

"Well," I picked up, "we were getting a lot of work through our connection with Webb Webster, but the competition in Columbus was fierce. The top bands—The Big Five—got the best jobs and everybody else was fighting over the leftovers."

"Who were The Big Five?"

"The Dantes, The Fifth Order, The Rebounds, The Grayps, and one or two others at different times. The only real way to set yourself apart from the others was to win a battle of the bands."

"What's that?"

"Different places would sponsor these contests in which a bunch of bands would play a few songs each and the audience would choose the winner. They had them at the Ohio State Fairgrounds, Valley Dale Ballroom, Northland Shopping Center, and various other venues. The Rebounds won the first Northland battle in 1965 and got a recording contract with Tower Records. That was a really big deal, especially when their recording of 'I'm Not Your Steppin' Stone' started climbing the charts. Unfortunately, the Monkees released their own version a few weeks later as the flipside of 'I'm a Believer.' It earned them a gold record while The Rebounds' version stalled."

"That sucks."

"Yeah, but that's the music business. Before I got into music, I wanted to be a writer—a novelist or maybe, a screenwriter. My initial resistance to rock and roll was because I couldn't tolerate the lyrics to most of the songs. They weren't literate enough for my tastes. Of course, I've since repented, but back then I was hung up on meter and rhyme and intelligence, I guess. But as I found myself performing some of these songs that I felt were beneath me, I began jotting down my own lyrics just to see if I could do any better. That's how 'The Shiek' came about. I was inspired by this footage of Rudolph Valentino I saw on 'Fractured Flickers' or something."

"So how did you get to make a record?"

"That was our manager's doing. He was friends with Shad O'Shea who owned Counterpart Records in Cincinnati. We did some recording at Musicol Studios in Columbus and Webb took the tapes to Shad. They picked the best song—or what they thought was the best—and that became our first real release—"What's Love?" We pressed maybe a hundred-and-fifty copies at first on the Musicol label—just enough for the band and our friends. Most of them wound up in my parents' basement. But then Shad reissued it on Counterpart and we were on our way. Number one in Columbus and sold about twenty or thirty thousand copies in all."

"That must have been exciting."

"You better believe it. But then we needed a follow-up, so Shad pressed up some copies of 'The Sheik.'"

"It's kind of a strange song."

"We were kind of strange guys," I replied. "I was trying to make a statement by projecting myself into the mind of a thirty year old woman. I was also under the influence of Jefferson Airplane and It's A Beautiful Day."

She laughed. "I love it."

"Why?"

"Why not? What's not to love?" She began singing lightly, gaining confidence by the time she reached the bridge.

"Be careful what you wish for,
Sometimes your wildest dreams may come true.
It's not imagination,
This secret yearning that draws me to you.
All consuming passion,
While flickering shadows dance on the screen.
Why must you be so lonely?
Night-blooming flower that no one has seen.

"Across the burning sand,
In some uncharted land,
You call —to —me.
Beneath a moon of blue,
A secret rendezvous
With des—ti—ny.

"Anywhere you go, I will follow,
Anywhere you hide, I will seek,
Anywhere you turn, I will be there.
You can't evade me,
Your love has made me
The Sheik.
Woh-oh.
The Sheik.
Who-oh.

"The echoes down the hallway,

And whispered voices from an empty room.
Footsteps close behind you,
Come, let me take you away from this gloom.
Beyond a thousand lifetimes,
Here at a place preordained by the fates,
Surrender to the moment,
Within the darkness your dream lover waits.

"Across the burning sand,
In some uncharted land,
You call —to —me.
Beneath a moon of blue,
A secret rendezvous
With des—ti—ny.

"Anywhere you go, I will follow,
Anywhere you hide, I will seek,
Anywhere you turn, I will be there.
You can't evade me,
Your love has made me
The sheik.
Woh-oh.
The sheik.
Who-oh."

By the end, Audrey was swaying from side-to-side, dancing in her seat. She stopped and gave me a wide-eyed smile as if to say, "What teenage girl could resist that?" It might not have been The Beatles, but it rhymed, scanned, and sounded like nothing else on the radio at the time, especially with its faintly Arabian rhythm. Zack even played a little electric violin on it while I added some recorder doodlings, having picked up a nice tenor model at a garage sale.

"What can I say? We were romantics at heart"

"That's probably what the girls liked about it."

"That makes me feel better. Where were you when we needed you?"

"I wasn't born yet," she said with a laugh.

With that splash of cold water, Audrey had put every-thing back in perspective. I was old; really old. And she was young, young enough to be my daughter if I had one. So to relieve my discomfort, I resumed my story.

"After that, Webb—that wasn't his real name, but all the deejays adopted these Anglo-Saxon monikers—Webb got us booked on these regional TV shows like 'Upbeat' in Cleveland. We also played some of the surrounding states. We opened for The Byrds, Strawberry Alarm Clock, Mitch Ryder, The Turtles, and other hot bands. Those were heady times for a bunch of teenagers from Columbus."

"You must have had more girlfriends than you knew what to do with."

"Not so much. First, we were working all the time. And second, I was going through this really awkward stage when it came to looks. I would have fit right in with those guys in The Zombies."

"You don't look so bad, now. In fact, I think you're ra-ther distinguished looking—not like the typical aging rock star."

"Yeah, well, I grew out of it after about thirty years."

CHAPTER 11

Blessed Are

That first day, we drove as far as Kingsport, Tennessee. If I had ever been there before, I didn't recall. Once nicknamed "the Model City," it looked much like everyplace else. Same restaurants, same stores, same gas stations—and same boarded up restaurants, empty stores, and abandoned gas stations.

So many towns look alike, you almost have to get out of the car and walk the streets to see the differences, to identify the quirky things that set them apart. In Kingston's case, it was a renovated carousel. But I was more interested in the town's location on the Clinch River—as in Ralph Stanley and the Clinch River Boys. Being from the east, Audrey had never heard of them. All she knew about bluegrass music was the "Beverly Hillbillies" theme.

After dinner, we went to a local mall to shop. The carnival in the parking lot seemed to be getting most of the business. Audrey was throwing her money around like a farmer spreading manure. Maybe that's one of the stages of grief. I came away with a couple of shirts, a pair of pants, and some socks and underwear. And, oh, yeah, a sweater she said was me. And I just thought it was a sweater. I wouldn't have known that without her.

The plan had been to get two rooms, but the hotel was full. Instead, we had one large room with two double beds. We broke open the mini-bar and sat on the edges of our respective beds, facing each other. Most of the day, I had done all the talking as we played a one-sided game of twenty questions but now it was her turn. She was in a reflective mood and started telling me her life story or, at least, the *Reader's Digest* version.

"Zack was the best thing that ever happened to me. Before he came along, I wasn't a good person. You wouldn't have liked me."

"You keep saying things like that. Are you trying to scare me?"

"No. But it's true."

"Then I guess it's a good thing he came along." Not wanting to intrude on her grief, I let her steer the conversation. "So how did you two meet?"

"How did I meet Zack? He bailed me out of jail."

"What were you doing in jail?"

"Waiting for someone to bail me out. It was just a misunderstanding."

"They call that a 'meet cute' in romantic comedies."

"There was nothing funny about it."

"So what happened?"

"I was out with some girlfriends. We were at this bar, and there was an argument with some guy. The police got involved because someone got scratched or kicked or something, and the next thing we knew they had run us all in for hooking."

"You? A hooker?"

"It was the eighties. We all dressed and talked like hookers."

"How did Zack get involved?"

"He was there with a client or something and had watched the whole mess play out. When he realized they were making a mistake, he bailed us all out and got the charges dropped."

"And after that you began dating?"

"Not right away. I had been in a relationship. More like a boxing match, really. But I kept thinking about what he did for me. I had never had a man do anything for me without expecting something in return. About a year later, we ran into each other. By then, I was free. My life consists of two parts: BZ and AZ. Everything that came before is dead and buried. I was a different person then. For years, I was scared Zack would discover my secrets, but he never asked me to tell him anything I didn't want to. He never, ever judged me. That's why I fell in love with him."

I took that as a warning that I shouldn't inquire about her past, either. And I understood. I had done some things I didn't like to admit to myself, although I had never been to jail.

"Well," I said, "I'm happy that you found each other—and had that time together." I was also sad for myself. I hadn't ever met anyone like Audrey, even though I felt like I had spent most of my life looking. Maybe the problem was I failed to recognize her when I did find her. Maybe I wouldn't have recognized her now if Zack hadn't recognized her first. I found myself staring at her, unable to think of anything to say.

"How did you wind up in New York?" Audrey asked.

"After the band broke up, I decided I wanted to see if I could make it as a professional musician. My mother had died, my father's job took him away from home for months at a time, and Zack was going to Columbia, so I thought I'd give New York a try. Keyboard players are always in demand, especially those who can sight read and play using more than one hand at a time. Of course, it turns out there's a lot more of them in New York than I had anticipated."

"Did you keep in touch with Zack?"

"At first. But our schedules didn't line up. Besides, he had his studies and I was scrambling for jobs. And we didn't live near each other. There aren't many apartments in New York that can hold a piano—at least not ones I could afford—and not many neighbors who would tolerate one. Fortunately, I used to live around the corner from this church and I struck a deal with the pastor. In exchange for playing a jazz service one Sunday a month, he would keep the piano tuned and I could practice whenever I wanted. He even gave me a key."

"A church key?" she said, suppressing a smile.

"Yeah, but it didn't work on bottles."

"You sure he just didn't want you to come to church?"

"A gig's a gig."

"So you got paid?"

"In a way. You know what it would have cost me to rent practice space in New York?"

"I'm guessing a lot."

"I would have had to give up eating."

"So are you a church-goer?"

"Sometimes. Not really. I was raised a Lutheran."

"What's that? Is it like Catholic?"

"You are from New York, aren't you? Everyone here assumes you if you aren't Jewish, you're Catholic."

"Everyone I knew when I was growing up was one or the other."

"What about you?"

"Both. Or neither. I thought about joining a church before Zack died. Now, it doesn't seem so important."

"I like church. I like the idea, that is. I don't care for the politics. After a while, I even formed a five-piece praise band with two girl singers up front."

"So sing me another of your praise songs."

"I really didn't write them for me to sing."

"Sing one anyway."

"Okay. But, remember, I'm not a soprano. This one is based on the Beatitudes—the Sermon on the Mount. Do you know it?"

"I'm not sure."

"It doesn't matter. It's a handful of proverbs that Jesus told his followers, but the message is universal." I began singing, hesitantly at first, "Bless-ed"— (two syllables, not one), —trying to remember the verses from years ago.

"Blessed are

The poor in spirit,
For theirs is the kingdom of heaven.
Blessed are
Those who know sorrow,
For comfort to them shall be given.
Blessed are all
Who claim nothing in life,
For they the whole earth shall inherit.
And blessed are those
Who for righteousness hunger,
For they shall be satisfied.

"Blessed are
Those who show mercy,
For mercy shall surely be shown them.
Blessed are
All the pure hearted,
For they shall see God in his heaven.
Blessed are those
Who keep striving for peace,
For they shall be known as God's children.
And blessed are those
Who for righteousness suffer,
For heaven is their reward.

The melody was light and delicate, lifting up the lyrics like a gentle wave.

"And blessed are you,
Regarded with scorn,
Reviled and ill-treated
For his sake.
Rejoice and be glad,
For this you were born,
And riches await you
In heaven,
In heaven."

When I had finished, Audrey sat quietly, saying nothing, hardly even breathing. It was getting late.

"Well," I said, "I should probably turn in. We've got another long drive ahead of us tomorrow."

"This has been fun, Will. You're a good friend. And thanks for church."

"You're not so bad yourself," I said, and then wondered what I had meant. I really couldn't trust myself to say the right thing, knowing the feelings that had begun to stir. Later, I learned that her flower child parents had never exposed her to religious teachings of any sort. They figured she could find her own way, leaving her hungry. She asked me to show her where the Beatitudes were in the bible she found in the hotel room. Fortunately, the Gideons had anticipated that and cited them just inside the front cover.

ↄↄↄ

About two in the morning, I woke to the sound of Audrey snoring, her shadowy form little more than an arm's length away in the adjoining bed. It wasn't a window-rattling snore, more of a loud sigh. I could have covered my head with a pillow, but I was too revved up to sleep. Lying awake in the darkness, I thought about how I came to be sharing a hotel room in Kingsport, Tennessee, with one of the most stunning women I had ever seen. The whole thing was so improbable. I already knew she would be easy to fall in love with if I had met her under different circumstances, but there was protocol to observe. She was, after all, the grieving widow of the person I had always considered my best friend, even though we had been separated much longer than we were ever together. Besides, she deserved more than I had to offer.

I don't think I slept much after that. We had decided to get an early start and put some miles behind us before stopping for breakfast. Audrey had already stashed her suitcase in the trunk by the time I came strolling out to the car with my own bag.

"Hi," she said cheerfully, flashing a smile as bright as a sunrise.

"Good morning. Sleep well?"

"Not really. I'm too excited to sleep."

"Me too," I replied, which was only partially true. I had tossed and turned all night because that is what I do in hotels.

The morning went by in a flash. I didn't realize I was hungry until a little after twelve, so we pulled into the first restaurant we came to that didn't look like a bait store and wasn't part of a chain. When I saw they served pancakes, I anticipated the tables would be sticky. I was right. I didn't know where to rest my arms.

"So what do you do with the songs you write now?" Audrey asked after we had ordered.

"Not much. It's not like I write them intentionally, but bits and pieces come to me from time to time. That part of my life is behind me. I knew this singer once. When he was younger, he had been signed to Columbia records and had written a bunch of songs for his debut album. But that deal fell through as they usually do. Years later I ran into him and asked him if he was still writing songs. He told me he wasn't. When I asked why, he said because there were already enough good songs. And he was right. There are thousands of good songs. There are some great songs, even, that hardly anybody knows about. Still, they aren't my songs and I can't be totally happy singing someone else's. It would be like sending someone else's love letters. So I'll haul one out every once in a while, usually around closing time, and play it for old times' sake.

"You, know, back when we were getting started, most bands didn't write their own stuff. A guy named Jack C. Sender who worked as a floor director at WLW-C wrote the songs The Fifth Order recorded. The Rebounds covered songs that had been written for others. And The Dantes got theirs from elsewhere, too. But the one local band that didn't was The Gears. They were our label mates on Counterpart, as were The Fifth Order, and they had two guys, Bob Allwood and Joe Daniels, who were teaching themselves how to write pop songs. So I decided I could do it, too. Zack, of course, was all for it. He could see which way the wind was blowing."

"What about Evan and Wes? Did they want to write songs, too?"

"Not so much. They would make suggestions from time to time. But since we weren't collecting any royalties anyway, they weren't concerned about the money—not then, anyway."

"So then you did 'What's Love?'"

"It was already in the can. But Webb had decided to dub in some horns. He hired a brass trio from somewhere to punch it up. At first we were upset—The Gears had one song ruined by horns, or at least we thought so at the time—but we finally had to admit that it gave us an even bluesier sound. We started adding a horn section for some of our bigger dates, county fairs and the like, and eventually full-time. We had morphed into a grittier version of Blood, Sweat and Tears or Tower of Power."

"I wish I could have heard you."

"The records probably made us sound better than we were. All of us were still learning our instruments. Zack, of course, was already unbelievably good and Wes had developed into a solid bass player, but Evan and I were still novices. The amazing thing is that we were all teens, amateurs, really, earning far better money than the adult musicians who were seasoned professionals. The whole music industry had been flipped upside down. You had fathers quitting their jobs to manage their kid's band. They would turn their living rooms into practice studios. They were buying Volkswagen vans and trailers to haul equipment around in. It was crazy. We were told about these places in New York—Paul Sergeant's and the Shed House—and we would go there on weekends to buy clothes: Tom Jones shirts, John Sebastian glasses, McCreedy and Schreiber shoes. They even hung the band's picture on the wall beside all of the other rock stars. The British Invasion was in full swing and we thought we would turn the tide."

When I placed my order, the waitress asked if I wanted grits. I didn't and told her so. Now, I saw that I had been served a plate of them anyway. Wouldn't penalize her for that, but I never understood the appeal—just watered-down corn chowder.

On the road again, I was starting to feel like I was making some sort of religious pilgrimage, only it was less about getting closer to God and more about getting closer to the person seated next to me. Audrey was intently studying the map. She had turned out to be a good navigator which, in my experience, is a rare thing. She was a pleasant traveling companion in other ways, too, and I couldn't help thinking how lucky Zack had been to find her. My own love life was a checkered affair and I accepted at least half of the blame for that. The bigger half.

CHAPTER 12

You May Be the Only

S potting the exit for Nashville made me think of Gene Cotton, a Columbus folksinger. He used to perform at this coffee house, the Cracked Cup, in the 1960s. He was a few years older than I and released his first 45 while I was still playing "Chop Sticks." Not long afterward, he crossed over into Christian music almost before anyone knew that was a thing.

Gene later settled in Tennessee. I remembered he had a recording of "Let Your Love Flow"—before it became a monster hit for the Bellamy Brothers—and a duet with Kim Carnes. However, my favorite was "Like a Sunday in Salem." He was sort of rock, sort of country, sort of pop. And because he was a local boy who made good, some of us thought maybe we could, too.

"What're you thinking about?" Audrey asked. At some point during the last half hour, I had lapsed into silence. As I said, I am not a talker by nature, and telling Audrey my life's story, or parts of it, was taking its toll. Apparently sensing that, she had been content to leave me be until now.

"Life."

"Life?" she asked.

"I used to eat a box or two a day."

"No, seriously."

"I am serious. I really liked that cereal when it first came out."

"So why were you thinking about it, now?"

"Okay, you got me. I wasn't thinking about the cereal. I was thinking about real life."

"What about it?"

"Sometimes it's just not fair."

"No argument here."

I knew she was probably thinking about Zack again. And I was thinking about her thinking about him. Even though she wasn't rending her garments and gnashing her teeth, I could see she was still grieving in a low-key sort of way.

"So what happened next?" she asked.

I scrambled to pick up the loose ends of my narrative. "Next? Well, eventually, I landed in New York and got hired as a jingle writer for a small ad agency."

"Jingle writer, huh? I heard you can make good money doing that."

"Some do. I still get royalties on occasion for such things as a sports show theme or a potato chip commercial. While I can't survive on them, they do help me to make an occasional rent payment." I was beginning to wonder if I was sounding as pathetic as I felt.

"Are you enjoying this trip?" she asked me.

"Very much."

"Me, too. It must be the company."

It certainly was, I thought, as we drove on for four more hours. We had been listening to the radio, mostly country songs, when Audrey asked me if I had ever written any country songs.

"Not really," I said. "Two or three things, maybe."

"Like what?"

I had to think. When The Byrds went country, I followed along as a fan, but I was already in the Blues Attack and committed to R & B and heavy blues. But then The Rolling Stones did a parody of a country song on their *Beggar's Banquet* album, so that opened the door for me to write my own. "Well, there's this one." And I began to sing it with as much twang as I could muster, stopping now and then to get back on the tracks when I'd run off.

"You go to church each Sunday,
But never in between.
And always shake the preacher's hand,
To make sure that you're seen.
You love to quote the Bible—
At least the parts you've read—
And loudly holler out 'Amen'
When you're not sure what was said."

Once I had locked onto the melody, the rest of it started
to flow.

"Now, you always pray in public,
Though not when you're alone,
If the Lord should ever call you
It'll be by telephone."

The chorus was the whole reason for the song.

"No, you just can't be a Christian,
When it suits your needs.
'Cause you may be the only gospel
Your neighbor ever reads.

"Well...
You'll gladly sit in judgement
When God is out of town,
Or maybe just too occupied
To know what's going down.
You savor all the gossip
On how we sinners live,
While watching the collection plate
Just to see how much we give.

"Now, I know you must be thinking
You're holier than me,
But I can't keep from wondering

If Jesus would agree.

"Even the best pilgrim sometimes
Gets lost in the weeds.
'Cause you may be the only gospel
Your neighbor ever reads.

"Well…
When they break out the hymnals,
You loudly clear your throat,
To ensure the congregation
Won't miss a single note.
You always a make a big display
When all eyes are on you,
But don't give God a second thought
After church is through.

"Now, I suspect you're thinking
That you're some kind of saint,
But I am here to tell ya, friend,
That's one thing that you ain't.

"Keep practicing the Golden Rule
In all your words and deeds.
'Cause you may be the only gospel
Your neighbor ever reads"

"You sure you didn't want to be a preacher?" Audrey asked when I had finished.

"That was Wes."

"But you have a tendency to stick sermons in your songs."

"Well, the way I see it there're are only a handful of important themes and religion is one of them."

"What are the others?"

"Growing up. Friendship. Falling in love. Falling out of love. Anger. Injustice. Death. And, of course, dogs."

"No cats?"

"Only if the cat's name is Kalamazoo."

"So, have you written songs about them all?"

"Probably. At one time or another."

"That's impressive."

"I didn't say they were all good. In fact, I sometimes feel that none of them are."

"Well, I like them—the one's I've heard."

Just then, we arrived in Oxford. In spite of being the home of "Ole Miss," the state's largest university, Oxford, Mississippi, was hardly any bigger than Oxford, Ohio, although it put on decidedly more airs. And when school was in session, it puffed up like a toad, doubling in size. It was William Faulkner's hometown and he wrote about it extensively, renaming it "Jefferson" for his tales of the fictional Yoknapatawpha County. A kid could easily traverse its pleasant streets on a bicycle, but when you were my age, a car was a necessity, especially in the Mississippi heat.

"Any idea where we're going?" Audrey asked.

"Not really. How many barber shops you think they have?"

"A half dozen at most," she said, checking her cell phone. "Probably fewer. Are you counting salons?"

"I doubt it. I'm just hoping the one we want is still in business. I think it's called Johnson's."

We had cruised through the center of town on the main drag when Audrey pointed down a side street. "What about that?"

I made a right turn and spotted a blue sign about a block away with an old fashioned barber pole on it. Pulling to a halt in front of it, I read the sign: *JOHNSON'S BARBERS*. Through the window, hung with yellowed venetian blinds, I could see three or four chairs inside. It was nearly five o'clock. Not knowing when it closed, I parked the car where it was, jumped out and walked quickly to the front door, pausing only when I heard Audrey call, "Wait for me."

As soon as she had caught up, I pushed opened the door and entered the shop. There were two elderly black men sitting in oak chairs along the wall. A third, dressed in a pale green shirt, was perched in one of the barber chairs like the monarch of some tonsorial kingdom. "Can I help you?" he asked as Audrey and I stood in the middle of the room, taking it all in. The place looked, I suspect, much as it had a half century before. The scent of aftershave wafted through the air. The radio was tuned to some black gospel station.

"We're looking for the family of Elmore Johnson— Spoolie Johnson."

"And why would that be?"

"I guess you could say we're fans of his and we have something that belonged to him. Something his family might want."

"So why don't you give it to him?"

I noticed that the men along the wall were grinning for some reason. "Give it to him? You mean he's still alive?"

"Well, he was this morning." They all started laughing then. "You can find him over at Greendale."

"Greendale? What's that?"

"Old folks home. But you better hurry." This caused another ripple of laughter.

We took the barber up on his offer to draw us a map, jumped back in the car, and headed across town. Less than ten minutes later, we sitting in the nursing home parking lot. After climbing out, I removed the guitar case from the trunk. "We won't mean anything to him, but maybe he'll recognize the guitar. You know how musicians are."

"I know how one musician was. I'm still learning about the second."

We entered the lobby, which smelled of industrial disinfectant, and approached the main desk. "We're here to see Elmore Johnson," I said.

The woman leaned back in her chair and spoke to a woman behind her who appeared to be a nurse. They all wore pastels uniforms and nametags, so it was hard to tell.

"You know where Spoolie is?"

"Dayroom, last I saw him."

Looking back my way, she said, "Just go down this hallway, turn left and then keep turning right until you get there."

"Thank you."

"What have you go there?" she asked as I turned away.

"It's a guitar. It belongs to Mr. Johnson. We're returning it."

"Well, you can't leave it here."

I assured her we wouldn't, although I didn't know what we would do with it. We'd deal with that when we had to. When we reached the dayroom, we asked an attendant to identify Elmore Johnson. He pointed to a man in a wheelchair in a group of other old folks, some of whom looked at us hopefully like puppies awaiting adoption. Guitar case in hand, I approached him while Audrey lagged a step behind.

"Mr. Johnson?" I said, careful not to startle him.

"Yes, sir," he said in a surprisingly strong voice.

"My name is Will Black. I was a friend of Zack Taylor. Does that name mean anything to you?"

"It might. I suspect I heard it somewhere."

Johnson had salt-and-pepper hair and a scraggily Fred Sanford beard. His skin was smooth as linoleum and he could have been fifty or one hundred and fifty for all I knew.

"I'm sorry to tell you this, Mr. Johnson, but Zack died. He passed away a few weeks ago."

"You don't say?" He paused and seemed to be concentrating on something. "He was just a little fellah last I saw him—if we're talking about the same Zack Taylor. His parents were northern folks and they used to bring him around every summer."

"That's the one."

"Are you going to introduce me to your friend?"

I had forgotten about Audrey for a moment, but I didn't have time to make amends before she stepped to the forefront. "I'm Audrey Taylor—Zack's wife. Widow," she said and extended her hand. "It's an honor to meet you, Mr. Johnson. Zack thought the world of you."

Springing out of the wheelchair like a man touched by a faith healer, Spoolie clasped her hand in both of his. "Where are my manners? 'Spoolie' Johnson, at your service, ma'am." He bowed slightly. "I'm sorry for your loss. Your husband was—well I really can't say. I mean I never knew the man, just the boy. But he was a fine boy. A mighty fine boy."

I knew that Audrey was as surprised as I was by how spry Spoolie appeared to be. In an instant, he had shed at least ten or twenty years as readily as a duck shedding water. It was a startling transformation, like the girl turning into a gorilla at the carnival.

"We thought you were a patient here," Audrey said.

"Me? Nah, I'm just visiting some friends. This here's Jake and the ugly one is Rufus," he said, gesturing at the two men seated near him. One nodded, the other waved. While it wasn't obvious before, I could see that there was an enormous difference between their physical and mental states and Spoolie's. Funny how context can change everything. Then he directed his attention to the guitar case. "What'cha got there?"

"Here," I said, handing it to him. "This is for you, Mr. Johnson. Zack wanted you to have it."

Taking the case from me, Spoolie rested in on the arms of the wheelchair, snapped the latches and swung open the lid. "Now, that," he said, taking a step back, "is a gee-tar."

"Do you recognize it?" I asked.

"Like I would an ex-wife. This one's Felicia. I named all my guitars. Looks like Zack took real good care of her, too." Without removing it from its case, he strummed his fingers slowly across the strings. It made a faint sound like a toy harp. "But I can't accept it."

"But Zack wanted you to have it. He made me promise," Audrey said.

"Sorry, ma'am."

"But why?"

"It might be hoodooed."

I could see the look of disappointment in Audrey's eyes, but how do you argue with superstition?

"Why would that be?" I asked.

"I let Felicia go," Spoolie explained. "And she went to him. He died. Now, she's come back to me."

We sat there is silence for a couple of minutes, then a thought occurred to me. "Isn't there something that can be done to remove the hoodoo?"

"Don't know," Spoolie drawled, rubbing his scruff of beard with his long, thin fingers. All of us stood there in thought, pondering our dilemma.

Then a voice broke the silence. "You need a potion." It was either Rufus or Jake. I wasn't sure which from the brief introduction and hadn't thought it would matter. "You could take it to Doctah Root."

"That would cost some," Spoolie said.

"I've got money," Audrey volunteered, too eagerly, I thought. I had begun to think we were being scammed.

Spoolie seemed to be mulling it over as he ran a finger up and down the guitar's neck.

"Where do we find this hoodoo man?" Audrey asked.

"Walmart." Again, it was Rufus or Jake. "Works there. At least he did last time I got out." I wasn't sure whether he meant someone had taken him or he had escaped.

"That's it, then," Audrey said. "Let's go see this doctor."

CHAPTER 13

Mississippi is a Foreign Country

You should never meet your heroes, they will only disappoint you. Or you will disappoint yourself. Trust me on this. I had been carrying this unrealistic picture of Spoolie Johnson in my head, but it hadn't mattered because I expected him to be dead. Now, I was having to come to terms with a living Spoolie Johnson who, guitar playing aside, seemed wrong in every respect. Not wrong, really, but certainly different. But, in the end, that was my fault.

Snapping the guitar case shut, I grabbed it by the handle. Then we all trudged, single file, out to the parking lot and piled into Audrey's car for the trip to Walmart. She was talking to Spoolie, who sat in the backseat, while I drove. I had the feeling he enjoyed being chauffeured.

"Zack said you taught him how to play guitar," Audrey said.

"I might have showed him a thing or two," Spoolie allowed. I wasn't sure if he didn't remember or was being cagey. "He wasn't much bigger than a turnip. Heard me playing on the corner once and asked his daddy to buy him an electric guitar like mine—like Felicia."

"Was it hard giving her up?"

"Some, but Mr. Taylor made it easier. He paid me a fair price. Besides, I've had a lot of guitars over the years—guitars and women." I caught his sly smile in the rearview mirror. "I remember the special ones." I wasn't sure whether he was talking about women or guitars.

The thing about Spoolie was that I couldn't get a fix on his age. Sometimes he seemed impossibly young, others as old as the moss strewn oaks that lined the streets of Oxford. And he seemed more like a parody of a bluesman than the actual item. It felt like he was saying what he thought we wanted to hear, mentally checking of a list of things old bluesmen are likely to have in common.

"Was Zack a good student?" Audrey asked.

"He took to it natural. Had the gift. Always wondered what happened to the boy."

"He formed a band—with Will. They even recorded some records."

"Is that a fact? So you're a musician, too, Mr.—whadya say your name was?"

"Black."

"You'll have to forgive me. Names get away from me at my age."

I wanted to ask him what age that might be, but instead I said, "I'm a piano player."

"Any good?"

"I make a living."

"Is that the same thing?" I didn't know if I should be offended or what, but then Spoolie cracked a wide grin. "I'm just messing with you, Will."

☙❧

When we reached Walmart, Spoolie ducked inside while Audrey and I waited in the car. "What do you think of him?" I asked.

"He's a character."

"That he is."

"And charming in his way."

"You think so? I'm not even sure we've got the right guy."

"What do you mean?"

"I think he may be conning us."

"Why do you say that?"

"Well, to begin with, I'm closer to the grave than he is."

"Maybe he had good genes. Watches what he eats. Exercises."

"And it doesn't sound like he remembers Zack at all?"

"It's been a long time. And Zack was just a kid. He probably taught lots of kids how to play guitar."

"Maybe."

After a few minutes, Spoolie returned, sliding into the backseat. "He's says to come back when he gets off work."

"When's that?" I asked.

"Ten—ten-thirty."

"Then what?"

"Then he'll remove the hoodoo."

"We should get something to eat in the meantime," Audrey said.

"I could go for that," Spoolie chimed in.

Spoolie directed us to a barbecue joint. I wasn't sure if it was an actual restaurant or we had dropped in on some of his friends. It was an open air affair, more like a barn with the sides stripped off. There were random configurations of tables and chairs that looked as though they had been salvaged from an old institution of some sort, possibly a hospital. The smoker appeared to have been fabricated out of three fifty-five gallon drums.

We met the owner whose name, not so coincidentally, was Johnson. Everything was handled on a cash basis with no signs of a cash register. "How do y'all know Spoolie?" he asked after pocketing our money.

"Doesn't everybody?" I replied.

"That's a fact. Where're you folks from?"

"New York."

"New York," he said, dragging the words out. "That's a long way to come for barbecue, even if it's good barbecue."

"We didn't come for the barbecue. That's just a bonus."

"Well, I hope you come back and see us again real soon."

"So do I," Audrey said. "I've never been to Mississippi before."

"I find that hard to believe, missy. We like to think all of the pretty ladies are in Mississippi."

"Only for another day or two," I said. "Then we'll be heading back."

After grabbing a bite to eat, served on paper with plastic utensils, we checked into the hotel—the Broken Arms or something like that—to kill time until our meeting with Doctah Root. It was one of those faux southern colonial structures that was as real as a carnival midway.

"Always wondered what these rooms were like," Spoolie said, perching on the edge of my bed and then falling backward. He spread his arms like he was making a snow angel.

Audrey and I had adjoining rooms and she insisted on keeping the door open between them because she didn't like being alone in strange places. We could hear her changing her outfit.

"Your girlfriend's a real looker." Spoolie had his eyes closed and was facing the ceiling.

"She's not my girlfriend."

"No. Then what is she?"

"Just a friend."

"Then maybe she'd like to be my woman."

"I doubt it."

"Why," he said, opening his eyes, "she got something against black people?"

I shushed Spoolie, signaling for him to keep his voice down. I lowered my own to a whisper. "She mated for life— like a swan." I wasn't sure he understood, so I added, "It's just that she took Zack's death pretty hard. She just needs some time to heal."

"Maybe she needs some Spoolie."

I was reminded of how embarrassing old people could be at times. They often said and did rude things as if their filters were malfunctioning. Audrey walked into the room, smoothing her skirt with her hands.

"Sorry I took so long. I wasn't sure what to wear to—to whatever this is."

"Candle-burning," Spoolie said.

"That sounds nice."

"Who is this Doctah Root?" I asked.

"He's a holy man—conjuror. If the guitar's got the hoo-doo, he can fix it if anybody can."

"Well, it's almost ten," I said. "We better get going."

༄༅༄

Standing outside the main door of Walmart was a gaunt fellow in a cape, vest, and top hat sprouting a pheasant feather. Looked like he bought his clothes at the House of Frankenstein. I assumed he was Doctah Root and Spoolie must have assumed I assumed it because he didn't bother with introductions. The doctah handed Spoolie a leather bag and slid into the backseat beside him.

"Did you bring the money?" the good doctah asked.

Spoolie looked at me. "I might have forgot to mention that. He gets one hundred fifty dollars."

"For what?" I asked.

"To remove the hoodoo."

"What?"

"That's okay," Audrey interjected. "Will he take a check?"

A few minutes later, we were idling beside a bank machine while Audrey drew $150 out of her account. Turns out Doctah Root only accepted cash on the barrel head. Something about bad mojo. Having removed that obstacle from our path, we drove on into the night as Spoolie fed us directions.

"Turn right here. Okay, now go straight. Right again at the fruit stand. Now, left."

If I didn't know better I'd have thought he was being paid by the mile. I was certain we had backtracked at least once. And then we were in the middle of nowhere with wisps of fog drifting across the road like phantom sheep. After driving around for at least half an hour when I finally asked, "Where are we going?"

"Copeland."

"What's that?"

"Burying ground."

"Of course." I suddenly had a vision of headless chickens flopping around in the dirt.

The thing about Mississippi is that no matter how peaceful and serene things might appear, you know there is a lot of creepy-crawly things right beneath your feet. There was a miniature hell mouth waiting under every rock. As we rolled on through the darkness, I kept imagining I could see the glint of yellow eyes staring at us. Or maybe I wasn't imagining it.

Our road trip had been uneventful until we met up with Spoolie. I don't know what I expected. Actually, I do. I thought he would be dead and we'd simply hand the guitar off to his next of kin, make a U-turn, and head back to New York. Instead, we were following one of those poorly marked detours that usually lead you smack into a clan of hillbilly cannibals, at least in the movies.

A few more miles and Spoolie said, "Okay, now slow down. It's right up here on the right." I strained my eyes to see anything that might suggest a cemetery, but a curtain of trees lined both sides of the county road. "Slow down. Slow down. Here."

I allowed the car to glide to a stop on the edge of the pavement and turned on the flashers. There wasn't a shoulder or a drive of any kind to pull off onto. "Where should we park?" I asked, but Doctah Root had already flung open the door and was standing beside the car.

"It'll be okay here," Spoolie said.

I wasn't certain whether I should feel reassured by the

lack of traffic or not. On one hand, there didn't seem to be anyone else out driving that particular stretch of road. On the other, they certainly wouldn't be expecting a parked car in the middle of nowhere. As we staggered single file into the woods, I kept expecting the car to erupt into a ball of flame behind us.

Flashlight in hand, Doctah Root led our little expedition, threading his way through the ranks of live oak trees. He was followed closely by Spoolie who carried the guitar, still in its case. Audrey needed my hand to steady her. Like most women I've known, she dressed for style, not practicality, and her shoes were definitely not cut out for the uneven terrain. But, then, neither were mine, apparently, as I slipped on the moist earth and nearly pulled her down with me.

Copeland Cemetery, as a weathered sign nailed to a tree read, was an old family plot that had been reclaimed by nature. There were several broken headstones, one of which was being absorbed into the trunk of a tree. There were also occasional depressions in the earth that were, I suspected, old graves or the work of groundhogs or both. It was spooky, to be sure, but so is most of the south. A circle had been scratched on a bare patch of earth and, possibly, a star as well. There were also some dark stains here and there that were likely paint, but could have been blood.

From his bag, Doctah Root removed a salt shaker—the kind you would find in any restaurant—and began using it to outline the circle. When he was finished, he instructed Spoolie to hand him the guitar. Grasping it by the neck and the body, he raised it above his head, chanted something I didn't catch, and then carefully placed it in the center of the circle.

The air was refrigerator chill. I could see Audrey was shivering, so I put my arm around her. Although she seemed surprised, she smiled faintly and did not resist. We both stood there watching as Doctah Root and Spoolie began lighting candles and arranging them around the circle. The breeze caused the flames to change directions like little pennants, but they all continued to burn.

I had grown up in the Lutheran church and we had our own fair share of rituals, but I remembered how foreign it seemed the first time I attended Catholic services with their incense burners and holy water sprinklers. This wasn't much different. It wasn't Robert-Johnson-selling-his-soul-to-the-devil-at-the-crossroads-strange, but it was strange enough.

The doctah now held a stick with some dried leaves tied to one end of it. As soon as he set fire to them with a cigarette lighter I knew from the aroma that it was sage. He blew out the flames, leaving a smoky trail that he used to inscribe wispy symbols in the air. As he did so, Spoolie began accompanying him on a tiny drum, tapping out a primitive rhythm and making guttural sounds. It would obvious that this wasn't his first time attending Doctah Root's church and I had the feeling some of the money would find its way into his pocket.

Sometimes when I get approached by a panhandler spinning a tale of woe, I will actually give him a few bucks even when I know he's lying. If he gave me something other than the run-of-the-mill hard luck story, I would reward him for his originality. As we were returning to the car, I was torn between feelings of anger at having been conned and admiration for how Spoolie and Doctah Root had pulled it off on such short notice. And, yet, Spoolie's whole demeanor changed once Doctah Root had removed the hoodoo. I believed that he actually believed. All the way back to town, Spoolie plucked away on the guitar, his fingers dancing up and down the fret board and skipping over the strings. And what I could hear on the unamplified instrument sounded fantastic.

We dropped both men off in the parking lot of Walmart. It was after midnight. Spoolie had turned down our offer to drive him home, saying he would catch a ride with the doctah. I had the distinct impression that he didn't want us to know where he lived.

That night as I lay in bed, I couldn't help but wonder why Doctah Root's show hadn't triggered any ideas for songs. It was as though some kind of barrier had been erected that prevented me from using the experience for my own purposes. As much as I wanted to versify it, I couldn't—not in any meaningful way.

I didn't believe that the guitar had been hoodooed or that Doctah Root had any power to remove it. But, I reminded myself, I was a traveler in a foreign country. They did things differently here. I just had to accept it. And, suddenly, with a nod to the L.P. Hartley's novel, *The Go-Between*, I had my inspiration. Not about the hoodoo, but about Mississippi. I was reminded of its dark history.

Flipping on the lamp by my bed, I sifted through the drawer of the nightstand until I located a ballpoint pen and a notepad. I began to write, singing a melody that I invented as I went along.

> "Mississippi is a foreign country,
> They do things diff'rently there.
> With their patterns of speech,
> And the manners they teach,
> You sense a certain something in the air,
> The air.
> Never knew folks could be so polite,
> Especially when you are white."

For it to work, you had to sing enunciate every syllable of "especially."

> "Mississippi is a land of secrets,
> Secrets buried in the ground.
> Yes, they bury them deep,
> In the hope they will keep,
> So you better not go nosing around,
> Around.
> Don't know quite to make of it all,
> Like Eden just before the fall."

I was thinking of the three civil rights workers who had been murdered there back when I was in high school. They had trained at Western College for Women in Oxford, Ohio. They called it "Freedom Summer."

> "Mississippi is a place of shadows,
> You never know just what is real.
> Now there's nowhere as great
> As the Magnolia State,
> If you judge it by the way that you feel,
> You feel.
> And the wiser man will soon realize,
> You shouldn't believe your own eyes."

Even before that, Mississippi led the nation in the lynching of black people. They were called "Strange Fruit" in the famous song sung by Billie Holiday.

> "Mississippi is a sort of dreamland,
> Place of faded memories,
> Where not so long ago
> The strange fruit would grow,
> Way up high in the silent oak trees,
> Oak trees.
> Though you may leave it you will one day find
> Mississippi's a state of mind."

Satisfied I was finished, I happened to look up. Audrey was standing in the doorway between our rooms, studying me. "Not now, but will you sing it for me sometime?"

I didn't realize I had been singing loud enough to disturb her. "Sure."

"Will you be able to sleep, now?"

"Probably." *Unless I get another idea*, I thought. I could still smell the aroma of sage on my clothing.

CHAPTER 14

Turn the Radio On

I did get another idea—or the shadow of one. I tried to ignore it, but I couldn't. And telling my brain to stop thinking about it just made me think about it all the more. Like saying don't think about purple giraffes. So I lay in bed for a couple of hours, pretending to be asleep and finally I was. But not for long. I spent the rest of the night running through dozens of songs in my head. Not a good start to the day.

Slipping out of the hotel at dawn, I went for a walk while Audrey slept in. We had no particular plans for the day. Our quest was completed. We had returned Zack's guitar to its rightful owner. Excalibur was back in Dozmary Pool. For the moment, we were simply killing time in Oxford, Mississippi, while making up our minds what to do next. I thought I would grab some breakfast. Or at least a donut. Might even try to choke down some coffee. Audrey was starting to convert me—Hallelujah! And the sweetness of the donut should help.

Oxford seemed like a nice college town, which meant it was probably subject to manic-depressive mood swings, depending upon whether or not school was in session. Unlike most people I encountered, I wasn't shuffling along Zombie-like, listening to my personal playlist through earbuds while checking the internet on my phone. No, any music in my head was born there and my eyes were wide-open to the sights around me, although I may have been nodding a little.

I was beginning to dread the thought of heading back to New York. I had enjoyed my unexpected vacation, the first in many years, and hated to think it would soon be at an end. I also realized that my life had been missing something and that something was Audrey—if only as a friend. I had never met anyone like her.

She was as incredible in her own way as Zack had been in his. Once again, he had come out the big winner in life's lottery—except, of course, he was dead and I wasn't. In one sense, as measured by years, I had outlived him, but, measured in life experience, I hadn't. Regardless of how my relationship—if you could call it that—with Audrey turned out, I knew I had to make some changes in whatever time I had left.

A half-dozen blocks away, I stumbled upon a place that advertised breakfast, but clearly was more of a barbecue joint. Seemed like you could get barbecue anywhere down here. Sandwiched in between the breakfast and lunch crowd, I was able to find a table in a low-traffic area in the corner. There was a paper placemat on the table which I immediately flipped over so I could use it to jot down some song ideas. This is what I usually did when I had time on my hands. Some people like to work crossword puzzles. I wrote songs.

For the next hour, I tried to write a song, to force the muse.

The problem was I was starting from zero. I was not reacting to some flash of inspiration. Nor was I revisiting some idea that had been incubating in my head for some time. And, of course, I wasn't relaxed precisely because I was trying to make myself come up with something. So after I had ordered, I tried to eavesdrop on nearby conversations while pretending to be staring out the window. I had sometimes found the nugget of an idea in some overheard expression or turn of phrase. But on this particular morning, no one was saying anything that I could use (unless you count, "You want grits with that?").

I was about to give up when I heard a couple talking. The man said he preferred a jukebox to a radio. The woman countered that she preferred the radio because even though she never heard what she wanted, she never knew what she was going to hear. Promising; I thought I might be able to do something with that so I started jotting down lines on the back of my placemat, beginning with:

> *Though you never get to hear what you want,*
> *You don't know what you'll hear.*

That would be the tag at the end of the chorus. Now, I needed a first verse. Where to start? At the beginning, of course.

> *Turn the radio on,*
> *And you're ready to begin,*
> *Turn the radio on,*
> *And give that dial a spin.*

It sounded like I was playing Russian roulette. Maybe this wasn't the first verse; maybe it would work better as the chorus. I needed a rhyme to go with "hear." What came to mind were "beer," "ear," "fear," and "disappear." This is what I now had:

> *Turn the radio on,*
> *And give that dial a spin.*
> *Turn the radio on,*
> *And let those good times begin.*
> *Though you never hear the song you want,*
> *And don't know what you might hear,*
> *Turn the radio on,*
> *And your troubles will disappear.*

This was increasingly sounding like the chorus, a strong chorus generally being the most important part of a song's success. It might be the only part you remember the first few times you hear it—the hook. So what is the first verse? Nashville songwriters have developed a number of formulas, but I'd never studied them. I figured I'd heard enough different types of songs that I had probably learned them through osmosis.

I approached songwriting from a storytelling standpoint with a beginning, a middle, and an end—like in country music. But I also was also inclined to going off on tangents. So how did I get to this point?

> *Back when I was traveling,*
> *And lived life on the road,*
> *I would get to feeling lonely*
> *And fear I might explode.*
> *Then I stumbled in a bar room*
> *To get myself a beer,*
> *And the barmaid said, "Sit where you like,*
> *We're glad that you are here."*

I like to take a stream of consciousness approach to writing the lyrics, at least at the beginning, knowing that some/most of the words are just placeholders. If I'm particularly inspired, I don't have to change them much. But as a rule, I will tear it down, rearrange large chunks, and rebuild it from the ground up several times.

So now I had a verse and a chorus, so I put them together and tweaked them a bit.

> *Back when I was trav'ling,*
> *My life was on the road.*
> *Sometimes I felt so lonely,*
> *I feared I might implode.*
> *But then I stumbled in this bar*
> *Just to get myself a beer,*

And someone said, "Sit where you like,
We're glad that you are here."

Turn the radio on,
And give that old dial a spin.
Turn the radio on,
And let those good times begin.
Though you never hear the song you want,
And don't know what you might hear,
Turn the radio on,
And your troubles will disappear.

I still didn't know what the story was, but I was pretty sure I wanted to delay the chorus until after the second verse. This would give me more time to set it up. I reread what I had written, reciting it over and over in my head to an imaginary tune. Then I found a clue buried in the line, "Though you never hear the song you want, and you don't know what you might hear." I remembered that the couple had been discussing the relative merits of a jukebox when compared to a radio. That would be the second verse.

I didn't see a jukebox,
Which left me quite dismayed,
Because I had been hoping
To hear some music played.
But then a barmaid winked at me,
Her eyes were all aglow,
And reaching high upon a shelf
Switched on the radio.

Now, I was getting somewhere, so I put all of the parts together and ran through it again.

Back when I was trav'ling,
My life was on the road.
Sometimes I felt so lonely,

I feared I might implode.
But then I stumbled in this bar
Just to get myself a beer,
And someone said, "Sit where you like,
We're glad that you are here."

I didn't see a jukebox,
Which left me quite dismayed,
Because I had been hoping
To hear some music played.
But then a barmaid winked at me,
Her eyes were all aglow,
And reaching high upon a shelf
Switched on the radio.

Turn the radio on,
And give that old dial a spin.
Turn the radio on,
And let those good times begin.
Though you never hear the song you want,
And don't know what you might hear,
Turn the radio on,
And your troubles will disappear.

I was ready to write the third verse which would complete my three act story while setting up the final chorus. I wasn't home yet, but I could see it from here.

Almost like a carousel,
That bar room sprang to life.
The cloud of gloom had lifted
And happiness was rife.
Then couples started dancing
While other sang along.
And before that record ended,
It was my fav'rite song.

Turn the radio on,
And give that old dial a spin.
Turn the radio on,
And let those good times begin.
Though you never hear the song you want,
And don't know what you might hear,
Turn the radio on,
And your troubles will disappear.

The waitress asked me if there was something wrong with my omelet because I had hardly touched it. I lied and told her that I was homesick. She said she was sorry and offered to take it off my bill, but I wouldn't let her and even tipped her extra out of guilt. But the truth was I had gotten caught up in the creative process and forgot that I was hungry. In the span of an hour, I had turned out a song. Now, I was feeling better. Fulfilled. And sleepy.

⁓⁓⁓

When I got back to the room, Audrey called to me through the open door. "Been doing something fun?"

"Just out walking," I replied as she wandered in and asked me to finish buttoning the back of her blouse.

As I did so, my phone rang. It was Spoolie. He wondered if we would could meet him at the barber shop. I relayed the question to Audrey and she nodded back.

A few minutes later, we were back at Johnsons. This time, I felt like I belonged there when we walked through the door.

"See ya found him," the barber, likely another Johnson, said. It did not look like he had moved from the chair since the day before. And I could have sworn the same collection of old men were seated along the wall. They looked like a shelf lined with Toby mugs.

"Spoolie asked us to meet him here," I said.

"He's in back."

With all eyes on us, Audrey and I walked to the back, past the row of barber chairs, to a doorway hung with a blue curtain. Pushing it aside, we passed through.

I had been a professional musician for forty years, much of it in New York City. I had played with some of the biggest names in the business—household words, even. I worked pit orchestras in musicals and concert venues. For a few years, I was in demand for session work and got to play with the cream of the crop, musicians' musicians. However, until that day in Oxford, Mississippi, in a small room in the back of Johnsons Barber Shop, I had never heard anyone truly play the guitar. In that moment, I knew that Elmore "Spoolie" Johnson was the greatest blues guitarist who ever walked the earth.

Pushing the sound through a tiny practice amp, Spoolie weaved an aural web like some sort of sorcerer. Muddy, Buddy, B.B., Howlin' Wolf, and every English guy you could think of—they were all in there somewhere. Every note seemed to conjure up another name: Blind Lemon, Son House, John Lee Hooker, Lightnin' Hopkins. The cries of the field hands, the moans of the work gangs, the laughter of the juke joints, the joy of the churches. Sweat and smoke, perfume and pomade, barbecue and stale beer. It was the most wondrous music I had ever heard. If I were to die right then, I would be a happy man.

And then, here and there, I could hear Zack. All of the great riffs he had played on our records, the incredible runs I thought he had invented, were flying out of Spoolie's guitar, played by Spoolie's fingers, not note for note exactly, but just as good and often even better. Where Zack would bend a string, Spoolie seemed to melt it. Where Zack raced up the fret board, Spoolie got there ahead of him and waited for him to catch up. I decided in that moment that I had to get Spoolie into a studio if it was the last thing I ever did. This treasure I had stumbled upon had to be shared with the world.

"Whadya think?" Spoolie said. He had suddenly stopped playing when he realized we were there. "Doesn't sound half bad, does it? Now that Doctah Root took the hoodoo off it."

I looked at Audrey. She was smiling from ear to ear like—like—well, I didn't even want to go there. "You're great, Spoolie," I said. "But I'm sure you know that already. What I'm wondering is why everybody else doesn't."

"What do you mean?"

"You should be a star. You're as good as anybody. Better, even."

He laid the guitar down on a table. "I play for myself."

"But you have a gift."

"A gift, huh? Well I ain't in a giving mood. I appreciate you're bringing me the guitar and everything, but my life was just fine before you showed up and I expect it will be fine after you go back to New York City."

"At least let me record you, Spoolie. I know some people in the industry and I'm sure they'd offer you a record deal." That was actually a white lie. I did know some people, but they weren't in any position to offer him a deal. But they would likely know somebody who could.

"No, thanks. I've had my fill of record deals. A bunch of fast-talking Yankees took my music and I never seen a dollar."

That sounded about right, from everything I had read. There was a long history of musical carpetbaggers. "This time it would be different," I said. "I don't want to make any money off of you, Spoolie. Any money that's made, I'll see to it you get it all. Just let me take you into a studio, roll some tape, and then I'll shop it around."

"How much?"

"How much what?"

"How much you gonna pay me to record?"

"I don't have any money. I'm just a musician myself."

"I'll pay you," Audrey said. "I'll pay you whatever you think is fair."

As negotiators go, Audrey left a lot to be desired. On the other hand, she got what she wanted. And, as she had told me, Zack left her with more money than she could ever spend.

"Well," Spoolie said, "the last time I got seventy-five dollars a song."

"I'll double it," Audrey said. "In advance."

CHAPTER 15

Rain on the Just

A few miles outside Oxford was a studio where the Black Crowes sometimes recorded. We didn't use that one. There was another where Elvis Costello and Buddy Guy once laid down some tracks. We didn't use that one, either.

After Spoolie consulted with Doctah Root who consulted with himself, we were directed to a farmhouse where some aging flower children had setup their own little studio to do home recordings. Judging by 1) their tie-dyed wardrobe and 2) the ubiquitous smell of marijuana, they probably played in one of those jam bands that somehow managed to sound like every other collection of stoned hippies. I thought of them as the Doobie Twins.

"I've never been to a recording session before," Audrey said.

As I watched them make preparations, setting up mics and running snarls of cables, I said, "Well, I hope you're not disappointed."

"Why?"

"Just don't get your hopes up."

"Well, at the very least, it'll be a good souvenir of our visit." She snapped some photos with her phone.

Spoolie decided I should accompany him on a bunged-up electronic keyboard that produced a respectable B-3-like sound. It would have been nice to have a drummer, too, but I wasn't about to waste time shopping for one. The hairier

Doobie Twin, who looked like he had sprung from Al Capp's inkwell, said he could play drums, but he didn't appear to be in any condition to tell time, let alone keep it. So I decided to use a click track and would dub in the percussion when we got back to New York.

I left the song selection to Spoolie. At this point, I wasn't interested in their commercial prospects. The goal was to simply showcase his talent. I was also wanted to see whether he could play with someone else. Could he handle the give-and-take of it? So many of the old blues legends were bands unto themselves, but nowadays most people wanted a fuller sound. The strength of The Beatles was that there were four of them.

In the course of an hour, with me in one room and Spoolie in an adjoining one so we could get good isolation on the tracks, we recorded a half dozen songs, only two of which I recognized: "Hellhound on My Trail" and "Black Snake Moan." Whether the others were originals, I had no idea. But there was one that stood out. It was a murder ballad: "Rain on the Just."

As I watched Spoolie through the window, I was transfixed by the passion he put into his playing. It was like I was witnessing the second coming of Jimi Hendrix. He wrung notes out of that guitar I didn't think possible. And the chorus was one of the most haunting things I had ever heard: *Rain on the just / Rain on the just / Without a woman's love / The heart turns to dust.* His voice had an edge like someone dragging a broken bottle along a concrete wall. I could hardly wait to get it back to New York too see what we could do with it.

After we completed each one, I asked Spoolie if he wanted to do a second take. He didn't, even when he threw me a curve and I muffed a chord change. No matter, I would strip the keyboard track out and redo it later. And it didn't matter to him because he had already been paid. I was disappointed that Spoolie didn't trust me more than he did, but that was understandable. He had been burned by other white men who only saw him as a commodity to be bought and sold. For all I knew, he might have been victimized by black men, too. The music business is like that.

Although we had booked the Doobie Twins for a four hour block of studio time, we were done in less than half that. They said we could use the remainder if we ever came back, but I knew we wouldn't. After Audrey settled up the bill, they handed me the tapes and a hastily mixed CD. I figured I would have ample time to listen to it in the car on the trip back home. With the right production, I thought it could open some ears to Spoolie's talent. Beyond that, who knows?

All the way back to the barber shop, Spoolie picked at his guitar, playing tunes that were so faint that we could barely hear them in the front seat. I thought it was a shame so few people would ever hear him. Even if I could swing a record deal, we'd be lucky to sell a thousand copies unless he got out on the road and promoted it. The music business goes back and forth. First recordings supported ticket sales, then concerts supported record sales, now it was back to recordings pushing the concert appearances. But you needed both. It was the very rare artist who could just do one or the other.

After dropping Spoolie off and obtaining contact information, Audrey and I returned to the hotel. The next day we would start driving back to Tarrytown. We had agreed to take our time and explore the side roads. Be spontaneous. However, that was before the recording session. I was now anxious to get back to New York and begin shopping the tapes. And yet…and yet I still wanted to spend as much time as I could with Audrey, get a chance to know her better and give her more of a chance to know me. At my age, I no longer believed I had all the time in the world.

Just before I was ready to turn in, Audrey came into my room. She was wearing a robe and her hair was wrapped in a towel. I was lying on the bed, flipping through the TV channels, searching for the news.

"He's really good, isn't he?" she said.

"Yes, he is."

"Better than Zack?"

"They're both great," I said, as though Zack was still with us. "But Spoolie's the whole package. You know what I mean?"

"I think so. Poor black blues versus rich white blues."

"Spoolie is his own instrument. He's like a Stradivarius."

"I think Zack would have traded places with a black man if it would have made him a better player."

"I think you're probably right." Jazz musician Mezz Mezzrow had tried his best to be black, marrying a black woman, playing in black groups, and living in Harlem. When he got busted for marijuana, he pleaded with the jailer to lock him up among his own kind—in the black cell block.

"Too bad Spoolie never got to play with the Blues Attack. Two guitars: just think of that." She sat down on the edge of the bed and shook down her wet hair. I felt as though a mermaid had climbed into my boat.

Later, as I lay in the darkness, trying to turn my mind off, I kept thinking of what it would be like to play with the guys one more time. The band had come to an abrupt and not a very happy end. Still, I believed the last chapter of our story hadn't been written. We had unfinished business.

છ૭ઈ૭

Audrey waited in the car, snuggling a pillow, while I checked out. Somehow she had managed to pack her suitcase, grab some coffee, and find her way to the Mercedes without fully waking. I'm not sure I got any sleep. I know I looked at the clock at least every hour. After the recording session, my mind was in overdrive, making plans for what to do with Spoolie's songs. For certain, I had over-promised and, now, I was determined to do everything within my power not to under deliver.

We drove the first couple of hours in silence except for the thumping of the windshield wipers like twin metronomes. Apparently, Audrey had something on her mind, too, and wasn't ready to talk about it. But I'm not the most talkative guy, anyway. That's what I liked about working piano bars. I didn't have to talk when I was playing and I could play for an hour without a break if I liked.

Finally, she spoke up. "I've been thinking about Spoolie. He couldn't be as old as Zack thought."

"I've been thinking about that, too," I said. "Zack was just a kid. He probably hadn't met many black men."

"So how old would you guess he is?"

"Ten or fifteen years older than me at most. What do you think?"

"Maybe. Like they say: black don't crack. But what about the seventy-eights?"

"Well, I know they were still making them in the late 1950s, maybe later on smaller labels. That was mainly for distribution in the south. So Spoolie could have recorded them when he was in his early twenties or younger. Might have done it at a local radio station."

"That would explain it, I guess." Her eyes were closed and arms folded. Just when I thought she had dozed off, she asked, "So why did the band breakup?"

"The Blues Attack?"

"No, The Beatles," she said, playing Hepburn to my Tracy. "Of course, the Blues Attack."

"Didn't Zack tell you?" I wanted to tread lightly on this subject and not contradict anything he might have said.

"He talked about it a few times, but only in general terms. I got the sense that he blamed himself as much as anybody."

"Everyone had a hand in it, at least that's how I remember it, now. Back then, I didn't feel that way."

"Tell me about it. I want to hear your perspective."

"Where do you want me to start?"

"The last tour."

The last tour. It was the Japanese movie, *Rashomon*, all over again. Four characters with four different, self-serving stories about what happened. And because we couldn't agree on how it ended, there was no way we could fix it. That's probably the closest we came to being The Beatles. "I assume you know how it came about."

"Tell me anyway." She leaned back in the seat and closed her eyes.

"Well, we used to run into this group from time to time, Sir Timothy and the Royals. They were this band from Mansfield who got by more on personality than musicianship. We never considered them to be a first-tier band, although the teenage girls probably would have disagreed. Imagine our surprise, then, when one day we learned they had signed a record deal. And they had this song, 'Beg, Borrow, and Steal' climbing the charts. Even made the Top Forty. Only it wasn't their song."

"Whose was it?"

"It had been recorded by another band, The Rare Breed, for a New York company called Super K Productions. When it failed to do anything, the producers re-released the record under the name The Ohio Express and hired Tim Corwin and the boys to perform under that name. Next thing you know, they had an album out, although they really only played on a handful of the songs. In fact, all of the hits that came out under The Ohio Express name were recorded by others.

"But we didn't know that at the time. All we knew was that The Dantes, The Grayps, The Fifth Order, and Zack Black and the Blues Attack were still stuck in Ohio while The Ohio Express had an international audience and gold records to show for it. It was kind of humiliating, really. Not that any of us wanted to be associated with bubblegum songs like 'Yummy, Yummy' and "Chewy, Chewy.' But a little attention would have been nice."

"Didn't you have a chance to sign with Super K?"

"Yeah, but there were no guarantees. Super K looked at a lot of Ohio bands, including The Fifth Order, but Billy Carroll's father—Billy was the lead singer—his father was an attorney and he wouldn't let them sign the contract. After we heard that, we decided to hold out for one of the big labels to call—Columbia or Capitol or RCA. After a while, we realized they probably weren't going to. Nevertheless, Zack and I had been working on original material when we found the time. Ever since *Sergeant Pepper*, concept albums had become all the rage, but we didn't really have a concept. Certainly, not like J.D. did with *The Ultimate Prophecy*."

"Who?"

"J.D. Blackfoot. He was a local singer/songwriter who got signed by Mercury Records and recorded this legendary psychedelic album that went nowhere. His real name was Benny Van-something."

"I think Zack had—I think it's in Zack's collection."

Zack's collection. I wondered exactly what he did have socked away in his museum. I hoped that Audrey would allow me to rummage through it some time.

"Well, depending on condition, you might be able to get a hundred bucks for it. Maybe more. It has a real cult following."

"Oh, I wouldn't sell it."

"I wasn't suggesting that. I was just pointing out that it has some value to collectors, more than most albums of that era."

"More than a Spoolie Johnson record?"

"I don't know. I don't know enough about old blues seventy-eights. But I wouldn't be surprised if the really rare ones went for quite a lot."

"You were telling me about your album."

"We had two singles to our name—the first one, 'What's Love,' started getting airplay. Once our name had gotten out, we started getting jobs in neighboring states, and not just teenybopper-things. That's when Stan Billups heard about us. He was the A and R man for Trojan Horse Records. It was a division of Horseless Carriage Enterprises, which, he hinted, had some General Motors money behind it. Tax write-off or something. He apparently liked what he heard and, more importantly, we liked what we heard."

"He made us this proposition. He would be put us on a nominal salary. We would take the band out on the road, work on new material, and after six months of touring the Midwest, we would go into the studio and record an album. And that's what we did—the first band signed by the label. We used our advance—five thousand dollars—to fix up our van. During those six months, Zack and I became a songwriting machine. We wrote fifteen new songs, eleven of which we used on *Save Your Goodbyes*. Even though we were living on White Castles, we had become a team, all pulling in the same direction. Those were the best days of our lives."

Out of the corner of my eye, I caught Audrey staring daggers at me, so I hastily added, "As a band, I mean. I'm sure Zack would say his life with you was—"

Audrey burst out laughing. "You don't have to be that careful about my feelings, Will. I'm not going to fall apart. I'm stronger than I look."

"I'm not," I said, and she laughed again.

I've never been very good when it comes to consoling people. I never know what to say. If there are some magic words, no one has ever shared them with me. So each time I just stumble through it as best I can.

"Playing five or six nights a week, we had honed those songs to perfection—at least as perfect as four guys good make them. We didn't want to do any overdubs. We thought the record should be a document of our live shows. But—and this is where the cracks began to show—Zack and I had developed this grander vision. We wanted horns like Blood, Sweat, and Tears or Tower of Power. So suddenly we weren't four guys anymore, but seven—three of whom were strangers. We were fortunate to pick up some of the Jazz Workshop alums. I quickly wrote some horn charts which were derivative of James Brown and other soul artists. They weren't great, certainly nowhere as good as what Ladd McIntosh had turned out for the Jazz Workshop, but our studio time was limited.

"By the time the album was out, we—Trojan Horse Recording Artists Zack Black and the Blues Attack—were booked on a nationwide tour that started in San Francisco and would wind up in Columbus, opening for The Doors. Thirteen dates altogether. A baker's dozen. We fully expected to be stars by the time we got home. Everything was in place."

"You opened for The Doors?" She was fully awake now.

"No, but I'll get to that. So, we were four guys who had worked and sacrificed for almost five years to be in a position to conquer the world. We felt we had paid our dues and deserved the rewards, if any, but now we had to add a horn section—three more guys who would share in the money, but hadn't shared in our struggle. And one of them, Leroy Hairston, was black.

"I guess I had always known or suspected that Evan was prejudiced. I was hoping I was wrong, so I turned a blind eye to it, hoping Evan and Leroy could work it out. Besides, other cracks began to show up. Namely, writers' credits. Zack and I had written all the original material. Sure, when we arranged a song, everyone contributed, but it was our names that were on the album as the songwriters, and we were the ones who stood to earn any royalties as composers.

"We weren't the first band that had this problem, of course. Most bands are composed of songwriters and frustrated songwriters who think they should be contributing their fair share of the material. But the thing is this: not all songwriters are equal and certainly not all songs are. In the meantime, Zack and I tried to buy time by assuring Wes and Evan that we would divide the songwriting chores equally on the next album. And we reminded them that you don't really make money until the second album, anyway."

"I thought it was the whole Yoko-thing that broke up most bands."

"We didn't have any Yokos," I said, which was a small lie, but she didn't need to know everything. "Say, are you hungry?"

"Maybe. What's on the menu?"

"You choose."

ᏋᎦᏋᎦ

We stopped at this little roadside café that appeared to be well-maintained from the outside. We just hoped they gave as much attention to the food. It was filled with locals and we both got the once-over when we entered the place and sat down at a booth. A waitress sat two glasses of water on the table and handed us both a menu. I hoped my glass was cleaner than it looked.

"The specials are listed on the board," she said. "What can I get y'all to drink?"

After establishing what they didn't have, Audrey went with coffee and I stuck with water.

"So," Audrey started, "were there any grown-ups in this band?"

"Remember, we should have been in college. Instead, we were off trying to be rock stars. There aren't many guys that age who could have handled it any better than we did. Look at how many didn't make it. If there had been a second album, I think we would have called it *Darwin Knows Best* or *Leave It to Darwin*."

"How about *Dar-Win, Dar-Lose*?"

"You're not just a pretty face, are you?" I joked, at the same time reaching across the table and touching her hand. I immediately withdrew it, feeling a little guilty at having violated the unspoken treaty between us. She was Zack's wife—still.

When we left the café, I knew we would be having an early dinner. The best tip I could have given our waitress would be to find another job.

Back on the road, I slipped Spoolie's CD in the player and started skipping through the tracks until I found what I was looking for. It began with my piano intro—da-duh-da-duh-duh—and then Spoolie sang:

"I was born a bad man,
Didn't do the things I should,
Even when I promised that I would.
Then I met a woman,
Who said she understood.
Sun shines on the evil and the good.

"Rain on the just,
Rain on the just.
Without a woman's love
The heart turns to dust."

At first, I only listened to the keyboards, critiquing my own performance. But Spoolie's playing and singing were so incredible that it gave me chills.

"The moment I first saw her,
My heart began to sing,
For her I would do 'most anything.
Didn't have the money,
To even buy a ring.
Night falls on the pauper and the king.

"Rain on the just,
Rain on the just.
Without a woman's love
The heart turns to dust.

"I've tasted good and evil,

And never felt no shame;
People used to tremble at my name.
Vowed that I would find a
Way to beat the game.
Good men and the bad men die the same.

"Rain on the just,
Rain on the just.
Without a woman's love
The heart turns to dust."

As I listened to him put on string-bending clinic, I knew there was no question about it. Spoolie was a monster guitar player.

"They sent me down to Parchman
That's where they'll take my life,
Because I killed another with my knife.
I swear upon the Bible,
When I took her as my wife.
I never meant to cause her any strife.

"Rain on the just (rain on the just),
Rain, rain on the just (rain, rain on the just).
Without a woman's love
The heart turns to dust."

The more I listened to the recordings, the more I thought of all the hullabaloo that preceded Johnny Winter's appearance on the music scene. Spoolie may not have been as exotic as a long-haired, tattooed albino, but neither was Stevie Ray Vaughn and, somehow, his music broke through all the noise. Could we make it happen for Spoolie?

CHAPTER 16

O-Hi-O

Audrey booked a couple of rooms in Fort Mitchell, Kentucky, just across the river from Cincinnati. Normally, I have no problem driving late into the evening if I know there's a bed waiting at the end of it. And I could have kept driving for a few more hours, even made it to Columbus, but she couldn't find any vacancies. Must have been some big event going on—like Buckeye football or the Quarter Horse Congress. Seriously.

This time we weren't even on the same floor together. It was just as well. We were both tired, at least I was, so we dispensed with the late evening conversation and turned in. That night I had a dream. I couldn't remember much of it, but it could have been a *Twilight Zone* episode. I had returned to my hometown, but no one recognized me. Even my parents didn't seem to know who I was. Everyone I encountered treated me like I was a stranger. But then I realized everyone was dead except me. When I awoke, my heart was galloping like I had run up a flight of stairs. I lost interest in sleeping any longer.

A newspaper had been slipped under the door, so I read the parts that interested me then got cleaned up and went down to the continental breakfast. As I was finishing up, Audrey joined me, and I sat with her while she ate. Neither of us was particularly talkative, which was okay with me. However, she looked so winsome, I had to remind myself not to gawk at her. It must be a terrible burden, being beautiful.

After gassing up the car, there was no reason for us to stop before Columbus. The anticipation was building and I didn't really know why. My parents were long dead. I didn't have any relatives there. And I hadn't kept in touch with anyone. I expected that much of the old had been replaced with the new. My childhood had already largely disappeared before I left. Yet, there was still an undeniable attraction.

Ever since I was a kid, I had loved driving across the bridge spanning the Ohio River from Kentucky. And I still did, although it was a different bridge altogether. It was especially magical at night with all the lights. Funny how some things stay with you, are engrained in your being. I had lived in New York longer than I had lived in Ohio, yet I never considered myself a New Yorker. I was still a Buckeye at heart. And now I was coming home. I began to sing:

> "Night and day the river flows,
> With no thought to where it goes,
> On a voy'ge from which there's no return.
> Dancing over ledge and stone,
> To a song that is its own,
> And whose words no one can ever learn.

> "So the people named her long ago:
> O-hi-o."

"What's that?" Audrey asked.

"It's a song I wrote years ago for Ohio's bicentennial. There was a contest."

"Did you win?"

"If you've been paying attention, you'd know I'm not the guy who wins—ever."

"What did?"

"I have no idea."

"Sing the rest for me. Please."

I hadn't really meant to sing it all, but something about being back in Ohio had triggered emotions that surprised me. I struggled to remember the words.

> "Ancient as the rolling hills,
> From whose shady pools and rills,
> Springs the source from which it all begins.
> Always changing yet the same,
> With a spirit none can tame,
> In the end the river always wins.
>
> "Cold and deep her mighty waters flow:
> O-hi-o."

I stopped. "You don't really want to hear all of this, do you? It's kind of long."

"Sure I do. Go on."

> "Fed by nameless creeks and streams,
> Ever coursing through our dreams,
> Bringing life and sometimes bringing death.
> Running wild and running free,
> As it pushes to the sea
> With a beauty that can take your breath.
>
> "It may be your friend or be your foe:
> O-hi-o."

Friend or foe. I remembered how there were always two camps: those who couldn't wait to leave Ohio and those who never planned to do so. Of course, a musician always believed you had to go elsewhere to be discovered, to really make it big. New York, Nashville, San Francisco—somewhere that had a true music scene. But I had known a few—more than a few—who had landed record deals while still in Ohio. While still in Columbus, for that matter. I even knew—or once did, anyway—good musicians who stayed in Columbus and lived nice, comfortable lives. They taught and they played and they put out albums if they wanted to. The albums didn't sell, of course, but few do. I suspected they had more to show for themselves than those who kept reaching for the brass ring.

> "Here the past and future meet,
> Bitter waters with the sweet,
> In the land our ancestors once trod.
> Keeping secret all it knows,
> Though its banks it overflows,
> Like some wondrous brown and muddy god.

> Timeless though the seasons come and go:
> O-hi-o.
> Cold and deep her mighty waters flow:
> O-hi-o.
> So the people named her long ago:
> O-hi-o.
> O-hi-o.
> O-hi-o."

Had I been wrong to leave? I wondered.

"You should have won," Audrey said. "It's beautiful."

"Too bad you weren't one of the judges."

"I am a judge."

"So what do I win?"

"I haven't decided. What would you like?"

"I haven't decided."

"Well, we have that in common, anyway."

I thought we were finished talking about the band, but Audrey picked up the conversation where we had left off the day before. "So why didn't you become rock stars?"

While I really didn't want to revisit all the uncomfortable details, there was no reason why she shouldn't know. Still, I felt a need to hold some things back. "The thing is, when we were out on the road, we were pretty much oblivious to what was going on outside our little cocoon. We assumed that if we did our part, the label would do its. But that's not what happened. Early on, there had been some mention of the fact that 'What's Love?' wasn't available in the stores when we played San Francisco. Shad had stopped pressing it on Counterpart when Trojan Horse bought the masters. He had stopped pressing 'The Sheik,' too, so copies of it are even scarcer.

"We were told there was a glitch in distribution and it would be resolved. But it turned out that Trojan Horse was having a cash flow problem. It was behind in paying its bills, so the record pressing plant was holding our forty-fives hostage. The label had flooded the country with promo copies, but there wasn't any store stock. People were hearing us on the radio and coming to the shows, but couldn't buy the forty-five anywhere. It was breaking big, but we couldn't make the charts."

"That sucks."

"But I learned an important lesson. Don't ever believe lawyers, actors, salesmen, and other people who make their living by lying."

"That an expensive lesson."

"Yeah. Later we found out they never even got around to putting out the album. It only existed as a handful of test pressings and promo copies for radio stations. I never even had a copy of my own."

"Well, at least we can fix that."

"What do you mean?"

"Zack has several cases of them. He bought them from the pressing plant. I guess they were still holding onto them after the label went under."

I couldn't believe it. All these years I had assumed it was gone forever, a lost relic from an Indiana Jones movie. I immediately wished we were at Audrey's house so I could see it.

"What's it look like? The album cover, I mean."

"It has this wooden platform. There are four open trapdoors with ropes hanging through them."

"That's it, all right. *Save Your Goodbyes.* It's a scaffold and four people have just been hanged. It seems particularly apt, now."

"On the back, there's a photo of these mannequins lying on the ground—like the ones Zack has posed with the band equipment."

"Wow. Christmas came early this year."

"I'm sure Zack knew everything he had, but I don't. You're welcome to look through it anytime."

"It's funny," I said. "Afterward, we— the band—got sued."

"What for?"

"It's the way record deals are structured. We basically defaulted on a loan—the money the company had put into us. We had to file bankruptcy, dissolve the band, to keep from having to pay them back thousands of dollars—the cost of recording the album, sending us on tour, all that. We never saw a dime. Try to explain that to Internal Revenue. We may not have been rock stars, but we had some rock star headaches."

ᏕᏗᏕᏗ

As we approached from the south, the Columbus skyline was virtually unrecognizable. The old Lincoln Leveque Tower, once the third tallest building in the country— (it had always reminded me of a finger pointing up), —was now just another skyscraper, and not even the largest. The city was starting to look like a chessboard on which nearly every pawn had been replaced with a bishop or a rook. There was also a jumble of highways heading off into all directions, encircling the city like the rings of Saturn.

My plan was simple: drive to Columbus. Beyond that, I hadn't given it much thought. Audrey wanted a tour of the old neighborhood and I felt I could manage that, once I found it. I just kept driving north on I-71. Unless they had changed it a lot from when I was a teenager, it should still lead me to where I wanted to go.

Zack and I had been best friends since fifth grade. Although I had lost touch with him after the break-up of the band, there was never anyone else in my life to replace him and I suspect he felt the same. If you compared the scrapbooks our mothers kept, you would be hard pressed to tell which was which. I was a Boy Scout and he wasn't. He was in the Civil Air Patrol and I wasn't. And we went to different churches—Lutheran (me) versus Presbyterian (him). But, otherwise, our histories were nearly identical. The difference was in the details. He usually won the competitions I placed in, so the newspaper articles featured Zack, usually including a photo, while I was buried somewhere in the article. Still, by driving Audrey around Columbus and showing her the settings of key events in Zack's life, I was also showing her my own.

I decided to drive straight up High Street, the main north-south corridor through Columbus since pioneer days. It bisected the city like a knife through a birthday cake. The south end was still sad, but I was happy to see the success of German Village—the largest privately funded preservation effort in the country—was spreading out into adjoining neighborhoods. The downtown was also looking prosperous, although Lazarus, the department store which had once anchored the local economy, was now an office building of some kind.

Negotiating the system of one-way streets, I circled around the block until I reached the river and followed it south to the Broad Street Bridge. I wanted to show Audrey the first stop on our impromptu tour: Veteran's Memorial. It actually was intended to be the last stop on the band's cross-country tour, our grand "Welcome Home" finale. But we never made it that far. And, now, it was gone. Where the limestone building—which hosted everything from big name concerts to Kenley Players productions—once stood was now a large excavation, gaping like an open wound. I could imagine that an angry giant had wrenched it out of the ground.

"It may not look like much, now, but that was where the band's homecoming was to take place," I said.

"Is that where Jimi Hendrix played?"

"Yeah. The Dantes and The Four O'Clock Balloon opened for him. How did you know?"

"Zack has the poster."

Of course he did.

We passed through the revitalized Short North area—no longer a no man's land, apparently—which now sported lighted arches like giant croquet hoops spanning the street. Before I realized it, we had reached "The Campus." Although the city had several colleges and universities, "The Campus" always meant the neighborhood around The Ohio State University. I slowed down as much as I could without impeding the traffic flow to see if I could spot any of the bars the band used to play at. I didn't really expect any of them—Stache's, Mean Mr. Mustard's, The South Berg, Moonshine Co-Op, the Castle—to still be in business, but the buildings were gone as well, most of them anyway, replaced by modern, impersonal-looking structures. I was beginning to feel the way I did when I came home to visit my parents and found out my mother had tossed out all my old comic books.

"My city is gone."

"What did you say?" Audrey asked.

"Nothing. Just thinking out loud." A line from a Pretenders song had come to mind. If only for a moment, Chrissie Hynde and I were in synch. I was particularly disappointed to see that Larry's was gone. It was where Phil Ochs, the singing socialist, got his start. There should have been a historic marker or something.

Our Magical Mystery Tour wasn't going at all like hoped. I drove Audrey passed Zack's childhood home on

Cooke Road, passing my more modest one on Maize, and then swung around on Karl Road to show her where we both went to school: Brookhaven High—where the upper middle and the lower middle classes met. When Zack and I were there, it had the highest household income of any school in Columbus, but also the lowest college enrollment rate. Too many well-paying union jobs at the time.

As we pulled up the drive, I was surprised to see the school was closed—closed as in shut down, never to reopen, at least not under that name. While I never felt any strong attachment to my high school, I always thought it would outlive me. After all, it was fifteen years younger. My class had been the first to go all the way through it.

"You didn't know it was closed?" Audrey was probably beginning to think I was the worst tour guide ever.

"I might have heard something," I said. Actually, I didn't recall having heard anything. I always ignored those solicitations from my classmates, none of whom I remembered at all. Maybe if I had gone to the reunions, I would have been fighting to keep the place open. Instead, I assumed it was a combination financial, demographic, and political decision that took a lot of guts to make. No elected official likes to close a school.

"Are you enjoying any of this?" I asked.

"Sure."

"You must be one sick puppy."

She laughed, which is what I had hoped she would do. "I imagine this is kind of painful for you."

"There's got to be something left. And I'll find it if I have to go to hell and back. Or Grove City, anyway."

She laughed again. "Ooh, Grove City. That sounds dangerous."

"We'll just hope it doesn't come to that."

Reversing direction, I headed south down Karl Road and then hung a right onto Oakland Park Avenue. There, just before the street abruptly ended at I-71, was the sign for Musicol Recording Studio, obnoxious as ever. And twenty feet away was a Cape Cod house with a two story cinder block addition, all painted pea soup green. It occupied a corner lot in what was ostensibly a residential neighborhood except for a fluke of zoning. When I was a kid, I had wished I lived next door, although my parents would have hated it.

"The band did some recording here once upon a time," I said.

"I've seen that logo before on some of the records in Zack's collection."

I was now reinvigorated by the simple fact that at least there was something still standing from my childhood. Looping around the block, I drove east on Oakland Park, headed for Sunbury Road. If there was one place in the city that was a shrine to music in Columbus it was the Valley Dale Ballroom. Dating back to World War I, it was a relic from the Big Band era which was known throughout the country for its coast-to-coast radio broadcasts. Over its history, everyone from Frank Sinatra to the Velvet Underground had played there.

As we were zipping along the serpentine curves of Sunbury Road, it suddenly sprung into view as we came over a slight rise. "That's it," I said. I'm sure Audrey detected the excitement in my voice.

"Valley Dale Ballroom?"

"Yeah. The musical Mecca of my generation." The building itself was hard to describe. It could easily be mistaken for an old roller rink. Half sunk in the ground, it looked sort of like a Quonset hut built out of white-painted stone-that-didn't-quite-look-real. There were pennants of various colors flapping from eight flagpoles. "It was a hopping place from the 'twenties through the 'sixties. Jerry Rasor and Chuck Selby used to hold battles-of-the-bands here."

"Jerry Rasor. The 'Dance Party' guy?"

"Yeah. He was the king. Really nice. So was Chuck. He was a veteran Big Band leader. That's probably why we were all so naïve when we started swimming with the real sharks in the music industry."

"Think we can get in?"

"Do you want to see it?"

"Sure. It's part of Zack's history—and yours."

After parking the car in the asphalt lot, we walked around the building until we found an open door. Walking in uninvited, we immediately bumped into a maintenance man.

"Hi," I said. "Mind if we look around?"

"You interested in renting the place?" he asked.

"Maybe," Audrey said, moving past him. "Maybe buy it."

The guy's eyebrows nearly leaped off his face.

"My band played here many years ago."

"Really? What band?"

I hesitated to tell him. I wasn't sure what concerned me more—that he would make a big deal out of it or that he wouldn't? "Zack Black and the Blues Attack."

"Oh, yeah."

I didn't hear a question mark, so I assumed the name didn't mean anything to him. By now, Audrey was standing in the middle of the wooden dance floor, taking it all in. Even with just the work lights on, the ballroom was beautiful in an old fashioned way. It always reminded me a showboat turned inside out, with its two levels of seating and a grand chandelier. Draped fabric hung from the ceiling, obscuring the latticework of beams. On either side of the stage were small booths that were once used for live radio broadcasts. Everything was painted a dazzling white; the effect was magical.

"I just do maintenance," the guy said. "If you have any questions, you'll have to ask the person who does the booking."

"Yeah, we'll do that," Audrey replied. "What do you think, Will? Won't it be perfect for our reception?"

Audrey caught me off guard with her question, which

was no doubt her intent. I don't even know what I mumbled in response. Something stupid, probably.

"Has it changed much since you were last here?" she asked.

"It's not as crowded."

"You probably miss all the screaming teenyboppers."

"Well, I don't miss the screaming." But sometimes I still dreamed about it.

I was ready to leave Valley Dale before Audrey was, but also glad she wasn't in any hurry.

CHAPTER 17

Music is My Mistress

Sitting in the rummage sale that is Studio B, we listened to Spoolie's tape.

Audrey had decided she wanted to hear it before we got back to New York and not just through the car speakers. So on a whim we dropped by Musicol Recording Studios and hired Clay, an audio engineer, to help us. We hadn't even finished listening to the first track when Clay, who had been nodding along to the music, said, "He's good."

"That's what we thought," I replied as I gazed absent-mindedly at the psychedelic carpeting. I thought I could make out faces in the pattern. I would later learn that it has been salvaged from a convention center decades earlier.

"What're you going to do with it?"

"My plan is to replace the keyboards, overdub the drums, and add some Memphis-style horns—the whole Blues Brothers package."

"I can help you with that."

"Thanks, but I was going to wait until we got back to New York."

"Why don't we do it here?" Audrey spoke up. "Give us a reason to hang around town for another day or two."

"We've got guys with the musical chops," Clay said. "Hell, even Eric Clapton lives here."

I had read that Clapton, the British guitar god, had married a girl from Columbus and built a home in the suburbs so she could be close to her parents. Says he enjoys driving around the countryside. Can't say that I would have predicted that. "We've already got a guitarist," I shrugged.

"So did Clapton, but that was before he heard Duane Allman. Besides, you'll be able to get New York quality at Midwestern prices. We've got cats here that can hold their own with anybody."

"Let's do it," Audrey said. "It'll be fun." She looked at me as if to obtain assurance that she hadn't spoken out of turn. I couldn't think of a good reason not to, especially since it meant extending our trip a few days more.

"I'll round you up a regular Murderer's Row," Clay said. "And I can block off some studio time the day after tomorrow."

"Sure. Why not." It wasn't so much a question as an expression of resignation. I wondered who he considered Murderer's Row.

As we were getting into the car to leave, Audrey said, "I hope I didn't overstep my authority."

"You could never do that."

"If it doesn't work out the way you want, we can do it again in New York. Don't worry about the cost. I just thought that since you and Zack were both from Columbus, why not use Columbus musicians for luck?"

"Luck? Do you think we had luck?"

"You got signed. How many people do that?"

I could think of a few, but there weren't as many as there should have been. Johnny Ulrich, for one, played piano better than just about anybody and only real jazz connoisseurs, those who bother with private label pressings, knew it. The man was music. He couldn't turn it off. But fame didn't hold any attraction for him. He was happy living and playing in Columbus and might not have been in New York or Los Angeles or Chicago or any of the other cities where you are only one step away from the spotlight.

⌘⌘⌘

That night, I wanted to take Audrey to some place uniquely Columbus for dinner, so I drove to Schmidt's Sausage House in German Village. Negotiating the labyrinth of brick streets severely tested my newly resurrected driving skills, not to mention my parking abilities.

Schmidt's had been around since the 1880s and its signature dish is a large, spicy sausage called the Bahama Mama—Van Johnson, the movie actor, used to have Bahama Mamas shipped to him in Hollywood. As we walked in the door, past the dessert case filled with softball-sized cream puffs, I noticed a photograph of the featured entertainment, three guys in lederhosen with an accordion, tuba, and drums. They called themselves The Katzenjammerz. Only the spelling was original.

"You're in luck," I said to Audrey. "Now, you'll get to hear what real musicians sound like."

She smiled, more out of tolerance than amusement. We were led to a booth, passing the band along the way, but I didn't really pay much attention to them. I'm not a fan of polka music, having heard enough of "Roll Out the Barrel" and "She's Too Fat For Me" as a kid. I just hoped that Audrey would appreciate the novelty of it.

"What should I order?" she asked.

"That depends on how you feel about German food. It's all good and it's all fattening. It's what I grew up on. Up and out."

"I think I'm part German. And part English and part Irish and part Greek and—"

"Greek?"

"My family came from Liverpool—like The Beatles. Lots of sailors in that town."

"Have you ever been there?"

"No. I never liked The Beatles, actually. I was more into the Stones. I guess that's why the blues appeals to me."

I was beginning to regret coming to Schmidt's because the band was making it hard for us to talk. I was about to ask the waitress to move us to another table when the drummer caught my eye or, rather, I caught his and then he caught mine. In my mind, decades peeled away like layers of old wallpaper. He was older, of course, and heavier and had less hair and his cheeks were puffed out like he had stuffed a couple of lemons in his mouth, but it was definitely him. He looked like an insurance salesman. A Bavarian insurance salesman.

Audrey must have noticed I was distracted for she asked, "What's wrong?" and then followed my glance. "Do you know him?"

"I used to. That's Stuka."

"Your drummer?"

"Yeah."

"Why did you call him that?"

"He sometimes would wear this German helmet when he would play—I think his father brought it home from the war—and the Stuka was a German bomber."

"Are you going to say anything to him?"

"What should I say?"

"I don't know. I'm not your counselor, although I was a bartender."

"Just as good. Better, maybe."

Fortunately, our food arrived before I had to plan my next move. "Don't let it get cold," I said, and during the next few minutes we held the talking to a minimum while slowly committing gastronomic suicide and loving every mouthful of it. But I knew I was only postponing the inevitable. As it turned out, the decision wasn't mine.

When The Katzenjammerz went on break, Evan sauntered over to our table. "I thought you looked suspicious. I almost had them toss you out."

"How have you been, Evan?"

Evan still had a trace of the bad boy's smile that used to drive the teenage girls mad and the fathers insane. I suspected it still worked, but on a much older demographic.

"Weren't you going to say hello?"

"I was getting around to it."

"Dropped your pocket," he said, pointing to the floor. And, stupidly, I glanced down before I caught myself. Evan laughed, of course, and Audrey couldn't help but laugh with him.

"You never get tired of that one, do you?"

"Nope. You're looking good."

"So are you."

"Well, now that we've got the lies out of the way, we can relax." He smiled, but it seemed strained. "Who's your friend?"

"This is Audrey Taylor—Zack's wife."

"Glad to meet you, Evan. Zack told me a lot about you."

"I'm sure he did. How is Zack?"

"He died," I interjected before Audrey could respond.

"Died? When?"

"A couple of months ago?"

"How?"

"Cancer," Audrey said.

"I'm sorry for your loss," Evan replied. "Zack and I sometimes had our differences, but he was a genius."

"Thank you."

"In fact, he carried this guy," he said with a laugh, punching me in the shoulder. "So what brings you to Columbus, Will? Last I heard you were doing the piano bar-thing in New York."

"Zack had some last wishes," Audrey said. "Will agreed to help me carry them out."

"Are you staying long?"

"No," I answered. "We've got to get back."

"Too bad. We could have shared a few laughs about how we turned gold into garbage."

"What about Wes? Do you ever see him?"

"Not since he went all Funkadelic. Not much call for someone to play 'Maggot Brain' at wedding receptions and bar mitzvahs."

"You're kidding."

"No, God's truth. In the 'seventies, he started playing

with all these salt-and-pepper groups. Some of them even got signed to record deals, but first they would dump him in favor of a brother. He's still around town, though you probably wouldn't recognize him."

"Why's that?"

"He's changed."

"We all have."

"Not like him. It's like he's gotten in touch with his inner Martian or something."

"Inner Martian? What's that mean?" Audrey asked.

"If you saw him, you'd know."

"So what have you been doing with yourself?" I was asking to be polite. I wasn't really all that interested.

"Well, I'm married. You remember Betty, don't you?" He fumbled with his wallet. "I've got a picture, here."

Betty had been Evan's high school sweetheart. The eyes and the smile were the same. And the hairstyle hadn't changed, although the color seemed to be darker.

"Got three kids. Two girls and a boy," Evan said. "Of course, they're grown, now."

"We all are."

"Ain't that the truth? Well, I gotta get back to work. Look me up next time you're through town."

After Evan had returned to his drum kit and the band resumed its incessant oompahing, Audrey said, "That was uncomfortable."

"Evan's a good guy—at least I think he still is. He lost his way, too. We all did. Bright lights, big city. You know the story."

"I don't know all of it."

"For that I am grateful. We might not be here if you did."

"You make it sound like you were all a bunch of serial killers or something."

"Or something."

"You're going to tell me the whole story eventually."

"We should split a cream puff. They're really incredible. Vanilla or chocolate?"

"Well, are you?"

"How can I say no?" Of course, that was an evasion, too. I was buying time.

ɞ∕ɷ∕ɞ

When we got back to the hotel, I didn't feel like turning in, yet. Nothing new there. Neither did Audrey, so we stopped into the lounge to get a drink. There was a small combo—piano, drums, guitar—playing to an indifferent crowd of eight or ten. Everyone, musicians and customers alike, seemed bored. As we entered, the piano player announced they were going to take a short break. No one seemed to notice or care.

"Play me something," Audrey said.

"I don't want to impose on their gig."

"You won't be imposing."

Audrey quickly intercepted the pianist as he was making a beeline for the bar. "Hi!"

"Hi, yourself," he replied, his eyes sweeping over her like a prison searchlight.

"My friend," she gestured toward me, "plays piano, too. Would it be okay if he played something while you're on break?"

The pianist gave me a less-than-benevolent look. "Sure," he said, realizing that he had nothing to gain either way. "Just so he keeps his hand out of the tip jar."

As he continued on his mission, I sat down at the piano, inviting Audrey to share the bench with me. No one seemed to notice or care that there had been a change in personnel. And there was only a buck or two in the jar. "So what would you like to hear?"

"A love song. One of yours."

"A love song, huh?" I thought for a moment. "Some

songwriters write nothing but love songs," I said. "The problem with that is there are so many love songs that you have to be at the top of your game if you don't want it to sound sappy. It's hard to find a new angle. Ask Paul McCartney. The harder he tries, the worse they sound. So I've tried to avoid that trap by writing love songs about things other than women."

"What things? Men?"

"No. Although some of the great love songs were written by gay men. Cole Porter's 'Night and Day' or Lorenz Hart's 'My Heart Stood Still.' We think they were about women, but who knows?"

"I hope the person they were writing them for. It would be awful to have someone write you a love song and you never knew it."

"I'm sure it happens. I may have done it myself. Anyway, this is one of my few." It was an up-tempo tune and I jumped into it with both hands (and one foot):

> "Of all the dames,
> In all the places,
> Cities and towns
> And wide open spaces—
> Now, what do ya think the odds are
> I'd meet you?"

As soon as I started, it was like an alarm went off. Everyone in the place, customers and staff, suddenly whipped their heads around to see what had happened.

"You have to imagine the percussion part," I told Audrey. "It was like one of those Motown songs where it sounded like somebody was stomping across the stage on metal roller skates.

> "Of all the dreams
> Down through the ages,

In fairy tales
And history's pages,
What do ya think the chance is
Mine'd come true?"

Audrey directed my attention to the guy whose piano I was borrowing, standing, drink in hand, his mouth agape.

"Yet, here we are,
You and I,
Both together,
Flying high,
Like two eagles
In the sky would do.

"'Cause you light the stars,
And you hang the moon.
You took my words,
And gave them a tune.
No point in finding
Some new rhyme for June
Without you.

"Yes, you warm my heart,
And you calm the seas,
Come on like a monsoon or
Tropical breeze.
Filling the silence
With sweet memories
About you.

"Under your spell, your spell,
I always feel so witless,
Because your charms, your charms,
Your charms are so resistless.
And to quote Marvin Gaye:
Can I get a witness?

> Music is my mistress.
> Music is my mistress.
> Music is my mistress.
> Music is my mistress."

I then ripped through the whole thing again as Audrey laughed and clapped her hands. By this time, the pianist was seething like a cartoon villain. I could imagine his face turning red and veins bulging from his temples. It was a fun image, even if it wasn't entirely accurate.

After I completed the third lap, I came to an abrupt halt and concluded with a shave-and-a-haircut, intentionally omitting the two-bits. "And so forth," I said as I dropped my hands to my sides. The whole lounge broke out in applause as the pianist, murder in his eyes, hurried to reclaim his seat. Pulling a twenty out of my wallet, I stuffed it in his tip jar. "Hoping you don't mind. I warmed it up for you."

Audrey was laughing like a loon all the way back to the room. "You call that a love song?"

"Wouldn't you?"

"Sounds to me like you can't make your mind up. Is it music or the girl?"

"Why can't I have both?"

"You can—as long as the other doesn't find out."

ܳܲ܀

Since I found it increasingly hard to sleep in, I was up before the continental breakfast was ready. The funny thing is, I didn't seem to need as much. Maybe it was because I had stored up a surplus during the period when I wasn't doing anything with my life. I was like a bear coming out of hibernation.

Audrey, on the other hand, liked to sleep in and there was no reason why she shouldn't. Leaving her in the arms of Morpheus, I went for a drive. I had no particular place to go—that's an old Chuck Berry tune—at least not at first, but I felt myself being drawn to the old neighborhoods like a magnet to a refrigerator. We had lived in three different houses as I was growing up. As I cruised up and down the once familiar streets, they called up scenes from my childhood. My parents had died half a lifetime ago, but I caught glimpses of them now in my mind's eye. Their faces weren't clear, but I knew it was them, doing things that were mundane at the time, but wonderful in my recollection.

I was amazed to discover how much had changed over the years. But I had changed, too, although I tried as best I could to ignore the signs. I wanted to believe that the old man who looked back at me in the mirror was someone else. Some people age more gracefully than others. Musicians, with their Peter Pan-ish approach to life, frequently don't age very gracefully at all, hiding behind the fashion and argot of their grandchildren. Nothing sadder than a one-hit-wonder who is still trying to live off a song that provided him with fifteen minutes of fame when he was twenty-two. Billy Joel and I cut our hair at about the same time. I thought we were both the better for it.

CHAPTER 18

Turtles All the Way Down

As promised, Clay had rounded up a drummer, two saxes, and a trumpet player. He could have picked them up at the Salvation Army for all I knew, but several were regulars in something called Vaughn Wiester's Famous Jazz Orchestra. Apparently, it was a local institution with a mix of veteran and up-and-coming players. I remembered Wiester from the Dave Workman Blues Band. He played in the horn section.

Introductions were made, first or nicknames only, and I promptly forgot them. I am terrible at names, but assumed they would be noted on a recording log should I need them later. And Audrey would see that they got paid. We had stopped at the bank beforehand.

"I've been playing the songs for them," Clay said as we strolled into the studio. "Thought they might have some suggestions."

"That's good. I didn't have a chance to do any arrangements," I replied, "but I do have a few ideas I'd like to flesh out."

"Where'd you find this guitar player?" the tenor man asked.

"Mississippi."

"He's a keeper."

"That's what I thought."

"That you on keys?" This time it was the drummer asking the question.

"Guilty."

"Not bad."

I didn't know whether that was faint praise or not. Maybe he was a hard grader. Wanting to make the best of the time we had booked, I limited the small talk and started discussing my ideas for the first song. I've always felt the best sound comes from everyone playing live together. In this case, we had to try to marry the sound of these four players with what Spoolie and I had already laid down. While it was not the optimal situation, we had to make do with what we had.

Feeling I should set the tone for the session, I said, "Like Steve Cropper says, have some fun. Let's not make work out of this."

Cropper, of course, played guitar in the Stax Records studio band, not to mention the Blues Brothers. If they didn't recognize the name, we were probably in trouble.

The first time through was a little rough, but by the fourth or fifth I was satisfied. This was just going to be a demo, after all. We continued onto the other songs. After we wrapped up the first three, we took a break. A couple of the players went outside to smoke, but the drummer hung back to make some adjustments to his kit. I had been impressed with his playing and took the opportunity to tell him so.

"You're good," I said. "Who was your teacher?"

"Evan Bishop. He played with Zack Black and the Blues Attack. You remember them?"

Our Evan. I guess I shouldn't have been too surprised. Columbus isn't exactly the size of New York, but the coincidences were starting to stack up. "Yeah," I said.

Then Audrey piped up. "This is Will Black. He cofounded the band."

"For real?"

"Yeah. And my husband was Zack Taylor."

"Wow. You guys are legends. What happened?"

That's what I've been trying to figure out, I thought. But I said, "We took a break."

"Well, if you ever get back together, I'd buy a ticket."

"I appreciate that. I would hate to get stuck with them all."

✀✀

At the end of the evening, we had our six songs in the can. Clay went ahead and made a sample mix for us, while promising he'd send us a better one when he had more time to work on it. Handing me several tape boxes, he said. "I think these might generate some interest."

"We'll see."

On the way back to the hotel, Audrey was strangely quiet.

"Something bothering you?" I asked.

"No. I was just riding the high as long as I could," she said. "That was fun."

It had been fun. Music was fun—when it's just music. But when it becomes a business, the fun quickly dissipates.

"Do you ever think about getting the band back together?"

"I might have once or twice. But there wouldn't be any point without Zack. Besides, no one cares about music anymore."

"I do."

"You and three others, maybe. But the general public doesn't."

"Why do you say that?"

"Because I have been watching the steady decline for the last forty years."

"Why do you think that is?"

"Several reasons. First, you no longer have to seek it out. It's everywhere whether you want it or not. Second, people expect it to be free. And when they don't pay anything, they don't place the same value on it. And third, most of it is garbage. It's as empty and soulless as a gum wrapper. The main thing it is used for is to block out the rest of the world. It's just a reason to wear earbuds."

"But your music isn't like that. People would want to hear the Blues Attack again. I know they would."

"Most never heard us the first time. They don't ever play regional hits on those oldies broadcasts."

"Just the same. I think you should do it."

"But who would play guitar? Who would sing Zack's songs?"

"Spoolie."

"Spoolie? You want Spoolie to replace Zack?"

"Not replace. But you know Spoolie can handle the guitar parts."

"But to what end? What would be the point?"

"Just think about it," she said.

So I thought about it. For a moment.

∽∾∿

Throughout Ohio, Pennsylvania, New Jersey, I made numerous suggestions that would have delayed our return home, if only for a few hours. Roadside attractions, scenic detours, country roads, an abandoned farmhouse—anything, really. But Audrey hadn't gone for any of them. So evening found us zipping across the Hudson River on the Tappan Zee Bridge to Tarrytown and beyond. I assumed she would invite me to stay the night although nothing had been said about it. I almost felt that she was giving me the cold shoulder for some reason.

"You've been unusually quiet," I said.

"Have I?"

"Something bothering you?"

"No. I've just been thinking."

"A penny for your thoughts."

"Is that all they're worth to you?"

"A dollar, then. But that's all I can afford."

"I've been thinking about Zack."

Oh, I thought. *You sure stepped on that landmine, buddy.* I assumed we were getting beyond that, but instead we seemed to be back where we started.

"What about him?"

"What he would want us to do?"

Now, I had no idea what she was talking about. All kinds of ideas started to jump out, each more ludicrous than the one before.

"Do about what?"

"Spoolie."

That wasn't the answer I was hoping for. I assumed the Spoolie project would continue as we—or, rather, I—had planned. We would try to get a record label interested in him, maybe one of the indie labels that specializes in blues like Alligator or Delmark.

"Don't laugh, but I think Zack would want Spoolie to take his place in the band."

"Why not just give Spoolie his own band?"

"But if you got the Blues Attack back together, you could finally finish your tour."

There was only one argument that could convince me to put the band back together again and that was it. I knew from the moment she broached it that I would do it against my better judgment. There was something irresistible about the thought of finishing the tour that the four of us had started together back when we were little more than kids. And maybe it would allow us—all of us—to gain some closure on that chapter of our lives.

"I don't know," I said, because I really didn't know—didn't know how to go about it. It would mean uprooting myself from a life I had grown comfortable and complacent in. There would likely be no money in it for any of us. The only one who really might have anything tangible to show for it would be Spoolie, and I had no idea whether he would agree. Then there were Wes and Evan. I didn't know whether they would be interested in taking a flyer on something as improbable as this. "I don't know how to run a band. That was Zack's wheel house or bailiwick or forte or whatever you want to call it."

"But you were the arranger."

"I didn't say I couldn't lead a band. I've worked as a music director off and on. I just can't deal with the other stuff. I'm not a babysitter or a therapist. I don't want to wipe noses and butts. That's why I've been a solo most of my career."

"I didn't know you held them all in such high regard."

"It's what they are. It's what most musicians are. Being married to one person is hard enough. Try being married to three or four or more at the same time."

"I didn't know you were an expert on marriage."

"I'm not—unless you become one by falling on your face."

"What's the worst that could happen?"

"We break up again."

"And what's the best?"

I thought for a moment. "I think all of us believed and probably still believe that, with a few breaks, we could have made it. This is our last chance to prove it to ourselves— prove that we were, that we are, as good as anybody."

"So why don't you take it?"

"I don't know. Even if we were Moby Grape, we couldn't make it, now."

"Moby Grape?"

"Yeah. They were one of the greatest bands of their era—my era—and yet they wound up with nothing." I don't know why I always came back to them when talking about groups that should have made it. There were others, of course.

"Why?"

"Well, you had five guys, all of whom could play, sing, and write songs. Three strong guitarists. And they had this sound that merged: rock, folk, jazz, country—you name it. Columbia Records was so high on them that released five singles from the first album all at the same time. That's ten songs! Nearly the whole album."

"So what went wrong?"

"Everything. First, the radio stations didn't know what to do with five singles. Which one should they play? They were in competition with themselves. And then they got all kinds of bad advice. Their manager wanted a million bucks for them to appear in the *Monterey Pop* film, so they got the worst slot on the bill. They wound up losing the rights to their music and even their name in a series of legal battles that, last I heard, are still going on and probably will be until they're all dead."

"Sounds like a good checklist of things not to do."

"The point is, Moby Grape still plays out now and then, but nobody cares. And we weren't Moby Grape."

"So why bother?"

"What?" Was she trying to use reverse psychology on me or something?

"So why bother? If that's the way you feel about it."

"One—no, two reasons."

"And they are?"

"Spoolie. If we can get him before the right people, he could be another Hendrix. I'd just like to be a part of that. And if he's playing our songs, that's even better."

"What's the other reason?"

"You."

"Me."

"Yes."

"Why?"

"You asked me to."

"And would you do anything I ask?"

"Don't ask."

"So do it as a favor to me, Will. I will cover all of the costs. I'll even put the band on salary so that none of you have to sacrifice your livelihoods over this."

"We're talking thousands. Tens of thousands, Audrey."

"Don't worry. I've got the money, Will. Scrooge McDuck-money. I'm swimming in it. Besides, it would really mean a lot to me."

"Do I have to give you an answer right now?"

"No, of course not. We're both tired. When we get back to my place, let's sleep on it. Tomorrow we can discuss it some more and see whether it's even possible."

"I don't know if I can sleep on it. You've given me a lot to think about."

"It's turtles, right?"

Turtles. She was using my own songs against me.

"You remember 'Turtles,' don't you?"

"I remember," I said. It was a song I had written about philosophical conundrums. Not exactly top forty material, but I always leaned more toward Tom Lehrer than Allan Sherman. I was trying to recall it and then Audrey started singing the first verse. It had sort of a Latin jazz feel to it. Think "Oye Como Va."

"Ev'ry night when I'm lying in bed,
Can't stop these questions running thru my head.
Like someone's giving me the third degree,
But still the answers keep eluding me.

"Is the universe real? (Is the universe real?)
Can we ever know? (Can we ever know?)
Why is there something rather than nothing?
And where does the time go?"

"Now, you," she said. Feeling I really didn't have a choice, I took the second verse and chorus.

"Met this wise man walking down the road,
He asked me, "Can I help you carry your load?"
Soon started sharing his philosophy,
And then I told him what was troubling me.

"Is there life after death? (Is there life after death?)
Do we have free will? (Do we have free will?)
How do we know what is wrong and what is right?
And how does time stand still?"

Audrey joined me on the bridge.

"But then he said the words that eased my strife,
Lifted my spirits and changed my life.

"It's turtles,
All the way down.
Turtles, turtles, turtles,
All the way down.
The first one stands on the second one's shell,
And the second one stands on the next as well.
'Cause it's turtles,
All the way down."

"You sing," I said. "I'll do harmony." So we continued.

"Now, ev'ry night when I'm lying in bed,
I find myself counting turtles instead.
So if you're having trouble falling asleep,
Just count your turtles and forget about sheep."

"Now, here's where we dropped in the opening guitar riff, from 'Satisfaction,' only with horns. Turns out Keith Richards originally planned to use saxes.

"'Cause it's turtles,
All the way down.
Turtles, turtles, turtles,
All the way down.
The first one stands on the second one's shell,
And the second one stands on the next as well.

> 'Cause it's turtles,
> All the way down."

"I love that song," she said when we had finished. "How did you come to write it?"

"I don't know. I guess I had read something about William James, Henry's brother. One day this little old lady came up to him after he gave a lecture on the solar system. She objected to his saying that the earth resolves around the sun. 'Then how do you think it works?' he asked her. The little old lady replied, 'We live on the crust of the earth which rests on the back of a giant turtle.' Trying to be kind, James asked, 'Then what does the turtle stand on?' She told him a second turtle. Patiently, James asked, 'And what does the second turtle stand on?' At that, the woman exclaimed, "Isn't it obvious, Mr. James? It's turtles all the way down!'"

"That's funny."

"I thought so. We intended to use in on the second album, but never got beyond the demo stage. Not bluesy enough. All of the philosophical questions were Zack's, I think."

"He mentions time twice."

"I never noticed."

"I think he knew that his time was limited. Did you ever think that?"

Her question made me think about Jim Croce. He wrote "Time in a Bottle," contemplating his own mortality, after his wife told him she was pregnant. It became his second number one record after he died in an airplane crash.

"Are you asking me whether I ever thought he thought he would die young?" I replied. "I don't think any of us did. We took life for granted. Personally, it was only when I started losing some of my friends that it dawned on me that my days—all of our days—could be numbered as well."

"I'm still trying to figure it out, you know? And I keep thinking that maybe someone else will have the answer. But it's turtles."

"Sometimes we just have to accept that we'll never know."

As I guided Audrey's car up the long drive I had this feeling that I was William Holden in *Sunset Boulevard*. The character he played, the screenwriter, was from Ohio, too. And, like me, he didn't have a lot going for him when he got sucked into the whole Norma Desmond-thing. The situation with Audrey and Spoolie was almost Hollywood-crazy. But Audrey wasn't crazy. She was as grounded as the Spruce Goose.

While Audrey unlocked the door, I played bellhop with the luggage. Ever since Mississippi, she had carried the tapes of Spoolie around in her purse and added those from Columbus, protecting them like they were the crown jewels. After we were inside, she took the tapes down to Zack's lair and locked them in a fireproof, climate-controlled vault. It was where he stored all of his most valuable recordings. I hoped to someday be able to spend some time checking out his collection. But for now I would just enjoy living in his house and the company of his wife.

It had been awhile since we had eaten, so I sat at the bar in the kitchen as Audrey whipped something up. The refrigerator was well-stocked. Audrey had called ahead to let her housekeeper know we would be back in a day or two, so she had done some shopping. I'm a sucker for garbage omelets, practically lived on them when I worked a gig on a cruise ship, and Audrey turned out to be a pretty good chef. Of course, the wine probably colored my judgement a little.

I thought we had agreed not to discuss the band anymore that night, but Audrey couldn't seem to help herself.

"How long do you think it would take to get the band prepped for the road?" she asked.

"Hard to say. At least we're all still working musicians. But we'd have to learn the songs all over again. And the horns—that's a whole other unknown. There's a lot to think about. Just the logistics of putting together a tour is a big headache."

"So we'll just hire people for that. We don't have to do it all ourselves."

Trojan Horse, our label, had been aptly named. It wasn't what it represented itself to be—a major player in the music industry. Oh, there had been money to get started, just not enough to keep it rolling. But we wouldn't even have that. This time, it would all be on us. Though we had said we would sleep on it, I knew that the decision had already been made. Audrey wanted the band back together and I wanted what Audrey wanted.

CHAPTER 19

Seen the Elephant

There had been times in my life when I didn't own a piano. And unlike the friends of the late Joey Nichols, mine didn't chip in to buy me one. But that speaks more to the kind of guy Joey was than it does my friends. Or me, for that matter.

Consequently, I got in the habit of playing the piano whenever I had the chance, just to keep from rusting up like the Tinman. If it wasn't at the church, it was a bar or hotel lounge. On occasion, I'd drop by this music store and give impromptu demonstrations on some of the floor models. Once I even dated someone longer than I should have because I had designs on her piano.

At Audrey's, I had my choice of two pianos—the Steinway and a Baldwin upright—a B-3, and several synthesizers. So whenever I found myself with some time on my hands or couldn't sleep, you could be sure to find me at one of them. Having driven straight through from Columbus, I was much too wound up to go to bed. Audrey, too, apparently.

Sometime after midnight, she came wandering down to the basement, sylph-like in a chiffon robe. I certainly didn't mind. Audrey was a good audience and a delight to be around. She was like the perfect date. We both knew we weren't going to allow our relationship to develop into something more serious—and for the same reason, although we were coming at it from differing perspectives. However,

I did wonder how my life might have been different if I had settled down with someone like her.

Draping herself over my shoulder, she said, "Play me a song."

"What'll it be?"

"Play 'Misty' for me."

When I turned my head up to see her in the face, she looked deadly serious, but then broke into a throaty laugh. And so did I. Obviously, she had seen the movie, too. So I started off playing it, hoping she would feel like singing, but when she didn't I quickly transitioned into something else and then something else after that. She walked behind the piano and peered at me over the top board. "Every girl should have her own piano player," she said. "I wish I had known that when I was younger."

"That would certainly sell a lot more pianos," I said, tossing in some rolled chords for emphasis.

Audrey continued listening quietly. As the song came to an end, I said, "Something you said before stuck with me."

"What was that?"

"You said, 'The next time you write a song, don't do it without me.'"

"Yes, and?"

"What else wouldn't you want someone to do without you?"

"I don't know. Eat at my favorite restaurant. Take in a Broadway show. Go to Paris…"

"Those are all good, but would you want to put them in a song?"

"I don't know. Maybe." For a moment, she scrunched up her face like she was thinking hard about something. Then she said, "Fall in love."

"All right. Fall in love. 'Don't fall in love without me.' That's the grain of sand we can begin to form our pearl around."

"So we're musical oysters, now?"

"In a way. When I get an idea for a song, it's kind of an irritant."

"You're kind of taking the romance out of songwriting."

"No, not at all. It feels good to scratch an itch, right? So whether it's in the chorus or the verse, we don't know yet, but that is going to be the last line in the lyrics: 'Don't fall in love without me.' Now, how do we get there?"

"I don't know."

"Unless we want it to be a straight ahead, plain old boring love song, we need some kind of conflict. Why would he or she fall in love without that person?"

"Maybe they're not ready. He loves her, but she's not ready to commit."

"Or it could be the other way around. So he—or she—has to acknowledge that. He has to let her know that he's willing to wait until she is ready. This is where I just try to get some words down to sketch out the musical idea. Something like…" I began to sketch out my idea for her.

> "You can go where you want,
> See what you want to see,
> Do what you want,
> Be what you want to be.
> Something goes here
> And something goes here and here—me.

"It has to rhyme with 'me.'"

> "Duh-duh-duh-duh-duh-duh
> Don't fall in love without me.

"Okay, so let's see what we've got," I said. "Let's change 'Do what you want' to 'Do what you like.' That sounds better to my ear and avoids the lazy rhyme of 'want' with 'want,' which we don't need anyway. Agreed?"

"Yeah. Kind of reminds me of the Mamas and Papas song."

"I can hear that, but it won't when we're done. Now, let's tackle the 'duh-duh-duhs.' It has to be a good set up for the last line. 'But whatever you do, don't fall in love without me.'"

"I like it."

"Now the hard part. This is the transition from the first four lines. Fortunately, lots of things rhyme with 'me.' We've used the more obvious ones: 'see' and 'be.' What's left?"

"Free?"

"'Free?' Sure. What about 'free'?' What needs to be free?"

"The girl."

"More poetic."

"Her heart?"

"Good. Free for what—to do what?"

"Sing, dance."

"Sing and dance. So let's make it 'The heart needs to sing and dance.' No, 'laugh, sing, and dance to truly be free. But whatever you do, don't fall in love without me.' So what do we have?

> "'You can go where you want,
> See what you want to see.
> Do what you like
> And be what you want to be.
> The heart needs to laugh, sing, and dance
> To truly be free.
> But whatever you do,
> Don't fall in love without me.'

"What do you think?"

"It's great," she said.

"Good. So, let's put it aside. Let it incubate for a while before we tackle the rest." I folded up the paper on which I had written the lyrics and handed it to her.

She looked at it for a few moments like it was some sort

of holy relic. "How long does it usually take—to finish a song?"

"They're never finished. You just stop."

"How do you know when to stop?"

"That's the hard part. You want to stop when it's as good as it's going to be. But most of the time you don't know when that is."

She thought about it for a few minutes.

"I'm hungry," I said, breaking the silence. "You want something to eat?"

She nodded her head. We retired to the kitchen, shared a piece of coconut cream pie, and then headed off to bed, separately.

ℰↁℰↁ

When I rose around ten, Audrey was already up and about. After our late night snack, neither of us was particularly hungry so we decided to get a little work done then drive into Tarrytown for lunch. To the best of my knowledge, I never actually agreed to put the band back together, but after our conversation the night before, it was sort of assumed. I suggested we start by developing our itinerary.

Returning to Zack's vault, Audrey pulled out a couple of scrapbooks. Some fan—I suspected—had assembled a book that was going to document our big tour. There were only about a dozen pages completed, but it told me what I had largely forgotten. After St. Louis, we had been booked into Chicago, which we played, followed by the Grande Ballroom, Detroit; Electric Factory, Philadelphia; Boston Tea Party, Boston; Syria Mosque, Pittsburgh; and Veterans Memorial, Columbus. Most, if not all, of those places had likely vanished from the face of the earth. And I didn't know if we could get booked into them, anyway.

"Why not?" she asked.

"It's different when you're touring to promote an album and have a major label behind you doing publicity. We're going to be asking these places to take a chance on an unknown. These places all had lots of seats. They'd need guarantees that we aren't in a position to provide them. Frankly, we don't know if anybody will show up to see us."

"So why don't we re-release the album. Then you could tour to promote it."

"First, we don't own the tapes and, second, we still would be unknowns."

"You may not own the tapes, but I do."

"What?"

"Zack bought back the masters."

If I looked stunned, it was because I was.

"I read that vinyl sales are making a comeback," she continued. "We could put the album out the way you originally planned with the cover art and everything."

I had to admit the idea appealed to me, having a copy of the album I could hold in my hand. Something I could pass onto my imaginary progeny.

"They still do vinyl pressing at Musicol," she added. "It's in the brochure Clay gave us."

"What about the recordings with Spoolie? This was all about getting him exposure."

"Make it one of those double albums, the kind that unfold like a book."

"A gatefold LP." I immediately thought of the Mothers of Invention *Freak Out!* album, which must have been one of the earliest.

"Yeah."

I could see it now. One record would be *Save Your Goodbyes*, the second the tracks we did with Spoolie and maybe some of the demos we had done. But what would that one be called? Almost before I had asked myself the question, the answer came to me: *Hello, I Must Be Going.* Both Zack and I were big Marx Brothers fans and that was a nonsense song Groucho sang in *Animal Crackers*. Since this would be the band's farewell tour, it made sense.

"I like that idea."

The cover art was also starting to take shape in my mind. I saw a long hallway with all these open doors, one for each member of the band. We would be walking through them. The first door, the closest, would be Zack's and he would have already passed completely through it so he wouldn't be visible at all. The next one would be mine and all you would see is my hand waving. The one after that would be Evan and we would just see his trailing leg. And so on until we got to Spoolie and he would just be entering the door, fully visible at the end of the hall.

Over lunch at one of Tarrytown's trendy little cafes, we—Audrey and I—began planning the tour like it was a military campaign. I could see she had a talent for organizing things on paper in contrast to my usual habit of trying to keep everything in my head. Basically, I would concentrate on reforming the band and whipping it into shape. I would also work with Clay on producing the double album, both on vinyl and CD. We would have to add in some vocal and instrumentals tracks on the new stuff. Fortunately, we had access to Zack's home studio and would only have to bring in someone to engineer.

Audrey would do pretty much everything else, starting with researching new venues in St. Louis, Detroit, Philadelphia, Boston, Pittsburgh, and Columbus. I would leave that entirely up to her. She would also look into renting a tour bus and a truck for our equipment, hiring a couple of drivers, portable lighting, hotels, etc.—all the logistical stuff that I would rather take a beating than have to deal with.

We also sketched out a budget, including salaries for all the band members except me. I drew the line at being placed on Audrey's payroll. After expenses were deducted, we would split any profits from the shows, not that we expected there to be any. The same with album sales. We would press five thousand copies, numbered and signed by all the members of the band. I just hoped we didn't have ten cases of them leftover at the end of the tour.

The one topic we had been avoiding was Spoolie. He was the key to pulling this off on the scale we were planning, but we weren't sure how he would feel about it. Like many black musicians, he was suspicious of white men in the music business. The legacy of exploitation was as long as it was undeniable. That's why your Bo Diddleys and Chuck Berrys always demanded cash in advance before going on stage. They had been burned too many times in the past. I didn't know Spoolie's story, not much of it, anyway, but I suspected he had been burned a few times, too.

I wouldn't need money while staying with Audrey, but I didn't want her to be my Sugar Mama, either. The next day, I went to an ATM and withdrew some cash from my meager savings. It was the first time I had been away from Audrey for any length of time since I took that walk in Oxford. Being around her was intoxicating. Her charm, her beauty, her smell. She appealed to all of my senses, making it hard to think straight. And yet in many ways she was still a stranger to me. There was a darkness about her. At first, I attributed it to mourning, but as the days went by I came to believe she was hiding something.

When I returned to the house, I found her downstairs. She was sitting on an overstuffed couch listening to *Save Your Goodbyes*. I could recognize a setup when I saw one. She had the album cover, some publicity photos, and a few newspaper clippings on the coffee table. Things I didn't even know existed. Maybe they were there as much for her benefit as mine, but she had to know they would affect me as well. We had spent enough time together, now, that she would know I had a sentimental streak a mile wide. My word for it was mawkward: mawkish and awkward—an embarrassing sentimentality. It was on clear display in Columbus.

I dropped onto the couch beside her. I hadn't heard those songs since I played the test pressing for the horn players we hired so they could learn their parts. I had never heard them on a top-of-the-line stereo system. It was like hearing a studio playback. The sound held us suspended. We heard it not just through our ears, but through our core. At that moment in time, it was the most beautiful thing I had ever heard. Later, I would come to despise every flaw.

"You should have been stars," Audrey said softly.

"Well, as a great philosopher once said, 'We are all of us stars, and we deserve to twinkle.'"

"Who was that?"

"Marilyn Monroe."

"She didn't really say that, did she?"

"I hope so. It would be tragic to have lived the life she did and not learn anything from it."

"I'm not sure Zack did."

"Did what?"

"Learned from it. He was a star in nearly everything he did, but I don't think he ever saw himself that way. He never really stopped to appreciate it all. Not until the disease made him slow down. And then it was too late."

Much of my life I had spent comparing myself to Zack, hoping to best him in something, no matter how trivial. It didn't happen, yet Zack never felt he was better than I was. He knew he had more opportunities because of his family, but he also worked harder. If our abilities had been the same, he still would have won because he had more drive. He was the active one, I was the reflective. He was the doer, I was the thinker. We made a good team because he was comfortable in the limelight and I avoided it. He knew I would have liked to have been more like him, but did he ever want to be more like me?

"He sounds like Spoolie," she said as Zack's guitar soared on "Seen the Elephant," the heaviest song on our album. In concert, we turned it into an extended jam that always left everyone sweating and, I always imagined, hairline fractures in the concrete. *Spinal Tap* had nothing on us when we turned our amps up to eleven. "So tell me about how you came up with this one."

"Well, it's like this. Wes challenged me to write a song based on the fable of the blind men and the elephant. The problem is that it's a fairly complex idea to convey within the format of a pop song. And when I had finished it, I wasn't satisfied because it didn't do anything more than tell the original story. I hadn't made any kind of a statement. That's why I tacked on the final verse."

"It does kind of take you by surprise."

"Yeah, it's kind of a long setup for the punchline." As I explained my thought process, we listened to it again. It kind of sounded like a ZZ Top boogie-blues with horns.

> "Once there were six blind men,
> Not so long ago,
> Heard tell of a circus
> And decided they would go.
> Though they couldn't see it,
> They knew that they would find,
> Many other ways to
> Entertain the mind.
> They'd use their other senses,
> Which had served them well:
> For they could taste, and they could touch,
> And they could hear and smell."

"On one hand, I was pleased that I got all the senses in," I explained. "But on the other, it's still kind of cluttered."

> "So they bought six tickets,
> And sat right by the ring.
> Had the best seats in the house,
> Up close to everything.
> They could taste the popcorn,
> And they could hear the cheers,
> And they could smell the greasepaint,
> Mixed with laughs and tears.
> But there was one thing missing,

From their little jaunt,
'Cause you haven't seen the circus 'til
You've seen the elephant!"

"This time, I had to mention all the remaining senses except touch. And also, I had to introduce the hook: 'We haven't seen the circus 'til we've seen the elephant!'"

"Sounds like you work from an outline."

"An outline in my head, maybe. But it's mostly just second nature. Now, I wish I had found a way to dispense with
the third verse, but I needed it to set up the chorus. Usually,
the second verse would have done that. So all at once I'm
working with a four-act rather than a three-act structure. I
sweated over this, but there was nothing I could do."

"When the show was over,
The blind men went backstage.
Past the painted wagons
And the tiger's cage.
Past all the performers,
Until at last they found,
Where they kept the elephant,
Tethered to the ground.
And when the trainer asked them,
"What is it that you want?"
They said: 'We haven't seen the circus 'til
We've seen the elephant!'"

"Now, when we get to the chorus, that's where my hands
were really tied. I had twelve lines to convey six ideas from
the fable. And I had to make it rhyme and scan. I amazed
myself that I got it to work at all."

"You make the listener work awfully hard."

"That's not a good thing, usually," I said.

"The first one grabbed a leg and said,
"I think this is a tree.""

> Replied the second with the tail,
> "It feels like rope to me."
> Another holding on a tusk,
> Declared, "It's like a spear."
> "This must be some kind of fan,"
> Said one who felt an ear.
> The fifth man seized it by the trunk,
> "It's like a snake," he cried.
> Proclaimed the last, 'It's just a wall,"
> As he touched its wrinkled side.'"

"I didn't write protest songs," I said. "I left that to the Dylans and Ochses and Paxtons. But given the tenor of times, I could let the opportunity pass to say something about the state of politics."

> "Once there was a blind man,
> Or maybe two or three,
> Went to join the circus
> In Washington, DC,
> Soon as they were settled,
> They set out on a spree.
> Seems the men weren't really blind,
> They just refused to see.
> Although they're always talking,
> It's mostly a smoke screen.
> As they fight about an elephant
> That none of them has seen!"

Audrey had listened quietly and remained quiet for a couple of minutes after the song ended. Finally she said, "I wish I could see inside your head."

"Why is that?"

"Because it must be beautiful there."

"There is beauty and there is horror and everything in between. You have to choose which room you want to enter

"I'm not sure I have that choice."

While we sat there listening to the rest of the album, I couldn't help but wonder how many times she had heard it. She seemed to know every song better than we ever did. It was as though the music was oxygen to her and she needed it to survive.

Audrey didn't mention Zack or Spoolie or the band again, but she didn't need to. As I lay in bed that night, trying to get the sleep I knew I would need tomorrow, I couldn't turn my brain off. I kept thinking about how—it was no longer a question of if but how—we could get the band back together. And for the moment I forgot about all of the problems that would inevitably arise. I was ready to be a rock star again. Or a wannabe one, anyway.

CHAPTER 20

Chic Was From Chicago

Just like some divorced couples, bands will periodically get back together. But it's an iffy proposition and the motivation is usually a monetary one—for bands, that is, but it probably applies to couples as well. When it works out it, it's presumably because they learned something the first time around. I didn't know whether the members of the Blues Attack, myself included, had learned anything, but I was going to find out.

"So what's on the agenda for today?" Audrey asked when she came down for breakfast. She found me sitting in my customary seat.

Funny how quickly we fall into patterns.

Opening the refrigerator, she removed a bowl of sliced fruit and set it on the island like a magician making a big "reveal."

"I thought I'd start by giving Clay a call. If he doesn't know how to get in touch with Evan and Wes, he'll probably knows someone who does."

"What do you need me to do?"

"Make a budget," I said.

While she was attending to her daily coffee-making ritual, I peeled the foil off a carton of yogurt.

"Budget? What for?"

"Because I need to know exactly how much you're willing to pour into this project."

"Money's no object. I told you that."

"Well, we can't tell that to a bunch of musicians. They need to know up front what they can and can't expect to get out of it."

"Sex, drugs, and rock and roll. Isn't that why all boys join bands?" When I didn't answer, she turned her attention back to the coffee maker. "Okay. I'll call Sammy."

"Who's Sammy?"

"My accountant."

"I can imagine how that conversation will go."

"Is that because you're underestimating me or overestimating Sammy."

"I would never under underestimate you."

"Good."

I called Oxford that afternoon, leaving a message at Johnsons barber shop. I told them to say I had good news, thinking that might pique Spoolie's interest. But most of the day I spent sorting through the band's catalogue, putting together suggested set lists. I would give Wes and Evan some say, but I had strong feelings about what we should play, given that Zack and I wrote it all.

℮⁊℮⁊

Around midnight, Oxford time, my phone rang. I was having this great dream and by the time I roused myself and swept away the jumble of images clouding my mind, I had missed it. I called back immediately, expecting Spoolie to answer. He didn't. Doctah Root did.

"Mr. Black," the doctah said in a voice marinated in graveyard dews and damps. "I understand you want to talk to Spoolie Johnson. What would that be for?"

"Well, I was hoping I could talk to Spoolie himself."

"This isn't a good time."

"Why is that?" I was immediately concerned that he was experiencing health problems or something.

"He's sleeping."

I was about to say, "So was I," but realized that wouldn't accomplish anything. So I said, "He could have called earlier."

"He didn't want to bother you."

Doctah Root was a shrewd one, as I knew from our previous dealings. It was becoming apparent that whatever I worked out regarding Spoolie would be a package deal—I would get both of them or neither.

"All right, doctah, here it is. I am putting a band together. We want to do a six city tour to showcase Spoolie's talents. It will be a great opportunity for people to get to know him and see what he can do. If things go the way I think they will, he could come out of this a star." I was overstating it a bit, but I was optimistic this would open some doors for him.

"I don't know that Spoolie would want to do that."

"Well, would you ask him?"

"Oh, I'll ask him. But he doesn't like to travel."

"Just let me talk to him."

"He'll still want my advice. But I'm not sure what I should say."

I was quickly coming to the realization that I was being shaken down. "What do you need to know to help you make up your mind?"

"How much will Spoolie get?"

"Audrey has agreed to put everyone in the band on a generous salary."

"What else?"

"Well, after expenses, we'll split the profits—if any. And, of course, Spoolie will get lots of publicity. I would almost guarantee he'll come out of this with a recording contract with one of the major labels."

"That's it?"

"I think that's a lot."

"I don't know," Doctah Root said. "It seems like my boy isn't getting his fair share."

"What would be fair?"

"Double."

"Double what?"

"Double what everyone else is getting."

I figured that the doctah was angling for his cut of the pie—that he would get half of whatever Spoolie got. On that basis, I had kind of rationalized it, that and the fact that he could have my share since I wasn't planning on accepting anything from Audrey anyway. So, I said, "All right. Spoolie will get paid twice what the others get. So, now will you recommend Spoolie signs up?"

"I believe I will, Mr. Black. Of course, for myself, I'll only expect the same share as everyone else."

If I could have reached through the phone and choked Doctah Root, I probably would have. I was seeing red, my eyes glowing like a bad flash photo.

"But they're being paid for being musicians!"

"So will I."

"What do you play?"

"Tanbu."

The tanbu was a drum—an African drum; I knew that much. But I didn't know whether Doctah Root could play the thing. I'd deal with that when the time came. And I would explain to Audrey later how the band had added a percussionist and Spoolie would be receiving twice what the other guys were getting.

The simple fact is I had never been a shrewd negotiator—not for myself, not for anyone. And for all I knew Doctah Root had cast one of his spells on me. After I shared a few more details with him, he said he would get back to me after he had the chance to discuss the proposition with Spoolie. He couldn't guarantee he would go along with it, but I suspected Spoolie would go along with whatever he said.

After he hung up, I tried to go back to sleep, but failed dismally. All I could think about was the ever increasing number of factors that were going to be beyond my control. If it weren't for Audrey, I would have already walked away.

It had been years since I wanted to join another band, let alone go on the road for several weeks.

Frustrated because I was now wide awake and didn't want to be, I finally slipped down to the museum and into the recording studio. Before deciding which of the various keyboards I wanted to take out on tour, I wanted to try them all. I suspected there was a story behind each one, but without Zack around to tell them they were probably lost to the ages.

Sitting down at a Fender Rhodes piano, I played a few random figures, just to get a feel for the sound. Since Donald Fagen played a Fender Rhodes, I found myself easily slipping into a Steely Dan tune. Next thing I knew, I was doing a song we had dropped from the album. It began with this loping baseline: "Dum, dum, dum, duh-duh-duh, dum, dum, dum, duh-duh-duh." Zack usually sang it, but now it was my turn.

> "Chic was from Chicago,
> That's how he got his name,
> A raw-boned guy,
> Quiet and shy,
> And football was his game.

> "Chic moved to Columbus,
> When he was just a kid.
> And those who knew,
> Said there were few
> Could do the things he did.

> "He could pass,
> He could kick,
> He could tackle.
> He could dodge,
> He could bob,
> He could weave.
> He was smooth,

He was quick,
He was agile,
Like nothing
You'd ever
Believe.

"Chic played for East High School,
A field now bears his name,
Give him the ball,
He'd do it all,
And only lost one game."

I grew up as a big Ohio State football fan and remained
one even after moving to New York, which wasn't difficult,
given that New Yorkers don't really have anything that
passes for college football. I had practically grown up at
Ohio Stadium, where the Buckeyes played. It was once
known as "The House that Harley Built," although I'm sure
younger generations wouldn't know that. James Thurber
said that Chic Harley ran like a cross between music and
cannon fire. We tried to impart that feeling to the song.

"Chic became a Buckeye,
Wore the scarlet and gray,
And there's no doubt,
They talk about
His exploits to this day.

"His first year on the gridiron,
The team went seven-and-oh,
Winning acclaim
With ev'ry game,
The pride of Ohio.

"He could pass,
He could kick,
He could tackle.

> He could dodge,
> He could bob,
> He could weave.
> He was smooth,
> He was quick,
> He was agile,
> Like nothing
> You'd ever
> Believe."

Rhyming "tackle" with "agile" wasn't something I was proud of, but it was the best I could do.

> "In Chic's second season,
> They had eight wins and a tie.
> On the old sod,
> He was a god,
> But then he said goodbye."

I had intended this to be one of a series of songs about Ohio heroes, but I only finished three or four. It still needed some polishing.

> "The year was nineteen-eighteen,
> And Europe was at war,
> Chic had to fly,
> Took to the sky,
> The Army Service Corps.

> "When Chic returned to college,
> The team went six-and-one.
> Still there were cheers,
> Filling the ears,
> Of our All-American.

> "He could pass,
> He could kick,

He could tackle.
He could dodge,
He could bob,
He could weave.
He was smooth,
He was quick,
He was agile,
Like nothing
You'd ever
Believe.

"If there's a football heaven,
Above the clouds somewhere,
You're sure to find,
Nobly enshrined,
Chic Harley's playing there.
You're sure to find,
Nobly enshrined,
Chic Harley's playing there.
You're sure to find,
Nobly enshrined,
Chic Harley's playing there."

As I finished the song, I flashed back on something my mother had said: Will can always entertain himself. She valued that in a child. And it was true that I seldom got bored, but I sometimes did get lonely. I just didn't realize how lonely until I met Audrey. In the brief time I had known her, I was beginning to sense that she was filling an emptiness that I wasn't even aware I had. Already, I was in no hurry to return to my old life. I wondered if Zach truly appreciated what he had had?

Audrey was a list person. I am not. But I would be the last to say that they are a bad thing for the kind of person who likes that sort of thing. And since Audrey had agreed to take care of all the arrangements outside of the band, I was more than willing to let her do so, with or without a list.

The next day, Audrey set up an appointment with a graphic artist. The purpose was to review his work and, if we liked it, discuss my idea for the album art. He turned out to be a she and we liked her work very much. She understood the concept we had in mind and appreciated how it needed to relate to the first album and yet be different. We spoke in all kinds of vague generalities and hand gestures which seemed to communicate something, although I wasn't sure how or even what. When she mentioned René Magritte and Norman Rockwell, Audrey nodded, so I did, too. At the end of an hour she said she understood, and we reached an agreement, confident she would deliver what we wanted.

Similarly, we met with candidates for the other positions we would need to complete our little traveling circus. I seemed to remember that on the original tour we had done much of the heavy lifting ourselves. Of course, our equipment needs were fewer back then and much more primitive. As I recall, Grateful Dead was getting about $2,500 a gig and we were getting $1,500, which was pretty good money—twice what we could have made as a bar band. Still, the economics didn't make sense to me then or now.

As big as Audrey's house was, it didn't have nine separate bedrooms—only a paltry seven—so we had to purchase two—no, three, allowing for Doctah Root—more beds. Some room-sharing would have to take place and I hoped that wouldn't create any unnecessary drama. I decided to fly Evan and Wes in first, then Spoolie and the doctah a week later. When the four of us were in synch, we could add the horns. Besides, if there was any unresolved issues involving Evan, Wes, and me, I wanted to be able to address them before we threw anyone else into the mix.

I spent the rest of the day in Zack's archives, immersing myself in the history of the band. Over the years, I had met people who knew more about us than I did. I had not been able to step outside of myself and look at Zack Black & the Blues Attack through the eyes and ears of a fan. Now, I wanted to see exactly what it was that people saw in us. Personally, I felt our original material was as strong as that of all but a handful of our contemporaries. While we may not have been The Beatles or the Stones, we were at least the equals of The Kinks or The Zombies and better than The Dave Clark Five or Herman's Hermits. And while we all acquitted ourselves quite well on our instruments, Zack took us to another level. We didn't need studio cats over-dubbing anything we laid down.

What I learned, though, is that a large part of our appeal, as much as our music, perhaps, was our appearance. Fan letters revealed that Zack was the "dreamy one," Evan was the "funny one," Wes was the "cute" one, and I was the "serious" one— (based, I assumed, on the fact that I was the introvert). It made me think how the Zombies were deemed too nerdy-looking, which may have kept them from being as successful as they should have been.

Our fan club sent out a newsletter which kept our followers up to date on such important matters as our astrological signs—Leo, favorite color, black—and what we were looking for in a girlfriend—personality. If I had ever seen any of this PR stuff, I didn't remember it. I was pretty sure I hadn't provided any of the so-called personal "facts."

What I was really hoping to find out was what it was they liked about our music. On that, the letters and newsletters were silent. They told us over and over again how much they loved us, but not why. When Audrey wandered in to check on what I was doing, she quickly hatched this plan to reach out to our old fan club members when we played Columbus. She would set up a website with names—there was a fan club roster on file—and try to place a newspaper article directing readers to it. She even thought she could get a reporter to interview a few of the "girls"—who were all probably great-grandmothers by now. I could see she had a real knack for promotion.

We needed a trumpet and two saxes or, maybe, trumpet, sax, and trombone. Of course, with three horns, you ran the risk of stepping all over each other in the way two horns wouldn't, but it was worth what you gained in power. At times, one could solo and the others riff behind him in unison, but the harmonies would have to be worked out and written down. In truth, I could have picked up the phone and called any number of New York musicians I had worked with who would fit the bill. But I preferred auditions because you never knew what would come through the door. A couple of well-placed ads generated the interest I had hoped for.

I wanted the horns to be aggressive, in-your-face, a wall of screaming brass. As usual, we had a number of sax players to choose from. They're the gunslingers. I think, for most people, the sax is the easiest horn to learn, certainly easier than a clarinet, and it looks cool—almost as cool as a guitar. But like every instrument, it's hard to play it well. The expectation is if you play sax, you double on flute or clarinet or both. But I was looking for a real honker and squawker—and a reader. If you couldn't read, you couldn't be in the Blues Attack. So Audrey booked us an off-off-Broadway theater in the city, rather than asking them all to make the trek to Tarrytown.

It was almost a stag party—nearly three dozen guys and one young woman. I didn't notice her at first because she was kind of short and was dressed in jeans and a shirt. She also wore a cap pulled down over some braids that stuck out like strings of firecrackers.

Everyone started off playing a couple of minutes from a chart so I could get a sense of their tone, timing, sight-reading ability, etc. And then I had them do something of their own choosing. Some of them went for technical difficulty, but others chose fun little things they could really cook on.

Before he even played a note, I was already drawn to one of the sax players, Floyd Druthers. As he was unpacking his instrument, I saw that it had a deep, golden patina like it had been buried in the ground for fifty years. I knew it would have the rich quality I was looking for. I never trusted a horn player that played a shiny yellow horn because I suspected he was interested more in flash than tone quality. Floyd didn't disappoint. He was black, but Evan would have to deal with it.

Technique was important, but we needed guys who played with freedom. That's what I liked about one of the trombone players. There were three or four—one electrified with pedals for effects like Bill Bendler did back with Strongbow—a Columbus band—but this guy was strictly acoustic. All horn players want to sound like vocalists and all vocalists want to sound like horns, but this guy really did sound like he was singing through his trombone. After he played "Skylark," I didn't care what other tricks he had up his sleeve—or slide. I wanted him—Sven Johnsson—in the band.

That left me with the choice of another sax or a trumpet. I was leaning toward a trumpet because it could always cut through the noise. And that brought me back to the girl. She was too young—and too black—to take on the road with a bunch of old white guys like us, Floyd excepted, that is. She could try out if she wanted to, but then we would take the guy, even if he hadn't been as good.

While we tried to be cool, I think she knew the deck was stacked against her. After she had shown us what she had already seen in the studio, she proceeded to throw in a whole lot more. She could play in any style, imitate any trumpet player you ever heard of. She could play Miles, Dizzy, Louis. She had chops like I couldn't believe for someone her age, man or woman. She wasn't going to make it easy.

"You know," I said, "we're basically a blues band. High energy, big sound, lots of grease."

"You don't think I can play blues?" she fired back. "I know more blues than anyone in this room. I'm black and I'm a woman. That's like being black twice. I've got more blues in me that Albert King, B.B. King, and Freddie King put together. I'm the abandoned child, the long-suffering wife, and the murdered lover. I'm all the things those so-called blues musicians put in their songs when they are feelin' sorry for themselves. When I blow my horn, everyone from Gabriel to W.C. Handy to Louis Armstrong comes out the other end. What do I know about the blues? I am the blues!"

As I said, she wasn't going to make it easy. "You ever been on the road with a band before?" I asked.

"Why?"

"There's nothing glamorous about it."

She surveyed the room before focusing on Audrey. "She goin'?"

"Yes, she'll be traveling with us."

"If that China doll doesn't break, I know I won't."

"No, I don't suppose you will."

"So am I in or am I out?"

"You aren't out, but we're going to hear a few more players before we make up our mind."

"Well, in that case I'll assume I'm in—as long as you listen with your eyes closed and your minds open." With that, she slipped her horn into a canvas bag, snatched up her coat, and sauntered out of the room.

She was right of course. Our horn section consisted of Floyd Druthers, reeds; Sven Johnsson, trombone and French horn; and Sarah Mannix, trumpet, Flugelhorn, and lots of sass. I would make sure she got lots of room.

CHAPTER 21

Elijah's Wooden Book

Evan and Wes flew in on Saturday. I'm not sure Wes would have needed a plane.

I had given them detailed instructions on how to get from LaGuardia to Tarrytown via the transit system. Neither had ever been to New York City before, so it would be an adventure and also a test. When their train pulled into the station at Tarrytown, I was waiting for them with the Mercedes.

Wes, the altar boy, had changed. All of us make bad decisions over the course of our lives. Fortunately, most of them are forgotten. But with tattoos, the bad decisions continue to be on display for everyone to judge and re-judge. Some people remind me of one of those old steamer trunks, covered with stickers chronicling the various ports of call. That was Wes. He also had several piercings and his earlobes were gauged, which made me wince. In in an earlier era, they would have landed him in a *Ripley's Believe It Or Not* cartoon. Since pop music had turned into a freak show, I'm sure Wes fit right in, even if he was as old as the rest of us. I felt like it was a reunion of the *Lost Boys*. None of us had grown up. Not really.

"What? No limo?" Evan asked in mock disappointment.

"I used it as a decoy," I said. "Throw the fans off the scent."

"Good idea. Wes gives off a lot of scent."

Not surprisingly, Wes did not look pleased by this remark. "This yours?" he asked as he deposited his suitcase in the trunk of the car.

"No. It belongs to Audrey."

"Yeah, tell us about her—the Widow Taylor."

"I'll let you find out for yourselves." I tried to get a good look at his eyes, checking his pupils for dilation.

"Zack always had his choice of women," Evan said. "But I never thought he'd settle down with just one."

"Well, you're in for a lot of surprises," I said.

As we drove through the countryside, Evan rode shotgun and cracked jokes while Wes slumped in the backseat like a figure in a Dali painting. Both were dealing with the strangeness of the situation in their own ways. There was a lot of history among the three of us, some of it not very positive. It was like one of us was carrying a bomb and only he could relax. I began to wonder why I ever thought this would work out.

"So who's this guy you've got replacing Zack?" It was Wes who finally broke the tension.

"His named is Elmore Johnson, but he goes by Spoolie. He's the one who taught Zack how to play."

"So how old is he—like a hundred?" Evan asked.

"I don't really know, but he doesn't look his age. He could pass for one of us."

"If one of us was black," Evan said.

It hadn't taken him long to introduce race into the discussion.

"Yes," I replied. "If one of us was black—and could play guitar like the lovechild of Buddy Guy and Sister Rosetta Tharpe."

"Is he really that good?" Wes was leaning over my shoulder, now.

"I think so."

His breath smelled of alcohol.

"I assume he will get an equal share."

"Yes."

"But we—the band—didn't decide that."

"No, we didn't. But unless I overlooked something, 'we' haven't made any decisions in forty years. In order to get this whole thing rolling, decisions had to be made and I made them."

Then Evan spoke up. "Look, Wes, if Will hadn't taken the lead, we wouldn't even be here. The way I see it, he's given us one last chance to show people Zack Black and the Blues Attack was worth all of the effort we put into it. I don't want to blow it."

"Don't get me wrong. It's not that I'm not grateful. I just feel it's better to lay all of our cards on the table."

"So what cards are you holding, Wes?" That was my question.

He didn't answer, though, for I had passed through the gates of Audrey's estate and they both got their first look at Chateau Zack.

"Holy moly," Evan said. "You didn't tell me we were dropping in on the Vanderbilts."

Audrey greeted us as soon as we entered the house. Floating down the grand stairway a la Scarlett O'Hara, she said. "Hi, I'm Audrey," as she alighted at the bottom. "Hope your trip was pleasant."

Wes gave her the once over at least twice then whispered to Evan, "She could make you take back things you never even stole."

If Audrey heard what he said, she didn't let on. No doubt she had developed an immunity to such remarks. "You must be Wes."

"How'd you guess?"

"Because we—" she said, turning to Evan, "—have already met. Nice to see you again, Evan."

"Same here."

"Zack has told me so much about both of you."

"And neither of us has really changed much in the past forty years," Evan replied, sweeping a hand over his balding head. "Except I've gotten better looking."

He would take to wearing a bandana when performing to

hide his naked dome and to keep the sweat out of his eyes.

"Well, welcome to my home," she said with a sweep of her hand. "While you're here, I hope you will treat it as your own. Feel free to raid the kitchen, play pinball, watch TV, whatever you like. Zack would want that."

"That doesn't sound like Zack," Wes said.

I would have assumed it was the liquor talking, but Wes had always been blunt.

"Perhaps not. Zack always regretted the way things ended. Had he lived longer, I am sure he would have told you so himself. He really did care about you—all of you. If I didn't think so, you wouldn't be here."

"Looks like old Zack did all right for himself," Evan said.

Whether he meant the house or Audrey, I wasn't sure.

"I suppose he's playing the harp, now. Blues harp, of course," Wes cracked.

"I don't know why not," Audrey said, fixing Wes with her stare. "He was a good man."

"He was that," I chimed in. Audrey was handling herself pretty well, but I thought it was time to change the direction of this conversation. "And he is why we have this second chance. After Audrey shows you to your rooms, let's meet in the kitchen and we can discuss the plan for the next few weeks."

As we sat around the island in the kitchen, eating pizza and drinking beer, I told them what I had in mind for the band's reunion tour. "I wanted the three of us to have a chance to get on the same page before we brought anyone else in. I figured we would take a week to relearn our songs and get back in synch. Then Spoolie will be here. I've planned a week of practice time for him. He already has a copy of our album, so, hopefully, he will know Zack's parts when he arrives."

"What about the horns?" Wes asked.

"I've lined those up, too. They'll be joining us later."

"You really think folks are going to want to see us?" It was Evan this time.

"I do."

"Not just those hoping to see a train wreck?"

"What if?" I answered. "Our job is to make sure they won't be disappointed when there isn't one."

Noticing Wes had finished his beer, Audrey asked him if he would like another. "Better hadn't," he said. "I may have overdone it a bit on the plane."

"Yeah," Evan added, "he has this theory about flying: you should be higher than the plane at all times."

"I don't care for flying myself," Audrey said.

"So," Evan said, "are we still Zack Black and the Blues Attack or are we the Spoolie Johnson Band?"

"We are Zack Black and the Blues Attack. However, I think we should add 'Featuring Spoolie Johnson.'"

"Why does he get separate billing?"

"Because we're—the three of us—the Blues Attack. All that's left of it, anyway."

"And you really think this guy is better than Zack?"

"Better than anyone, maybe."

"He should be able to keep up with us, then," Evan said.

I took Evan and Wes down to the studio. They were impressed. No surprise there. But that's not why I had brought them there. As we made small talk, I slipped Spoolie's CD into the player. "Listen to this," I said and I pushed the play button.

The first thing they heard was my counting off, "One, two, one-two-three-four" and then we launched into the first song. It wasn't long before Evan took a seat behind the drums, grabbed some sticks, and started playing along. Although it wasn't plugged in, Wes picked up a bass and began singing the bass part while fingering it.

When the first song ended, I paused the recording. "What do you think?"

"Not bad," Wes said.

"Not bad? He's fantastic," I replied.

"You've never heard me play guitar."

"Well, I have," Evan chimed in. "And you're lucky we let you near an instrument."

☙☙

There was no need to call our first rehearsal. It simply happened. As soon as Evan and Wes saw the museum, they pushed aside their mannequins and commandeered the bandstand in the center of the room. I had already cued up a dub of the album, so when Audrey began rolling the tape, first Evan and then Wes started playing along. Although they couldn't have been more different as people, they had always been a good rhythm section. The heart of the band. Zack was the soul. That left me the brain or the spleen or...something.

"Is this the key we're going to play this in?" Wes asked.

"I thought we'd try to keep everything in the original."

"Why?" Evan asked, looking like a Teutonic Buddha. "Who'd know?"

"We would."

"That'll be hell on the vocals." Even more than his solid bass playing, Wes's contribution to the band had been the vocal arrangements. "You should have given me a heads up. I might have quit smoking—like thirty years ago."

"Well, maybe the new guy will bail us out," Evan said.

All we knew of Spoolie's vocal abilities was what we had laid down at the Doobie Twins' studio. And singing alone is a lot different than doing the harmonies Wes had worked out. I assumed we would pick up another singer if necessary, but I didn't really want to do that if we could avoid it. That would change the focus of the band which had always been on the dazzling musicianship—or that's what I liked to believe.

"This is like *Music Minus One*," Evan said. *Music Minus One* was a series of albums, each of which had an instrument missing. The idea was for you to play along with the album, filling in for the missing instrument.

"Yeah, I wore out *Play Guitar with the Ventures*," Wes said. "Volumes One and Two. When I was starting out I used to tell people I played with The Ventures."

When we recorded the album, it was with the idea of performing it live so we avoided studio trickery. The horns were a concession to that. Wisely, I had opted not to use synth-horns or any of the other developing technology at the time. I thought it was cheesy like Insulbrick on houses. I think most people would admit most of that stuff sounded pretty bad once the novelty wore off.

In short order, we had knocked off the first three album cuts. It hadn't taken us long to find our groove again. I had been somewhat concerned that Wes and Evan might have gotten lazy over the years, but they were as good if not better than ever. If Wes had an alcohol problem, it hadn't impaired his playing. I could hardly wait for them to meet Spoolie and see what he would bring to the band. I was hoping there would be chemistry.

"I've been thinking about how to introduce Spoolie," I said.

"You could just say, 'Audience, Spoolie,'" Evan said with a smile. "'Spoolie, audience,'" echoing a line from *Alice in Wonderland*—or was it *Through the Looking Glass?* I couldn't remember.

"We could," I replied, "but I was thinking something more visual. Zack has the footage from when we were on 'Upbeat.' I thought we could begin by projecting that on a screen behind us. Then each of us would enter, one at a time, take up our instruments, and start to play along. When it gets to the close-up on Zack's solo, we would freeze the image and the music, and then Spoolie would walk on and we would all kick out the jams."

"And everyone will think, 'Gee, those guys are sure old and one of them turned black.'"

"Yeah, that's exactly what they'll think, Evan."

"I feel like we're handing this guy the keys to a Corvette, and we don't know if can even drive. Playing in a band's different than busking for pork chops on the street corner."

It was going to be a challenge, keeping Evan's inherent racism in check. "We need him and he needs us. We can't put the band back together unless we have all the pieces."

"Yeah, but he's strictly aftermarket not OEM."

Audrey's timing was perfect. She entered our sanctuary with a tray of snacks and sat it down on the counter. She had everyone's attention and not just for the food. "Anybody hungry?" she asked a la Donna Reed and countless other TV moms. All she was missing was the high heels and pearls.

I got up from the Hammond, walked over to where the refreshments were, and twisted the cap off a bottle of water. My focus should have been on how well things had gone so far, but I was having trouble getting around the little "digs" Wes and Evan kept giving me and each other. That would have to change.

"How's it going?" Audrey asked.

"Fine." As a rule, I was not overly generous with praise.

"Is this really going to work?"

"I have every reason to believe so." Even as I said that, I was thinking how this was probably a mistake. I never really had anything in common with Wes and Evan. We were never friends—not like Zack and I were. The only shared interest we had was the band.

"Mind if I hang around to listen to you practice. It's getting kind of lonely upstairs."

"Hey, it's your house," I replied. "We're just guests."

After setting down the refreshments, Audrey took a seat while I thought about what we should play next.

"There's a song on the album—'Elijah's Wooden Book,'" Audrey said. "What's the story behind it?"

"It's just like the song says. Elijah was this barber in Columbus who started whittling Bible stories out of wood. He had a room in his barber shop filled with them. Zack and I liked the idea that he was creating his art for himself because he had it in him and had to get it out."

"It almost sounds like church music."

"Yeah, well, I always liked gospel. I sometimes went to black churches just to hear the choirs. I probably stole the opening from something I picked up there." I began go play. "This starts off Bach, morphs into Billy Preston, and then slides into Sister Rosetta Tharpe."

"Who's she?"

"The godmother of rock and roll," Wes said.

"Let's try 'Elijah' next," I suggested.

"This should be interesting. Acapella three-part harmony on a song none of us has performed in over forty years."

"All right," I said, "I'll step it down a little," and depressed a key on the organ to give them the pitch. We all hummed to find the pitch and then Wes gave us the upbeat with an upward stroke of his hand. We began to sing:

"They called the boy Elijah,
And Elijah had the call,
To be a faithful servant,
And preach God's word to all.
But Elijah was hardheaded,
Didn't do the things he should.
So God declared he'd have to turn
His sermons into wood."

We were a little off at the start, but soon found our places. (Reminded me of a Three Dog Night concert I heard once.) Even as we hit the slight sustain on "wood," Evan began counting out four beats on his drumsticks and the whole band launched into the chorus:

"And ev'ry text he didn't preach,
He whittled out of pine or beech.
Then painted them in colors bold,

For all his neighbors to behold.
Soon folks from all around would stop
Inside his humble barber shop,
To ask if they might take a look
At Elijah's wooden book.

"By trade he was a barber;
He worked hard all his life.
A skilled man with a razor,
An artist with his knife.
For when he wasn't cutting hair,
Then you'd be sure to find,
Elijah setting down in wood
The pictures in his mind.

"And in a garden make-believe,
He put Adam and his Eve,
While animals by twos embark,
With faithful Noah on the ark.
Zacchaeus climbing up a tree,
And our Lord's nativity,
Are gathered here for all who look
In Elijah's wooden book."

I felt a twinge of arthritis in my left hand and eased up a bit on the rhythm. On an electric keyboard it wouldn't be noticeable, but I would have to remember not to pound the keys on the acoustic piano like I had always done on Elton John's "Burn Down the Mission."

"God called Elijah to him
When he was ninety-two,
And welcomed him to paradise
With the usual ballyhoo.
Rewarding him for his great faith,
Throughout his earthly strife,
By giving him a pair of wings

And a brand new pocket knife.

"Elijah thanked God with a grin,
And knew right where he would begin.
He set about to decorate
The posts which hold the pearly gate.
Now, when in heaven you must stop,
Inside Elijah's barber shop,
And ask if you might have a look
At Elijah's wooden book."

As we finished, Audrey clapped enthusiastically. "That's wonderful. I mean it. It's just great."

I noticed that she had been quietly singing along with us throughout the song and didn't muff a word, which was more than the rest of us did.

"I hope there are a lot more like you in the audience when we play," I said. But she was right. Over the years, we had all grown as musicians. We were seasoned professionals. The challenge was to make ourselves relevant. "I can't wait to hear what Spoolie might do with it."

Evan had helped himself to a second sandwich and was sipping some cranberry juice. I was glad to see neither of them requested alcohol, although there was plenty available. "So I guess you're our band mother," he said, brushing some crumbs from his mouth.

"Band mother—what's that?" Audrey asked.

"Well…" I began.

"A Mrs. Stickel," Evan said with a laugh.

"Yeah, Mrs. Stickel," Wes said.

"Who's Mrs. Stickel?"

"Mrs. Stickel had two sons and the sons had this band," Evan said.

"The Lapse of Tyme," Wes added.

"Yeah, the Lapse of Tyme," Evan replied. "Anyway, Mrs. Stickel did everything she could to help with the band. She let them rehearse in the basement. Then when they

couldn't get the B-Three down the stairs, she let them rehearse in the living room. Then when they got a second B-
Three, she gave up the master bedroom. The Stickels took
out a loan to buy a van and Mrs. Stickel would drive them
to their gigs."

"She also sent flowers to the neighbors when they got
too loud or practiced too late."

"No wonder with all those horns."

"Horns?"

"Yeah, they were the first band to add horns. That's
where Workman got the idea for his band."

"Workman?"

"Dave Workman—lead guitar for The Dantes."

"Them I know."

"That's probably why we added horns, too."

"That's why everybody added horns. Anyway, whatever
they needed, Mrs. Stickel got it for them. That's a band
mother."

"So I'm your Mrs. Stickel?"

"It's a compliment, really. She was cool. Everyone liked
Mrs. Stickel," Evan said.

"You're a little old to be my sons."

It took us about thirty to forty minutes to nail each song,
allowing for the absence of horns. If I had had any doubts
about whether Wes and Evan were still up to it, they were
quickly dispelled. We sounded tight and good, better than
we probably ever had. I had seen enough reunion shows
where it was obvious the members hadn't been playing
much over the ensuing years. I didn't want to be associated
with that. Fortunately, or perhaps, unfortunately, none of us
had put music aside for more stable careers. We weren't the
weekend warriors who got together a couple of times a year
to brush off the cobwebs, shake of the rust, and play for our
own amusement. We were all professionals, although our
bank accounts might not reflect that fact—or, maybe, that's
what they did reflect.

After a few more hours, we decided to call it quits for

the night. I was satisfied with our progress and I certainly didn't want to push them too hard. I was counting on their own professionalism to do that. At the same time, I was hoping that Spoolie would be challenged to bring his A-game when he saw that he was going to be fronting a first rate band. And I wanted to put some ice or heat—I never knew which—on my hand.

As we were about to file out of the practice room, Wes shuffled up next to me. "She yours, now?" He said it with such a heavy layer of innuendo that I would have had to punch him in the mouth if Audrey had been standing there.

"It's nothing like that."

"Then what is it like?"

"I barely know her. She asked for my help after Zack died, and I couldn't very well turn her down."

"I guess you're Zack, now." Wes's tone insinuated that he wasn't particularly receptive to that idea.

"It's still our band—yours, Evan's, and mine. That hasn't changed."

"It's been forty years. Everything and everyone has changed."

I hoped he was wrong, but my gut told me he wasn't. Later, I noticed Evan was bunching his shoulders and rubbing his neck.

"Something wrong?" I asked.

"It's the back. Time is catching up with me."

"What do you do for it?"

"Lots of weed." I must have reacted in some way, because he quickly added, "Just kidding, Will. The doctor gives me these muscle relaxants if it gets bad enough."

I hoped that was true.

Over the next few days, we continued to practice until we got each song where we wanted it. Then in the evenings, Wes and Evan recorded their parts on Spoolie's tracks. It was a good way for them to get accustomed to his playing. It was music minus one all over. As soon as I was satisfied, I dropped the recordings off at a local studio to have them mastered and then ordered 500 promo copies for the media package Audrey was putting together.

CHAPTER 22

Panama Hat

Driving in the city is like dancing in a mosh pit and trying not to spill your drink. That's why I didn't own a car—that and the fact I couldn't afford one, not in the city. But Spoolie wanted to be picked up at the airport. Correction: Doctah Root wanted him to be picked up at the airport. Apparently, he couldn't be bothered with figuring out the trains to Tarrytown. I guess I could understand, given the difference between the pace of life in Oxford and New York City. So Audrey and I took her car to fetch them while Evan and Wes hung out back at the house. I was praying they had grown up some over the past forty years.

Spoolie, the doctah, and two skycaps were waiting for us at passenger pickup. They had four suitcases between them and a small mountain of assorted trunks which, I was to learn, contained Doctah Root's impressive collection of African drums, at least those he chose to have with him when he traveled. Spoolie hadn't even bothered to pack a guitar. I guess Felicia decided to stay home or maybe the hoodoo had returned like a bad cold.

While the Mercedes could accommodate the suitcases, I had to arrange for the drums to be transported to Audrey's house in a passenger van. However, before we could depart from the airport, Doctah Root insisted that we all have dinner in the terminal. He said they had not eaten since they left Oxford that morning and could put it off no longer. So after we loaded up the suitcases, I parked the car in short term parking and we began to scour one terminal after another until we found a restaurant that was to his liking.

In the end, the doctah ate parts of three different entrees while Spoolie had a cheeseburger and fries. Audrey was amused by the whole affair. I was not and made little effort to conceal my anger.

When she had the chance, she quietly jostled me and whispered, "It's all right. I can afford to humor them."

That only made me feel worse.

By the time we reached Tarrytown, Mohammed, the driver, was parked in front of Audrey's house, waiting— meter running—with his van. Neither Evan nor Wes had the money—cash or credit—to pay him. As Audrey showed Spoolie and Doctah Root where they would be staying, I helped Mohammed unload the cases off to the side of the driveway, thanked him for his assistance, and sent him off with a nice tip. For now, I would leave the doctah's drums stacked where they were.

Evan, Wes, and I were down in the museum when Spoolie and Doctah Root joined us about ten o'clock that evening. After the flight, they were exhausted, Doctah Root said, and had retired to their rooms for a nap. I didn't know whether I would see them again that day and was pleased that they had shown enough interest to stop by to see what we were up to. Spotting Zack's guitar, Spoolie stepped up onto the platform and took it in his hands, turning it over and examining it from every angle. Finally, he looked at Audrey, who was sitting on the couch. "Do you mind?" Apparently, he had decided this one was hoodoo-free.

"No, of course not. That's why you're here."

He turned on the amp, set the dials where he wanted them, and gave it a strum. It was a little out of tune, of course, so he plucked each string with his thumb and turned the tuning keys until he was satisfied. I don't know if he had perfect pitch, but it sounded pretty good to me. He then played four or five chords in quick succession, adjusted the amp again, and smiled. Nodding at Audrey, he launched into an intense version of "Dust My Broom."

All of us watched him, spellbound, as he wrung sounds out of that guitar I wouldn't have believed possible. Over the course of four or five minutes, he made it sing, he made it whisper, he made it scream like a banshee. He bent strings so many ways I expected they would be knotted like shoelaces. He turned sound into colors and colors into pictures that danced in the air. When he finished, we all stood there, stunned.

"How's that?" he asked.

No one said anything until I finally spoke up. "It was amazing, Spoolie. Truly amazing."

"This here's a nice little guitar. This your husband's?"

"Yes," Audrey replied.

"Well, a guitar is like a woman. You can love it and leave it, but you can never own it. Know what I mean?" He looked around the room. Once upon a time, he would have drawn a laugh, Now, no one said or did anything. He strummed the strings again. "So whadya want to do now?"

"We've been working on this new number. A fun little trifle. I thought I'd set it up by telling the audience something like this: 'There's always a risk when you play new material in a concert because most people are there to hear the old material. But, of course, we are the old material.' At this point Audrey will walk out of the wings and cross behind me. I supposedly wouldn't know what she's doing, but keep talking. 'I know what you're thinking. How do these guys still sound and look so good? Well, there's really no secret. The older your fans are, the worse their eyesight gets. And their hearing. Which brings me to this song. I had my last birthday a few years back and I handled it like most of you probably do. I resolved to stop aging. We call this one 'Panama Hat' for reasons that will soon be obvious.' At that moment, Audrey will drop a Panama hat on my head. And when I turn to look at her, I'll see the rest of you are wearing them, too. So I I'll turn to the audience and say,

'Now, I know what they mean by 'dress for success.'"

With that, I began to sing and play, trying my best to channel Dr. John.

> "When I turned fifty-nine and a half,
> Bought myself a Panama hat.
> Thought it might be good for a laugh.
> Took it on home and that was that.
> 'Till I went walkin' out one day
> And I heard this young boy say,
> 'Wish that I could look like that
> Sharp-dressed cat in the Panama hat!'

"Now, the horns will jump in," I said, "and give us a real N'awlins-style second line feel, sort of like a box of assorted junk bouncing around in the back of a pick-up truck." I played the part on a kazoo. It sounded a little bit like Edgar Winter's "Frankenstein."

> "Buh-buh buh-buh buh-bum-bum-buh

> "Pushin' sixty and I'd paid my dues.
> Got a case of the birthday blues.
> Figured I had nothin' to lose,
> Bought myself some alligator shoes.
> So whenever I went out,
> All around me folks would shout,
> "Did ya get a look at who's
> All decked out in alligator shoes?"

> "Buh-buh buh-buh buh-bum-bum-buh"

I was pleased to hear the band cookin' behind me.

> "Still I was feelin' like an old coot,
> When I spotted an ice cream suit.
> Knew at once it would be a hoot.

Picked out a blue silk tie to boot.
As I went walkin' out that day,
I could hear the young girls say,
'My, oh, my don't he look cute
All tricked out in his ice cream suit!'

"Buh-buh buh-buh buh-bum-bum-buh"

Spoolie's confidence was growing by the minute as he learned the song. I could see him watching my left hand to pick out the chord changes. I was a little fearful that he might only play lead guitar, but he was equally adept playing rhythm. It was evident that he knew when to play, but, more importantly, when not to.

"Panama hat,
Ice cream suit,
Alligator shoes,
Silk tie to boot.
Panama hat,
Ice cream suit,
Alligator shoes,
Silk tie to boot.

"When I turned fifty-nine and a half,
Bought myself a Panama hat
Thought it might be good for a laugh.
Took it on home and that was that.
'Till I went walkin' out one day,
And I heard this young kid say,
'Wish that I could look like that
Sharp-dressed cat in the Panama hat!'"

"Buh-buh buh-buh buh-bum-bum-buh…"

As the song was winding down, I sailed my hat across the room and, after a beat, the rest of the band did likewise.

When we had finished, Audrey, our audience of one, applauded wildly as we all sat looking at one another, flush in the confidence that we still had it. We then looked at Spoolie for some indication of what the thought of it. He seemed to pay no notice to us, but kept fiddling with the guitar. Finally, he muttered, "Bridge needs adjusting."

"Is that something you can do," I asked, "or should we get somebody?"

"Nah, I can do it." Then he looked at us like a cat up in a tree. "You boys are all right. What else you got?"

For the next couple of hours, we performed much of our album for Spoolie, and I was pleased to see that he had learned Zack's parts, although he reinterpreted them some. But that was okay. Zack would have done the same thing. What I didn't know how to broach was the topic of who sang lead on each number. Zack was a big-voiced tenor in a tenor world. He had a bright, ringing tone and could go high without screaming. Naturally, he took the lead on most songs. I, on the other hand, was a bass who struggled to stay in the baritone register.

My singing had a muffled quality like I was wearing a cardboard box on my head. Wes, the choirboy, was also a tenor, but could bail me out on baritone or shore up Zack when necessary. He was the most versatile singer in the group, but lacked power. And Evan, a baritone, handled the novelty numbers. He was our Ringo. On a few songs, Audrey was starting to sing harmony as needed, but was more than content to keep to the shadows.

Feeling we had developed some rapport, at last I asked Spoolie straight out: "We're going to need another lead singer. Is that something you would want to do?" I intentionally made it sound as though I was confident he could do it if he wanted to when, in truth, I was not confident at all.

For the longest time, Spoolie seemed to be mulling it over. Finally, he said, "I only sing my own songs."

"Fair enough," I responded. "We're planned to work

some of your material into our set."

I noticed Wes's eyebrows rise like a pair of draw bridges. It's an old story—how black music was appropriated by white artists and exploited by white businessmen at the expense of the black musicians. They were paid a pittance, they lost their publishing rights, they received no royalties and no recognition—all done in the interest of making the music more palatable and safer for white teenagers. That and also the pursuit of the dollar. Everybody from Pat Boone to Elvis Presley to the Rolling Stones covered records that had been originally recorded by Fats Domino, "Big Mama" Thornton, and Willie Dixon, among others—including Spoolie Johnson, as Doctah Root would not-so-subtlety remind us while making one of his not-infrequent suggestions.

I met a keyboard player once, Rich Bradburn, who had been in a pick-up band that backed Bo Diddley when he came to Columbus. They met with Bo for about twenty minutes before the gig. One of them asked him what they were going to play. He responded, "Bo Diddley music." And that was that. No run-throughs or anything. Before he would go onstage, he demanded payment in advance—cash. Afterward, he jumped in his car and was out of sight before the cheering had stopped. Braduburn chalked it up to Bo's having been stiffed too many times over the years. I suspected he also didn't want people knowing he carried so much cash on him.

It wasn't just Bo and it wasn't just with local musicians. Keith Richards of the Rolling Stones ran into it while working with Chuck Berry on *Hail, Hail, Rock and Roll*. Keith idolized Chuck and wanted to do something special for him. So he put together this all-star concert in New York City and filmed it for a documentary all of which was intended to highlight Chuck's importance in the development of rock and roll. Right in the middle of rehearsals for the New York concert, Chuck disappeared.

Turned out he had slipped away to Columbus to earn a

few more bucks for a gig there, leaving all of these big name musicians in the lurch. Like Bo, Chuck had scraped to get by for so many years that he didn't trust anyone or anything in the music business. He didn't know when his next job would come along, so he grabbed the money whenever he could. Obviously, cash in Columbus was more important than a hope and a promise in New York.

Spoolie never complained about a thing. Apparently, that was the good doctah's job. From the moment they arrived in New York, Doctah Root was making demands in the form of suggestions that Audrey and I scrambled to accommodate, beginning with room assignment. Even a mansion is only so big, but the doctah informed us that it would be best for Spoolie if they had a wing to themselves, with adjoining rooms. A suite would be best. So Audrey and I created one, converting a craft room into another bedroom.

Working out the logistics was the easy part. Getting Wes and Evan to understand why Spoolie was receiving special treatment was more of a challenge. Up to this point, I had gotten them to buy into the Three Musketeers all-for-one, one-for-all mantra. Now, I was bending it a little bit. White guilt, I guess. I felt it, they didn't. But I bent over backward to try to see things from Spoolie's position and I thought I did.

It was hard to be friends with someone who didn't want any friends. But Spoolie trusted Doctah Root. It was Doctah Root who didn't trust anybody. And I didn't trust Doctah Root. I wasn't sure he was always acting in Spoolie's interests. But he had this shamanic quality that was almost religious in his control over Spoolie, so I had to read him carefully.

When it came to playing, Spoolie was a dream. He learned the songs quickly and was every bit as good as advertised. However, he wasn't a robot. He didn't play note-for-note copies of Zack's leads. We had to allow him to improvise some—put some Spoolie in it. He also sang with a bluesy tenor, kind of reedy, but serviceable. What he lacked in range he made up for in technique. Of course, his voice had sounded a little different on the old 78s

Although he was used to being the center of attention, he soon was open to filling in on some of the vocal arrangements Wes worked out. The only thing we were lacking was someone who could still hit the high notes like Wes and Zack used to do.

Although I had resisted, it was starting to look like we might have to play our songs in a lower key than we had recorded them in. That wasn't unusual for classic rock groups working the oldies circuit. A Howard Kaylan of The Turtles might still be able to stretch for the high notes, but most of his contemporaries couldn't.

CHAPTER 23

Now, Comes the Mystery

A s soon as he arrived at Castle Taylor, Spoolie picked up his guitar and never put it down. At Audrey's invitation, he had examined all of the guitars in Zack's collection, selected five he might play, and settled on one that became his consort. He had it with him from the moment he climbed out of bed to the moment he fell back in. He attached a rainbow-colored guitar strap that must have had sentimental value because he refused to swap it for any of the dozens of custom made straps Zack had lying around, real pieces of hand-tooled leather art that must have cost several hundred dollars each. It didn't matter. Spoolie was his own person.

We could hear him coming before we saw him, the frantic whisper as he plucked and fingered and tapped the strings, racing up and down the neck, pausing now and then to bend a note. Walking into the kitchen, he would swing the neck to the left as he opened the refrigerator door on the right, the fingers of his left hand still dancing about on the strings. All of us would watch in amazement as he transferred a carton of orange juice to the island and proceeded to pour himself a glass and drink it, all in one continuous motion and without a break in the unheard music.

With Spoolie in the band, Evan and Wes must have felt the pressure to up their game. I found them practicing at all hours, playing along with the tapes I had brought back from Mississippi, trying out different runs and fills. One day, I had shown Evan a video I found on the internet of a drummer twirling two sticks in each hand. After that, he would carry two pairs of sticks with him and practice the trick when he thought no one was watching.

Doctah Root had unpacked his drums, all eight of them, and soon occupied a footprint that was every bit as large as that held down by the rest of the band. There was a papa, mama, and baby drum, as well as an assortor, which was nearly as tall as he was. Despite my initial reservations, he proved to be as good a percussionist as he was an eccentric one. And he would certainly enhance the band's appearance.

Wes was clearly spooked by the human skull and other voodoo paraphernalia that was arranged on an altar behind the doctah and moved over to a position on the opposite side of the band from him. Evan wasn't too thrilled about his presence, either, since he knew Doctah Root's sideshow antics would detract from his own playing. I would have to work out a truce of some sort to keep them both happy, assuming they couldn't work it out themselves.

That afternoon, while the rest of the band was off somewhere, I slipped into Zack's inner sanctum to spend some time alone with my thoughts. Sitting down at the piano in the studio, I began working on an idea that had been germinating since the moment I learned Zack was dead. It was a meditation on his life, our friendship, and all the remaining questions, unanswered and unasked. I began to play, knowing that no one would be able to hear me in the tomb-like chamber.

"Now comes the mystery,
No more secrets, all will be revealed,
Unsealed,
Behold the final page.
Goodbye to history.
All the scars and brokenness are healed,
Repealed,

The Ending of the Age."

I had been raised in a Christian home and though I drifted away from the church as an adult, a part of it never left me. At odd intervals of my life I had sought it out. Maybe it was just the music or the stained glass or the ritual, but I always felt welcome there. It was comforting. I knew what I believed, but as close as Zack and I had been, I had no inkling of where he was on his spiritual journey.

> "As the faith that once sustained us,
> Mortal coil that once restrained us,
> Fleshy prison that constrained us,
> Fall away.
> For the journey is completed,
> Want and fear have been unseated,
> And even death has been defeated,
> So make way,
> For judgment day."

I had just started the second verse—

> "So ring the curtain down,
> Time to meet the author of the play"

—when I became aware that I was not alone. I stopped playing and looked behind me where Audrey was standing in the doorway, trying to be unobtrusive. "I'm sorry," she said. "I didn't mean to interrupt."

"That's okay." I dropped my hands to my sides. "I don't know what comes next."

"It's beautiful. And sad. It's about Zack, isn't it?"

"I don't know. It could be about a lot of people."

"Even you?"

"Perhaps."

"Want to talk about it?"

"That's what I'm doing. I turn to music when words fail."

By this time, she was standing in front of the piano. "Something bothering you. Will?"

"I was thinking I don't belong here. This is Zack's world."

"I know how you feel."

"But you are part of his world—a large part. Maybe the largest. Or were."

"So were you. Just as he was part of yours. I don't have that part…" Her voice trailed off.

"It shouldn't have ended, not this way. I should have been there for him."

"You were. In the end, it was the music that the two of you created that kept him going. I think it may have been the truest statement of who he was and what he believed."

And yet, I thought, *the words were mostly mine. The musical ideas were mostly mine*. Not at first, but later. Of course, Zack had helped give them shape and they never would have been what they were without him, but I was more than an equal partner. It had taken me years to see that. If he was speaking, it was through me. I resumed playing.

"I wasn't completely honest. It is about Zack. I was thinking we could perform it in his memory toward the end of each show. What do you think?" I started singing the second verse in a very slow, deliberate manner.

> "So ring the curtain down,
> Time to meet the author of this play,
> Display,
> The world beyond the veil.
> All things are certain, now,
> As the meaning of the lines we say,
> Convey,
> The truth that will prevail."

I noticed Audrey was mouthing the words, so I said, "Sing this part with me."

I fed her the words one line at a time and then sang them with her.

"As the faith that once sustained us,
Mortal coil that once restrained us,
Fleshy prison that constrained us,
Fall away.
For the journey is completed,
Want and fear have been unseated,
And even death has been defeated,
So make way,
On judgment day.

"That's good. Now, back to the beginning.

"Now comes the mystery,
No more secrets; all will be revealed,
Unsealed,
Behold the final page."

Audrey was a singer—a soprano. She may not have thought so, but her voice was strong and pure. What she lacked in technique, she more than made up for with passion and honesty. There were no tricks. And I began to think. Paul McCartney put Linda Eastman in the band so he could see more of her. I wanted Audrey in the band for the same reason and more. We needed another singer, someone who could compensate for the high notes that were now beyond our reach.

"Goodbye to history.
All the scars and brokenness are healed,
Repealed,
The Ending of the Age."

When we finished, we both were teary-eyed. "You really can sing," I said. "I'm not kidding, Audrey. I want you to sing in the band. I want you to sing this song. We're going to need as much help as we can get to replace Zack. I can't sing his songs. You can."

"No, I couldn't. I'm not good enough. Besides, people don't want to hear me."

"They don't know what they want to hear until they hear it. And believe me they will want to hear you."

"But I don't like being the center of attention. Let me sing backup."

"You will. But for this song, we'll have you step out front."

Of course, I was lying. I didn't intend to let her off with just one solo. But that was my opening. If I could get her to sing one song, I could get her to sing them all. But she said, "No. It's too personal. I would rather keep it for myself."

"All right," I said, hoping she might change her mind later.

⌘

By the time the horn players showed up, we had become this incredibly tight foursome—make that fivesome including Doctah Root. Everyone knew his part and knew how he fit in. For a lead guitarist, Spoolie was also an amazing rhythm player. You'd think that all of them could be, that it was actually a step down in the talent spectrum. But, in truth, many of them really didn't know chords and harmonies and such. They had spent all of their time copying these runs they learned off of records until they could play them backward, forward, and in their sleep. Art Ryerson, another Columbus boy, was an exception. He spent most of his career in the studio, playing rhythm, but also was an incredible lead guitarist when the occasion demanded it.

Our brass section consisted of two guys and a girl—make that young woman. And by the way the rest of the band reacted to her, I could see that a fight or two was inevitable unless I shut them down early. The first chance I got, I took Sarah aside and told her that she couldn't date anyone in the band. She replied that she didn't intend to; she had a boyfriend at home. Nevertheless, I asked Audrey to keep an eye on her for me and she agreed.

The sax player, Floyd, doubled on flute and clarinet, not that we had need of a clarinet. He was a jazz cat of the first order but worked with rockers to support his jazz habit. He had toured with some of the big names, playing stadiums in major cities all over the world. When he auditioned for us, Floyd played Acker Bilk's "Stranger on a Shore," a song I often played on piano when I was in a melancholy mood. I never liked the lyrics, though; they weighed it down. Floyd had wonderful tone on sax and clarinet. He flute was breathy a la Ian Anderson.

On trumpet, flugelhorn, French horn, and percussion, we had Sven. He also knew his way around a keyboard and, I suspect, could play about any instrument you put in front of him. What English he knew was mostly slang and profanity picked up in jazz clubs on both sides of the ocean. He looked like a Norse god with a bad drug habit which, apparently, he did have—once. However, he swore he had been clean and sober for more than a year. I didn't believe him, but I decided to take a chance. He was the best of the blowers who came through the door. We would joke that it was good he spelled Johnsson with two Ss so we wouldn't confuse him with Spoolie. Later, he came close to starting a mutiny when he brought a jar of lutefisk on the bus.

The brass were incredibly quick studies. All of them had done time in pit orchestras and Sarah and Floyd had been inside a recording studio on occasion, mostly doing jingles. They viewed their time in the Blues Attack as a well-paying job. Whether they liked our music or not, I could never tell. However, when they learned they were making the same as the rest of us—except for Spoolie, that is—they were surprised to say the least. During the big band era, a few groups had operated as collectives with each musician getting an equal share—Glen Gray, for one—but most were dictatorships with a wide range of salaries.

To top it all off, all of the horn players were passable singers. More than passible, really. Sarah was especially soulful. Wes would be able to haul out the vocal arrangements that we thought we had to leave in the studio. I was quite satisfied, assuming, of course, they didn't have a lot of emotional baggage we'd have to deal with.

At the end of our first rehearsal with the whole band, I was pleased to see Evan was making small talk with the horn players, seeing if they had crossed paths with any of the same people, when he mentioned someone and one or two of them laughed. Maybe I had misjudged him. Maybe he wasn't as prejudiced as he used to be. Or maybe he just hid it better.

Evan had dropped the name of another Columbus musician.

"Yeah, I know what you mean. I played with him on a few freelance gigs," Floyd said.

"He was a Toby," Wes said.

"A total Toby," Evan added.

"A Toby? What's that?" Audrey asked.

"Toby Banfield," Evan replied. "He's a drummer. He was the first guy from our circle who went to California to become rich and famous."

"Did he?" she asked.

"Not rich, exactly, but he was almost famous." The guys all laughed at some secret joke.

"What? What? Aren't you going to let me in on it?"

"It's not really funny," I said.

"Yes, it is," Evan said.

"Yes, it is," I admitted. "As Evan said, he was a local drummer. And he went out to California in the 'sixties, right out of high school. Wound up in Los Angeles, Hollywood, and played with everybody at one time or another. For a short time, he played with Jim—aka Roger—McGuinn, Dave Crosby, and Chris Hillman. After he dropped out, they picked up Michael Clarke and became The Byrds. At least that's what he claimed."

"He was replaced by a guy who had never played drums before. Clarke drummed on a cardboard box," Wes said.

"Toby also played in a band with Arthur Lee and Bryan MacLean. It wasn't too long after that that they became Love."

"What bad luck," Audrey said.

"That's what Toby said. Twice he came real close to making it. There were other examples, too. He was in Buffalo Springfield before they became Buffalo Springfield. I think he may have been in Strawberry Alarm Clock before anybody heard of them. Each time, he left, the band picked up a new drummer, and immediately got signed to a record deal. Last time I saw Toby he told me that he did some serious soul-searching when he turned thirty. He had spent half his life chasing his dream and he had come so close that he felt he couldn't give up. So he headed back to California to keep plugging away."

"So that's what a Toby is? A person who chases his dream?"

"No," Wes said. "A Toby is a person who doesn't know that he has no talent. The bands kept dumping him because he was holding them back. He was a terrible drummer. Everybody knew it but him. He couldn't keep time worth a damn."

"And nobody told him?"

"It wouldn't have mattered," I said. "He wouldn't have believed them. After all, he was sure he had almost made it big."

"Well, if I was a Toby, I'd hope I knew it," Evan said.

"That's good," Wes said, "because I've been trying to work up the courage to tell you."

Evan hurled a stick at him, followed by a string of profanities accompanied by some nimble verb conjugations.

"Being a Toby's not the worst thing," I said.

"What is?" Evan asked.

"Remember Tyler."

Both Evan and Wes grew quiet and looked at each other knowingly.

"Who was Tyler?" Audrey asked.

"Tyler wasn't a 'who,'" Wes said. "Tyler was a band. Columbus's first super group."

"Zack never mentioned them."

"I'm not surprised," I said. "Hits a little too close to home."

"Why is that?"

"Because it's easy to see ourselves in Tyler."

"But why?"

"Well, I'll tell you. Or, at least, the way I heard the story. It began one summer when Frank Pierce and Dick Mackey holed up in a basement writing songs on a four-track tape deck. Frank was a drummer and keyboard player and Dick was a singer. They had been brought together by friends who thought they had a lot in common. Both of them were dissatisfied playing the local music scene and wanted to produce some songs to please themselves. But when word got out what the two of them were up to, curious musicians started dropping by to see if they could get involved. Soon, they were encouraged to lay down some tracks at Owl Studios. They weren't intended to be demos, but the engineer thought they were really good. So some tapes got mailed off to Los Angeles. After a while, when they didn't hear anything, they forgot about them.

"Then out of the blue, they got a call from Jon Peters, Barbara Streisand's former hairdresser and boyfriend. He flew a guy to Columbus to sign Pierce and Mackey to CBS records. Along with Ted Lenker, the two of them went to California to record a single. However, after it was done, the producer brought in Joe Walsh to replace Lenker's guitar licks note-for-note because he had better name recognition.

"Later, the band was featured in a 'World Stage' broadcast in which the audience watched them on a huge screen even as the band was watching the audience on their own. By then, the band had degenerated into a nightly soap opera. Pierce told me it all fell apart because their manager 'hated me, loved Dick.' Fans were afraid to miss a show because they never knew what was going to happen. Car wrecks, screaming matches, fistfights, you name it. And their music had become this schizophrenic mix of the Eagles, Beach Boys, and Steely Dan."

"Wow. But how were they like you?"

"Some people say Columbus's first super group was Zack Black and the Blues Attack," Evan said.

"Well, you're not in Columbus, anymore," Sarah said. "Just saying."

She was right.

CHAPTER 24

Crash, Bang, Boom

I got you a gig." Big smile.

Audrey had dropped that bit of information into our conversation like a jar of pickles ripping through the bottom of a grocery sack. Most days, those would have been magic words. But whether I wasn't sure I heard her correctly or just out of habit, I responded with, "What?"

"I got you a gig."

"A gig? What for?"

"I thought we needed to air you boys out. You can't spend all your time woodshedding."

She was right. We had grown quite comfortable in our surroundings and who wouldn't? Anytime of night or day, we were free to eat, drink, and play to our heart's content and we were even getting paid for it. We were the most risk-averse band in history.

"Where?"

"The Set Back Inn. On Main Street. You'll like it there."

Although I hated to say so, it was a good idea. It was important to see how we were going to handle ourselves in front of an audience. I was never a fan of the shoe-gazing set. People wanted to be entertained and I saw my job as doing what I could to entertain them. I preferred the days when musicians would dress up when they played. The whole t-shirt-and-sandals-look never did anything for me. Give me the suits, ties, and black hats of the old fashioned

R & B bands any day—the Roy Miltons, Jimmie Lunce-fords, James Browns. "What's it like?"

"It's a bar. No food, lots of history."

"Do we get drinks?"

"All the water you want."

I assumed she was kidding, but in a way I hoped she wasn't. No point inviting trouble. When I told the band, they were all enthused, but the younger ones more than the older. That's to be expected, I guess.

"Time to put on the paint," Evan said.

Everyone looked at him with a puzzled expression except for Wes who threw a rag at him that he used to wipe down the strings on his bass.

"Is that musician talk?" Audrey asked.

"Not exactly," I replied. "I think he's kidding Wes about his time with The Toads."

"The Toads?"

"Another Columbus band. Joe Brown, their bass player, convinced them to paint themselves green."

"Yeah," Evan said. "This was way before KISS. They would mix green food coloring with Covergirl makeup and smear it over their hands and faces. What they didn't take into account was that it would get all over them if they started sweating."

"It also stung when it got in your eyes and stained your clothing," Wes said. "I filled in for Joel a couple of times, but it didn't pay enough for all the aggravation."

"Were you any good?" Audrey asked.

"Yeah, they were good," I said. "They had a great young guitar player, Chuck Wilson. I remember when 'Lucy in the Sky With Diamonds' came out, Chuck didn't know that the introduction was played on an organ, so he figured out how to reproduce it on guitar. Unfortunately, nobody cared if they were good. They were wanted only because they were green."

"Well, I hope we don't have to resort to that," Audrey said.

I hoped so, too.

ᘒᘒᘒ

It was late afternoon. We were at the Set Back Inn, loading in. Just before we were scheduled to take the stage,
Audrey came up to me with a scrawny kid trailing behind
her. He was exceedingly pale as though his whole body had
been covered with bandages for a month. After she was certain we weren't engaged in anything that he shouldn't witness, she called for him to join us. "This—" she said, pre-
senting him like he was an Oscar, "—is Artemis Gordone.
He's your sixth Beatle."

"So, what do you play, Artey? Keyboards? We could
always use someone to replace me."

"No, sir. I don't play an instrument."

"He's a master of social media. And it's Artemis. He
doesn't like 'Artey.'"

"Social Media? Like FaceBook and Twitter? What do
we need that for?"

"Because nobody's heard of you."

"That's not true."

"Tell him how many mentions you found of the band on
the internet," Audrey said.

"Twenty-three."

"So what's that mean? Wouldn't each mention translate
into a hundred or two hundred people?"

"Tell him how many followers you have."

"1.7 million."

"Is that good?"

"That's great. That's why I've hired Artemis to generate
some interest in the band. Using his network, he will make
sure that someone shows up to see you."

"But he's just a kid. What are you? Fourteen?"

"Seventeen."

"He probably doesn't even like our music."

"It's okay."

"Okay? You think it's just okay and that's supposed to build interest?"

"Artemis has a podcast that has listeners all over the country."

"The world."

"The world. He interviews bands. What's more, he knows others who have podcasts in major cities all around the country. He's going to interview you on his show and then he's going to get others to interview you when you're on the road."

"Podcasts? We need radio and newspapers."

"You need to reach your audience, Mr. Black. Do you even know who your audience is, let alone where it is?"

"Artemis can find them for us."

"I don't like being some high school project," I said.

"I'm not in high school. I dropped out."

"So you live in your parents' basement?"

"No."

"Artemis is my neighbor. He bought the house next to mine."

"He bought it? How did he do that?"

"I told you. He's a master of social media. His services are in high demand. We're lucky to get him. He's only doing it because Zack gave him his start."

"So, now he'll be joining us on tour?"

"No," Artemis said. "That would not be an efficient use of my time. I can handle everything from right here in Tarrytown."

"Okay, when does he start?"

"He already has. He'll be covering this event and the whole tour."

"It'll all be virtual."

❧❧❧

Audrey had booked us as The Next Big Thing, so that's

what it said on the sandwich board outside. I actually thought it was a pretty good name. There used to be a band in Columbus called Tonight Only. I thought that was pretty clever, too.

I don't know what the Wednesday night regulars at the Set Back Inn were expecting, but I'm certain it wasn't Spoolie Freakin' Johnson. While the band was setting up, many of them stole furtive glances at Doctah Root, who sat in the farthest corner of the bar in full Ju-Ju regalia. He looked like an army sniper fitted out for the jungle camouflaged in moss and feathers. So they barely noticed the grizzled bluesman with a gray Fedora tilted over his eyes, plugging in his guitar, adjusting his pedals, setting the knobs on his amps, completely absorbed in his own little world. Not until the music started, that is.

As we took our places, Wes leaned toward me and said, "Don't let me catch you thinking!"

I started to laugh and Evan followed up with a rim shot on the snare drum.

"What's that about?" Audrey asked.

"It's something Zack used to say. 'Don't think! Don't let me catch you thinking!'"

"What did he mean?"

"He wanted us to play with feeling. We would rehearse the hell out of each arrangement, so when it came time to do it in concert, he expected us not to have to think what came next. That was hard for me, because I had written most of the arrangements and I was always listening for mistakes. But Zack didn't care about mistakes, not when we were performing."

We kicked off with our take on "You've Got Me Hummin'," which owed more to Cold Blood than the Sam and Dave original. It provided room to introduce everyone in the band, starting with a rapid-fire volley of five notes from the brass, answered by five climbing bass thumps, like you'd dropped the tone arm down in the center of the record. Then on "You" the rest of the band kicked in at full volume.

Wes sang the lyric like he was shouting orders in a greasy spoon. I didn't remember him being that good, but, then, we had all been kids. Now, his voice was marinated in whiskey and cigarettes and who knows what.

When we got to the guitar break, Spoolie held one note for four bars then followed it up with about a hundred more in the next four. Jaws dropped. A beer bottle hit the floor and caromed off the chair legs like a hockey puck. Like most bars, the people, most of them, anyway, were there to socialize and not to listen to some band they never heard of playing songs they didn't know. But Spoolie wasn't about to let them ignore us. It was a slap in the face followed by a kick in the stomach. He wasn't holding back, saving the best for last. He was setting the bar impossibly high from the get go. We had no choice but to join him on a rocket to the moon.

The next song up was the old Ides of March hit, "Vehicle." Only we gave it the Vanilla Fudge-treatment, slowing it way, way down so that we all had room to move around. It had a grittier, more menacing feel, especially with Spoolie bending and sustaining notes longer than I would have thought possible. It was also a showcase for our wall of brass.

It was nine-forty-five before we wound up the second number. We had been playing the same song for twenty minutes and each of us was soaked with sweat.

As Spoolie fine-tuned his guitar, the manager of the place sidled over to me, leaned close to my ear, and said, "Do you think you could keep them a little shorter. The bar practically shut down during that first song. Everyone was listening and nobody was buying."

I smiled. The Set Back Inn was crammed with people. More were standing outside, hoping to get in. "You usually packed like this on a Wednesday night?" I asked.

"Not usually."

Next, we did a pretty much a straight-up cover of Sugarloaf's "Green Eyed Lady," with lots of interplay between

Spoolie's guitar and my organ. I used to date a woman with green eyes and I flashed back on her as we bounced along.

Four songs into our first set, we threw in an original, just to test the waters. The crowd had hung with us so far, even though we hadn't been doing note-for-note copies of other people's hits. I was thinking how I had always wanted a band with muscular vocals, a top-notch horn section, and first rate players. Now, I did, but I was having trouble enjoying it because I knew it wouldn't last. This was a band that came with an expiration date.

There were people who were there that night who would be telling their grandkids about it. I would have been one of them if I had had any. There was no question in my mind that Spoolie was the greatest unknown guitarist in the world, but that's a pretty stupid thing to think. After all, I hadn't heard most of the others by a long shot. But he was good, real good, and I knew at that moment he could be a giant—if he wanted to be.

What I really wanted to do was just stop playing and listen, but I didn't have that luxury, not in this band, anyway. So I just tried my best to keep up with him. We forgot about the arrangements we had carefully worked out and just went with it. Spoolie was in charge. He didn't even need us, but he shared the spotlight, giving each of us an opportunity to show off.

Some people tried to dance, but had to be satisfied with shuffling their feet in one place. A few moved out to the sidewalk, propping the door open so they could still hear the band, which only brought more people into the place.

From the moment we decided to get the band back together, it was apparent that Audrey wanted to contribute in some way beyond just being our financial benefactor. So convincing her to sing backup, while probably not what she had in mind, proved to be easier than I anticipated. Everyone in the band was supportive, especially Sarah, and she soon grew acclimated to this new role. But I wasn't going to be satisfied with allowing her to languish in the shadows.

At the end of every rehearsal, I would suggest she sing a song of her choosing just for fun. It took some coaxing at first, but after a couple of times she found herself enjoying it. What everyone but Audrey knew was that I was setting her up.

Because of space limitations at the Set Back Inn, Audrey was standing at a microphone that was off to the side, partially hidden by the jukebox. She was more a part of the crowd than she was the band, which seemed to make her feel even more at ease. As we began our second set, she had resumed her place and was waiting to hear what song I would announce next.

"Welcome back," I said, taking a seat behind the B-3. "I hope you aren't done listening because we aren't done playing."

As I thought it would, that remark was greeted with a roar of approval.

"We're going to start off our next set with something a little different. This song features the newest member of our band, the lovely Audrey Taylor." As I looked at her, I could see a flash of terror in her eyes, but I knew I wasn't asking her to do something she couldn't handle. "Please join me in welcoming to the stage…Audrey Taylor."

The crowd sensed that she would need some encouragement and readily gave it. Nervously, she stepped onto the bandstand and walked over to Wes's mike which he moved closer to the center. He then helped her adjust the height.

"So, what will it be?" I asked.

She thought for a moment before saying, "Flat Tires?"

It was more of a question. At that particular instant, she would have preferred to have been anywhere else.

Turning to the audience, I said. "This is a Joni Mitchell tune—'You Dream Flat Tires.'" And then Evan counted it off with his sticks.

It was a smart choice showed off Audrey's voice to good effect. She may have been a little hesitant at first, but the patrons of the Set Back Inn were cool and showed that they were behind her. There was also plenty of room for Spoolie to add some sonic spice, while Sarah and Wes sang backup on the bridge. By the time the song was over, Audrey was an equal member of the band. We would keep "Flat Tires" in the show, adding just a touch of horns.

We ended the night with "High Heeled Sneakers." And if Tommy Tucker heard it, I'm sure he was pleased. The band played the text and Spoolie played the subtext, the notes flying out of his guitar. As we left at the end of the night, I was sure the notes were still spiraling up through the cosmos like a swarm of birds.

On the drive back to Audrey's house, Wes said to Evan, "All we were missing tonight was Don B singing 'Batman.'"

"Yeah," Evan replied. "Then we would know we had arrived."

"Don who?" I asked.

"Don B. Don Bovee. I guess he's after your time. You tell him, Wes."

"Don Bovee is this character who hangs around campus. I haven't seen him in a while. He's got a lot of problems—mental, physical—but everyone likes him because he's a real upbeat guy. And funny as hell."

"Musicians have kind of adopted him as a mascot," Evan added. "And when he sang 'Batman,' he really came alive. It was just pure joy. "

"Even though he has more problems than most of us ever face, he's always philosophical about it. He accepts his limitations. He has this expression he says all the time. If you're having a bad day or something and start complaining, Don will say, 'You lucky you get that much.'"

"Yeah, 'You lucky you get that much.' That's Don."

"Maybe he'll join us in Columbus," Audrey said. "Do 'Batman.'"

જજજ

Not quite ready to turn in when we got back to the castle, I slipped down to the museum to unwind—quietly, I thought. Having already consumed an injudicious number of beers, I opened a bottle of water instead and sat down at the B-3. A tableau of images chronicling the incredible journey I had been on since that night at Joe's Pier 52. Then I heard Audrey's voice behind me. "Do you think Zack would be pleased?"

Turning to look at her, I said, "I was wondering the same thing. But I suspect not."

"Why? The crowd liked you."

"Zack was like a football coach, always looking for ways of improving."

"Do you have trouble winding down after you play?"

"Not normally. But it's been a long time since I played in a band, especially a band I was this invested in."

"Does that cut down on the enjoyment?"

"In some ways, yes."

Audrey picked up one of the arrangements that was lying around. "Who was Jeannie?" she asked, looking at a piece of music entitled "Jeannie's Song."

"Jeannie Cummins. She was a big band singer and a friend."

"Play it for me."

On the album, it started out very quietly, just me and the piano.

"When her husband passed on,
Jeannie lived alone,
And learned to manage quite well on her own,
On her own.
He was a musician,
She sang in the band.
Until he died, they'd lived their lives
Much as they had planned.

"Jeannie had few neighbors,
But she didn't mind.
It helped her leave her troubles far behind,
Far behind.
She was never lonely,
Even late at night.
Because she loved to lie awake
And gaze at the moonlight.

"But then a strange thing happened,
It was an awful shame,
And afterward she never,
She never was the same."

Then out of nowhere, Evan was all over the drums, exploding like Keith Moon.

"With a crash, bang, boom,
He smashed into the room.
This man she'd never seen before,
Hurled himself through her glass door,
And now was lying on the floor,
More dead than alive.

"And as she drew near,
She thought it was a deer.
This quivering and shapeless mass,
Awash in blood and broken glass.
She knew she must do something fast,
Or he'd not survive.

"Jeannie later learned that
The man had lost all hope,
And could no longer find the strength to cope,
Strength to cope.
Searching for a way out
Of his soul's quagmire,

He bought some gas, then struck a match
And set himself on fire.

"But then a strange thing happened,
As he went up in flame,
And afterward he never,
He never was the same.

"With a crash, bang, boom,
A light broke through the gloom.
In his agony and his pain,
One thought burned inside his brain,
Kept repeating the same refrain,
"God, please let me live."

"With a mother's charms,
She held him in her arms.
And tried to soothe this broken man,
Hoping somehow he'd understand,
Even the most defeated can
Still have much to give.

"A doctor later told her,
Just by hearing her talk,
The man had kept from going into shock,
Into shock.
In the weeks that followed,
She became his friend
And so this tragic story would
Have a happy end.

"Though over time they lost touch,
No one was to blame,
Still neither one was ever,
Was quite the same.

"With a crash, bang, boom,
He smashed into the room.
This man she'd never seen before,
Hurled himself through her glass door,
And now was lying on the floor,
More dead than alive.

"And as she drew near,
She thought it was a deer.
This quivering and shapeless mass,
Awash in blood and broken glass.
She knew she must do something fast,
Or he'd not survive.
Or he'd not survive.
Or he'd not survive."

When it was over, Audrey grew quiet after having sung all the lyrics to herself. I was beginning to think ours was the only music she ever listened to. I hoped not. That would have been concerning.

"It's a true story," I said. I don't know why, but I had always thought of it as an Irish ballad. "I was thinking the whole album would be sort of a musical *Spoon River Anthology*."

"What's that?"

"It's a book of poems. They are supposed to be the epitaphs of the people who lived in the town of Spoon River."

"But nobody dies in your song."

"Maybe. Or perhaps he dies and is reborn." I was joking, as I usually am, but Audrey thought about it for so long that I wondered if I hadn't stumbled upon a deeper truth.

CHAPTER 25

I'm From Columbus

At the post-mortem-cum-brunch the very next day, everybody agreed that we had knocked it out of the park. Which didn't mean everyone was happy. Without coming out and directly saying so, Wes apparently felt that he had been shut out most of the evening. I think he saw himself as a lead bass player like Jack Bruce, as well as the lead singer. As such, he felt he should have been highlighted a little more.

I had been in groups where we didn't use a bass player, just my keyboard bass, and we did just fine, but we did need his vocal chops. I could carry a tune, but rarely sang lead except on special numbers because my voice was too low and, to my ear, not particularly pleasant. So I was willing to give in a little.

"You're right. Last night was just for fun," I said. "From now on, we'll stick closer to the arrangements"—which wasn't true and I knew it. I no longer thought of following them to the letter because I wanted to make certain that Spoolie didn't feel confined.

Practice that evening was as flat as the open bottles of beer that had begun to collect around the mansion like so many brown stalagmites. I know Audrey must have been getting annoyed—at least, it wouldn't have surprised me if she was—but she kept silent. Instead, she picked them up from time to time and I tried to remember to help her. The music trumped everything, even good manners. That was the rock and roll way, wasn't it? That's how bands could get away with trashing hotel rooms and treating their fans like dirt.

I could see now that Spoolie didn't intend to give much of himself in our practice sessions—which was okay because I didn't want him to burn himself out. I'd rather he save something for the concerts. On the other hand, we were serving up mashed potatoes without gravy—cold mashed potatoes at that. It was hard to judge when we were ready. The only time he really kicked it up a notch was when I suggested we play something from his songbook. Even though we didn't know most of the tunes he'd drag out, it didn't matter because they were all blues numbers. But they were fun and they challenged the band in ways our set pieces weren't anymore.

The truth was we were as ready as we were ever going to be. Audrey thought so, too, and we decided to book another tune-up show before we hit the road. This one would be at Pierson Park which was located on the Hudson River over-looking the Tappan Zee Bridge and the Palisades. There was a free sunset concert series where people would come and sit on blankets. They featured mostly jazz and blues groups, but she thought we were close enough. The stage was a slab of stone and concrete with a sort of awning to provide shade, but little protection from the elements. I didn't learn until later that she had paid another group to switch dates with us.

Audrey proved to have a knack for marketing. What with the word-of-mouth from our Set Back Inn gig and a number of strategically placed flyers up and down the main drag, we had a respectable audience—four or five hundred people, I would guess—at six-thirty in the evening! It wasn't the Set Back crowd that was for sure. This time, there were a number of kids—toddlers to teens. I questioned the judgement of some young parents who had babes-in-arms right up close to the speakers. In fact, I felt a need to make an announcement right after we were introduced.

"We're a rock and roll band," I said. "And we play loud. Too loud. That's why I'd advise you to take young kids about as far back as a football field. You'll still be able to hear us and we really aren't much to look at."

Of course, most of them didn't heed my advice, but squatted on their little piece of turf, protecting each square foot as fiercely as any soldier on Omaha Beach. But during "You Got Me Hummin'," all but a few die-hards did move back. And, I'm happy to say, most of them hung around until the end. It had been the second and last performance of the Next Big Thing. Starting tomorrow, Zack Black & the Blues Attack was back.

☙☙☙

The plan was to go our separate ways after Tarrytown and reconvene in St. Louis two days before our first show. Admittedly, it was a risk, but I felt everyone would benefit from some time off.

Audrey had booked us into a hotel with a conference room we could use as a rehearsal space. The two of us would drive the bus to St. Louis; the equipment would be sent ahead. We would then pick up a truck and driver to follow along on the tour.

Make that the three of us.

At the last minute, Audrey transferred Zack's ashes from the box on the mantel into a Tupperware container. She informed me she planned to leave a little bit of him behind at various stops along the way. I was glad she wrapped the container in a white plastic bag because that made it easier for me to ignore.

Just as we were leaving, Audrey received a message from Artemis. Cellphone video of her singing "Flat Tires" at the Set Back Inn was posted on YouTube that same night. She was surprised and embarrassed, but the embarrassment would wear off and her confidence grow when she saw the number of hits it was racking up, and not just because she was a good-looking woman. Although I'm sure that didn't hurt.

For the first couple of hours, we didn't talk much except when she told me which routes to take. I was acclimating myself to driving the bus. The largest vehicle I had driven before was a Cadillac Fleetwood and this was more than twice as long as that, so I was giving it my full attention. After weeks of practicing every day, I was also enjoying the quiet, the charming scenery rolling by, and being enrapt in my own thoughts, when Audrey spoke up.

"Tell me about your tour."

"My tour?'

"The band's tour. The big tour. What do you remember about it?'

"Didn't Zack tell you?"

"Not really. Never got around to it, I guess."

That was a relief, actually. I could only assume what he might have told her and I'm not sure we would have been in total agreement.

"Well, as Churchill said, 'History is simply one damned thing after another.'"

"Did he really say that?" Audrey asked.

"Probably not, but someone did."

A guy once wrote a history of rock and roll in Nebraska called *'Til the Cows Come Home.* I'm pretty sure we're not in it. Someone would have had to notice us when we played the Pla Mor Ballroom, but the good folks of Lincoln did their best to keep their distance.

"We opened in Lincoln, Nebraska, at this old dance hall called the Pla Mor. The Pla Mor was Lincoln's answer to Valley Dale. Count Basie, Lawrence Welk, and other legendary big bands had performed there. A local R and B band, I don't remember the name, was also on the bill. They had a three-piece horn section, a girl singer out front, and a no-holds-barred stage show. From time to time, a horn player would jump on the shoulders of one of the other band members and keep playing as he was carried about the dance floor. Another band member would leap around, wearing a silly hat and smacking the dancers with a Whiffle Ball bat. It was the kind of stuff that only a much-loved local band could get away with. Needless to say, we didn't make quite the same impression."

"They didn't like you?"

"We were kind of stiff in comparison. Afterward, we drove straight through to California. I think we were on the road for at least twenty-four hours and crossed a half-dozen states. We passed through Las Vegas in the middle of the night. There was this cotton-candy-glow on the horizon more than a hundred miles away from all the neon. It looked like the city was burning."

We needed to get some gas, so I pulled into a station on the Pennsylvania Turnpike. Audrey went inside and bought something to eat and drink while I filled the tanks. As soon as we were back on the road, she said, "So tell me about the next show."

"How we managed to get from one gig to the other without getting killed was a miracle. We were basically a bunch of teenagers with very little experience behind the wheel. As a group, our judgment was poor. And we were flatlanders at that. None of us had ever driven in the mountains before. I decided I would be the primary driver and, to my relief, nobody really disagreed. I did have a clean driving record, but that was more luck than skill. So we all piled into a used VW bus that had been given a psychedelic paint job.

"We hauled all our equipment in an orange U-Haul cargo trailer. That added a degree of difficulty to the task of driving. And we had to be extra certain it was well-balanced each time we packed it, particularly with my B-Three and the Leslie acting like a four hundred fifty-pound tail wagging the dog. It would have been easy to flip it and, likely, the van on one of those hairpin turns. Fortunately, we didn't."

"So where did you play?"

"After Nebraska, there were some things I wanted to work on, but the very next day we were booked at the Rose Palace in Pasadena. I didn't think we were going to make it through the mountains. Then we barely had a chance to do a sound check. Still, I think we were a little tighter the second time out, but the acoustics were terrible."

"Is that the one that was recorded?" Audrey asked.

"There weren't any recordings. I wish there had been."

"Maybe not an authorized one, but there's a bootleg."

"A boot? Where'd you hear that?"

"Zack has it."

"You're kidding."

"Nope, I've heard it."

"Where'd he get that?"

"I don't know. But I'm sure he documented it."

A live recording of the Blues Attack—for a moment, I just let the realization sink in. Over the years, I had occasionally thought of what I wouldn't give to have heard us play. It's different when you're on the stage. The sound is all around you, but it's not directed at you. We were playing for the people out there in the dark and I envied them as much as they envied us.

"That's the problem with being in a band. You don't really get to hear yourself, not the way you would if you were out in the audience. We didn't have monitors or anything back then. I'd like to hear it sometime."

"Of course. It really belongs to you—all of you. I'm just the caretaker. So tell me about the Rose Palace."

"I don't remember a lot about it. It was this big building, sort of a warehouse, really, that they used to build the floats for the Tournament of Roses Parade. But most of the years it was available for other uses so someone decide to book bands there. It held several thousand people, all ages—not that they came to see Zack Black and the Blues Attack. I forget who we were on the bill with—a couple of bands that I hadn't heard of before or since. But they were good. All of those hippie bands would come down out of the hills and blow everyone away." Actually, I could remember a lot about it. "If we could have held the music at that level, I might have been satisfied. But things started going sideways."

"What do you mean?"

I didn't want to share the gory details with her, not since she now knew every one of us. "There were distractions," I said. "We took our eye off the ball or the prize or whatever metaphor you want."

"Zack, too?"

"Yeah."

"And you?"

"Guilty as the rest."

That wasn't true, though, not completely. I had not sampled the drugs or the groupies. Zack hadn't either, as far as I knew. We were far too busy focusing on the business at hand. But we knew what was going on and pretended to be oblivious to it.

"Where did you play next?"

I had to think a moment. "San Francisco. The Fillmore. That was seven or eight hours north. Didn't realize how long California was. In Ohio, you can drive from one border to the other in three hours or less."

"So tell me about the Fillmore," Audrey said.

"I don't know about the others, but I was nervous— really nervous," I said. "It was our first date on our big national tour—thirteen cities in three weeks. Sharing the bill with some local favorites. One was called Beefy Red, I think. Great, great musicians. Promotional tie-ins with local radio stations. Newspaper photo ops. The star-making machinery had been set in motion. I wanted us to be perfect, but we had only rehearsed with the horns a half-dozen times and I was worried. I was pacing around in the dressing room, trying to calm down, when I saw this wall that had been signed by all these musicians who had played there. I started reading them. Many I recognized, but many I didn't.

And then I spotted several that jumped out at me: Bill Bartlett, Steve Walmsley, Ivan Browne. It was the Lemon Pipers."

"'Green Tambourine', right?"

"Yeah. It went to number one. But, the thing is, they were just regular guys from Ohio, too. I even met Bartlett a time or two. He was a terrific guitarist, by the way. Didn't deserve to be saddled with the bubble gum label. But I figured if they could hold their own at the Fillmore, so could we."

"And did you?"

"Well, we didn't fall on our faces. And the people seemed to like us."

Dissatisfied with the way the local deejay had introduced us at the Rose Garden, we wrote our own. This time Evan began thumping his bass drum as the deejay shouted into the mike, "They're not The Beatles…They're not the Rolling Stones…They're not even Freddie and the Dreamers…They're *Zack Black and the Blues Attack!*"

Then I launched into my Jerry Lee piano intro, followed by a swooping vocal on "I-I-I-I-I-I-I'm from Columbus…"

The song became our icebreaker. It was a way to introduce the band and elicit audience involvement from the get-go. I did what I called a Gabor Szabo arrangement with lots of percussion and an extended jam. It began with a steady four-on-the-floor beat.

> "I'm from Columbus—
> It's etched on my soul
> Like a sailor's tattoo.
> I'm from Columbus—
> Its spirit imbues
> Ev'rything that I think, say, and do-oo-oo-oo."

Dragging my thumbnail across the keys in a quick downward glissando, and I transitioned into the bridge.

"Though I've been away
I still feel I'm part of
The hoi polloi.

"And I look at the world
Through the wondering eyes of
A Midwestern boy-oy-oy-oy."

I then returned to the verse:

"I'm from Columbus—
A special kind of place
Where dreams really
Can come true-oo-oo-oo."

A wall of horns supported me on the chorus:

"I'm from Columbus,
I'm from Columbus,
I'm from Columbus,
I'm from Columbus."

Then Zack took up the second verse, bending a string so it sounded like a siren.

"Yes, I'm from Columbus—
It's where I call home
And I that know it always will be.
I'm from Columbus—
It's where I first learned
The best things in life are free-ee-ee-ee.

"And though it may lack
What sophisticated people
Once called razzmatazz.

"It's still a place
Where anything can happen
And it usually has-as-as-as.

"I'm from Columbus—
The heart of Ohio
Keeps on calling to me-e-e-e."

Everyone joined in the chorus.

"I'm from Columbus,
I'm from Columbus,
I'm from Columbus,
I'm from Columbus."

Suddenly, the horn players all moved over to percussion, playing congas, bells, shakers, what have you, while Zack jammed on guitar, turning it every which way but loose. It was something I had seen the Sons of Champlin do, switching off on instruments, and I always wanted to incorporate something similar in our show.

And then Zack stopped. We would turn the volume down as he walked to the edge of the stage to address the audience. "This is where you come in," he said. "I need you to sing along with me: 'I'm from Columbus, I'm from Columbus, I'm from Columbus, I'm from Columbus.' Do you think you can do that?"

If they roared back "Yeah!" then we knew we had them. If not—well, then we were in for a long evening. But Zack was a very persuasive guy and it wasn't much of a challenge for him to get them to sing along, first the girls, then the guys.

"I'm from Columbus,
I'm from Columbus,

> I'm from Columbus,
> I'm from Columbus."

"Okay," Zack would say. "Now, I am the conductor and you just follow me. If I raise my arms like this, you raise your voices. If I lower them like this, you lower your voices. And if I raise my arms way up high like this, then I want you to lift the roof off this place. Got it? Let's try."

> "I'm from Columbus,
> I'm from Columbus,
> I'm from Columbus,
> I'm from Columbus.
> I'M FROM COLUMBUS,
> I'M FROM COLUMBUS,
> I'M FROM COLUMBUS,
> I'M FROM COLUMBUS."

Zack then signaled for them to stop, while we continued to play. He then sang, "I'm from Columbus," then pointed to each of us in turn to do likewise. Then when we each had sung our part, we sang it together in four-part harmony. After a brief pause, I launched into the final verse.

> "I'm from Columbus—
> I'm from Columbus—
> It's etched on my soul
> Like a sailor's tattoo.
> I'm from Columbus—
> Its spirit imbues
> Ev'rything that I think, say, and do- oo-oo-oo.

> "Though I've been away
> I still feel I'm part of
> The hoi polloi.

> "And I look at the world

Through the wondering eyes of
A Midwestern boy-oy-oy-oy.

"I'm from Columbus—
A special kind of place
Where dreams really
Can come true-oo-oo-oo.

"I'm from Columbus,
I'm from Columbus,
I'm from Columbus,
I'm from…"

"When the song was over, Zack said, 'I didn't expect to see so many people from Columbus in San Francisco.' And the crowd went crazy. He followed up with, 'But hometown shows are always the best, right?' And I thought they were going to tear the place down. That night, I think we might have been as popular as Quicksilver Messenger Service."

"That must have been gratifying."

"It should have been, but I think it may have also been the beginning of the end."

"Why is that?"

"We started to believe we were stars. It had come too easy. The irony is, nobody remembers that show."

"Why?"

"We weren't supposed to play there. It was a hurry-up job to fill a date that had opened up unexpectedly. No ads, no posters, just a few flyers. People showed up just because it was the Fillmore."

"I'm sure someone remembers it. Aren't there any bands you remember that other people don't?"

"A few, I guess. B and W Commonwealth."

"Who were they?"

"This band out of Westerville. I think they were Otterbein students. I caught them at the Northland Battle of the Bands one year. I remember they did a cover of 'It's a Legal Matter, Baby' that I really liked. But they didn't win. They didn't even place. I only knew one other person who remembered them and he died years ago."

"Well, I suspect there are more than two people who remember when the Blues Attack played the Fillmore."

"Perhaps."

"Too bad it's gone. I think I read they turned it into a car dealership or something."

"Well, they can't blame that on us."

CHAPTER 26

Color Wheel Blues

Where did you play next?"
I had to think a moment. It seemed like several lifetimes ago and the answer had slipped my mind. I was bobbing for apples and not getting any bites. Finally, it came to me. "The Whiskey A Go Go. Yeah, that was it." I felt like I had won the jackpot on some TV game show. They could call it "Senior Moments."

"Los Angeles?" Audrey asked.

"Yeah. Shows you how well it was planned out. Our manager must have thought that everything in California was within a couple of hours' drive of everything else. So we had to turn around and head back down the coast. The Whiskey was in West Hollywood. Still is, I think. It was a smaller venue, but we were there for two nights. And we should have been at our best because it was more like what we were used to, but the cracks were already beginning to show. I remember Evan cut his hand somehow—there was a broken glass—and blamed one of the horn players. He wrapped it in gaffers tape and had to get stitches later."

I was remembering other things, too, but I didn't want to tell her those. I was making some major edits on the fly.

"Met Arthur Lee. That was cool."

"Who?"

"Arthur Lee. The leader of Love. One of my favorite bands."

"So many Lees. Arthur, Albert, Alvin. I can't keep them straight."

"Zack taught you well."

"How do you know I didn't teach myself?"

"Did you?"

"You don't think a girl can know as much about music as a guy?"

"No reason why she can't. I just haven't met many."

The Whiskey A Go Go, located right on the Sunset Strip, was legendary. Johnny Rivers had recorded a live album there which put him and the club on the map. It had launched the careers of many Southern California bands, from The Byrds to Frank Zappa.

"It was at the Whiskey," I said, "that I introduced a new song into our set. I usually didn't do a lot of planned patter between songs, but 'Color Wheel Blues' was different. I would play a standard blues vamp and then start to talk over it. I'd say that some time ago I decided to sit down and write a blues song based on my own life experience. After all, I was a white, middle class kid, a high school graduate, and had been out on my own for a year or two.

"At the time, I was living in a band house near campus, playing out every weekend. I was responsible for no one but myself. I knew what it was like to not have a clean shirt—to not know where my next beer was coming from—to have to skip dessert. When Robert Johnson sang, 'If it wasn't for bad luck, I wouldn't have no luck at all,' I could relate. He was talking about me.

"That usually got a laugh. If it didn't, I knew we were in trouble. Then I'd say that I started out by making a list of all the different kinds of blues that I had experienced on the mean streets of Columbus. It was kind of short. So I expanded it to include all the other places I had been, mostly on vacation. Places like the Smokey Mountains, the Atlantic Ocean, and Disneyland. And I started to realize that I didn't have much to complain about, certainly not like Robert Johnson and Howlin' Wolf and Lightnin' Hopkins did. But

I wasn't going to let that stop me. I knew I could still write a blues song—the ultimate blues song, even. And I did. But it didn't turn out quite the way I imagined it would."

I decided to listen to the song—the third to the last track—and slipped it in the slot in the dashboard. I then pushed the button to jump ahead. Finally, I found it and turned up the volume. Wes was singing. It was a standard blues progression.

> "Used to date an artist;
> Loved her more than life.
> Little did I know that she
> Would cause me so much strife.

> "But then she introduced me
> To the world of tints and hues.
> I've got those red, orange, yellow, green,
> And every shade that's in between blues."

"Following each chorus, Zack would play a few licks taken from some iconic bluesman, say B.B. King or T-Bone Walker or Muddy Waters. Might even throw in a bit of 'Sunshine of Your Love.' It was already becoming a cliché."

> "She would always want me
> To tell her how I feel.
> But then she had to show me
> That wicked color wheel.

> "Well, wish I'd never told her
> Which color I would choose.
> I've got those red, orange, yellow, green,
> And every shade that's in between blues."

"If the crowd reacted positively, Wes would say, 'You think that was good? Well, just hold onto your—whatever.' I would deliver the rapid fire lyrics with the horns squealing behind him."

"Baby, Bondi, Carolina,
Midnight, Alice, Royal China.
Navy, Oxford, Egyptian, Teal,
Azure, Cambridge, Turquoise, and Steel,

"They're all part of my palette.
Lord knows I've paid my dues.
I've got the red, orange, yellow, green,
And every shade that's in between blues.

"Things were once so simple,
No reason for complaint.
Now, I'm so conflicted,
Can't buy a can of paint.

"Faced with all those choices,
I know I'm bound to lose.
I've got those red, orange, yellow, green,
And every shade that's in between blues."

"Then he'd say, 'Now you quick studies may think you know this part, but you don't.'"

"Cobalt, Brandeis, Ultramarine.
Air Force, Dodger, and Tourmaline.
Persian, Powder, Electric, True.
Prussian, Iris, and Sapphire, too.

"They're all part of my palette.
Lord knows I've paid my dues.
I've got the red, orange, yellow, green,
And every shade that's in between blues."

"For the finale, we would slow it way down."

"Yes, they're all part of my palette.
Lord knows I've paid my dues.
I've got the red, orange, yellow, green,
And every shade that's in between blues.

"You want another verse? All right, let's do it.

"Told her it was over,
Couldn't take it anymore.
Grabbed my keys, my coat, and hat
And headed for the door.

"Said she, 'Now, wait a minute,
Does this purse go with my shoes?"
I've got the red, orange, yellow, green,
And every shade that's in between blues.
That's all.'"

When the song was over, I noticed Audrey was looking at me like I was a raccoon that had stolen into her kitchen through the dog door. "You're strange. You know that, don't you?" she said.

"Strange in a good way or a bad way?"

"Good—I hope. I've had my share of the bad."

I'll admit it wasn't the best thing I'd ever written, but the hip crowd at the Whisky dug it. Maybe it's because they knew they were poseurs, too. I've always believed that the deadliest thing in rock and roll is when musicians take themselves too seriously. The best songs weren't usually the most polished; the best bands weren't necessarily the most talented. Robert Johnson was a poet and a thief. In the grand tradition of folk musicians everywhere, he wrote some great couplets and copped some others. His gift was in knowing what to do with them.

೧೨೮

I am not one to skip meals, but I was enjoying Audrey's company so much that I hadn't noticed that I was getting hungry. I'd like to think she felt the same. Mid-afternoon, we stopped to get sandwiches and called ahead to Columbus to make reservations for the night. Less than an hour later, we were back on the road and Audrey picked up our conversation where she had left off. "So what came after the Whiskey A Go Go?"

"Kansas City." I was never certain whether we played Kansas City, Missouri, or Kansas City, Kansas—or what difference it would have made. "Drove all day and all night again. We were booked into the El Torreon Ballroom, an old dance hall that been integrated since it opened its doors half a century earlier. Maybe that's why so much of our audience was black—either that or they had thought that we were a black act. It was like the scene in the movie where Buddy Holly takes the stage at the Apollo Theater, except they didn't really like us that much. At least not at first.

"We started out playing our usual set, but it was soon apparent that they had come to dance and our music wasn't doing it for them. After the third number, Zack called a quick huddle back by the drum kit and we agreed to dig deep into our library and pull out all of the black music we knew. It would be rough and raucous because we weren't seasoned musicians by any means. However, we hoped that what we lacked in technique would be more than made up for by passion. I wouldn't go so far as to claim we had soul.

"Leaning into the microphone, Zack screamed, 'Are you ready to dance?'

"'Yeaaahhhhhhh!' they answered.

"'I mean are you ready to dance!'

"'Yeaaaaahhhhhhhhh!' came the response, even louder.

"'Then what's stopping you?' Zack shouted, bending a few notes on his guitar. Then Wes clacked out the count with his drum sticks and we launched into our "High Heeled Sneakers/She's About a Mover" medley. In moments, the entire dance floor was in motion, churning like a giant cement mixer. Obviously, we had done something right. All of us realized that it would behoove us to ride that groove as long as we could, so we stretched the song out for ten or twelve minutes. From there we moved on to Wilson Picket and some Sam and Dave, milking each song for as long as we could. Zack and I traded off leads, doing a call and response and guitar and B-Three. Steeped in the blues as he was, Zack played every riff he had ever heard, while I threw in the greasiest organ sounds I could muster.

"At the end of the evening, we were surprised when we were called back for an encore. Zack then threw us for a loop by announcing "Kansas City," a song we had never played together and, I suspect, some of us had never played at all. After Zack sang the first verse, a young black woman was lifted onto the stage. She took command of Zack's mike and proceeded to bring the house down with her singing. I don't know who she was, but I was sure I was witnessing the birth of a major star. I was wrong. I never saw her again, but her performance gave me chills.

"We brought the whole thing to an end with a reprise of 'Hi-Heel Sneakers' with the crowd singing along. To my way of thinking, Kansas City was both the highlight and the lowlight of our tour. It was where we received the best reception, but we lost our focus. We were no longer Zack Black and the Blues Attack. We were a bunch of white guys trying to pass for black. There were already enough English bands doing that."

"I would have loved to have been there," Audrey said.

"You would have been kind of young."

"You know what I mean." She hit me playfully on the shoulder. "So where did you go after Kansas City?"

"Some place in Minneapolis. Straight shot up through Iowa. Took us most of a day. It was crazy. The Guthrie I think it was called. It was right downtown by the river."

"What river?"

"The Mississippi. That's the only time I was ever in Minneapolis. I should go back some day and see what I missed. We shared the bill with Stoned Soul Picnic, a boogie band from Kansas or Colorado or somewhere that had a debut album slowly moving up the charts. Anchored by two drummers, they seemed like a pale imitation of Canned Heat to me, but still they ranked above us on the food chain. Their single, 'Country Fried,' was getting some airplay, and they also had a well-deserved reputation for an anything-goes stage show. We knew we had our work cut out for us if we were going to compete with them. However, we were tighter players and our bluesy mixture of Three Dog Night and Blood, Sweat and Tears gave us a muscular sound. Hannibal could have gotten by with half as many elephants if he had had a B-Three.

"When I took the B-Three on the road, I felt like a vampire lugging around at four hundred fifty-pound casket. Throw in the Leslie speaker and it tipped the scales at nearly six hundred. I was always the first one to arrive and the last one to leave. Sometimes, I had to find a way to lift the behemoth up onto a 'stage' that might be six inches or three feet above the main floor. A few times, I had to leave the 'squawk box,' as Zack dubbed it, sitting at ground level, while the rest of the band towered over me."

"Didn't you have roadies?"

"Roadies? Sure," I answered. "Us. We did it all and didn't even think twice about it."

"So you must have been getting better with all that playing."

"I still felt like an amateur. The key to getting the right sound was learning how to set the registrations. I spent a lot of time fiddling with the B-Three's drawbars, percussions, and vibratos, trying to emulate my keyboard idols. After hearing Richard 'Groove' Holmes do it, I added wah-wah pedals. My time probably would have been better spent learning the B-Three itself, but it was a time of gimmicks."

"So did you boys 'play nice' together?"

"We played okay. Stan Billups, the guy who signed us, was there. I think he had heard from someone that there was trouble brewing. Next thing I knew, he had Zack off in a corner. It was quite an animated conversation. When I asked Zack what was going on, he told me they were concerned because record sales weren't taking off like expected. Of course, he didn't mention the distribution problems with the album. The single was starting to get a little bit of play in some markets, but had dropped completely off the charts in San Francisco. Not surprisingly, several Ohio stations had placed it in rotation, but also one in St. Louis. We started pointing to our show at the Kiel Opera House as being our big coming-out party.

"I was still pushing for some rehearsal time, hoping we could tighten up the arrangements a little more. As it turned out, we had a couple of days' lay over in Chicago. We weren't booked there until after St. Louis, but the plan was for us to pre-record some radio promos. The hotel we were staying at had a ballroom free, so we spent one full day rehearsing—at least that was the idea. Instead, Wes and one of the horn players decided to go AWOL. When they finally turned up, I went off on them."

"You went off? That's hard to imagine."

"Yeah, well, I did, but it wasn't exactly spontaneous. I had already worked it out in my mind, rehearsed what I was going to say—at least the first minute or so. The adlibs came after that. Sort of like free jazz."

"I wish I could have heard that."

"No, you don't. We probably wouldn't be sharing a car right now."

"So did you get the reaction you were hoping for?"

"Not exactly."

ℰℛℰℛ

When we reached Columbus, we were about halfway to

St. Louis. We didn't really have time to do much sightseeing, but I assured Audrey we would on the return trip. She seemed disappointed, as though she had plans. And, I suspected, many more questions to pepper me with. Not all that talkative by nature, I was getting fatigued. I had nearly exhausted my quota of words for the day.

We had left Columbus bright and early that morning, headed for Indiana. Next stop St. Louis.

Indiana is a lot like Ohio or like Ohio was twenty years ago. That's its charm. At least that's what I thought when I was growing up. As we cruised through the Indiana countryside, I saw reminders of things that had long vanished from the Ohio landscape. In an earlier age, the United States had developed from the east to the west. Later, it had been from the coasts to the middle. Soon, it would be everywhere at once. But not yet. Not in Indiana.

"So what happened in St. Louis?" Audrey asked, picking up the conversation from where we had left off the day before.

"St. Louis didn't happen. Wes and the horn player quit or were fired. I forget which. So we had to cancel. Zack and I thought we could keep going if he played bass guitar on some songs, while I would cover it with the B-Three on others. And we hired another horn player, hoping he could catch onto the arrangements quickly. We rehearsed for two days, using a test pressing of the album so he could learn the songs, and then played our Chicago date. It was called the Electric Playground or something like that."

"How'd that go?"

"Better. But, then, disaster struck."

"What happened?"

"Zack lost his voice. Strep throat. He had been hiding it from us, or trying to, but he reached the point where he just couldn't sing a note. We had no choice but to cancel the other dates. The tour was over. And Zack Black and the Blues Attack was no more."

"You never played together again?"

"Not as the Blues Attack. Zack and I thought we'd give it one more try. We scrapped the horns, found a new drummer and bass player, and got hired as a last-minute substitute for the Cincinnati Pop Festival. It was this day-long rock concert which took place at Crosley Field, the old home of the Cincinnati Reds. In fact, I think they only played a few more games there and then they tore it down. The line-up was kind of fluid. There were supposed to be fourteen or sixteen bands, I think, ranging from Mountain, Ten Years After, and Traffic to all of these Michigan bands like The Stooges, Grand Funk Railroad, and the Bob Seger System. It was actually pretty cool.

"Michael Quatro, this keyboard player from Detroit, was one of the guys behind it. We had crossed paths somewhere and he remembered us when he needed to add some bands to the line-up after a couple dropped out. It was supposed to start at ten o'clock in the morning, but it was raining so the bands couldn't start setting up until it stopped. The first band didn't take the stage until around noon. I think we went on second or third. We were only allotted forty-five minutes to play, nobody knew who we were, and, since we were an afterthought, we weren't on the posters or flyers. A local TV station videotaped the whole thing, but they edited it down to an hour and a half for broadcast on television. Of course, we didn't make the cut, although you could see us in the crowd."

"Zack has some photos."

"He does? Where did he get those?"

"I don't know. A friend, I think."

"I bet it was Thomas Berger."

"Thomas Berger?"

"Yeah, he knew him from high school. He came to see us once or twice. Thomas had been in the band briefly. If I remember right, he might have hung out with us at Cincinnati." As a performer, Thomas Berger was the least talented member of Zack Black and the Blues Attack. He was a passable rhythm guitarist and an okay back-up vocalist.

However, he had the least ego investment in the group of anybody. When everyone else was butting heads, they turned to Thomas as the final arbiter of what should be done. He was a good songwriter and his opinion was nearly always respected. Unlike the rest of us, Thomas didn't go into the music business." I was thinking we could have used as a mediator. Maybe he could have held us together.

"Zack also has some video," Audrey said. "Do you remember Iggy stage diving?"

"Yeah, the crowd lifted him up and carried him around like he was a flagpole or something. He stepped right back onto the stage. Then somebody handed him a jar of peanut butter so he smeared all over his chest and then began throwing globs of it out at the crowd."

"What else happened?"

"Alice Cooper got pied. This was back before he had his big stage show or had scored any of his hits. He was holding up this pocket watch, trying to hypnotize the crowd, when someone hit him in the face with a cake. So he just mashed it all over his own face. He ended his set by draping sheets over all of the guys in the band."

"The video shows Alvin Lee doing his 'Going Home'-thing, just like at Woodstock."

"And Suzi Quatro played with her sisters. Suzi was the cute one. The band was called Cradle. And when Mountain was playing, this longhaired hippy guy jumped up on stage and was dancing, flinging his hair around, and it got tangled in Leslie West's guitar. He kept playing and the guy got jerked around each time Leslie turned or moved his guitar."

"Wish I could have seen it."

"The really dumb thing was they had erected the stage on second base and they expected everyone to remain seated in the grandstand. Of course, that didn't go over very well. Finally, about half of the people rushed the field. There were a couple of dozen cops guarding the infield and, probably, ten thousand people or more coming toward them, dancing on the grass. So they stopped the concert until everyone went back to their seats."

"Did they like you?"

"Like us? I don't know. I didn't like us. I don't think Zack did, either. I remember we left around midnight as Traffic was doing 'John Barleycorn.' We were trying to beat the crowd. We dropped Thomas off in Oxford. I think he was graduating from college the next day. I hadn't thought about any of this in years."

We were making good time on I-70. It was a straight shot across Indiana and Illinois and they had fewer highway patrol troopers.

CHAPTER 27

Goods Days/Bad Days

Sunlight stabbed my eyes as we pulled into St. Louis late Wednesday afternoon.

Inching across the Mississippi on the Stan Musial Bridge, I finally caught a glimpse of the Gateway Arch off to the left. It had been a long wait. Back when the Blues Attack were originally supposed to play here, the Arch had been open just a few years, and I was looking forward to checking it out. But after the band imploded, I went directly home without passing Go. Over the intervening years, I had never gotten any nearer to St. Louis than switching planes at Lambert Field. Meanwhile, the Arch was showing its age, due to graffiti, pollution, and patches of corrosion. I could relate.

For my sake, Audrey had booked us into a hotel in Fenton, a St. Louis suburb, making it easier to park the bus. Although I had grown up in the Midwest where people who don't drive are regarded with suspicion, she didn't have much confidence in my driving skills—and rightly so. I hadn't owned a car in decades and my reflexes weren't what they once were. From here on, I would leave the driving to a professional. Still, I had enjoyed being behind the wheel these past few days. I had scared myself only a couple of times and, if I scared Audrey, she had kept quiet about it. After a late dinner, we turned in for the night, knowing we would have a full day ahead of us. The real work was about to begin.

All day Thursday, band members began turning up like stray cats—all except Spoolie and Doctah Root. Audrey's calls and messages to both went unanswered. At rehearsal on Friday, they still hadn't made an appearance, so I began planning for how we would cover for them if necessary. But I didn't share my plan with the rest of the band because I didn't want to alarm them. Instead, I did something I never liked to do: I lied. Sort of. I told them Spoolie had been delayed—which was obviously true—but I expected he would join us soon—which was more of a hope.

Audrey had arranged for us to rehearse in the hotel's ballroom. A convention had ended at noon on Friday, so we had the place pretty much to ourselves. During a break, one of the horn players bumped into Spoolie and Doctah Root in the lobby. They had just checked in and were heading out to get something to eat. When he brought up rehearsal, Spoolie just shrugged. The doctah, however, told him not to worry. They were ready. Of course, that didn't go over well with the rest of the band. I found myself falling back on the old bromide that artists tend to be difficult people.

"So you're saying they're artists and we're not?" Wes responded.

"No, Wes, I'm saying for every Willie Nelson, there's a Van Morrison. Talent has nothing to do with it." Of course, I didn't know either Nelson, purportedly a mellow fellow, or Morrison, generally regarded as anything but, and was just going on what I had read. All the while the words were coming out of my mouth, I was hoping they wouldn't get back to Spoolie. My gut told me that it wasn't his doing. He was under the spell of Doctah Root. Besides, there were no indications of an attitude problem in his playing. As Jack Kerouac said, "The only truth is music." By that measure, Spoolie wouldn't have had any trouble beating an E-meter, even if L. Ron Hubbard himself were at the controls.

Just when we were about ready to call it a day, Spoolie and Doctah Root strolled into the rehearsal room.

"Hope you folks are ready to play," the doctah said.

"It'll only take me a moment to set up."

I gave the band a wan smile. There was mutiny in their eyes. As the doctah went about arranging his drums and Spoolie was checking his tuning, I gave everyone else a ten-minute break. As they filed out into the hallway, I quietly reminded them they were getting paid—very well—and that I expected them to be professionals. When we reassembled twenty minutes later, we focused on ensuring that Spoolie and the doctah knew their parts. We then would be able to sleep in until sound check the next afternoon.

c∙∂c∙∂

We had hoped to play as many of the original venues we had been booked into as we could. In St. Louis, we were supposed to play the Kiel Opera House. It was this schizo-phrenic building that was half sports arena and half concert hall with a stage in the middle. The arena portion was torn down a few years back, but after standing empty for a time, the concert hall was renovated and reopened as the Peabody Opera House. Different name, but basically the same place. I even saw a few handbills for our show in windows and tacked up on telephone poles as we cruised through the downtown.

As our bus swung wide onto Market Street and the thea-ter came into view, Evan said, "I know this place. I was here with J.D. Blackfoot in 1982. Me, George Mobley, Pat Jeany."

"I've heard about that concert," Wes said.

"It was amazing," Evan continued. "J.D. developed this huge following in St. Louis after some disc jockey on KSHE started playing his *Song of Crazy Horse* album. The people of St. Louis couldn't get enough of it. By the time he was booked to play here, the fans were going crazy. There must have been four or five thousand people crammed into the hall. When we arrived, the limo got mobbed, everyone was screaming. You'd have thought we were The Beatles. Just before we went on, this guy from the city with a decibel meter shows up. J.R. Goings, J.D.'s road manager, asked him what he was going to do with it. He said if the music got too loud, he would have to make the band turn it down. Then the disc jockey goes on stage and says, 'Let's give a St. Louis welcome to J.D. Blackfoot!' The crowd let out this unbelievable roar that spiked the meter. The official looks at Goings and said, 'never mind,' and walked away."

I had first crossed paths with J.D. back when he was calling himself Benny Van. He had played in The Ebb-Tides before he landed a recording contract. His first single was a catchy little song called, "Who's Nuts, Alfred?" But Zack Black & the Blues Attack weren't J.D. Blackfoot. We were touring in support of an album few people had ever even heard. But word had gotten out, courtesy of Artemis Gordone, our social media guru, that this might be something special. Thanks to Audrey, our promotional package was better than we could have hoped for—certainly better than anything the label ever provided. One St. Louis radio station even made a point of playing cuts from our album.

For the opening band, Artemis had recommended this local blues group, The Spanksters. By his calculations, they would draw about 1,200 followers on their own and would dovetail well with our sound. He had also found—or invented, I'm not sure which—this quote by someone whose name meant nothing to me in which he said "Hole in the Heart" had the greatest blues lick ever recorded. Not surprisingly, there was a noticeable buzz in St. Louis in anticipation of the debut of Elmore "Spoolie" Johnson. And, oh, yeah, the Blues Attack. This fact did not escape Doctah Root's notice.

We were all in the green room, waiting to go on, when I noticed he had cornered Audrey. I couldn't hear what they were saying, but when he became quite animated, I decided to insert myself into their conversation. "Is there a problem?" I asked.

The doctah looked at Audrey who looked at me. "No," she replied. "No problem."

Root gave an enigmatic smile, said, "I better check on Spoolie," and slipped away.

"What was that about?"

"Nothing," Audrey said.

"Nothing?"

"He just informed me that Spoolie won't play unless he's paid in advance—in cash."

"I hope you told him to forget it."

"I told him it was too late, now, but I would pay them as soon as the show was over. And that he would be paid in advance for the rest of the concerts."

"That's blackmail."

"What does it matter? If that's what it takes to keep Spoolie happy, then that's what I'll do."

"What if the rest of the band hears about it?"

"I intend to treat them all the same. You want in on it?"

"I told you: I don't want your money."

"What do you want?"

I don't know why she was upset with me.

"To be your friend."

Audrey looked at me as though she were reading a Chinese menu. "We better get ready," she said before she walked away.

I suspected the illusion she had about what it was like being in a band was starting to crumble.

ↄ৹ↄ

At precisely nine o'clock, we took the stage of the Peabody and launched into "You've Got Me Hummin'." That showed we were a high energy band and had come to play. From the moment Spoolie cut loose with his first solo, the crowd was his. It was like Jimi Hendrix at the Monterey Pop Festival. Nine minutes later, I thanked the crowd for—

finally—welcoming us to St. Louis. I also told them to feel free to take pictures and shoot video, knowing some of it would likely be posted to the internet. I also gave them a hashtag if they wanted to tweet anything. When she wasn't singing, Audrey shot video with her phone and emailed it to Artemis back in New York.

"As some of you may know, tonight we are kicking off the second leg of our national tour. The first leg came to an abrupt end some forty-five years ago just before we were scheduled to play St. Louis. I always knew we'd be back to pick up where we left off. I just didn't think it would take so long. Now, there are a few here tonight who still have your original tickets. Would you raise your hands, please?" This had been Audrey's idea. Frankly, I was amazed that so many people had hung onto them—although I suspected many were counterfeit.

Looking out over the sea of faces, I said, "Thank you for your extreme patience. In your honor, we want to play this new song that will give you some idea of what we've been up to." I had written the song just for our reunion. It was autobiographical in spirit, if not in fact. "Let's do it," I said, and Evan began counting off,

"One, two, three, four."

I began to sing and play one phrase at a time, coming to a momentary stop at the end of each line.

> "When I was a boy, growin' up, goin' nowhere,
> Didn't have a dream or a hope, but I didn't care.
> All I really wanted was a sharp girl and a fast car.
> But they took my car, said I was a public menace,
> And I lost my girl to some guy who taught her tennis.
> Only thing she left me was a battered old Harmony guitar."

When I paused, Wes played a few simple chords on a cheap acoustic guitar. Then as I transitioned to the bridge, the rest of the band began to join in, a layer at a time, as the tempo slowly increased.

> "Well, sittin' in my room, I was feelin'
> mean and lowdown,
> Starin' at the walls, waitin' for the sun to go down,
> I picked up that guitar and
> I taught myself a chord or two.
> Never hurt so bad, didn't know just how to say it,
> So I made a song and I began to play it,
> All about that girl and the changes that
> she put me through."

The angst had been real; but, again, not the girl. She was pure imagination. Unlike Audrey. I wondered what would become of her—of us—after we got back to New York. Was she going to mourn Zack forever or would she ever be open to a new relationship? Even if she were, I had no reason to believe that she would choose me. I had nothing to offer her but a constant reminder that I wasn't Zack. And so I sang,

> "Year or so went by and I'd put a band together,
> Just a bunch of friends, couldn't make our
> minds up whether
> We should stick to country or maybe switch to rock 'n roll.
> Then we got a job workin' with a local deejay
> At this record hop just a short stop down the freeway.
> Didn't pay much money, but I tell ya
> it was good for the soul."

I drug out the word "soul," coming to another complete stop. We then went back to the bridge with Hal Blaine's drum intro from "Be My Baby": three bass drum beats followed by a snap of snare and tambourine.

The deejay did his thing, talkin' jive and spinnin' platters,

Had those kids believin' music's all that matters.
Then he went on break, sayin' hope that
you enjoy the band.
After all these years, my memory's grown hazy,
Don't know what we played,
but the whole place just went crazy,
And when the song was done,
we had them eatin' out of our hand."

And then the chorus. The band came on in a full-Bruce Springsteen circus bandwagon-style with the sax wailing over the top. Through it all, Wes continued to play acoustic guitar, but with increasing sophistication.

"Those were the good days and the bad days,
The never-felt-so-happy-or-so-sad days,
And no one ever gave a thought to
what the future might bring.
Those were the best times and the worst times,
The never-felt-so-lucky-or-so-cursed times,
If I could do it all again I wouldn't change a thing."

Spoolie then dropped in a spiraling lead that hinted of things to come.

"We were flyin' high, had more jobs than we could handle,
Workin' night and day, burnin' both ends of the candle.
Thought we had it made,
but the fates had somethin' else in store.
Disco came along and at first it just seemed funny,
'Till we couldn't find a job for love nor money.
No one seemed to care for our kinda music anymore.

"I almost cut my hair and took a job in retail.
Would have chucked it all except for one small detail;
Music was my mistress and I just couldn't say goodbye.
So I left the band, tried my hand at workin' single,

Playin' song for tips wherever folks would mingle.
Some days I went hungry, but,
ya know it sure beat livin' a lie.
"Those were the good days and the bad days,
The never-felt-so-happy-or-so-sad days,
And no one ever gave a thought to
what the future might bring.
Those were the best times and the worst times,
The never-felt-so-lucky-or-so-cursed times,
If I could do it all again I wouldn't change a thing."

When I thought of it, I threw a glance back at Audrey, standing at her mike, bobbing and swaying, while singing back-up. It looked as though she had gotten over her jitters and was fully absorbed in the music.

"My luck began to change, signed up with this record label,
And we laid down tracks whenever we were able
To come in off the road, if only for a day or so.
Livin' in hotels and workin' out of Nashville,
Funny when you think how a pocketful of cash will
Change the way you look at life and the people you know.

"Then one day I heard a song we had recorded,
On the radio, and at last I felt rewarded,
For the many years I'd worked to keep the dream alive.
Now, maybe I won't ever play the Grand Ole Opry,
But I'll never let nobody try and stop me,
Long as I can sing my songs then I know I'll survive.

"Those were the good days and the bad days,
The never-felt-so-happy-or-so-sad days,
And no one ever gave a thought to
what the future might bring.
Those were the best times and the worst times,
The never-felt-so-lucky-or-so-cursed times,
If I could do it all again I wouldn't change a thing.

"Those were the good days and the bad days,
The never-felt-so-happy-or-so-sad days,
And no one ever gave a thought to
what the future might bring.
Those were the best times and the worst times,
The never-felt-so-lucky-or-so-cursed times,
If I could do it all again I wouldn't change a thing."

Spoolie had been playing the guitar for more years than I had been walking the earth. And he was scary good. Any guitarist seeing him for the first time might consider giving up the instrument. But on top of that, he was a showman. Although I didn't know his history, it was evident that he understood how to capture and hold an audience, likely from years of working the Chitlin' Circuit. He was dynamic, he was flashy, and he played as well as anybody I had ever seen. He didn't set fire to his guitar, but he didn't have to. It had already been done. The challenge for me was to keep playing when what I wanted to do was just sit back and watched the show. Anyone who didn't come away thinking they had just seen one of the fifty best concerts of all time must have had a personal agenda.

∽∾∽

Afterward, in the commotion backstage, I spotted someone who looked familiar. He threaded his way through the press of people. "Remember me?" he asked.

"Why wouldn't I? You haven't changed a bit." It was J.D. Blackfoot—or Benjamin Franklin Van Dervort, as he was known when I first met him.

"Never have forgiven you for not joining my band," he said, trying to look stern.

"But if I hadn't, you wouldn't have picked up Sterling Smith."

Smith had been with The Grayps, a contemporary of

ours, and later played with The Beach Boys. Last I heard, he was working with choreographer Twyla Tharp.

"Yeah, but you would have made it to St. Louis a lot quicker if you had."

"It feels good just the same."

"Well, I just wanted to tell you that you did Columbus proud tonight, Will."

After I had introduced J.D. to the rest of the band and they began swapping stories, Audrey pulled me aside. She wanted to spread some of Zack's ashes at the Gateway Arch and, of course, she asked me to go with her. Although I had known this day was coming, I wasn't sure how I felt about it. I hadn't quite accepted the fact that all that was left of my best friend was in a Tupperware container that could have held celery.

When it comes to bad-date scenarios, a man, a woman, and a green Tupperware container holding the ashes of the woman's late husband has to rank close to the top. But this wasn't a date, at least that's what I kept reminding myself. We were just friends and what we had in common was our connection to the ashes.

There was plenty of greenery in the park beneath the arch, so we could spread the ashes without drawing attention to ourselves, assuming that was what Audrey had intended. I'm not sure how important that was to her, but I wasn't interested in making a big show of it. Solemn and discreet would suit me fine. We had the band bus drop us off as close as possible to the park and then drive off somewhere to wait for us to call when we wanted to be picked up. Until that moment, the members of our entourage hadn't been aware that Zack was along for the ride. Doctah Root didn't look comfortable with the idea.

The thing about "cremains" is they don't look like you expect them to; they don't look like ashes. When we opened the plastic container, I saw something that resembled coarse sand and fragments of crushed bone. It seems that Zack had almost, but not quite, returned to dust. Add a few pebbles

and a toy-rake and you could have had one of those miniature Zen gardens.

Audrey pulled a plastic spoon out of her pocket. It was
still wrapped in plastic, so I knew it had come from a fast
food restaurant—likely Wendy's, judging by the shape of
the bowl. There was a slight breeze, so I suggested that we
stand upwind of where Audrey intended to spread them out.
As she scooped up several spoonsful of ashes and let the
breeze carry them off, I thought of the strawberry scene
from *The Caine Mutiny* in which Captain Queeg, crazy as a
loon, ladles sand out of a tin can. I also noticed that the ashes tended to adhere to various surfaces, especially skin. I
don't know how Audrey felt about have Zack sticking to
her like chalkboard dust, but it made me feel strange.

"Is there anything you want us to say?" I asked.

"No, but there should be music. A song."

I had played a lot of weddings, but no funerals, so I
didn't have any songs at ready. "Dust in the Wind," the
Kansas song came to mind, but I wasn't sure it would be
appropriate. Though I knew little about Zack's or Audrey's
religious convictions, I began to sing softly: "Amazing
Grace! How sweet the sound / That saved a wretch like
me."

Funny thing. Many of the musicians I knew had strong
spiritual yearnings—and not just because there was money
to be made playing in church bands. I think it had something to do with the music—and the acoustics. Couldn't
beat a church for acoustics. I remember one sax player,
Gene Walker, who used to carry an old child's story bible
around with him because the pictures aided his understand-
ing of the text. Although their lives might not reflect it, they
really wanted to believe in an afterlife.

I especially liked the last verse, which wasn't originally
part of the song. "When we've been there ten thousand
years / Bright shining as the sun. / We've no less days to
sing God's praise /Than when we've first begun."

Audrey said nothing, but clung to my arm all the way back to the bus.

೧ჟ೧

The show was barely over before Artemis had flooded social media with images and video of the band. In the coming days, we would be hyped as much as any celebrity you could name. But the spotlight was squarely on Spoolie. He was being hailed as "The Greatest Blues Guitarist You've Never Heard Of."

Actually, I knew it would happen. I was just surprised by how quickly. I could derive satisfaction from the fact that we were playing my songs—mine and Zack's. But for Wes and Evan, it was déjà vu all over again. It had been the same thing with Zack Black & the Blues Attack: Zack was the star and they were the sidemen. Only now it was more like Jesus and his disciples. Instead of becoming rock stars, they were destined to be Mitch Mitchell, Noel Redding, and the other guys who backed Hendrix. A footnote.

CHAPTER 28

Going Thru the Motions

Y ou really got to marry this thing we call music," Wilbert Longmire once said. "You can't date it."
He would know.
A self-taught singer and guitarist from Cincinnati, Longmire got his big break playing with Hank Marr. He then ricocheted back and forth between sideman and headliner, occasionally flirting with, but never quite achieving, stardom—or what passes for it in the jazz world. I would have had more faith in the system if he had.

For Zack Black & the Blues Attack, the musical marriage was long over. Now, we were dating our exes. And we knew that when the tour ended, we would be breaking up again. Actually, that took some of the pressure off. Evan was calling it the "Making Nice Tour." It was supposed to be a joke, but I began to wonder almost as soon as we took to the road.

The morning after our St. Louis concert, we set out on I-70 for Detroit. It was about an eight- hour shot. Most of the band tried to catch some sleep, but Audrey was too excited. "This hardly seems real," she said. "I've never done anything like this before."

"The novelty will wear off soon enough," I said, although I was pumped up as well.

"I hope not."

"You did great. Everyone said so. The crowd loved 'Flat Tires.'"

"I was so nervous."

"It didn't show."

"I think I could get use to this."

"That'll change. I don't know any musician who actually enjoys being on the road. You live for the gigs. You die—very slowly—in between."

"Unless you pull a Buddy Holly," Wes said.

By now, it was apparent that no one was actually sleeping.

"Yeah, and wind up in a Don McLean song," Evan added.

Everyone laughed. Of course, they knew the story of Buddy Holly, the young Texas singer/songwriter who, at the height of his fame, died in a plane crash with Ritchie Valens and The Big Bopper. But he wasn't the only one.

"Hank Newman settled in Columbus after several of his friends died in auto accidents," I said. I took particular delight in my knowledge of music trivia.

"Who's he?" Audrey asked.

"The leader of The Georgia Crackers. They were fairly famous country band at one time. He opened this pizza place near the airport and major country stars like Patsy Cline, Loretta Lynn, and Conway Twitty would stop by to get advice from Hank. And every weekend, they would have a jam session."

"It's gone, now," Wes said. "Donna Newman kept it going as long as she could. She's gone, too."

I was sorry to hear that, although, given her age, it wasn't a surprise. I would have liked to have seen her one more time. And talked her out of her spaghetti sauce recipe.

"What's the worst thing that ever happened to you on the road?" Audrey asked.

We all had stories. The question was which ones to share with her.

"This didn't happen to me," Evan said, before I could answer. "But John Schwab told me he was playing with Mickey Wilson's trio one summer. They were working all over Michigan and Wisconsin and happened to be in Green Bay the day Vince Lombardi—the football coach—died. The whole town immediately shut down. It was closed up so tight that the band had to eat supper out of the vending machines at the airport."

"There were times I wish we could have afforded candy," Wes said. "I was in this band and we lived for weeks on bread and mustard sandwiches."

After that, everyone joined in—everyone, that is, except for Spoolie and Doctah Root.

First it was Sarah: "We used to have ramen noodles for every meal. The only difference was we put sugar on them for breakfast."

Then Evan: "Remember when Wendy's first opened? They used to have packages of crackers with the straws and napkins. We'd all fill our pockets with as many as we could carry."

Then Wes: "I think we were all flirting with malnutrition much of the time."

Then Floyd joined in: "Yeah. You play bars and you get free beer, but I would have rather had food."

Evan: "Beer is food, isn't it?"

Sarah: "Only if you chew it."

Wes: "We're lucky we didn't go to jail. I was with this one band and while we played our roadie would be out in the parking lot siphoning gas."

Floyd: "Sounds like you're lucky you didn't get shot."

Then Sven, who had been listening quietly, waded in, his accent so thick we could barely understand him: "We were playing that college town in Indiana. We didn't have money for a hotel, so we would try to find a place to crash for the night. These girls invited us to stay at their apartment. We figured we'd camp out on the couch or the floor even. But these girls had other ideas. And just as we were trying to decide who was going to sleep where, their boyfriends came in. Football players. Seems they had an away game that weekend, but the girls miscalculated when they would be back."

"Weren't you getting paid?" Audrey asked.

"Paid?" Evan interrupted. "Sure. In experience, but maybe they paid Sven in lutefisk."

Everyone laughed, including Sven.

Evan continued: "You quickly learn to save money whenever you can because you just know something is going to go wrong. Your radiator is going to spring a leak or your transmission is going to go bad."

Wes: "Or you'll hit a deer!"

"Or hit a deer," Sarah said. "When you're on the road, you're always going from one disaster to another. It can be rough."

"Well, we're riding in style, now," Evan said.

I think Evan—who was built for comfort, not for speed—appreciated that more than anyone.

☙❧

Between Audrey and Artemis, I found much of my spare time being devoted to podcasts and interviews with the media, all via cellphone. No major outlets, but Artemis said that didn't matter. He would make certain they got seen and heard. Usually, I made sure one of the other band members participated so it didn't appear that I was hogging all of the attention. But mostly they preferred to sleep. And Audrey begged off, saying she didn't like the sound of her voice.

Since we would be leaving Detroit immediately after the concert, I suggested to Audrey that we get the spreading of Zack's ashes over with before then. The question was where? I had thought we could spread them at Hitsville, USA, the Motown Museum, in recognition of Zack's love of black music. Sprinkle some on Berry Gordy's front lawn, right in the little flower garden that surrounds the historic marker. Besides, it was only fifteen minutes from where we would be playing. But Audrey vetoed the idea.

At the intersection of Jefferson and Woodward, right in the heart of the city, is a very bizarre monument to boxer Joe Lewis. It consists of a twenty-four-foot long right arm and fist made of bronze, suspended above the ground by four beams that meet to form a pyramid. If "The Fist"—its official name—had been raised upright, it would have looked like a Black Power salute. As it was, it evoked enough controversy. To me, it resembled a medieval battering ram. I could just imagine it being used to break down the doors of an office building. Audrey opted to distribute some ashes in a clump of grass and trees across from the Bronze Bomber's bronze arm. She then took a few photos with her cellphone, to memorialize it, I guess.

The MC5 recorded *Kick Out the Jams,* one of the most audacious debut albums of all times, live at the Grande Ballroom in Detroit. We swung by the place to take a gander at what we had missed. Most of the windows were blown out, but you couldn't blame the band for that. Or maybe you could.

The husk of a building sat along Grand River Avenue like an empty shoebox. From the looks of the neighborhood, the shoes had been gone for some time. It was a forlorn sight, all boarded up and scarred with graffiti, reflecting the neglect of many years. Trees sprouting from the roof suggested it had likely passed the point of no return. A faded sign on the wall didn't hold out much hope for its resurrection: "Future Home of Chapel Hill Ministries."

In lieu of playing the Grande, Audrey had booked us into the Fillmore Detroit, an elegant old theater in its own right, once known as the Palms. It could accommodate just over 2,000 people and had sell-out crowds on a fairly regular basis, which was understandable given the amenities. The main floor was tiered and the loge, mezzanine, and balcony had good sight lines. It was the sort of place that brought out the best in all but the most jaded musicians.

As we waited in the green room for our call to go on, I

noticed someone had written on the wall with a black marker, *"Everything in the universe has a rhythm, everything dances."* ~ *Maya Angelou.* I didn't know the quote, but repeated it several times so I wouldn't forget it. Then as soon as we walked out on stage, I wrote it on top of my B-3 with a marker.

The music world is divided into two camps: those who feel music is for dancing and those who feel it is for listening. Stan Kenton is often blamed for the division. Some musicians believe that if they cater to dancers, they are selling out. Certainly, they can't experiment with unusual—make that ridiculous—time signatures like Don Ellis. It's like playing with one hand tied behind your back. But Zack Black & the Blues Attack was formed as a dance band and I did not want to lose sight of that.

က်ခ

Immediately after the St. Louis concert, Spoolie had made himself scarce. However, he had relayed a message to me through Doctah Root: he wanted us to hire a guitar tech. And he knew just the guy. He had arranged for him to meet us in Detroit. His name was Johnson, too—Colton Johnson—and he was Spoolie's cousin or nephew or something. Evan wanted to call him "Little Spoolie" or "Spoolette," but I put a quick stop to that. As it turned out, he did know his way around a guitar and could even play some. If we had been in the market for a second guitar, we could have done far worse than Colton Johnson. He definitely showed potential.

During the concert, Colton sat in the wings and tuned Spoolie's guitars. He liked to have a freshly tuned one for each song and Colton was quite adept at sneaking out on stage and replacing the guitar that sat on a stand stage right. He was kind of like one of the ball girls at Wimbledon or a highly skilled bat boy. After the first couple of times, no one even noticed him.

I felt the best way to keep the band fresh was to change the set list a little for each show. I dropped "Good Days/Bad Days," and inserted a song in which we employed stop-time in the verse. After opening as usual, with "Hummin'," I told the audience of the Fillmore, "We've got something new here for you. Something we've put together just for Detroit. Something . . . funky. Take it away Mr. Bassman." Stepping front and center, Wes began laying down a bassline so funky it would have tied a centipede in knots. He then started singing:

> "Can't help,
> Thinking about how,
> Thinking about how
> We used to be.
> Can't stop,
> Looking for a sign,
> Looking for a sign
> You still love me.

> "What happened to the sparks?
> We thought they'd burn forever.
> But I guess that's not
> The way our story ends.
> It's so hard to accept
> That we were only lovers,
> And never, never, ever, ever really truly friends.

> "So we're going thru the motions,
> Pretending nothing's changed,
> Acting like we're both okay
> Even though we are estranged.
> We're going thru the motions,
> Smiling thru the tears.
> It's only muscle memory

After the smoke clears.

"Can't find,
Just can't find the strength,
Just can't find the strength
To say goodbye. Oh-oh-oh-oh.
Can't make,
Make myself not care,
Make myself not care
Although I try.

"What happened to the sparks?
We thought they'd burn forever.
But I guess that's not
The way our story ends.
It's so hard to accept
That we were only lovers,
And never, never, ever, ever really truly friends.

"So we're going thru the motions,
Pretending nothing's changed,
Acting like we're both okay
Even though we are estranged.
We're going thru the motions,
Smiling thru the tears.
It's only muscle memory
After the smoke clears."

At this point, I stood up and led the audience in clapping on the beat while Wes danced from side to side. He likely had picked up some of those moves from watching funk bands. Audrey was dancing, too, while really getting in the groove of being a backup singer.

"Can't help,
Thinking about how,
Thinking about how

We used to be.
Can't stop,
Looking for a sign,
Looking for a sign
You still love me."

Then I signaled for them to stop clapping as I began to slow it down.

"You still love me.
You still love me.
You
Still
Love
Me-ee-ee-ee-ee-ee."

Later in the show, I brought Sarah up front. During one of our post-rehearsal jam sessions, we had given every member of the band a chance to sing something. Sarah had floored us with a spot-on cover of Kim Weston's hit, "Take Me In Your Arms (Rock Me a Little While)." Since then, it had been in the back of my mind to work it into the Detroit concert. The arrangement was strictly Motown and the Fillmore audience ate it up. Before we left town, Sarah had received at least a dozen marriage proposals.

There's no denying Detroit's historical importance as a music center, especially black music and, later, rock and roll. My buddy Teddy Robinson had recorded a single in Detroit. I had never been able to track down a copy of it. Later, he recorded an album with Jackie Wilson, but then Wilson had a massive heart attack while singing "Lonely Teardrops" and was semi-comatose for the rest of his life. Some might say the same thing applied to Detroit. But whatever problems the city might have, they were the farthest things from the minds of the Fillmore crowd that night. They came to have a good time and we did our best to give it to them.

After the concert, Audrey asked me, "True song?"

"What?"

"'Goin' Through the Motions.' True song?"

"For someone, I guess."

"Not for you?"

"No. My relationships weren't that—danceable."

"So none of your songs are about you?"

"The emotions, maybe. The details, not so much."

"That's too bad."

"Why?"

"I thought if they were autobiographical, they would help me figure you out."

"Sorry to disappoint you."

"Oh, I'm not disappointed. It just means I'll have to try something else."

"Why bother?"

"I like puzzles."

"So I'm a puzzle?"

"We're all puzzles. Some of us just have more pieces."

"And sometime there are pieces missing."

"Pieces are always missing. But that doesn't mean you can't see the picture."

"I may use that in a song."

It was readily apparent that some members of the band read more into my relationship with Audrey than was actually there.

And I wanted to confront it head on. But Audrey asked me not to. She wasn't as concerned about her reputation as I was. Maybe it was a generational thing. I don't know. But I felt a need to be protective of her.

About two o'clock, I heard her whisper from the adjoining room, "Are you awake?"

If I hadn't have been, I don't think I would have heard her. "Yes," I replied.

"Do you think Zack is watching?"

"Watching?"

"That his spirit or whatever was there at the Fillmore to-

night and could see the band and the crowd and everything?"

I didn't know how to answer her. If there is a heaven and
people go there after they die, I don't know how it could be
a very happy place if they could still see what was taking
place back on earth. So I simply replied, "I don't know."

"I would like to think that he would be pleased."

"I think he would be. The band is really good." Actually,
it sounded better than it ever had. We had all improved im-
mensely, but it was a different band without Zack. I missed
his self-assurance and leadership. I was happier as a sideman.

CHAPTER 29

Kokovoko

The shortest route to Philadelphia took us north of Columbus via Youngstown and Pittsburgh. But that was okay. We'd be home—I still thought of Columbus as home—soon enough.

Forty years earlier, we had been scheduled to play Philadelphia's Electric Factory. It was an old tire warehouse which opened in 1968 as the Electric Factory & Flea Market. The Chambers Brothers had been the first band to play there. Then Jimi Hendrix, Country Joe, Vanilla Fudge, even Stan Kenton. But it was razed in 1973.

Twenty years later, a new Electric Factory opened up in an actual old electric factory. Audrey considered booking us into it until she learned the capacity was 2,500 to 3,000—standing room only. Given our target demographic—people my age—she decided against it. Instead, we would play the Tower Theater in Upper Darby, west of Philadelphia. It held about 3,000 and was a refurbished vaudeville palace.

"Look at this line-up: Angel, Hawkwind, and The Godz!" Wes was scrunched up the seat of the bus, his face bathed by the glow of his cellphone.

"I don't know those bands," Audrey said. She was leaning on my shoulder and I thought she was asleep. Apparently, not.

"Angel was this 'seventies glam-rock band. They looked like fashion models. The Godz were from Columbus. They often opened for Angel because they were on the same label—Casablanca, I think." I had practically lived in record stores for a good part of my life.

"Gotta keep a runnin'," Evan sang over and over, while beating out the rhythm on the back of the seat ahead of him.

"Sound like Christian bands." Audrey stirred at my side.

"Hardly," I said, wishing I could see more than the top of her head. "Angel was a bunch of pretty-boys in white spandex. The Godz were just the opposite. They were these four Neanderthals, shirtless, dressed in black leather, hair streaming down to their asses. Primitive as they come. Ranting, raging, and rocking out. Blood and destruction. There was so much carnage on stage you were sure some-one was going to die."

"So are you going to out-do The Gods?" Audrey asked.

"I don't think so," I replied. "They were—still are, I im-agine—a hard-rockin', head-bangin' biker band."

"The Godz are a rock and roll machine," Wes said, crushing an empty Coke can on his forehead.

"What he said."

"But what do you expect from a band led by a bass play-er." Evan had an impish smile on his face.

"What do you mean?" Audrey asked, falling into his trap.

"What do you call someone who hangs around with mu-sicians?" he asked, before supplying the punchline. "A bass player." Audrey almost laughed, but suppressed it after see the expression on Wes's face. But Evan was on a roll. "What do you call a beautiful woman on a bass player's arm? A tattoo. What are the hardest three years of a bass player's life? Second grade."

By then, Wes had had enough. "You can make those jokes about any musician."

"Maybe," Evan answered. "But a bass player isn't a mu-sician. All you need is a washtub, a broomstick, and a piece of catgut."

Everyone on the bus could barely contain their laughter.

Even though he knew Evan was kidding, Wes found a

need to defend himself. "Paul McCartney is a bass player," he stuttered. "But he's also a hell of a guitar player. People think George played all the leads, but it was Paul on 'USSR,' 'Taxman,' 'Good Morning.' It's just that The Beatles needed a bass player more than they need another guitarist, so Paul got stuck with it."

"I know Paul McCartney. And you're no Paul McCartney."

More laughter.

"I'm just saying, in a different band, I could have been Zack."

"That's what the world needs—another Wings."

Abruptly sitting up, Wes hurled a bag of cheese curls at Evan's head, and it exploded in a spray of orange punctuation marks.

✍✍

To me, Philadelphia was the jazz organ capital of America with the likes of Jimmy Smith, Jimmy McGriff, Shirley Scott, Trudy Pitts, and others. But my favorite was Don Patterson and not just because he was from Columbus. He might not have been as well known, but that was probably his own fault. Anyone who heard him at his peak couldn't fail to be blown away by his impassioned bebop lines. However, like many hard core jazz players, he had trouble staying clean and his battle with drugs likely wrecked his health. Many years before, Rusty had teared up when we talked about Don. But I wasn't surprised that Audrey had never heard of him.

"Did you ever meet him?" she asked.

"No."

"Do you wish you had?"

"Meet him? No. See him play? Certainly."

"So who would you like to meet?"

"I've tried to avoid being star struck."

"So you wouldn't want to meet The Beatles or the Stones or, I don't know, Alan Price?"

"Not particularly."

"Why not?"

"I wouldn't know what I'd say to them. Or they to me. Because if you're a star, people are willing to give you a pass on just about anything. John Lennon could be anti-Semitic, homophobic, abusive to women, abusive to his own son, maybe even killed poor Stu Sutcliffe, but that was okay because he talked peace and love."

"Is that all true?"

"Who knows? But I think there's enough evidence out there to show Lennon was far from the saint his fans want him to be. It's the same reason I don't want to be thinking about Miles Davis slapping women around while I'm listen to *Kind of Blue*."

I paused to allow my words to sink in. It was hard to tell what impact they were having on her. "Remember what Elizabeth Taylor said: 'Fame is the best deodorant.'"

"Elizabeth Taylor? Really? Did she really say that?"

"No."

"So who did?"

"Me."

"*You*?"

"Yeah, but it sounds better coming from a celebrity. People are more likely to pay attention."

An hour before the show, I slipped out in the lobby of the Tower Theater and stood beneath its vaulted ceiling as the crowd was being admitted. There wasn't much chance that anyone would recognize me. We were still pretty much an unknown entity. Looking up at the tarnished bronze light fixtures, I noticed the walls were peeling like a bad sunburn. While rock and roll kept a lot of these old palaces open, it didn't do much to restore them. The upgrades that were made, mostly for additional lighting, appeared to have been grafted on by Dr. Frankenstein.

I stood some distance from the merchandise table—

photos, T-shirts, recordings—on the off chance someone would make the connection between this senior citizen and the young man on the cover of our CD. After the show, all of us would come out to the lobby to sign autographs if anyone wanted them. I expected that many of them would wind up on eBay in a few days. The T-shirts seemed to be moving. I credited that to Audrey who had found a talented young artist who could have held his own with Wes Wilson, Stanley Mouse, and the other poster artists during the heyday of Haight-Ashbury. I decided to hold up one of the shirts and give him a shout-out at some point during the evening.

As we filed onto the stage, taking up our respective positions, I looked out over the audience and was pleased to see that most of the seats were filled. After the initial applause died down, they had grown quiet, patiently waiting for us to begin playing. In that moment, I thought of what Leopold Stokowski, the great conductor, once said: artists paint pictures on canvas, musicians paint pictures on silence. At the beginning of each show, we started with a blank canvas. Everyone was waiting to see what pictures we would paint, most of all me.

I don't know why, exactly, but a few songs into our first set, I felt something was off. We seemed a little too tightly wound to me, so I decided to loosen things up by dropping in "Nutbush City Limit," the old Ike and Tina standard. The band had jammed on it a few times during our rehearsals and everyone seemed to love it, but we had never considered using it in our show. Of course, Spoolie played the hell out of it, we all did. And the Philadelphians loved it. We were on track.

When the Blues Attack was in its heyday, there was no lack of bands writing songs about drugs and tripping, that is when they weren't writing songs while tripping. But Zack and I had nothing to contribute to that genre. Ours wasn't a drug-fueled band except around the edges. We insisted upon it. However, one of our songs was rumored to be a drug song, although my inspiration was *Moby Dick* rather than marijuana, mushrooms, or LSD. It was about the fictional home of Queequeg, the heavily-tattooed savage who befriends the novel's hero, Ishmael. Melville portrayed Kokovoko as an unspoiled island paradise.

"We're going to take a trip, now," I said and the audience began to hoot and holler. "No, not that kind of trip. Imagine yourself, if you will, in a Tiki Bar on some South Seas island, sipping some rum concoction from a coconut. A breeze is blowing, the palm trees are swaying, and the moon is glistening on the ocean. It is a perfect night for you and your special someone. Then you hear this."

Since Wes had turned himself into our own Queequeg with his tattoos and piercings, I decided to start the number with a pin spot on him as he began playing the gently rocking baseline and then Doctah Root slowly added percussion. I went full Martin Denny on the arrangement with shakers, cabasas, rasps, ratchets, and various bird and animal sounds, mostly produced by the horn section. It was all very mellow. Wes began to sing:

> "It can't be found on any map,
> The truest places never are.
> Far away to the West and South,
> Sailing by a wand'ring star."

For the chorus, Audrey provided harmony.

> "So set course for Kokovoko,
> Beyond your wildest dreams.
> Cast off for Kokovoko,
> Where nothing,
> Nothing,
> Nothing's
> Quite the way it seems.
>
> "Some still long for El Dorado,

Others yearn for Camelot.
There are those who spend life searching
For what was and what was not.

"Set course for Kokovoko,
Beyond your wildest dreams.
Cast off for Kokovoko,
Where nothing,
Nothing,
Nothing's
Quite the way it seems.

"Take care, forebear,
Kokovoko waits for you.
Some way, someday
We will rendezvous
In Kokovoko.

"Should you find the lost Atlantis,
Shangri-La or Xanadu,
Just make certain paradise is
Safely hidden inside you.

"Set course for Kokovoko,
Beyond your wildest dreams.
Cast off for Kokovoko,
Where nothing,
Nothing,
Nothing's
Quite the way it seems."

The song was a risk. It offered a respite from our usual
wall of horns and screaming guitar solos. Spoolie, in particular, enjoyed the opportunity to try out odd string effects,
employing a violin bow and tapping out notes with his fingers. And Doctah Root went crazy on his array of drums,
playing actual notes. I had written it as sort of a mental ex-

ercise. After I determined to write a song about Kokovoko, I gave myself thirty minutes to do it. While it wasn't my favorite song, I felt the arrangement put it over.

On the spur of the moment, I added another chorus with a slight modification.

> "Set course for Philadelphia,
> Beyond your wildest dreams.
> Cast off for Philadelphia,
> Where nothing,
> Nothing,
> Nothing's
> Quite the way it seems."

Some might call it pandering, the crowd loved it and, in turn, us. As we left the theater afterward, I noticed Audrey was singing it to herself. Or, perhaps, for Zack.

I didn't know that Robert Indiana's famous LOVE sculpture—the block letters L and a tilted O stacked atop the V and E—was in Philadelphia at John F. Kennedy Plaza. I assumed that it would be in, well, Indiana. But Audrey had happened across it on the internet and decided that LOVE Park, as the locals called it, would be a good place to deposit some of Zack's ashes. And so we took at cab.

Located across from city hall atop an underground parking garage, the sculpture sat on an elevated platform next to a geyser-like fountain. There were trees and flower beds as well. Audrey sat down on a bench immediately in front of some of the foliage and placed the Tupperware container beside her. The casual observer might think she had brought her lunch. I remained standing, using my body to screen her from anyone who might be watching.

When she was finished, I saw that her face was a jumble of emotions.

"I thought it would get easier."

"Well, I'm no expert, but if it was too easy, I might think that it wasn't that important."

"It just doesn't seem fair. It's not like he lived recklessly."

"Like a rock star?"

"Yeah."

"Rock stars are such clichés. They make it big, then lose it all due to bad management, bad choices, bad drugs—"

"Bad women."

"Bad women."

"Bad liver."

"Bad liver."

"Then a transplant."

"Then a transplant. I wonder if the same thing would have happened to us if we had made it big."

"What do you think?" Audrey asked. She was looking at something on her cellphone.

"About what?"

"The sculpture."

I remembered when it was first unveiled. It was simple, iconic, beloved by hippies, and looked good on a postage stamp. The concept was widely copied. I probably used it myself.

"Seems kind of dated," I said.

Still looking at her cellphone, she said, "This art historian says it is 'full of erotic, religious, autobiographical, and political underpinnings.'"

I looked at it again. "I always thought he took his inspiration from kids' ABC blocks."

"It doesn't turn you on?"

"Afraid not."

"Me neither."

Before we left, Audrey sprinkled a couple of spoonsful of ashes on the flowers. Again, she took a picture with her phone. We later learned the original LOVE sculpture is at the Indianapolis Museum of Art.

As we made our way back to the bus, Audrey said, "You never mention women when you're talking about the band."

"I never mention cheeseburgers, either."

"Is that all women were to you—cheeseburgers?"

"No, it wasn't like that at all. They were around, of course, but they didn't have any direct influence on the music. And there weren't all that many around," I said. "We had even less sex appeal than the Zombies. They at least had that English-thing going for them. We were just four Midwestern boys on our own."

"So no groupies?"

"Will you be disappointed if I say 'no'?"

"No, there weren't or no there were?"

"Yes."

"You just want me to change the subject."

"Why, what did Zack tell you?"

"Nothing."

"Nothing?"

"I never asked him."

"But you thought you would ask me."

"We don't have the same kind of relationship that Zack and I did."

I wanted to say, "Thanks for reminding me," but instead I said, "Well, I can't speak for the others, but the answer is 'no.'"

"*No*?" She acted shocked and, I supposed she should have. I didn't know many of my peers who hadn't indulged.

"We didn't attract the top-tier groupies because we weren't exactly a top-tier band. And even within the band, the keyboard player is seldom a groupie's first choice. Call me old-fashioned, but I was interested in relationships. And not just any relationships. I always had one girl in mind."

"No 'free love'?"

"No free love, no free lunch. Nothing in this world is free. Somebody pays. Disappointed?"

"I wouldn't say 'disappointed.'"

For a couple of blocks, she said nothing else, although I suddenly became aware I was holding her hand. Finally, she said, "So how did you unwind after a show?"

"Well, depending on what city we were in, I would go

out to a club where there was live music and see what I could learn."

"Music's never far from your thoughts, is it?"

"Music is life. The dead don't dance."

"Did you ever wish you had settled down with someone and lived more of a normal life?"

I pondered her question for a moment. "I've known many musicians in my life, and I've noticed that they all come to this decision point, generally about the time they turn thirty. Am I going to continue doing what I am doing, always scrambling to make a living, or am I going to give up on music and try to get a regular job? The life I chose is normal—normal for me."

"But wouldn't you have liked to have shared it with somebody?"

I knew the answer to that, but I didn't know how to tell her without sounding pathetic.

"Look," she said, holding up her cellphone for me to see. "Here's a video from tonight."

It was the band doing "Nutbush" and whoever shot it got about thirty seconds of Audrey singing backup. She looked terrific.

"Guess we know who the real star is," I said.

CHAPTER 30

Can't Hear the Music

We were a little late for the Boston Tea Party. It had closed the same year our band broke-up, although I'm confident that wasn't the reason. The building that had housed it still looked to be in good shape, like a plastic hotel on a Monopoly board.

Originally a Unitarian meeting house, the Tea Party bore the inscription "PRAISE YE THE LORD" on the proscenium arch above the stage. During its tumultuous four-year existence, the Tea Party was a psychedelic temple, attracting such names as the Grateful Dead, Cream, Pink Floyd, Jimi Hendrix, The Byrds, Led Zeppelin, The Who, the Velvet Underground—and very nearly the Blues Attack. Now, there was just a plaque to mark what was and would never be again.

Fortunately, there had been a cancellation at the House of Blues. Audrey knew somebody who knew somebody— Dan Aykroyd's name was mentioned. Anyway, she got us in. Located on Kenmore Square, close to Boston University, it could accommodate 2,400 or so. More than enough, not that we had any illusions that we would attract a college crowd. Norm and the guys down at Cheers would be more like it.

But I was wrong.

To begin with, the House of Blues had a box of genuine Mississippi mud directly beneath the stage. The fact that Spoolie was a genuine Mississippi bluesman whose legend—thanks to Artemis—was growing day by day gave him and, by extension, us—instant credibility. Then there was the fact that it was built smack up against the wall of Fenway Park. So there was a chance we'd snag some of the Red Sox fans, if not a foul ball, assuming there was a game. Or, more likely, tourists. Whatever the case, I wasn't going to be intimidated. I knew we belonged there—and not just by riding on Spoolie's coat tails.

The green room was nice. Small kitchenette, stocked refrigerator, a few chairs—the usual accoutrements. It hadn't been vandalized, which suggested they ran a tight ship. And the furniture didn't look like cast-offs from a homeless shelter. I would rate it four guitar picks.

Per a schedule taped to the door of the cupboard, we went on after All Thumbs.

"Anybody ever heard of them?" I asked no one in particular.

"Maybe they're local," Audrey said.

"Doesn't sound like blues," Evan added.

"Good name for a punk band," Wes shrugged.

"Or one made up of all bass players," Evan said with a smirk.

"When you think of Boston bands, which ones come to mind?" I asked.

"Aerosmith."

"The Cars."

"Boston."

"J. Geils."

"Pixies."

"Okay," I said. "Stop right there. Do you know what two of those have in common?"

"They're from Boston?"

"Yeah, they're from Boston. But the core of each one is a Buckeye. Take Boston. Tom Scholz, the guy who wrote the songs and played all the instruments, was an electronic wizard from Toledo who went to MIT. He recorded the first album in his home studio and added Brad Delp on vocals.

And Ric Ocasek and Ben Orr of The Cars first got together in Columbus." Even though I had been in New York most of my life, I continued to file away Ohio trivia.

"Yeah, and Kim Deal of The Pixies is from Dayton," Wes added.

"Is that so? Didn't know that one, but it makes my point. Clearly, Boston loves Ohio musicians."

"Well, we'll put that to the test." Wes was joking. I think.

"Boston, The Cars; I always thought those were stupid names for bands," Evan said.

"It's kind of hard to argue with success."

"Just the same. I think they could have come up with something a little cleverer."

"You mean like the Evan Bishop Band?" Wes said.

"Yeah," Evan replied. "That works."

"You don't want to overthink it. I was in a prog rock band, once. We called ourselves Morass. It was me on keyboards, a drummer, and a guitar. All of us sang. We covered Yes, ELP, King Crimson—you know, the usual suspects. I thought we were pretty good. We practiced hard, spent a fortune on photographs and ad slicks. Unfortunately, it didn't occur to any of us that people might not know what a morass is. We would do interviews and have to correct the deejays when they called us 'more ass.' We would show up at clubs and the sign would say 'More Ass.' Some newspapers wouldn't even print our name. And we would get catcalls all evening. Wound up having to dump the name, the photos, everything."

"That's not true," Audrey said.

"Every word. I swear." I gave her the three-finger Boy Scout sign.

"You weren't a Boy Scout!"

"Somebody had to be. Evan was, too."

"Do you remember some of the names we came up with?" Wes asked.

"Like the Hush Puppies."

"Red, White, and Blues."

"Kitchen Sink."

"Fly and the Ointments."

"Fly and the Ointments?" Audrey was incredulous.

"I wanted the Oxford Comma," I said. "Fortunately, I only got one vote."

"That doesn't sound like a blues band."

"Well, we were a blues band when we started out—but only for a minute. By the time we got in the studio, we had changed. Not really changed, but evolved. We still did some blues and there were blues elements in some of our originals, but Zack and I both thought of ourselves as Tin Pan Alley tunesmiths. We were trying to be a high-voltage Irving Berlin. Hummable melodies, singable lyrics. We were hoping that everyone would cover our songs. We probably should have changed our name, then, but we didn't want to risk losing our following—the 150 members of our fan club. But the problem was never the name."

"What was it?" Audrey asked.

No one spoke at first, but then Evan finally said, "Us."

ⓔⓢⓔ

The House of Blues was primed for Zack Black & the Blues Attack. And if they weren't, they were by the time Spoolie let go with a few fiery riffs. Not wanting to lose momentum, I decided to drop in this song that developed out of a blues jam we used to do, based on the punchline from an old joke. A clean one for a change. It was always a crowd favorite—a great sing along—but we hadn't done it in a long time. It had an easy-loping rhythm. *Dunt, dunt, BOW, dow; dunt, dunt, BOW, dow.* I took the first verse alone.

> "Once I had a day job, felt more like doin' time.
> Paid me next to nothin', surely was a crime.

Went home ev'ry ev'ning, weary to the bone.
Felt like I was livin' in the Twilight Zone.

So I told my buddy, 'I might just take a flyer,'
And he said:
'Can't hear the music,
But your monkey's on fire.'"

I wasn't sure I remembered all of the words, but I think I got them all out in the right order. Not that it mattered. By the second verse, the horns had found their parts and Spoolie added some rhythm. Wes took over the vocals.

"Home may be man's castle; that's not what I've found.
Wife gives me a hassle, dog kicks me around.
Tried to lay the law down, tell her what was what.
All I got was backtalk: "Keep your big yap shut!"

So I asked my woman, 'What's your heart's desire?'
And she said:
'Can't hear the music,
But your monkey's on fire.'"

Like the horn players, Spoolie had never heard the tune before and had held back initially, feeling it out, playing tentatively, not wanting to make any false moves. It was a good song for a character voice, so Evan took a verse.

"Had to find a place where I could sit and think,
Went down to the corner, bought myself a drink.
After several hours, knew just what was wrong.
Sittin' on this barstool's just where I belong.

"So I put the question to the drunkards' choir,
And they said:
'Can't hear the monkey,
But your music's on fire.'"

Up to this point, I hadn't given Spoolie any space. That's the thing about the B-3; it was like having an orchestra at your command. But I knew the song would be right up the old bluesman's alley, so at the end of the third verse, I said, "Take it, Spoolie," and let him go to work. He was like a pressure cooker on the verge of exploding. All of this steam came shooting out, enough to power a locomotive. His fingers were like greyhounds scrambling around the track. After that, we could add Boston to our short, but growing, list of conquests. The manager told us we were welcome back anytime. And the video of Spoolie soloing would go on to get a quarter of a million hits.

ᘒᘒᘒ

Whether by accident or design, Audrey had scheduled us a day off. We neither had to perform nor travel, so the two of us headed off to explore the city. We were drawn to Beacon Hill to see the original "Cheers" bar from the long-running television show. They had only used the outside for an establishing shot, but in an example of life imitating art, the bar was remodeled to look more like the show's set with life-size replicas of some of the characters like Norm and Cliff.

As we were walking around, taking in the sights, we came across a street piano in front of King's Chapel. It was painted blue and covered with mirrors.

"Play something," Audrey said.

"It's probably not in tune," I said, plunking a few keys. I really didn't want to play and hoped that it would sound horrible, but I'd played a lot worse. "What do you want to hear?"

"Anything. Whatever you think is appropriate."

Appropriate for what? I wondered. Since the piano was located in the entrance of a church, I decided to choose something religious. Taking a seat on the bench, I began playing the old Shaker tune, "Simple Gifts." I had always liked the way Aaron Copland interpolated it into *Appalachian Spring*. Along with Gershwin and Bernstein, he was one of my favorite composers.

When I looked up at Audrey, her face was beaming. I could see I had made a good choice. Instead of stopping when I reached the end, I morphed it into my favorite American hymn, "What Wondrous Love is This?" The beautiful melody supposedly goes back to a song about Captain Kidd, the pirate. I had forgotten that I could hardly play it without tearing up. Looking back at Audrey, I could see that it affected her the same way. She smiled through the tears. By this time, a dozen or so people had gathered around me, listening intently to the mournful tune.

When I finished, the crowd clapped politely. A man started to place a couple of dollars on top of the piano, but I waved him off, mouthing the words, "No thanks." I quickly rose from the bench, nodded my acknowledgement, took Audrey by the arm, and hurried away. The truth is I only like to perform in designated performance spaces—in the bar or on stage. I assume a different persona in those places, one who is more comfortable with public adulation. Otherwise, I'm like a shoplifter, hoping to attract as little attention as possible.

"That was wonderful," Audrey said as I hurried her along the Freedom Trail, the walking tour of old Boston. I released my grip on her arm and we walked side by side. I felt a little guilty at having manipulated her emotions, knowing how vulnerable she was. And it's not like we were alone. She was clutching the plastic box that held Zack's ashes tightly to her breast like a school girl carrying her books.

The Old Granary Burial Ground was, perhaps, an obvious place to sprinkle some of Zack's cremains. Paul Revere, Samuel Adams, John Hancock, and several other notables are buried there, as well as a woman, Mary Goose, known locally as Mother Goose. Many of the headstones were dark and, occasionally, illegible. They were adorned with carved images of winged skulls, the Grim Reaper, and Father Time.

As we meandered through the graveyard, looking for a suitable spot to make our deposit, I noticed one modern stone that marked the final resting place of Crispvs Attvcks and four other victims of the Boston Massacre, a practice that was not uncommon at the time. The fact that he was buried with white people was impressive, though.

I mentioned to Audrey that Shep Edmonds, a Columbus musician who founded the first African American-owned music publisher in New York's Tin Pan Alley, had named it after Attucks.

"Really?"

"Attucks Music Publishing. Edmonds was also a songwriter. A good one."

"Do you know any of them?"

"One. I haven't played it in a while, though."

"What's it called?"

"'I'm Gonna Live Anyhow Until I Die.'"

"That was Zack."

No matter what I said, everything always came back to Zack. I had experienced grief before, but nothing like what Audrey seemed to be going through.

Given the hour, we had had the cemetery pretty much to ourselves, but now tourists were beginning to arrive. I was anxious for us to finish our task and leave before it got much more crowded.

"We should probably get this over with." The words were barely out of my mouth when I heard a tinny tune emanating from Audrey's phone.

"Is this it?" she asked.

I listened intently. It was, I later learned, a field recording made by Alan Lomax in 1959 of a couple of elderly black men playing and singing Shep's song in a very spirited manner.

"That's it."

"I think Zack would have liked it."

As the song continued to play, Audrey dug into the ashes with her plastic spoon and slowly poured them over the old grave. Several people pointed and at least one took a photograph with her phone, but no one bothered us. I was just glad we weren't reported for littering.

എന

When we got back to the hotel, I immediately realized something was wrong from the look Wes gave me when he encountered him in the hall. So after I dropped, Audrey off at her room, I looked him up. "What's going on?" I asked him.

He was with Evan.

"You haven't seen it?" he asked.

He then held up his cellphone. Someone had recognized Audrey from the Set Back Inn video and posted a link to a newspaper article about a robbery. From there, things snowballed. Other postings appeared, revealing more details and even more rumors, as well as editorial commentary by the trolls who live on the internet.

Although her name was not mentioned in any of the stories, someone wanted people to believe that the runaway teen who was identified as an accessory to the crime was Audrey. And I wasn't sure they were wrong.

"Who robs a record store?" Wes asked incredulously. "How's that ever a good idea?"

I studied the article in disbelief. "Who knows about this?"

"Everybody," Wes replied.

There was a knock on the door. Wes opened it to find Sarah standing in the hall. "Has she seen it?" Sarah asked.

"I don't know," I said. "I don't think so. We were out walking."

"You want me to talk to her?"

"Why you?"

"Because I'm a woman, and I suspect I know a little bit more than you about how a woman might get herself in a mess like that."

Although I wanted to believe that I should be the one to talk with Audrey, feeling we had a special bond, neither could I disagree with Sarah's reasoning. It was with mixed emotions that I watched her knock on Sarah's door and, after a pause, gain admittance. I then went back to my room to wait, but kept the door open a crack so I could monitor the hallway.

After half an hour or so, Sarah stopped by. She peered in the door and then swung it open.

"How is she?" I asked.

"You best ask her that. I see it one way. Maybe you'll see it another."

"What did she tell you?"

"Nothing I haven't heard before."

"What did you tell her?"

"I told her if you ain't done nothing wrong sometime, you ain't done nothing. I think she got the message. But I don't think you should count on her for the show."

"You think she'd want to talk to me?"

"Not now. I'd say give it a day." With that, Sarah slipped away.

I spent the next hour or so not going to see Audrey. And writing a song to distract me from thinking about going to see her. Sarah's words had provided me with a hook. *If you've never done nothin' wrong, you've never done nothin'. / If you've never asked to tag along, you've never done nothin'. / If you've never had to try to be strong / Or been somewhere you didn't belong, / If you've never sung a silly song, you've never done nothin'.* When I was done, I wadded it up and threw it in the direction of the wastepaper basket. I missed.

CHAPTER 31

I Went to Hear Fats Waller Play

Something went wrong in Pittsburgh.

We were confirmed for the Altar Bar, a desanctified church, but that was before we found out it could accommodate no more than 600 people. Somehow, that particular fact had gotten lost. So Audrey arranged for us to move to the Rex Theater on the Southside even as we were on our way to Philadelphia.

The Rex had originally been a vaudeville house. Like the Tardis, it was bigger on the inside than the out. I think it maxed out at 900, including standing room only. Not what we had in mind, but the best we could do on short notice.

Forty years earlier, we had been scheduled to play the Syria Mosque, a 3,700-seat theater that looked as exotic as it sounded. Despite efforts to recognize it as a historic landmark, it was demolished years ago. Pittsburgh, I guess, has as little respect for history as Columbus.

I remembered traffic in Steel Town as being horrible. I remembered right. The drive in was like pouring marbles into a funnel. All the roads seemed to be under construction at once. As we were filing off the bus, I noticed Spoolie was massaging his left shoulder.

"Problem?" I asked.

"Slept on it wrong," Doctah Root answered for him. "Think we may get the boy a massage."

I had no doubt Root would take care of him, but it was jarring to hear him refer to Spoolie as a "boy." And I would have preferred to hear about his ailment directly from him, rather than through an interpreter.

⌀⌀⌀

Standing backstage, waiting to go on, we heard the local deejay say something about Columbus. One whole section of the crowd erupted in cheers and whistles. We later learned that about a dozen or so people had made the trip from Columbus to see us, including a woman who had once won a contest for a date with the Blues Attack when she was a teenager. She had a newspaper clipping, the menu from the Kahiki, and an autographed photo to prove it. Unbeknownst to us, Audrey had invited her to be our special guest for the show. We knew she would go home and tell 100 of her closest friends.

Pittsburgh was another town with an impressive musical legacy. I felt we had to honor that. But we hadn't prepared anything specifically Pittsburgh-related, so I repackaged one of our songs including some local references as I talked it in.

Three songs into our set, I slowed things down a bit and began my introduction. "There have been some pretty great musicians from Pittsburgh," I began. "One of the greatest—maybe the greatest—was called 'Fatha.' As a piano player, Earl 'Fatha' Hines set the bar pretty high. I think Count Basie once called him 'the greatest piano player in the world.' And then there was Johnny Costa. He was the guy who played piano for 'Mister Rogers.'"

There was a smattering of laughter.

"You might laugh, but true jazz musicians knew better. But we're an Ohio band. And Ohio has had its share of great musicians, too. This song is about one of them, Johnny Costa's idol, and a pianist Basie called 'The Eighth Wonder of the World.'"

Alone in the pin spot, I began to play the intro, a wistful
little thing that sounded nothing like the subject of the song.

> "I went to hear Fats Waller play,
> Where it was I can't recall.
> His rollicking style
> And that wide-eyed smile,
> Held me in their thrall.
> I remember it like yesterday
> And I know I always will.
> The night I heard Fats Waller play
> Some forgotten bar and grill.

> "Fats treated us to 'Viper's Drag.'"

I played a phrase from "Viper's Drag," although I don't
think many recognized it.

> "And 'Honeysuckle Rose.'"

I expected more of a reaction to "Honeysuckle Rose"
and got it, although I suspect the day was rapidly approach-
ing when nobody would recognize it, either. The whole
band gradually joined in, but stayed in the background.

> "I sat entranced
> As his fingers danced,
> While he struck a playful pose.
> Then all at once he hushed the crowd—
> And you could have heard a mouse—
> As he said, 'I only play piano,
> But tonight God's in the house.'

> "Then this blind man took his seat,
> Though he sounded more like three,
> By the way notes flew
> As the sound just grew

> Into a symphony.
> He held more music in each hand
> Than a Dixieland quartet.
> The night that God was in the house
> Was a night I'll not forget."

I double and triple tracked myself for the instrumental break, playing over top of tracks I had just recorded. That way I could almost, but not quite, sound a little bit like the Piano Monster himself. As the sound grew, the whole band joined into a swirling crescendo like at the end of The Beatles' "A Day in the Life." But instead of the crashing piano chord, there was silence. Then after a few moments, I began to play softly once more.

> "There were gasps and there were cheers
> As he worked the ivories.
> His fingers were
> A perpetual blur
> Racing up and down the keys.
> I remember it like yesterday,
> The wonder and the thrill.
> The night I heard Art Tatum play
> Some forgotten bar and grill.

> "I remember it like yesterday,
> And for a moment time stood still...
> The night I heard Art Tatum play...
> The night I heard Art Tatum play...
> The night I heard...
> Art Tatum...
> Play...

It was a good show, if not a great one. Audrey was there, but sang only backup and she wore a hat with a wide brim like the rings of Saturn, keeping her face in perpetual shadow. Obviously, she didn't want to seen. Since I hadn't expected her at all, I asked what made her change her mind.

"Sarah. She said I owned it to myself and to the band. She also said you can't worry about who might be out there and what they think of you."

She was right. I knew a guy who tried to continue playing in a band after he was hired as a police officer. But he soon grew paranoid from wondering if anybody in the crowd had a grudge against him. So he had to give it up. And that was way before social media.

୧୦୧୨

The Cathedral of Learning was a towering Gothic Revival skyscraper on the campus of the University of Pittsburgh, within walking distance of our hotel. Nearly as tall as the Leveque Tower in Columbus, the gleaming limestone pillar was a good site for depositing some of Zack's ashes, given his appreciation for the arts and education. So in the shadow of "Cathy," as Pitt students called it, we stood beneath a tree and measured out several heaping spoonsful of his cremains like so much Ovaltine.

While we were observing a moment of silence, I put my arm around Audrey without thinking and she leaned into me a little. At least I think she did. An occasional student passed by, preoccupied with their own concerns, and only occasionally casting a glance at the old man standing awkwardly with the beautiful, middle aged woman. A campus security officer also studied us from his cruiser, but must have decided we weren't a threat and drove off.

It had been over an hour since we left the Rex Theater. Though we had been talking almost continuously, we had yet to say anything of consequence. Nothing too deep, nothing too sensitive. And she was still wearing that damn hat.

"So who was the best band?" she asked. More small talk.

"We were," I said.

"Besides you."

"I don't know. There were a lot of good bands. But it might have been the Bones."

"The Bones? Who were they?"

"That's a long story."

"I've got time."

"And it's not a happy one."

"Oh."

"Did Zack ever mention Ballard Keith?"

"Who's Ballard Keith?"

"When we were starting out, I believed the two best teenage guitarists in Columbus were Zachary Taylor and Ballard Keith. And they couldn't have been more different. Polar opposites. Zack was from the north end, Ballard from the south. Zack had well-to-do parents, Ballard had just his mother who worked as a waitress or beautician or something. Zack was an excellent student, Ballard was a dropout. Zack had his choice of many fields, Ballard only had one—music. Like The Dantes and The Fifth Orders, we had top-of-the-line equipment while Ballard and the Bones made do with what they could beg, borrow, or steal."

"They stole equipment?"

"Ballard got his PA from a church. Walked in one afternoon and carried it out. Every penny he earned playing, he put back into new equipment. He knew he was as good as Zack or Dave Workman or Chuck Wilson, but he didn't have the gear—the guitars, the amps, the mikes, the lights—like we did. He believed that was the only thing holding the Bones back from being in The Big Five."

"Was he right?"

"Partially. He didn't have the management behind him, either. Not like we did."

"That's too bad."

"Ballard wasn't the patient type. He wanted money, *now,* so he could buy the stuff he felt would help make him a star. And then he met some guy who offered him a lot of money for just a few minutes of work and he took the job."

"What was it?"

"Arson. The guy owned some property and he decided he'd rather have the insurance money so he hired Ballard to burn it down. And he did. And he got away with it. So then someone else hired him to torch a building and he did it again. This time he wasn't so lucky. He got trapped in the fire."

"Oh, my god! Did he die?"

"No. But he was burned so badly he could never play guitar again."

Audrey was visibly shaken by the story, so much so that I felt maybe I should apologize. It would probably give her nightmares. But I didn't because there was more to the story and I felt if I said any more I might just tell her the truth.

Ballard had gotten into a jam and had to pawn his guitar and amp—took them to Uncle Sam's on East Main Street. Then he needed them back for a gig, so he asked Zack to loan him the money. Ballard said he'd pay him back as soon as he got paid for the gig. But Zack wouldn't do it. So that's when Ballard turned to arson. After the first one, he went back to Uncle Sam's, but the guitar was gone. Someone had bought it. I had forgotten all about what happened to Ballard until I saw his guitar—in Zack's collection.

಄ఞ಄

When we arrived back at the hotel, I escorted Audrey to her room and then stepped inside for a few minutes. I had learned that she was apprehensive about entering hotel rooms alone. Years before, she was startled when she walked in on somebody because there was a mix-up and the hotel had given her room to someone else. That was another thing she couldn't shake. The Ballard Keith story probably didn't help.

"Would you like a drink or something?"

"No thank you?"

"Would you stay while I have some coffee?" she asked.

"All right." I took a seat on the couch as Audrey fiddled with the coffee maker.

After a few minutes, she had brewed a cup and sat down next to me. "Has it been worth the wait?" she asked, taking a sip.

"What?"

"Everything. Getting the band back together. Finishing the tour?"

"I suspect I appreciate it more, now, than I would have back then. Rock and roll is wasted on the young."

"Why do you say that?"

"All that rage and anger—and for what? Boo hoo. Somebody dumped them. But it's not the end of the world. Until they've reached our age, they haven't earned the right to make angry music."

"Our age?"

"My age, then. Until they've had some life experience."

"Like what?"

"Hardship, injustice, disillusionment…thinning hair, incontinence." As much as I tried, I couldn't keep from smiling. "Should I go on?"

"Not unless you want to." She tried to remain stone-faced as well.

"The problem is it's all aimed at the young—younger than ever. They've taken over."

"Well, there's still hope. They won't be young forever. Maybe then they'll come around."

"Around to what?"

"Who knows? Joy, love, peace, beauty. Someone has to write those songs."

"Even if nobody is listening?"

"Especially, then."

Apparently, I had grown silent because Audrey suddenly asked, "What are you thinking?"

"I was thinking what it would have been like to play in The Ohio Express," I said.

"Were they angry?"

"Quite the opposite."

"Too bad you didn't get the chance."

"Oh, I did. I was asked to join them once."

"Why didn't you?"

"I guess I was a snob. I kind of looked down on them because they played bubblegum music. But if I had taken them up on the offer, I might have been at the Whisky A Go Go when Jim Morrison jumped on stage, grabbed Dale Powers' microphone, and shoved it down his pants."

"That really happened?"

"That's what I heard."

"Too bad for you."

"Yeah. Could have been present when rock and roll history was being made."

"Could have wound up with 'Yummy, Yummy' carved on your tombstone."

"I would come back to haunt...somebody."

Ever since Pandora's box had been opened as a result of the Set Back Inn video, I had been biding my time, thinking that Audrey would eventually get around to telling me about it. But my patience was wearing thing. I had been waiting for an opening, waiting for her to relax her guard, like Joe Louis dropping his left hand when jabbed with his right. When it happened, I struck. "So are you ever going to tell me?"

"Tell you what?"

"Why you're such an awful person."

"I thought you'd have seen the videos, read the stories. That's why I could barely bring myself to face you."

"I don't care about them. I want to hear it from you."

"I guess I owe you that." She then grew quiet, collecting her thoughts, or so I guessed. She took so long that I considered the possibility that she had changed her mind. Finally, she said, "I've made some mistakes in my life. Real big ones."

"Most people do at one time or another."

"Not like this. I was sixteen and I had run away from home."

"You and half the kids I grew up with."

"But not you."

"No, not me. But I'm sure you had a good reason."

"I thought I did. I don't think that's changed. I didn't have anywhere to go, so I was living on the streets. Then this guy—Ricky—finds me. He wasn't one of the creepy ones. He was closer to my age. Twenty-five, maybe. And he said if I needed a place to stay, I could crash with him. He seemed nice enough and I didn't feel I had many options, so I did. He never told me much about his past and I didn't ask. But I could tell there was a lot going on inside of him and not good stuff."

"So what did this Ricky do for a living?"

"Hustling, mostly. I didn't really know where he got his money, but it wasn't very regular. Much of the time he'd hang around the apartment, talking on the phone, making deals of some kind. If he thought I was listening, he would shut himself up in the bathroom."

"How did he treat you?"

"He was jealous and controlling, like a lot of guys. He wasn't mean, not at first, anyway, but we argued a lot and sometimes when he ran out of words he would lash out."

"He'd hit you?"

"Yeah. Sometimes. I owe him my nose."

"It's a nice nose."

"You should have seen it before I got it fixed."

"So what's this about a robbery?"

"The robbery. Yeah, that was bad. Real bad. I knew Ricky owed somebody money and it was worrying him a lot. He started asking me if I couldn't get some money somewhere. I think he didn't care where I got it as long as I got it. So I tried to get a job, but nobody would hire me. I don't think he believed me. I could tell that he was getting angry because I wasn't pulling my own weight. I thought about leaving, but I didn't have any place to go. And I didn't think he would let me."

"What do you mean by that?"

"He thought of me as his property. He didn't even want me talking to another guy. Then one day he tells me I'm coming with him to a record store. I asked him what for? He said he knew a guy who worked there who might loan him some money, especially if I played up to him."

"How were you supposed to do that?"

"Remember how I said we all dressed like hookers back then? Well, that was Ricky's idea. I don't think a lot of hookers work record stores."

"I would guess not."

"Well, I got the guy's attention all right, but it was the wrong guy. Ricky's friend wasn't there. So all at once Ricky pulls his shirt up over his face and points a gun at him. I couldn't believe it. I'm thinking what the hell's he doing? Then Ricky orders him to open the cash drawer and give him the money. Either the guy wasn't moving fast enough or he tried to grab something from under the counter, but Ricky hit him with the gun. Opened up this big gash on the side of his face. He starts bleeding real bad and I'm freaking out.

"So as the guy is fumbling with the cash drawer, this other guy appears out of nowhere. And he has a gun, a bigger gun. It looked like a cannon. When Ricky sees him, he turns in his direction. And the guy shoots him three times. I start screaming. I remember seeing the look in Ricky's eyes like a match was burning out. I had never seen a person die before. There was blood everywhere. I couldn't move. I couldn't think. Turns out the guy had been back in the storeroom, watching the whole thing on closed circuit TV. When the cops arrived, they took me to the precinct and charged me with being an accomplice to armed robbery."

"That's awful."

"I felt like I was in a movie."

"And that's where you met Zack?"

"Yeah. I was still in shock. I didn't know what they were

going to do with me. They didn't believe I was sixteen because I had a fake ID. They wanted to know who my parents were. I didn't want to go back there so I told them I didn't have any. They were going to book me as an adult. But Zack was there and overheard it. I don't know why, but he told his attorney to see if he could help me. And that was it. I don't even think Zack even spoke to me."

"So what happened?"

"Since I was a juvenile, I got put in a diversion program for a few months. From there I went to this group home and then probation. I didn't have any contact with Zack until after I was eighteen. Then one day, out of the blue, he checked up on me to see how I was doing. I think I was in love with him before I even knew his first name. The lawyer always called him Mr. Taylor. But none of it would have happened if Ricky hadn't died. And I'll always feel responsible for that."

"It was his decision to rob the store."

"But I should have known something was up. He wasn't a criminal mastermind. He was looking out for me."

"He was looking out for himself, too. And he was the adult."

"I could have gotten him some money."

"How?"

"I don't know."

"It wasn't your fault, Audrey. And it doesn't make you a bad person."

"I have a criminal record."

"You were a kid. You're not that person anymore."

"That's what Sarah said."

"Sarah's right. Zack knew that and I know that. Everybody in the band knows that—except you. You can't keep beating yourself up over it."

"I also lied to you. That makes it even worse."

"It doesn't matter. I understand."

"Can we just stop talking about it?"

"If that's what you want." I made a mental note never to

mention it again. But I knew it wasn't over. The internet wasn't ready to let it go of it quite yet. She would just have to accept it.

CHAPTER 32

What and What Not

Sometime in the early afternoon, we crossed the Ohio River at Wheeling, West Virginia, and rolled on into Ohio. Wheeling was an Indian word that means "place of the head," as I learned when I was a kid and delighted in telling anyone who would listen. Now, it was Audrey's turn to hear it. As we drove farther westward, the hills began to flatten like someone was smoothing out a giant throw rug.

I had been studying Spoolie. He looked old. Old and tired. Even under the best of circumstances—and we certainly had those—touring can wear you down. I think all of us were feeling it. As much as we tried not to let it, the business part of the trip was outweighing the pleasure.

Audrey was unusually quiet. I assumed she was tired, too; neither of us had gotten much sleep. The rest of the band was sawing logs, but she seemed pensive. I didn't know whether to disturb her, so I kept to myself across the aisle. We finally made eye contact and she smiled feebly at me, so I said, "Something on your mind?"

"Sort of?"

"Want to talk about it?"

"I'm thinking of selling the house."

I just let that hang out there with no comment.

"No one needs eight thousand square feet," she added.

"I've made do with five hundred," I said, rounding up a bit. "But it is an amazing house."

"It is—when you share it with someone amazing. But it's too much for one person."

"What about the museum?"

"I don't know. But I know I don't want to be the curator."

For once, I didn't want to express my opinion, especially unasked. But I couldn't help but wonder what would happen to his collection. It would be a shame to break it up.

"I could do something good with the money. Give it to charity. Build a hospital in Haiti or something."

"It's not a decision you have to make right now," I said.

"I don't deserve to be wealthy. What have I ever done?"

She was still beating herself up.

"Nobody does," I said. "But I always thought I'd like to give it a try."

The Columbus skyline appeared on the horizon like a fleet of ships when we were still about twenty or thirty minutes outside the city. It was the last stop on our tour and, in all likelihood, the final performance by Zack Black & the Blues Attack.

Nearly half a century before, we had dreamed about our triumphant homecoming. It was on our minds even before we set off for California and anticipated stardom. We had envisioned legions of screaming fans—or at least a fair number of local high school girls—turning out to welcome their conquering heroes back to where it all began.

Jump to the present and we were simply hoping enough people would show up so we wouldn't embarrass ourselves.

We were no longer young.

We didn't have a record deal.

We weren't getting airplay.

And, most importantly, we didn't have endorsements. If we were poster boys for anything it was reverse mortgages. Even then, Evan was the only one of us who owned a house. Other than Zack, of course, and now that had passed to his lovely widow.

"Vets"—Veterans Memorial—had been this enormous

auditorium in downtown Columbus, squatting like a lime-stone cake box on banks of the Scioto River. The Dantes and The Four O'Clock Balloon had opened for Jimi Hendrix there. And I think The Emeralds opened for The Doors. Jim Morrison had a terrific hangover. Before he went on, the promoter—a burly guy who was as tough as he needed to be—threatened to take the young punk back behind the woodshed if he didn't behave himself. He did—to a degree. Still, the curtain had to be rung down after he incited a small riot with his profanity-laced performance.

Elvis, Dylan, Bowie, Joplin, James Brown, The Beach Boys—Vets held a lot of memories. But mostly what I went to Vets for was Kenley Players, the summer stock theater that brought fading Hollywood and/or current TV stars to town to perform time-tested Broadway shows: Mickey Rooney; Ginger Rogers;, Jane Powell; Howard Keel; Carol Lawrence; Paul Lynde, the fan favorite; Anna Maria Alberghetti, who was dating a local newspaper writer; and Susan Johnson, a local girl who made big.

As far back as the Clintones, I had been looking forward to playing Vets. But it wasn't to be. It had closed during the summer of 2014, so our dream of playing there was kaput. Instead, Audrey booked us into the Lifestyle Communities Pavilion, the country's first combination indoor/ outdoor concert venue. It could handle 2,000 to 5,000 patrons by opening up the outdoor amphitheater. Having hosted everyone from Santana to John Legend, it definitely was not a step down in prestige. All of us were feeling good about it. Still, it was a reminder that you can't go home again, even if you never thought you left.

℘ↄℰↄ

Our bus pulled into town at about four o'clock. We had rooms at the Hilton adjacent to a shopping complex called Easton which resembled Hollywood's idea of a small town, though with a touch of Stepford Wives. It had all been farmland the last time I passed through. After checking in and unpacking, we split up into twos and threes and fanned out in search of dinner. There were restaurants in abundance. Audrey and I found one that featured its own wines. If it was a chain, it disguised it well.

"Until I met you, I'd never been to Columbus before," Audrey said after we had ordered.

"Zack never brought you here?"

"No. I got the feeling he didn't want me to see it."

"Why is that?"

"I'm not sure. But I think it held some painful memories."

"I can see that," I said. "Zack's father was a hard man. He had been a colonel or something in the military, accustomed to giving orders and having them obeyed. I suspected that's why Zack always excelled at everything. If he didn't, he would have had to answer to the colonel. On one occasion, I saw Zack's father punch him hard in the chest. In my neighborhood, that wasn't exactly rare, but using a closed fist was."

"What about his mother?"

"I think she did her best to blend into the wallpaper." I hadn't thought about it before, but maybe he knocked her around, too. "He didn't tell you anything about them?"

"We had sort of an agreement—I didn't ask him about his childhood and he didn't ask me about mine."

"I'm sorry."

"For what?"

"I always feel a need to apologize for having a pretty good childhood. Seems like everybody I know was damaged by their parents in some way or another, but mine were pretty great people over all."

"Both of them?"

"Yeah."

"That is unusual."

"I wasn't conscious of it at the time. I used to think people were making it up, but I've learned better."

"Well, here's to the survivors," Audrey said, raising her glass. We clinked our glasses in that awkward way that people do when it is not a scene from a movie.

ᐧᗑᐧ

Somehow, either Audrey or Artemis had tracked down one of the two sisters from Portsmouth who had operated our fan club. They had seen us play a dance at the local armory and volunteered to put together a fan club with membership cards, pinback buttons, bumper stickers, photos, and a monthly newsletter. They were so successful that we went back to Portsmouth several more times just to play gigs they had lined up for us.

Carole Metzler—that was her name—became our ambassador to the Columbus media. She did a number of interviews with local TV and radio stations, talking about what had inspired her and her sister, Connie Shump, to do it and why she was looking forward to seeing us after all these years.

To pay Carole back for all her help, Audrey arranged for Connie and her husband to fly in from Florida. Of course, all four of them were given front row seats. We were hoping that their enthusiasm would be contagious. Not surprisingly, they arrived early, wearing homemade buttons with pictures of each member of the band on them. As their husbands tried to look inconspicuous, the sisters delighted in their newfound celebrity when some of the other concertgoers recognized them.

"You've created a monster," I told Audrey, watching the action from backstage.

"They will remember this night forever," she replied.

"So will I."

"Oh?"

"Well, what could possibly top this?"

"I don't know, but you should always keep yourself open."

She was right. A year ago, I would have placed the odds of being back in Columbus and getting ready to perform songs I had written forty-five years before as a million to one. And the odds of sharing that experience with someone like Audrey as even more astronomical.

Maybe it was due to the novelty of it, but the local media had gotten behind us, transforming our humble concert into a must-see event. Ticket sales were so brisk that Lifestyles kept expanding the venue. We were getting thousands of hits on our YouTube videos. Audrey placed some radio spots, announcing that anyone who came to the concert with one of our 45s would get in free. Within a few days, there was a bump in the collectors' market for used copies with some bidders offering more than $200 apiece. We began to think we might even sell out.

Predictably, I was worried. I say "predictably" because I always expect the worst, especially when I am part of something as messy as a band. Like a parachute, the only way to know if it was going to work was to strap it on and jump. But my biggest concern was Spoolie. He had complained about being under the weather. Not to me of course, but through Doctah Root. However, he and the doctah made their way to the greenroom with a good ten minutes to spare.

As we stood in the wings, I took a peek at the crowd. "I was kind of hoping Don B would be here."

"Yeah, so was I," Wes replied. "It's become a rite of passage for every Columbus band."

"Artemis tried to arrange it," Audrey said, "but apparently Don's health isn't very good. He can't walk anymore."

"Guess it's up to us, then," Evan said. "We've got to carry the torch for him."

✐✐✐

From the moment we took the stage, the audience was ours to lose. I don't know what Artemis had promised on social media, but I doubted we could live up to it. But we were determined to do our best. However, right from the get-go, the horns missed the cue to kick off "Hummin'" and I had to cut them off. In an attempt to cover, I decided to go for the joke. "See what happens when you skip practice?" I tilted my head in their direction and gave them a pained smile.

"We didn't skip practice. You did," Floyd shot back.

"I know that. But did you have to tell them?" I made a grand sweeping gesture toward the audience.

The audience laughed—and I knew we had them back. So I gave the sign again and this the horns jumped in right on cue. We were off to the races, hitting on all cylinders, burning up the asphalt and whatever other clichés you might like. Still, I was worried—worried about Spoolie. Had we spent more time in his hometown, we might have learned more about what made him tick. But, he seemed determined to keep some parts of his life strictly private. I attributed it to many things—all the ways sociologists and politicians find to pigeon-hole people—and maybe it was. But I suspect there was more to it than that. Besides, the good Doctah Root had erected an impenetrable wall around him.

We were four songs into our set when it happened. Spoolie was in the middle of a solo that suddenly went off the rails. He was trying to play this run when his fingers seemed to stumble. It wasn't at all clean and precise the way I had been accustomed to hearing it. And then he just stopped cold. For a moment, it was like hearing dead air on the radio, although I am sure few people actually heard it that way. I tried to cover by picking up the rest of it on the keyboard as though we were trading licks.

I looked at Spoolie and he looked at me. I saw in his eyes that something was wrong. He appeared almost frightened. I was hoping I was wrong. As we finished the song,

Spoolie took off his guitar and placed it on the stand. I thought for a moment that he was going to pick up another guitar, but instead he staggered off into the wings where he folded over like a jackknife and then fell on the floor in slow motion. Immediately, he was surrounded by crew members.

"We have a, uh, technical problem and need—and need to take a short break," I stammered. "We'll be back in a few minutes." I then slid off the bench and rushed to Spoolie's side. He was already being tended to by Doctah Root, Colton, and several people I didn't know.

"Just get him to the bus," Root said. Spoolie didn't look like he could say anything.

"Someone call nine-one-one," I barked.

"Bus, first," Root responded. "Give him some privacy. I know what's best for him."

I immediately had visions of Doctah Root performing some voodoo ritual over Spoolie as his life ebbed away.

"I don't think we should move him."

"You a doctor?"

"No," I said.

"Then it don't matter what you think."

After an uncomfortable silence, I acquiesced. "All right. I'll help you get him there. But then we need to call nine-one-one."

He smiled at me in his inscrutable way and I chose to interpret it in the affirmative.

"What do you want us to do?" Wes leaned in over my shoulder. Audrey was beside him.

"Go back and play something, anything." This would be his chance to show if he was a bandleader he believed he was. "Audrey can sing."

"What?" She pulled back, her face contorted like someone had blown smoke in it.

"I need you to do this, Audrey."

"Sing? What? All I know is 'Flat Tires.'"

"Do some of the others we fooled around with. Do whatever you want to do. Just keep people entertained—and in their seats. The show's in your hands. Do it for the band. Do it for yourself."

I didn't wait for an answer, but left her standing there with Wes, her mouth agape.

Against my better judgement, we carried Spoolie out of the building and placed him on the couch in the bus. By then, I thought he was looking kind of gray, but it might have just been the lighting. As soon as we were in settled in, Doctah Root was on his phone, speaking to someone.

"I called for an ambulance," he said. "I told them no lights or sirens."

"What can we do for you?" I asked Spoolie.

"It's just his asthma," Doctah Root said.

Asthma? This was the first I had heard Spoolie had asthma. I certainly hadn't seen any evidence of it before.

"Or maybe his sugar. Just move back and give him some breathing room."

When I was a kid, people told me I should be a surgeon because of my long fingers, but I never seriously gave thought to becoming a doctor. The truth is I was never very good at reading people. I had trouble enough recognizing when they were angry or flirting, let alone sick. Spoolie could have turned purple and I probably wouldn't have picked up on it. Even now I wasn't sure whether I was looking at a sick person or not.

"You go back," Doctah Root said. "I'll look after him."

Reluctantly, I tore myself away. When I returned to the wings, Sarah was rocking out "Take Me in Your Arms," with Wes and Audrey providing harmony. Sarah was great. *Good enough to front her own band*, I thought.

I was just about ready to take my place back on stage when a man who with an English accent who looked about my age approached me. "Sorry to hear about Spoolie. I'd like to help, if I can," he said. Something about him seemed familiar. "I'm Eric Clapton."

Even though I had been away from Columbus for a long

time, I still had kept up on events in my hometown. I was aware that Clapton had bought a home here. I don't know how many homes he had, but he wanted this one so his wife could be close to her family. During their courtship and after, Clapton had been spotted in local clubs—and laundromats—from time to time and even sat it with some of his old blues-playing buddies when they came through. His photograph hung in a local barber shop. Now, here he was, as cool as the underside of a pillow. I extended my hand. "It's great to meet you, Mr. Clapton."

"I've always been a fan of Spoolie's," he said softly, "but I've never seen him before. In fact, I didn't realize he was still alive until I heard about this concert. Is he going to be all right?"

"His doctor says so." I couldn't believe I had referred to Root as his doctor, as if he were a legitimate medical practitioner. "But we could use a lead guitarist."

"All right," he replied. "I'll do my best."

Turning my attention back to the stage, I caught Audrey singing the last verse of "Now Comes the Mystery," the song I had written about Zack's death. We had planned for her to sing it in every show, but she hadn't felt up to it before. Now, as she finished, the audience was on their feet, expressing their love.

Pausing a moment to allow Audrey to enjoy her moment, Eric and I then quietly padded onto stage. As he took a guitar from Colton, strapped in on, and adjusted the foot pedals to his liking, I walked up to the microphone.

"Let's hear it again for Audrey Taylor," I said. "And also Sarah Mannix." After the second wave of adulation had subsided, I segued into our next set. "Unfortunately, our guitarist, Spoolie Johnson, isn't feeling well—and will not be able to continue this evening."

There were sighs and groans, but I did not let them dwell on it long.

"Now, I know this is a big disappointment for many of you and if you would like a refund, you will be given one.

However, if you will bear with us, we will try to make it up to you. It so happens, that one of Spoolie's biggest fans is with us tonight and he's been known to play a little guitar himself. Please welcome Columbus's own—Eric Clapton!"

The crowd erupted in cheers and whistles again. Clapton silently ran his fingers up and down the neck before plugging in. I later learned that he had seen some video of one of our concerts on the internet and was curious to see Spoolie Johnson firsthand. Since Colton knew our material, we decided he would play rhythm guitar, freeing Eric to drop in some licks whenever he wanted. It wouldn't be Spoolie, but it was certain to be memorable.

We launched into "Elijah's Wooden Book." Clapton held back at first, watching Colton closely through the first verse and chorus, before jumping in with both feet. While he did not make the songs his own, he did acquit himself quite well. And an occasional reference to his own catalogue never failed to bring a smile or a cheer, especially when he ended one song with the opening lick of "Sunshine of Your Love."

It was like Rusty once told me: the most important thing in music isn't knowing what to play, but what not to play. I guess the same is true in life.

CHAPTER 33

Tonight at Noon

Despite grave concerns about his health, I did my best to put Spoolie out of my mind. There was nothing more I could do for him, except offer up a quick prayer. With or without Spoolie, the show must go on. Besides, I was confident that Doctah Root wouldn't allow anything to happen to his meal ticket.

Rahsaan Roland Kirk was one of my musical idols. He occupied a place at the top of my personal musical pantheon, right up there with Art Tatum. Even though he didn't play keyboards, I still bought nearly all of his albums and managed to hold onto most of them during my frequent moves. When Rahsaan died in 1977, I walked around in a funk for a while, knowing I had missed the opportunity to ever see him play live.

So, as I often did, I dealt with my melancholy by writing a musical tribute, "Tonight at Noon." It consisted of vocals, percussion, and reeds, but no keyboards. Still, I felt it was as good as anything I had ever done. Possibly the best I could do. And Columbus would be its debut, a tribute to both Rahsaan and Zack.

We hadn't performed "Noon" before this because there was no way we could do it justice. It required a full gospel choir. A couple of weeks earlier, I had sent a recording to a friend of mine—Martha Abbott—and asked her if she could help out. I had met Sister Abbott decades earlier during a trip to Columbus. At the time, she was leading the Mt.

Herman Baptist Church Inspirational Choir. She sang, played organ and piano, and wrote much of their material, even though she was totally self-taught and couldn't read a note of music.

Although she must have been close to ninety, Sister Abbott said she would be there and she was—along with thirty of the best gospel singers in the city. Resplendent in robin's egg blue robes, they were assembled in the in the wings on both sides of the stage. Now, when I gave the signal for them to enter, they met in the middle like the closing of the Red Sea.

Stepping out from behind the B-3, I walked to a mike on the right, while the rest of the band—save for Evan, the doctah, and Eric—put down their regular instruments, picked up various shakers, scrapers, and bells, and took their places behind an array of mikes on the left.

"This is a new one," I said, "I hope you like it." Evan and Doctah Root began laying down what I had imagined as an African drum rhythm, although I couldn't vouch for its authenticity. Then Sarah started singing over the syncopated beat of jungle drums.

> "Rahsaan, Rahsaan, the wondrous one.
> Rahsaan, Rahsaan, our native son.
> Rahsaan, Rahsaan, was here and gone,
> But bright moments live on and on."

I began to rap/sing the first verse. The lyrics mixed quotes, song titles, and observations.

> "When you talk about your reeds and deeds,
> The conversation often leads
> Up to the topic of hip chops,
> And, like as not, that's where it stops.
> To contemplate the life and work,
> Of our man Rahsaan Roland Kirk.

The one, the only Kirkatron,
Whose pure vibration still goes on."

Now, the others merged their voices with Sarah's.

"Rahsaan, Rahsaan, the wondrous one.
Rahsaan, Rahsaan, our native son.
Rahsaan, Rahsaan, was here and gone.
But bright moments live on and on."

Stepping forward, Wes took the second verse.

"If you saw him play you'll not forget,
The one they called the Triple Threat.
On tenor sax, stritch, and manzello,
He really was an awesome fellow.
The Miracle, the One-Man Twins,
The saint who struggled with his sins,
Then cried out in the darkest night,
To let the music be your light."

As we finished, Sister Abbott, with a weep of her arms, brought in her choir on the chorus, increasing the sound tenfold.

"Rahsaan, Rahsaan, the wondrous one.
Rahsaan, Rahsaan, our native son.
Rahsaan, Rahsaan, was here and gone.
But bright moments live on and on."

Tears welled in my eyes as I was enveloped by the most beautiful sound I had ever heard. It was as though the heavens opened up and the angels appeared. And now Audrey joined me, layering her voice behind mine.

"Now, please don't you cry, beautiful Edith,
The Whistleman can still play you a tune.

Now, please don't you cry, beautiful Edith,
'Cause he'll meet you on the bandstand,
'Cause he'll meet you on the bandstand,
Yes, he'll meet you on the bandstand,
Tonight at noon."

I had intended for a flute solo here and Phil had been listening to Kirk's recordings for inspiration. He played a few breathy bars, interweaving several melodies that Kirk had used. I thought I recognized snatches of "Three for the Festival." But then a tenor sax came in over the top and baritone underneath. I looked around and saw some of the best horn players in the city coming on stage to join us. Without warning, it had become an all-star jam.

I was so caught up in the moment that I lost track of what I was doing. Finally, I took control back and brought the instrumental break to an end. Accompanied only by percussion, Wes and I began to sing the last verse:

"Born in blacknuss, he embraced,
The heritage of his whole race.
This boy who played the garden hose,
Would soon make music with his nose,
And mouth and throat and fingers and
Whatever else he had at hand,
'Till folks said he was living proof
That only jazz can speak the truth."

At Sister Abbott's invitation, everyone in the theater joined in with the choir.

"Rahsaan, Rahsaan, the wondrous one.
Rahsaan, Rahsaan, our native son.
Rahsaan, Rahsaan, was here and gone.
But bright moments live on and on.
Rahsaan, Rahsaan, the wondrous one.
Rahsaan, Rahsaan, our native son.

Rahsaan, Rahsaan, was here and gone.
But bright moments live on and on."

By then, the entire crowd was on its feet. They didn't want it to end and neither did I. So we played on and on...

But I couldn't help but think of Spoolie, hoping that he was going to be okay. I had been foolish to think I could take him on tour and not expect his age to catch up with him. But I wished he could have been standing with us now. This was for him as much as it was for any of us.

When we finished playing, the crowd erupted: clapping, whistling, stamping their feet. I didn't think they would ever stop and I didn't want it to.

But then Eric sidled over to me and whispered in my ear: "If you can't top this, you better give it to them again."

So I raised both of my hands and signaled for quiet. "Thank you very much," I said. "You don't know how much this means to us. Would you like to hear it again?"

The crowd immediately roared back at me. They would have lifted the roof off the building if it had one. And so we played the song again. This time, Eric wove this tapestry of sound in a call-and-response fashion that was one of the most impressive displays of guitar artistry I had ever heard. For a moment, it made me forget about Spoolie.

As the piece concluded, the reaction was almost as overpowering as it had been the first time. All of us luxuriated in it for what seemed like fifteen minutes as we were recognized and cheered individually and collectively. I didn't think they were going to stop, so finally I signaled for quiet. "Thank you, thank you, thank you all very much for welcoming us home. You've been great. Now, we don't have much left in our song book, so I think we'll close with one of the first songs we ever did."

We launched into our "High Heel Sneakers/She's About a Mover" mash-up. Clearly, Eric was happy to be playing something he knew and he played the hell out of it.

I thought that was the end of it, but the crowd was still

going crazy a good ten minutes after we took our bows and left the stage. Audrey said to me, "You've got to give them something else."

At that point, I didn't even know where the rest of the band was, but I walked back out, anyway and sat down at the B-3. I stalled for a minute or two, trying to think of another song to play. After adjusting the microphone, I began. "As someone once said, 'What a long, strange trip this has been'" and the crowd roared. I noticed that some of the others had begun to file back onto the stage and take up their positions, Eric included.

"When I came out here," I said, "I wasn't sure if I would have to do this song by myself or not. Apparently, these good folks wanted to spare you that." I indicated all of the other musicians with the wave of my hand. "So we're going to do an oldie. It wasn't an oldie when we first played it, but we all had more hair, then. Given what we've gone through to get here, I think it's particularly apt. It's called, 'Expressway to Your Heart.'"

With that, Wes kicked off the funky baseline like he was auditioning for George Clinton. Then Evan began firing off shots on the drum. I joined in on the organ and began singing the first verse. By the time we reached the break, the horns were behind me and Eric added a tasty little guitar figure at the end of the chorus.

As I began singing the second verse, most of the choir had shuffled back on stage and were swaying to the beat. When they joined in the chorus, it was glorious. We then moved into "She's the Kind of Girl." And then back again.

Martin Luther said—wrote, actually—that next to the word of God, music is the world's greatest treasure. Who am I to disagree, especially with the man who wrote "A Mighty Fortress is Our God"? It was a hit song 500 years ago and it is still being performed somewhere every Sunday. We'll see if the Beatles have that kind of staying power.

"Goodnight everybody!" I screamed, my voice in tatters.

And then some deejay whose name I never caught took command of the mike.

As we hustled off stage for the last time, I felt a tap on the arm. Only seconds before I had been standing alongside Eric Clapton and the members of my band. And for eleven minutes and thirty-eight seconds, the time it took to perform "Tonight at Noon," I believed we were as good as any band that ever walked the earth. It had been the pinnacle of my career and already the memory was being snatched away like the wind stealing your kite.

Glancing back, I saw Eric was on my wing. He was saying something. What I made out through the din was, "Could I meet Spoolie?"

Spoolie.

I had completely forgotten him, focused as I was on getting through the show. Now, I recentered him in my mind like a potter at a wheel. I began questioning people at random, people I hoped might know something, anything. But no one did. So I carved my way through the press of well-wishers back stage until I emerged outside where the tour bus was parked.

There was a rent-a-cop standing by the door to the bus, scowling at anyone who approached. He was appropriately big.

"How's it going?" I asked.

"What do you mean?" He was sizing me up, trying to determine whether I was anyone he should care about.

"Is he okay?"

"Who?"

"Spoolie. The guy in the bus." I gave a wave toward the door.

"Black guy?"

"Yeah."

"He's not here." By then, Audrey and Clapton had joined us.

"Where'd he go?"

He shrugged. "Beats me."

"Well, did an ambulance take him?"

"Didn't see an ambulance."

"What was it, then?"

"Limo."

I looked at Audrey and then at Clapton. I could almost see the question marks floating above their heads. In that instant, my IQ doubled.

"Hey, you can't go in there!" the guard said as I pushed by him and bounded up the steps into the bus. It was empty. I checked everywhere. Spoolie was nowhere to be found. All he left behind was a hotel notepad on which he written his name over and over again in cursive, as if signing autographs.

When I emerged from the vehicle, I found Audrey explaining to him that I had a blank check to do pretty much whatever I wanted. He looked at me warily, his hand on the butt of his holstered gun.

"No sign of either one," I said. But I knew Spoolie was okay, and that's what made me all the angrier.

While the Blues Attack had been dedicating its farewell performance to Spoolie, he had already given his. He had carefully orchestrated the whole thing, feigning symptoms—fatigue, pain, shortness of breath—in the hours leading up to his on-stage collapse. We all thought the venerable bluesman was ill, perhaps dying, but that's what he wanted us to believe. And Doctah Root was his accomplice, if not his Svengali. After shooing us away, he had called a limo. He then arranged with the roadies for their suitcases and his drums to be quietly stowed it as soon as the load-out began. Even charged it to Audrey's account.

လာလာ

In the weeks that followed, we learned that Spoolie Johnson—the *real* Spoolie Johnson—was likely a dead man long before we traveled down to Mississippi. According to a death certificate Audrey obtained from the Department of Health, Elmore Johnson, Jr., had passed away on June 1, 1965. So the Spoolie Johnson we had come to know, the Spoolie Johnson we had shared a tour bus with, the Spoolie Johnson we had come to regard as a friend and who could play the guitar like nobody since...well, since the real Spoolie Johnson...was a fraud. As I'm sure everyone in his hometown could have told us so.

Elmore "Spoolie" Johnson, III, although a phenomenal guitarist, was not the old man who taught Zack how to play all those summers ago. His father had. He was not the fabled bluesman. His father was. He did not record those wonderful 78s. His father did. But he knew every snap, crackle, and pop of them and could reproduce them note-for-note, mistakes and all.

There had been at least three generations of Elmores and each one had been nicknamed Spoolie. But to the family, they were always Big El and Little El. Anyone who came around asking for Spoolie—his professional name—was identifying themselves as a likely mark.

From the beginning, I had wondered why someone hadn't discovered Spoolie before. Now, I suspected they had, and their experience probably wasn't much difference than ours. But I didn't begrudge Spoolie any of it. It was his legacy. He had no reason to believe that we weren't going to exploit him the way the music business had exploited his father. Besides, Audrey could afford it and, when all was said, the experience had been priceless.

As improbable as it seemed, Zack Black & the Blues Attack had completed their long-delayed grand tour. We had known what it felt like to be stars or demi-stars if only for a few nights. And we had proven we could share the same stage with rock royalty.

Before he slipped away in the confusion, Eric Clapton told Evan that playing with the Blues Attack was one of the high points of his career. That's what Evan said, anyway, and I chose to believe it.

എൽ

Who really knows why a band breaks up? It's not like you can get into each person's head. I thought I knew why the Blues Attack did, but it's was just my viewpoint. There were three other guys involved and, likely, three other stories—stories I didn't care to hear. But then as we were saying our goodbyes, Audrey and I encountered Wes and Evan backstage. "Guess it'll be kind of hard to return to normal," I said. I was thinking of myself.

"Normal?" Wes replied with a grimace as though I had insulted not only him, but his mother, his sister, and his dog. "I don't know what that is. We're musicians, Will. There ain't no normal."

I turned to Evan. "You feel the same?"

"Me? I'm just a monkey. As long as someone keeps dropping nickels in my cap, I know I'll have another meal."

"Wow," Audrey said. "That's kind of dark."

"That's reality. It took me a long time to figure out why Zack wanted me in the band."

"Because you're a really good drummer." Audrey looked at me for confirmation.

"Good enough," Evan said, "but not great. There were at least a dozen drummers in Columbus who would have jumped at the chance to play in the Blues Attack. But Zack didn't want a great drummer. He didn't want anyone who threatened his leadership."

"That's not true, is it?" Audrey didn't look away from me this time.

"I don't know," I replied after an uncomfortable delay. There was a lot of truth in *Spinal Tap*, especially the part about drummer. They do explode on occasion.

"It's true," Wes said. "Zack was a control freak. Maybe you didn't notice, Will, but that's because he needed you. He couldn't handle the arrangements by himself. But he expected Evan and me to stay in the corner and do what we were told. It was Zack's ego that broke up the band. He didn't give either of us any breathing room."

"To be honest," Evan said, "neither of us wanted to get the band back together. The only reason we agreed was because we knew we wouldn't have to work with Zack again."

At first I was shocked, but that quickly changed to horror as I thought of the impact their words would be having on Audrey. I studied her face for some sign of what was going on inside her head, but she was as expressionless as a statue. Finally, she said, "That's not the man I knew. Zack never said an unkind word about either of you. His memories of the band were all good ones. I'm not saying you're wrong to feel that way. But I have to believe his opinion of you was higher than you suspected."

"I wish that were true," Wes said. "But you weren't there. We've perpetuated this myth that Zack was some sort of musical genius. But he wasn't. He was just a technician—a walking encyclopedia of other people's guitar licks. He may have had the charisma, but you had the real talent, Will. And Zack had you."

I kept searching Evan's face for some indication he was joking. With Audrey looking on, I felt I should say something to in Zack's defense, but I was having trouble coming up with the right words. So I simply started talking. "I think—I think Zack was trying to do what he thought was best for the band. He realized it might be our only opportunity to make it big, and he didn't want to blow it. None of us had any experience in that area. But I believed then, and I believe to this day, that we wouldn't have gotten as far as we did without his vision, without his drive, and without his genius. I remember hearing years ago that there are two types of ministers: those who build churches and those who sustain them. I think Zack was a builder."

After I finished, no one said anything for a couple of minutes, then Wes spoke up. "You must be the sustainer, then, because I enjoyed playing together these past few weeks more than I ever did back then."

"I did, too," Evan added. Then he turned to Audrey. "For what it's worth, I still think Zack was a better guitarist. He may have borrowed some riffs, but he was just as entitled to them as Spoolie was. They both had the same teacher. I just think he did it better."

I didn't know if that was Evan's prejudice talking or he actually believed it. After all these years, there was still so much I didn't know about him or Wes. It was like we lived on different planets and always had. I could anticipate what they were going to play, but not what they were thinking or feeling.

When we had finished loading up, I handed one of Zack's guitars to Colton and told him to keep it. I knew Audrey wouldn't mind, and I hoped he would treasure it more than Spoolie had. Then Evan shook my hand and Wes did likewise. We did not make any promises to keep in touch because we knew we wouldn't. The band had been the only thing we had in common and now it was over. But at least it had ended on a high note. As Don Bovee would say, "You lucky you get that much."

CHAPTER 34

Don't Fall in Love

W e didn't go out to celebrate the end of the tour. The concert had been celebration enough. Instead, Audrey and I soon returned to the hotel with a bottle of champagne to bask in the memory of the evening. And to decompress. Though weary to the bone, neither of us was quite ready to put the night to bed.

For the first time since we met, our schedules were clear. We had no plans—not for tomorrow, not for the days that would follow. And we were in no hurry to make any. While I uncorked the bottle, Audrey kicked off her shoes and lounged on the couch beneath a large window that overlooked the make believe town that was Easton.

"I was really proud of you tonight," I said, handing her a tumbler of champagne before pouring one for myself. "You killed it."

No response.

"Seriously. You *owned* the crowd."

She still didn't respond.

"You aren't mad at me for making you sing, I hope."

"No." She was barely audible.

"After everything that's happened, I felt you needed to do it for yourself."

"That's not why I did it," she said softly.

"No? Then why did you?"

"For you." She took a sip. "I did it for you."

"For me? Why would you do it for me?"

"Because ever since that night at Pier Fifty-Two, you've done everything I asked of you."

"I'm sure there are any number of guys who would have done the same," I said, seeking to dispel any possible intimation that I might be a saint, even a minor one.

"Not the ones I've met."

"Not even Zack?"

"I would like to think so, but I don't know." Lapsing into silence, she set the tumbler down on the coffee table, an oval of chrome and glass. "Funny," she said. "Seems like everything we've done since we met has been about Zack."

Yeah, funny. I found myself studying my drink like it was a crystal ball, perhaps hoping to divine the future. Zack had been the bond that united us. Now that we were seemingly moving beyond him, would there be anything to replace it? When I looked up again, Audrey had fallen asleep on the couch.

ⲉⳁⲉⳁ

Both of us slept in the next morning.

Since we had packing to do before check out, I ordered breakfast from room service. I then began cramming my dirty clothes into a plastic laundry bag I found in the closet.

"I still can't believe we met Eric Clapton," Audrey shouted through the open doorway between our rooms.

"Well, Ohio is kind of a retirement community for rock stars," I replied.

"Who else?"

I had to think. "Peter Frampton. He lived in Cincinnati for many years. Also Joey Molland of Badfinger. He was in Columbus for a while. And Jorma Kaukonen from Jefferson Airplane lives in Athens."

There was also a guy from Savoy Brown, but I was still fishing for his name when Audrey asked, "Why do you think that is?"

"Ohio girls." I meant it as a joke, but a joke is just the truth in disguise.

"What's so special about Ohio girls?"

"You'll have to ask Eric the next time you see him." I had begun arranging things in my suitcase. Audrey was presumably doing likewise

"That could be a while."

"You never know. You've already seen him one more time than you ever expected to." My packing technique was to take each article of clothing, roll it up as tightly as possible, and then pack it side-by-side with the others like sardines. Somehow, I thought that would reduce wrinkling. Also, I couldn't fold things worth a darn.

"You're right," Audrey said. "My life has been one unexpected thing after another."

When I didn't reply, Audrey quietly sauntered into my half of the suite. "So, has it been worth it?" she asked. "Getting the band back together?"

"Yes—and no."

"What's that mean?"

"You might say a band is like a marriage based on sex. And when you take the music away, you often find you had nothing in common."

"You didn't enjoy the sex—the 'group sex'?" She had a sly look in her eye.

"The music was great. But I realize, now, they were never my friends—Wes and Evan."

"What about Zack?"

"I think we were. At least I hope so. I'll probably always regret that we didn't keep in touch."

I was robotically folding a sweater and carefully arranging it in my suitcase, when Audrey approached me from behind, peered over my shoulder, and said, "You're not gay, are you." It was a statement; not a question

"No," I replied too quickly. "Why would you ask that?" I thought maybe I had misheard her and turned to study her face.

"Because of Zack."

"What do you mean?"

"Well, you were *close*."

I wasn't sure whether she had placed a peculiar emphasis on the word or my mind had. "We were best friends."

"That's not the way he saw it."

"What?"

There was a knock on the door and a voice announced, "Room service."

I opened it and admitted the food service attendant who carried a large tray into the room and placed it on the table. After I signed the receipt, she quickly departed.

"What do you mean, 'That's not the way Zack saw it?'" I asked, picking up where we left off.

"You know. The way gay men do."

"No, I don't know." I couldn't imagine why she thought I would. "Are you saying Zack was gay?"

"You didn't know?"

I must have missed something. She had to be using words that had meanings other than the customary ones. "No, he wasn't," I said. It was not a topic I had ever considered. "If he were gay, why would he marry you?" I found myself slipping into Perry Mason-mode, trying to entrap her with my shrewd questioning.

"I don't know. Gay men do that sometimes. I think he felt sorry for me. But he was in love with you."

"That's crazy. He had girlfriends. We used to double date."

"That was so he could be with you."

In an instant, I began to reevaluate all of our history together. Was it possible that I didn't know Zack at all? Thinking back, I didn't really know any gay people during that era. Sure, I suspected some people were gay, but that's all it was. A suspicion. Liberace was gay. Paul Lynde was gay. Brian Epstein was gay. But nobody I personally knew, that I was friends with, was gay—at least I didn't think so. Not before I got to New York.

"You all had different reasons for becoming musicians," she said.

"How do you mean?"

"Well, Wes is in it for the lifestyle. He's totally a creature of pleasure. Sex, drugs, and rock and roll sums it up. Evan, on the other hand, is in it for the money. He's a family man. Dresses like an accountant, but has too much personality for that. And he likes to keep his hands clean so he couldn't be a plumber or a mechanic. But you're the most hopeless one of all."

"Why is that?"

"Because you love music. Everything else is secondary. Eating, sleeping, intimacy."

"That's not true."

"You as much as said so yourself."

"Okay, but what about Zack? What was his reason?"

"I already told you. He was in love with you."

"But he loved the music."

"Music came second."

Even though I didn't want believe it was true, something told me it was—like the way all the clues line up once you know the ending of an Agatha Christie novel.

"When did you find out?"

"I always knew."

"But you married him!"

She grew quiet. I thought I might have made her angry, but she was evidently trying to figure out the best way to phrase her answer. "He made me feel the way music makes me feel," she said. "He made me feel like everything was okay." I thought I knew what she meant. I knew the feeling I got from music. Then she added, "Relationships are complicated."

That was something we could agree upon. "But why would you think I'm gay?"

"Well, you're not married or in a relationship, we've been together for weeks, even shared a room, and you haven't hit on me."

"You're the widow of my best friend!"

"Who was gay!"

"I'm not gay," I said. "So all this while you've been thinking I was gay?"

"Not really." She lifted her eyes as I approached her, but then averted her gaze. "But I was starting to wonder."

"I guess we don't know each other as well as I thought we did."

"I guess not."

"So what do we do about it?"

"What do you want to do?" Audrey asked.

"Well, you could start by telling me more about yourself. Why is everything about you such a mystery?"

"Isn't that what men want?"

"Why would you say that?"

"Men aren't interested in real women. Look at all the songs that have been written about Patty Boyd and Stevie Nicks and Rosanna Arquette. I doubt if any of them were written about the real person. Besides, guys only want to know things about your past so they can use them against you."

"Zack, too?"

"Zack wasn't like other guys. He wasn't the jealous type. He didn't care about who I might have been, only who I was."

I was going to say that's because he was gay, but I didn't. Instead, I asked, "So he didn't write a song about you?"

"No."

"That's too bad."

"Why?"

"Because in the time I've known you I've already thought of writing a half dozen."

"Well, don't."

"I can't promise that."

"Then at least don't use my name."

"I won't."

"Good."

"But Layla's been taken."

"I'm sure you'll come up with something."

"Besides, the only rhymes I can think of for Audrey are bawdry and tawdry. And I don't think those fit."

"Well, I'm thankful for that." And then she laughed.

We both laughed, and for the same reason. *Now, we were getting somewhere*, I thought.

ဇာဇာ

Our Columbus show had been everything I could have hoped for and more. And then we went our separate ways. Evan went straight home with his wife, Betty, who had been watching from the wings during the show. Wes went bar-hopping and hadn't returned. And the horn section had caught an early flight out. But Audrey and I still had a long drive ahead of us. I would be playing the role of Ralph Kramden, back behind the wheel of the tour bus.

Before we hit the road for New York, Audrey asked my advice on where to dispose of the remainder of Zack's ashes—nearly half the Tupperware container. It was not a subject I had given any thought to. I tried to think of places that may have had some significance in his life, but they were all pretty mundane. High school? His memories of Brookhaven probably weren't any fonder than mine. Northland Shopping Center? It had been razed, most of it, anyway, and what hadn't been was unrecognizable. Vet's Memorial? Also gone. In the end, I found my list consisted of exactly two places: Valley Dale and Evergreen Cemetery.

In its heyday, everybody played Valley Dale. Originally a stage coach stop, "the Dale" had been one of the best known ballrooms in the county during the 'thirties and 'forties with its live broadcasts heard over CBS and NBC radio. Then during the 1960s, bandleader Chuck Selby and TV's Jerry Rasor transformed it into a gathering spot for teens eager to hear the latest bands, learn the latest dances, and meet other teens. It was hallowed ground for my generation.

We slowly circled the building, looking for a suitable spot for Zack, but the ballroom wasn't exactly known for its landscaping. There was a hedge lining the steps to the front door and some bushes here and there, but most of it was paved. Audrey chose to sprinkle half of the remaining ashes along the banks of Alum Creek which flowed behind the parking lot. They were likely to be washed away by the next rain, but you don't really think about that at the time. Besides, Zack was never one to stand still. After she had poured out about half the ashes out, we stood silently for a moment before reboarding the bus.

Evergreen Burial Park, its official name, was located in the east side of Columbus in a semi-industrial neighborhood, only a couple of miles away. It was the final resting place of Rahsaan Roland Kirk. The monuments were fairly modest affairs. No statuary or family crypts. Kirk's grave was marked by a black stone cross with a tenor sax etched into it. Two years before he died, he had suffered a stroke which paralyzed one arm. Nevertheless, he continued to play concerts with just one hand. Death seemed to have been the only thing Kirk couldn't overcome. I thought of him as our city's greatest contribution to music. And I thought Zack might have been up there, too. So they belonged together.

Audrey emptied out the remainder of the ashes on Kirk's grave and then we stood there in silence for a long time as a couple of cabbage butterflies darted about. After a couple of minutes, I put my arm around her because I felt I had to say or do something supportive. I had no way of knowing what was going on in her head, but I knew what was going on in mine: this was it, we had reached the end of the trail. Once we got back to Tarrytown, I would return to my life and she would return to hers.

"It seems like all the time that's left to us is butterfly days," Audrey said. "It goes by so quickly. Sometimes I want to run through the streets warning people to hug your loved ones, your friends, your family because you might think you have all the time in the world, but you don't."

"*Our Town*," I said.

"Our town?"

"The play. You sound like Emily. She asks, 'Do human beings ever realize life while they live it?'" I didn't mention that Emily was dead at that point in the play.

"What's the answer?"

"No. At least that's the play's message. But I tend to agree."

She rested her head against my chest. After a few moments, she broke the silence. "The last thing Zack said to me was, 'Audie, you know what the hell of it is? Who'd have thought Keith Richards would outlive me?'"

Keith Richards will probably outlive us all, I thought.

And then Audrey laughed. And cried. And laughed again in spite of herself. And then she kissed me on the cheek and said, "Thank you, Will. Thank you for everything."

As we left the park a few minutes later, she pitched the Tupperware container into a trash barrel.

๛

The drive to New York normally took about eight hours, but I intended to keep well within the speed limit. I had no idea what the future might hold and wasn't in any hurry to find out. As we pulled away, I found myself lingering on the rearview mirror. I don't know what I expected to see as the hotel receded from view.

Audrey sat across the aisle in the passenger seat. I thought of how we had temporarily occupied the same world and would soon be returning to our separate ones. Steering the tour bus onto I-70 East toward Wheeling, I said, "When we get back to New York, I guess my work will be done."

"What do you mean?"

"The tour's over. There's nothing left to do." I squinted into the sun before dropping the visor.

"You're forgetting something."

"What?"

She held out an unfolded sheet of paper. "We still have a song to write."

The song. I hadn't given it anymore thought. "That could take some time," I said.

"That's okay. I've got time if you do." And she began to sing.

> "You can go where you want,
> See who you want to see.
> Do what you like,
> And be what you want to be.
> The heart needs to laugh, sing, and dance,
> To truly be free."

I found myself joining in for the last line:

> "But whatever you do,
> Don't fall in love without me."

That was all I had written, but she continued to sing.

> "You can keep your old friends,
> Dreams and opinions, too.
> Don't ever change
> The things that have made you you.
> I'm sure there is some common ground
> On which we agree.
> So whatever you do,
> Don't fall in love without me."

Surprised, I asked, "What's that?"

She handed me the piece of paper and I saw that more

lines had been added in her handwriting. "When did you do this?"

"Do you like it?"

"Yes," I said. I must have looked like an idiot, with a big old Jack Lantern smile spreading across my face. "Now, we need a bridge. Let me think." I tried to think of something. "I may not be perfect or I know that I'm not perfect or—"

"God knows that I'm not perfect," she said.

Her eyes had this proud and hopeful look like a child that has made you a birthday card out of construction paper.

"That's good," I said. And I mean it. "God knows that I'm not perfect / But this much I know is true. / I would—I would try with all my heart / To be the perfect one for you." As I gazed through the windows of her soul, I knew things could never go back to the way they were.

"You told me you make it a point not to believe lawyers, actors, salesmen, and other people who lie for a living," she said.

"That's still good advice."

"What about musicians?"

"Believe the song, not the singer."

"Why is that?"

"Because music is the only truth." I then began to sing:

> "God knows that I'm not perfect,
> But this much I know is true.
> I would try with all my heart
> To be the perfect one for you."

Audrey joined me for the verse.

> "You can go where you want,
> See who you want to see.
> Do what you like,
> And be what you want to be.
> The heart needs to laugh, sing, and dance,
> To truly be free. But whatever you do,

Don't fall in love without me."

And we sang that song all the way to West Virginia.

The End

I would not be surprised if many of the bands and musicians mentioned in *Hello, I Must Be Going* are new to most readers, even to those who grew up in central Ohio. As something of a local music historian, I never cease to be amazed at how little public awareness there is even of the best them. But such is fame. King Tut and Mickey Mouse will be remembered; most of us will not. To assist readers in identifying which characters and bands are real, I have included brief bios of many of them:

Abbott, Martha: A lovely woman, the late Sister Abbott treated me to an impromptu concert in her home one afternoon. However, after dedicating her talents to the Lord, I'm not sure she would have participated in something as secular as my imaginary homecoming concert.

Alfred, Chuz: The epitome of 'fifties cool, Chuz was one of the hottest tenor players around and when he released his 1955 album, *Jazz Young Blood*. Due to his fierce playing on the single, "Rockin' Boy," some record collectors thought he must surely be black.

Alwood, Bob: When Joe Daniels joined the Gears, he and Bob began writing original material for the band. Larry McKenzie, who released some of their recordings on his Hillside label, felt that "Explanation," in particular, was as good as any early Beatles song.

Bartlett, Bill: "Green Tambourine" may have been the first song featuring electric sitar to go to the top of the charts, and Bill was the guy playing it. Thirty years later, he charted again with a new band, new sound, and a top twenty hit, "Black Betty."

Behm, Kenny: During the summers, I used to spend several

weeks with my cousins in Dayton, Kenny and Denny Behm. Kenny was a very good organ player whose group, Marvin's Circus, was signed to MGM Records. However, I don't know of him ever carving the initials "K.B." on an organ.

Bendler, Bill: In between the OSU Jazz Workshop and the Danger Brothers, Bill electrified his trombone, added keyboards, and emerged as a singer for Strongbow. The band was signed to Southwind Records, only to have the label fold two weeks after their album debuted.

Big Five, The: There was general, though not universal, agreement on which bands constituted The Big Five. For example, The Regents were sometimes mentioned as being the fifth band and every band liked to think of itself as being in that select company.

Blackfoot, J.D.: Born Benjamin Franklin Van Dervort, J.D. legally changed his name in 1970. Although he is not a Native American, he was inspired by a dream to write his song cycle "The Song of Crazy Horse." H was once a guest on my radio show.

Bradburn, Rich: Rich joined the Columbus band Spittin' Image to provide arrangements for a planned second album on MCA Records. Founded as a county rock band, Image had been transformed by MCA into pop/new wave group before it dropped them.

Brown, Joel: Joel founded The Toads at Grandview High School, a Columbus suburb. It was his idea of painting the band green so they would stand out from their peers. He also had a good eye for talent.

Browne, Ivan: Before starting the Lemon Pipers, Ivan was a member of a Centerville band called Ivan & the Sabers. He was the first to quit the Pipers when he could no longer tolerate the "crap" they were forced to record.

B&W Commonwealth, The: The late Dave "The Captain" Diemer was the only other person I ever met who remembered the Brunswick & Wadsworth Commonwealth. He even placed an ad in the local shopping news seeking information and then passed it on to me.

Bryant, Rusty: I held Rusty in such high esteem that I was reluctant to approach him for a long time. When I finally did, we became good friends and were even starting to work on a book together before he passed away.

Cataline, Glen: Glen became a professional musician at the ripe old age of 12. When they formed The Gods, Glen was originally supposed to be paired with a second drummer, but that drummer and another band member died in an automobile accident.

Carroll, Billy: After Billy stepped out from behind the drums to concentrate on singing, he became the teenage heart throb of The Fifth Order. Later, he joined with J.D. Blackfoot for the *Southbound and Gone* album.

Cars, The: When Ric Ocasek and Ben Orr teamed up in Columbus, they formed a band called Id Nirvana. They opened for the Stooges and MC5, before relocating to Woodstock, New York, and recording an album as Milkwood.

Chatfield, Mark: At the age of twenty-eight, Mark was already regarded as "the old man in town" because of his early success with The Godz, Rosie, and Bob Seger. He also recorded an album entitled *Flint* with former members of Grand Funk Railroad.

Chickadee: Johnny Albert was a popular organist who sold

the pedals for his B-3 to Victor Wolfe. When pianist/singer Charles "Merry Christmas, Baby" Brown played the local Cadillac Club, he was forced to switch to organ so Johnny set the organ stops for him.

Chickadoo: When working in a duo with Chickadee, drummer Bobby Shaw was billed as Chickadoo. Shaw had many offers to go on the road and make a bigger name for himself, but was reluctant to leave Columbus.

Clapton, Eric: After Eric married Melia McEnery in 2002, he bought her a house in Columbus so she could be close to her parents. Although he is English by birth, he considers the United States his spiritual home. He has been known to drop into local clubs from time to time.

Corwin, Tim: As the only remaining original member of the band, Tim has kept the Ohio Express alive for half a century. In 2010, the Express recorded a cover of the "Scooby-Doo" theme song for a German label.

Cotton, Gene: During 1976-1978, Gene had four *Billboard* Top 40 hits. Since stepping away from music, he has devoted himself to helping underprivileged kids in the Nashville, Tennessee, area, where he has lived since the late 1970s.

Coyle Music: Coyle Music, which grew into a series of music stores, was founded by well-known Columbus musician William R. "Ziggy" Coyle. In business from 1952 to 1997, Coyle Music's influence on high school band programs was incalculable.

Cracked Cup, The: Opened in 1966, this coffee house was a joint ministry involving three Columbus churches: First Congregational, Trinity Episcopal, and St. Joseph Cathedral. But I think I saw the door motif at a coffee house in the Canton-Massillon area.

Cummins, Jeanne: Jeanne was a singer with the Bernie Cummins band and married the group's guitarist, Walter. After she settled in Columbus, she became a pioneer in local TV, performing on several morning talks shows hosted by "Spook" Beckman and others.

Dailey, Chuck: During the garage band era, many of the teenage guitarists who bothered with lessons were likely taught by Chuck. And if they paid attention, they could learn a lot. When I started interviewing musicians, Chuck gave me a list of twenty guitarists.

Daniels, Joe: Joe and Bob Alwood became the songwriting team for The Gears, both individually and together. Since Joe played keyboards, his songwriting approach differed from Bob's, who was a guitarist.

Dantes, The: Arguably the most popular teenage band to ever come out of Columbus, The Dantes were saddled with a dated name when the "British invasion" occurred. Members of the Ohio Express told me they modeled themselves after The Dantes.

Day, David: David was only thirteen years old when he was recruited to jam with several high schoolers, including Tommy Williams, Phil Davis, and Raymond "Bucky" Sharpnack. The resulting band was called The Rebounds.

Ebb Tides, The: At one time, The Ebb Tides included Benny Van who later became better known as J.D. Blackfoot and he is featured on one of their two 45s. They toured eleven states and parts of Canada with the "Shindig All-Star Review."

Edicates, The: A southside band, The Edicates was formed by longtime friends Glen Cataline and Tim Fleisher. They recorded a 45, "She's Gone," which sold 6,000 copies locally and landed them the gig as the house band on the "Dance Party" TV show.

Edmonds, Shepard N.: A highly respected composer of rag-time songs, Shep started Attucks Publishing in New York, which was the first African American music company in Tin Pan Alley. He was a primary source for Rudi Blesh's book, *They All Played Ragtime.*

Epics, The: Originally an instrumental band, The Epics, with Bill and Roger Pence, were the house band at the Blue Dolphin teen club. Before they broke up, they were signed by Lucky Eleven Records and their name was changed to The Plastic Grass.

Fifth Order, The: Formed as the Electras, The Fifth Order was the pride of Upper Arlington High School. Jeff Fenholt, the band's rhythm guitarist, originated the role of Jesus in the Broadway production of *Jesus Christ, Superstar* before becoming a televangelist.

Four O'Clock Balloon, The: The "stars" of the 1967 Northland Shopping Center Battle of the Bands, the Balloon was the first local band to really mine the West Coast psychedelic sound. Their set list drew heavily from Jefferson Airplane and the Mothers of Invention.

Francis, Dean: The leader of the Soul Rockers, Dean went on to success in the jingle writing field. However, it was the drum break on "Funky Disposition," that led to his developing a cult following in German dance clubs twenty years later.

Gears, The: The Gears were born when Bob Alwood got together with three members of The Trends. According to Jim Lynch, who joined later, the band "got in fights every weekend" while playing small towns throughout Ohio.

Georgia Crackers, The: A pioneering country group, The Georgia Crackers were heard nationwide on broadcasts originating in Columbus for over twenty years. They also were featured in several Durango Kid westerns during a stay in Hollywood.

Godz, The: Eric Moore and Glen Cataline had been playing in a band called Sky King when they befriended Mark Chatfield. The original concept for The Godz included lights, make-up, an enormous PA system, and dual drummers.

Goldslager, Joe, The: proprietor of Goldmine Records, Joe was a cantankerous character, but also a good friend. Just before he passed away, he quipped that he never would have thought that Keith Richards would outlive him.

Grayps, The: Born in Kettler's Confectionary, The Grayps once attracted 5,000 kids to hear them play at the Whetstone Park shelter house. They were charter members of the "The Big Five" and released a very rare 45 on the Cobblestone label. (Wish I had one.)

Howard, Arnett: There are few Columbus musicians who are as well-known as Arnett, which led to his tongue-in-cheek campaign for the office of mayor. I have known him for many years and have written one and one-half songs with him.

Hughes, Bob: During his lengthy career, Bob worked with Jackie DeShannon (when she was Jackie Dee), Joey Dee (actually DiNicola) and the Starlighters, the Sonny & Cher Show, and the Oxford Watchband.Hughes Blues—An "underground band" (i.e. below the radar), Hughes Blues used to play at the Sugar Shack during Bob Seger's breaks. It was led by Bob Hughes who said he was the first person in Columbus to ever bend a string.

Jeany, Pat: From his days with The Four O'Clock Balloon through his work with J.D. Blackfoot to his gigs with the Hipnotics, the Frank Harrison Group, and other contemporary bands, Pat was a steady presence on the local music scene.

Johnson, Susan: Born on the Hilltop in Columbus, Susan's childhood was sacrificed to her parents' ambitions for her. Performing professionally from the age of three, she went on to stardom on Broadway, where she is still remembered for her booming voice.

Kirk, Rahsasan Roland: As Ronald T. Kirk, Rahsaan was a musical prodigy in his early teens, besting seasoned veterans in local talent contests. He remains one of the most phenomenal instrumentalists in the history of jazz, able to play three different horns at once.

Lapse of Tyme, The: One of the first bands in the area to add horns a la Blood, Sweat & Tears, the Lapse of Tyme was too young to play bars, so they traveled throughout the state, working fraternity parties. They had a strong influence on the Dave Workman Blues Band.

Lemon Pipers, The: When I arrived at Miami University in 1966, a publicity photo of the Lemon Pipers was taped on the wall in Myers Music Store. Over the next four years, I watched a very good band receive a gold record for a song they despised.

Lenker, Ted: A guitarist and composer, Ted was a highly regarded member of the Columbus music community. And he certainly didn't need Joe Walsh to re-record his tracks when he was a member of Tyler.

Longmire, Wilbert: A self-taught guitarist and singer, Wilbert got his big break with Hank Marr, performing on the

Live at the 502 album. Later, his friendship with George Benson led to three albums under his own name on the Tapan Zee label.

Mackey, Dick: After moving through rock and roll and rhythm and blues, Dick gradually morphed into an outstanding jazz singer. He specialized in resurrecting forgotten songs of exceptional quality and performing them impeccably.

Marr, Hank: In 1961, Hank was signed by King Records to replace Bill Doggett who was switching labels. For many years, he traveled the country as music director for George Kirby, before returning to Columbus and becoming a jazz educator.

Maxted, Billy: Although he had a longtime gig at Nick's in Greenwich Village, Billy made Columbus his second home after football coach Woody Hayes invited him to attend his morning staff meetings. For fifteen years, he played the Grandview Inn.

McIntosh, Ladd: Ladd put the OSU Jazz Workshop on the map, taking first place at the first American College Music Festival in 1967. A talented composer and arranger, he is regarded as a pioneer in the field of jazz education.

Michal, Scott: A composer and music educator, Scott has collaborated with me on various projects, including the full-length musicals *The Last Christmas Carol* and *The Last Oz Story*, available through DramaticPublishing.com.

Mobley, George: George was with J.D. Blackfoot when he recorded his *Live in St. Louis* album in 1982 and also joined him for his farewell concert thirty-five years later. He was also a member of the Monster Band, a legendary Columbus group.

Molland, Joey: Joey came to Columbus in search of a personal manager following the suicide of his partner in Badfinger, Tony Evans. During the eighteen months or so he lived here, he recorded a new album, *After the Pearl*.

Musicol Studios: Founded by John Hull in 1964 to record southern gospel groups, Musicol has established itself as a boutique studio and custom record pressing plant. It began with John recording groups in the dining room of his home.

Nichols (Ginnetti), Joey: Joey was a popular performer in clubs and lounges all over Ohio. His sons also went into music, performing as the Nichols Brothers for many years before Jimmy Nichols made a name for himself in Nashville as a producer and bandleader.

*Ocasek, R*ic: Born in Baltimore, Maryland, Ric dropped out of college to concentrate on music. Settling in Columbus, he took a job at a booking agency where he met Ben Orr and invited him to join a new band he was forming, Id Nirvana.

Ochs, Phil: Phil grew up in Columbus and played his first gigs at Larry's Bar while studying journalism at The Ohio State University. Although not as well-known as many other protest singers, he was, in my opinion, both the most pointed and the most poignant.

Ohio Express, The: The Ohio Express was a capable enough band, but had few opportunities to show it on their recordings because most of them were done by studio musicians while they were out touring. They had to learn their "hits" the same as any other cover band.

Orr (Orzechowski), Ben: Ben, a Cleveland native, had been living as a musician since dropping out of high school, including a stint in the Grasshoppers, the house band for the

"Upbeat" television show. Then he met Ric Ocasek in Columbus and the rest is history.

O'Shea, Shad: I met Shad once and found him to be quite personable and generous (he gave me a handful of records and permission to use a Muffets' song on the soundtrack of a film I was making). He knew the music business inside and out.

OSU Jazz Workshop, The: In 1967, the OSU Jazz Workshop won the Duke Ellington Award as the best collegiate jazz band in the country, while Ladd McIntosh won the Stand Kenton Award for the best original competition. They were my idols.

Pierce, Frank: I met Frank through Dan Green and Sally Fingerett. We hit it off so well that we decided to write songs together, but barely got started before his jingle writing career took off. Like many others, I was left stunned by his unexpected death.

Powers (Ruggiero), Joey: Although "Midnight Mary" peaked at number 10 on the *Billboard* charts, Joey was unable to duplicate its success. Later, he ran a booking agency before entering the ministry and establishing an orphanage in St. Petersburg, Russia.

Powers, Dale: Dale was the lead guitar player and vocalist in The Ohio Express. After serving in the military, he returned home and worked in industrial sales. Then in 1996, he formed Race Ministries for the purpose of pursuing Christian evangelism through music.

Rasor, Jerry: A longtime fixture in Columbus TV, Jerry was a versatile broadcaster who could handle any situation, which made him the perfect host for "Dance Party," Columbus's answer to "American Bandstand." He also was a singer and prominent Mason.

Rebounds, The: Students at Brookhaven High School, The 'Bounds won the first city-wide Northland Shopping Center Battles of the Bands in 1965. This led to a record contract with Tower Records, a subsidiary of Capitol Records.

Banfield, Toby: Everybody knows a Toby. This isn't his real name and all of the facts have been changed, but otherwise the story is absolutely true. You will find Tobys in every field of endeavor. Just hope you aren't one.

Robinson, Teddy: I have never met or even spoken to Teddy. All that I know about him I gleaned from the internet and then invented the rest for the sake of the story. I hope he is every bit as good a person and musician as I imagine him to be.

Ryerson, Art: Trained on the banjo by a man who went door to door selling lessons, Art developed into one of the top session players in New York. He can be heard on thousands of recordings, from Elvis to Sinatra, Paul Whiteman to Raymond Scott.

Schwab, John: John is the keeper for the flame for McGuffey Lane, a country rock band from Columbus which was signed by Atlantic Records after its self-released album outsold the latest Rolling Stones LP in Ohio.

Selby, Chuck: During the 1950s, Chuck managed Valley Dale Ballroom and led the house band with his wife, Anne Young, as the featured vocalist. When the garage band era dawned, he embraced it, booking acts and hosting events catering to Columbus teens.

Sender, Jack C.: Although he wasn't a member of the band,

Jack became the designated songwriter for The Fifth Order, providing them with their "hits." Judging by a tape I heard, his musical tastes ran more toward Sinatra.

Sidewinders, The: Led by Jimmy Harris, the Sidewinders deserve to be remembered for more than their one novelty 45. On his own, Jimmy is represented by a single released on the short-lived Oliver Records label, a subsidiary of ABC-Paramount.

Sir Timothy and the Royals: A Mansfield group, Sir Tim was extremely popular in central Ohio, competing successfully with the top bands. They were then tapped to be the Ohio Express, replacing another group, the Rare Breed, whose 45 was already charting.

Smith, Sterling: An extremely talented keyboard player, Sterling would go on to play with J.D. Blackfoot before being hired by The Beach Boys. As a studio musician, he has recorded with Randy Meisner, Terry Reid, Bonnie Tyler, Steve Perry, Whitney Houston, and others.

Stickel, Mrs.: According to Mrs. Stickel, mother of Dennis and Craig, she was motivated by the need "to keep up with The Grayps and Dantes." She and her husband bought a van for her sons' band and "signed loans one after another" so they could constantly upgrade equipment.

Strongbow: Although Strongbow was a Columbus band, it worked much of the time in Michigan due to a connection with a Lansing deejay. Signed by Southwind, a division of Buddah, they released their debut album just two weeks before the label went bankrupt.

Tatum, Art: Partially blind from birth, Art became the jazz pianist by which all other jazz pianists are measured. A product of Toledo, he spent a brief time in Columbus while attending the school for the blind where he learned braile and studied music.

Toads, The: Known primarily for their green make-up, The Toads were a Grandview band which recruited hotshot guitarist Chuck Wilson. They released a highly collectable 7 inch EP with a color postcard of the band glued to the paper sleeve.

Tonight Only: Tonight Only was formed to play Wednesdays at Ruby Tuesday, a campus night club. It was the one night of the week that the members weren't playing in other bands. However, their brand of blues and fusion didn't appeal to everyone, as they readily admitted.

Ulrich, John: Ragtime pianist and historian Terry Waldo said that when he moved to New York City, he found himself surrounded by piano players, but none of them were as good as Johnny Ulrich.

Vanguards, The: As Joey Powers's backing band, The Vanguards toured Canada and New England in support of his hit, "Midnight Mary." They even relocated from Columbus to the East Coast. But after their ranks were dissipated by the draft, the band dissolved.

Walker, Gene: Before he did session work in the 'sixties for a number of artists on the Prestige label, saxophonist Gene Walker worked with Jackie Wilson, Lloyd Price, and Chris Columbo. As a member of the King Curtis Band, he traveled with The Beatles.

Walmsley, Steve: I first saw Steve when he was practicing with the Water Bears in the basement of Stanton Hall my freshman year. Most of the members were from Columbus, but Steve, who soon left to join the Lemon Pipers, was purportedly from New Zealand.

Walsh, Joe: Although he wasn't born in Columbus, Joe spent some of the happiest days of his childhood here and drops by the old neighborhood when he's in town. His song, "Indian Summer," is said to be about this period of his life.

Wiester, Vaughn: An alumnus of the Woody Herman Orchestra, Vaughn has been leading a 21-piece big band every Monday night since 1997. Before his retirement, he was a popular jazz instructor at Capital University and a much sought after arranger.

William, Tommy: The original bad boy of rock and roll, Tommy and I grew up in the same neighborhood. I was told that Ric Ocasek decided to leave Columbus because Tommy wanted to join Id Nirvana and wouldn't take no for an answer.

Wilson, Chuck: After leaving The Toads, Chuck wound up in a Marysville band, The Original Cast. In 1968, they competed on the "Happening '68" TV show— (hosted by Paul Revere and the Raiders) —in a battle of the bands, losing to the Heart Beats, an all-girl group.

Wilson, Mickey: An early rock and roller, Mickey was such a popular attraction in local night clubs that he finally opened his own, Mickey's Old Timers Bar. He told me when he was starting out, he played in a number of every-man-for-himself-type joints.

Wood, Mr.: My junior high science teacher, Mr. Wood once said to me, "You're not as smart as people think you are." Rather than being offended, I was surprised to learn that some people thought I was smart or that they even thought of me at all.

Workman, Dave: Lead guitarist for The Dantes, Dave developed into a serious student of the blues. Eventually, he hooked up with blues singer Willie Pooch to form the Dave

Workman-Willie Pooch Band, before later moving his base of operations to San Francisco.

About the Author

A graduate of Miami University and The Ohio State University, David Meyers can't seem to keep from writing stuff. His lifelong interest in history has led him to turn out more than a dozen non-fiction books on a variety of topics, including Lazarus Department Stores, the Kahiki Supper Club, and local music. He has also written scripts for a kids radio show, several cantatas, various articles, and a handful of works for the stage, including two full length musicals. In 2019, David was inducted into the Ohio Senior Citizens Hall of Fame.

His website is: https://www.explodingstove.com.